AGAINST ALL ODDS

Book 3 of the *Crossroads* Trilogy

By Jacqui Murray

From the *Man vs. Nature* Saga

Published by Structured Learning LLC

Laguna Hills, Ca 92653

This is a work of fiction. Names, characters, places, and incidents are the product of the author's imagination. Any resemblance to actual persons, living or dead, events, or locales, is entirely coincidental. The publisher does not have any control over and does not assume any responsibility for author or third-party websites or their content.

Printed in the United States of America

ISBN 978-1-942101-44-4

ACKNOWLEDGEMENTS

Special thanks to Hilary Melton-Butcher and Malvika Vazalwar for helping me understand the whistling/ singing languages of the world.

DEDICATION

To anyone wondering who this creature is called man and how did we become the alpha in the animal world

"(Man's) greatness does not consist in being different from the animals that share the earth with him, but in being...conscious of things of which his environment has no inkling." –GHR Von Koenigswald

OTHER BOOKS BY JACQUI MURRAY

Dawn of Humanity trilogy

Born in a Treacherous Time
Laws of Nature (coming Winter 2021)
In the Shadow of Giants (coming Winter 2022)

Crossroads trilogy

Survival of the Fittest (Book 1)
The Quest for Home (Book 2)
Against All Odds (this book)

Sequel to *Crossroads*

Coming 2023

Cro-Magnon trilogy

Rowe-Delamagente Series

To Hunt a Sub
Twenty-four Days
Book 3 (coming 2026)

Non-fiction
Building a Midshipman: How to Crack the USNA Application

Education

Over 100 non-fiction resources integrating technology into education available from Structured Learning LLC

PRAISE FOR JACQUI MURRAY

For Survival of the Fittest

SURVIVAL OF THE FITTEST is set in times so ancient that author Jacqui Murray had to delve deeply into past and current research to create the African world in which the book is set. I enjoyed her strong characters, particularly Xhosa, and how they interacted with other humanoid species, some with lesser language skills. Bravo Jacqui! A fine read and meticulous research. —S. Harrison

There are power struggles, deceptions, kindnesses, and wisdom. The world building is a fascinating foray into prehistoric landscapes. Though fiction, Murray deftly brought to life a time we have little record of. Highly recommended. —D. Peach

I'm completely hooked on this moment in history and storyline. I will definitely read the rest of this series and highly recommend it. —Amazon Reader

WOW I absolutely loved and enjoyed this book. I found it very hard to put down, held my interest and I can't wait to find the next book in this 3-book series. — Amazon Reader

Through meticulous research, author Jacqui Murray illuminates the gritty details of the lives and world of Homo Erectus as the People trek through Africa and beyond to search for more hospitable surroundings. With wisdom, courage and the ability to learn new ideas, Xhosa is a fierce and memorable character capable of leading the People to their new home. I am eagerly awaiting the second book of this three-book series! — Amazon Reader

I thoroughly enjoyed this well-researched prehistory read. The storyline drew me in and the character development was spot on. The protagonist Xhosa is an amazing leader. No matter the hardships, of which there are many, she always takes care of her people. So, grab your coffee or beverage of choice and settle in for an adventure of epic proportions. —S. Cox

I like this view of how the different species of man might have behaved and interacted. The style and material remind me of Jean Auel of "Clan of the Cave Bear" fame. The writing tugs me right into the lives of the primitive characters. … Just scan the sample chapters and see for yourself how the stimulating story events will keep you reading until "hand of Sun's travel" occurs many times. — Amazon Reader

For Quest for Home

Murray has created a story rich in history and has built a solid world with a colorful cast of characters. I found myself rooting for the protagonists and hoping the villains got their comeuppance. — Amazon Reader

I can't begin to imagine the hours of research, not to mention the actual writing time, that went into this wonderful gem of a story. I highly recommend this book. It's a must read for those who love prehistoric fiction. — Amazon Reader

Full of non-stop action that makes the book a page turner, The Quest for Home is also full of cultural details and practices that Murray always works into her stories. What they ate, wore, used for tools and how they interacted among themselves and with others—all that helps bring to life the world of Homo Erectus. The book is full of interesting well-developed characters. I'm looking forward to the next one in the series to see what challenges they will face in their quest to find a land they can call home. — Amazon Reader

Although I loved Xhosa's strength and interactions with her people, it's the wolf that held my heart. — Amazon Reader

I am a Clan of the Cave Bear fan. If you are, then you will love Jacqui Murray's latest novel in her Crossroads trilogy. Her historical fiction story is based on the migration of people who struggled to survive in the harshest of environments. The fight or flight emotion we humans have today came from this time in history. Also, if you are into DNA Genealogy you should know we all come from this time and these people. This fast-paced brutal look into the past can give you a glimpse into who you are and where you came from. — Amazon Reader

One of the few books of this topic that I found difficult to put down. I hope the next book comes soon. — Amazon Reader

Give me a strong, brave, and compassionate female protagonist any day of the week, and I'm your reader. Author Jacqui Murray does not disappoint. — Amazon Reader

TABLE OF CONTENTS

CHARACTERS

Xhosa's People
Ant
Bird, Lead Scout
Bone
Gadi
Hecate, Lead Hunter
Mbasa, Lead Warrior
Ngili
Nightshade, Lead Warrior
Rainbow
Siri, Primary Female
Snake
Starlight
Stone
Tor
Xhosa, Leader

Pan-do's People
El-ga
Lyta, Pan-do's daughter
Pan-do, Leader
Sa-mo-ke, Lead Warrior

The Hawk People (aka, former-Hawk People)
Dust, Lead Scout
Hawk (deceased)
Honey
Talon, Lead Warrior
Water Buffalo

Shore Dwellers
Acto, Leader
Qaj
Shaga

Big Heads (Archaic form of *Homo sapiens*)
Fire
Thunder
Wind

The Mountain Dwellers
Dawa and Davos, Leaders

Leopard and Deer
Viper

The Islanders
Betaaka, Leader
Isaalka
Kasiika
Tuuka
Zooka

The Cave Dwellers
Asal'rez and Rul'ez
Cucu'tez
Qu'tez
Re'ez
Zak'ez

The Wolves
Black Wolf (Ocha)
Red Wolf (Lone Wolf)
Spirit
The pups

Others
Fang
Scarred One
Seeker, born in what we now call Indonesia
Vaya
Zvi, born in what we now call China

Uprights
All Others

Tribes
Big Heads (archaic Homo sapiens)
*Hairy Ones (*Homo habilis)
*Hawk's People (*Homo erectus)
*Islanders (*Homo antecessor)
*Cave Dwellers (*Homo antecessor)
*Pan-do's People (*Homo erectus)
*Shore Dwellers (*Homo erectus)
*The Mountain Dwellers (*Homo erectus)
*Xhosa's People (*Homo erectus)

Animals

Big Panther—a Pleistocene Iberian predecessor to a panther and xxx to the Holocene leopard

Carrion birds—vultures

Gray Small Wolf—like the Mosbach wolf, a predecessor of the gray wolf but smaller, less aggressive, with a bushy tail

Equiis—an early version of a horse

Giant Owl—a Pleistocene version of the owl, much larger than today's owl

Horned Beast—the Iberian species of a rhino but with two horns

Goat—a predecessor to the Iberian Wild Goat that populated the Pyrenees

Kite—predecessor to Eagles in Spain

Okapi—a primitive mix of giraffe and okapi; as tall as a giraffe with less neck and more horns, and more muscular than okapi

Red Wolf—predecessor of a wolf living in Pleistocene Spain

Short-tailed Cat—predecessor to the almost-extinct Iberian Lynx

Short-toothed Cat—extinct species of a Sabertooth cat called Homotherium

Wild Beast—a paleo version of today's Wildebeest

Wolves—like the extinct North American native, the Dire Wolf

THE JOURNEYS OF THE *CROSSROADS* TRIBES

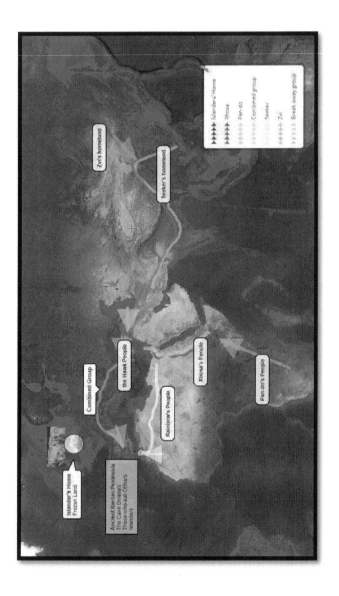

Author's Non-fiction Introduction

Although the story of Xhosa's migration from Africa, across Europe is fictional, the places and people are based on fact. Through the *Man vs. Nature* saga, and this trilogy, *Crossroads*, I try to bring to life the hardships endured by those early inhabitants of our planet.

Homo erectus, the star of *Crossroads*, is a gifted prehistoric hunter-gatherer who outlasted every other species of man and became the first to inhabit Eurasia. He possessed a sophisticated ability to reshape stones into intelligent tools, solve new problems, and make complicated plans. He fearlessly faced unknown dangers and was adventurous enough to think he could defeat them.

He lived 850,000 years ago.

Why did he thrive? He was an omnivore—ate almost anything, hunted rather than scavenged, and mastered the rudiments of fire (or not, depending upon the expert you talk to). His communication was robust and sophisticated though rarely verbal. Instead, he shared ideas, thoughts, and directions with a complicated collection of body movements, facial expressions, sounds, and hand gestures. Even today, "body language" is responsible for about half of what we "say". In this story, I often refer to "motioned" but that's synonymous with the dialog tag, "said".

Homo erectus individuals were more comfortable on two legs than climbing trees and adept at imagining what they couldn't see. Their differences from earlier *Homo* species continue to fascinate paleoanthropologists. For example, their skulls are the thickest of any human species. They left a homeland they dominated and ranged to the far corners of Eurasia. They were a violent people but not mean, overall, well-equipped to survive a treacherous world and eager to do so. While the first species of man, *Homo habilis* (the star of the trilogy, *Dawn of Humanity*), was timid and shy, you'd never accuse *Homo erectus* of that.

The *Crossroads* trilogy follows multiple *Homo erectus* populations as they travel Eurasia in search of a new home. Xhosa and her People are from East Africa (the Olduvai Gorge area), Pan-do from South Africa, Hawk from Gesher Benot Ya'aqov in Israel, Seeker from Indonesia, Zvi from China, the Cave Dwellers from the Iberian Peninsula, and the Islanders from Britain. They all flee their homelands for various historically accurate reasons, frequently because a different iteration of *Homo* is determined to eradicate them, sometimes because Nature turned on them. When forced to by circumstances, they put aside differences, trade knowledge, and work to achieve a greater goal.

Survival of the Fittest is Book 1 in the *Crossroads* trilogy and covers how these communities come together. *The Quest for Home*—Book 2—follows the catastrophes the combined group faces as they search for their new home. In Book 3—*Against All Odds*—they settle in an area we now call Sierra de Atapuerca in central Spain but their past comes back to haunt them.

The references to Lucy in Xhosa's dreams come from *Born in a Treacherous Time*, Book 1 of the *Dawn of Humanity* trilogy. When threatened, Lucy sometimes appears to guide Xhosa.

Both *Crossroads* and *Dawn of Humanity* explore man's journey from where we started to who we are today. Together, they are two of the four trilogies in the *Man vs. Nature* saga which chronicles how the family of man survived from inception to present day. The characters share the particularly human drive to survive despite extreme adversity, well-equipped predators, and a violent natural environment that routinely asks them to do the impossible.

Questions you might ask

Here are questions I get from readers about the *Crossroads* trilogy:

What are Others? And why capitalize it?

Others refers to all Homo *species including* Homo habilis, Homo erectus, *and archaic* Homo Sapiens. *Capitalization indicates Xhosa's respect for the individuals or their tribes. This is also true when animal species are capitalized such as Gazelle or Mammoth. If the characters refer to them in general terms, they aren't capitalized.*

Who are the "Hairy Ones" who Pan-do once shared a cave with?

These are Homo habilis, *mostly extinct by this point in time. When you read Pan-do's description of them, you'll understand why.*

What is the meaning of the term "People" (and why is it capitalized)?

The label "People" applies to a collection of individuals with shared common experiences, culture, and beliefs. Why is it capitalized? Because it is the proper noun for the community, like "Americans" or "Englishmen". In general, capital letters denote Xhosa's respect for the species and belief that they are equal to her. You'll see this with many animal names, also.

How do you know Xhosa's People are as smart as they seem in this book?

A study published in the journal Nature Human Behavior *places the appearance of human-like ways of thinking with the emergence of* Homo erectus. *The complex thought required to create their stone tools (called Acheulean) and their functional variety (which includes cutters, choppers, handaxes, cleavers, flakes, and scrapers) have long inspired many paleoanthropologists to believe* Homo erectus *was smart. A 2017 study that mapped student brains while they recreated these tools revealed that this work required the ability to "hold in mind" information—much as you and I do to plan complete complex tasks. 'The fact that these more advanced forms of cognition were required to create Acheulean hand axes ... means the date for this more humanlike type of cognition can be pushed back to at least 1.8 million years ago ...' [Indiana University. "Humanlike' ways of thinking evolved 1.8* *million years ago." ScienceDaily. ScienceDaily, 8 May 2017. <www.sciencedaily.com/releases/2017/05/170508184905.htm>]*

Not definitive but interesting!

Their speech is too erudite.

As a species, Homo erectus *lasted far longer than any other* Homo *species for a reason: They were not only highly intelligent for the day but made use of rich communication skills. Their sophisticated tools, especially the symmetry of the hand-axe, suggests to many scientists that they could use sophisticated communication. Because the capacity to "speak" with voices remains a hotly-debated topic, with opinions divided on whether the "speech" part of their brain—that allowed them to speak—was evolved enough for verbal words, I present communication often as body language with limited speech.*

A persuasive argument of why early man didn't want to talk with his voice is that these sounds are noisy and unnatural. That attracts unwanted attention from would-be predators. For these primordial humans, far from the alpha in the food chain, being noticed wasn't good.

Convince me they communicate effectively with gestures, body movements, and facial expressions.

I get this a lot. Let me give you two examples. First, have you ever been around someone who doesn't speak your language and still, the two of you communicate? It's probably via hand gestures, body movements, and facial expressions. Much can be said without voices.

Second, think of sign language. Sophisticated ideas are communicated with hands and facial expressions around the world daily. That's how Xhosa and her kind did it.

You used "said"—I thought they didn't speak.

In this trilogy, "said" is generic for communicating. It could be verbal but is more likely to be gestures, body language, or facial expressions. I also often use "motioned" and "gestured" to indicate hand signals that communicate their words.

I'm surprised by the sophistication and cleverness of some of their actions.

Homo erectus *could pass as a modern man dressed properly and if the viewer carried no precognitions about what he expected. But he lacked many of the social constructs we take for granted. Because these traits don't fossilize, we extrapolate what life was like from artifacts like their sophisticated tools.*

A recent study out of Gesher Benot Ya'aqov (in the Levant) provides evidence that in that part of Eurasia, Homo erectus *lived in a camp—called a homebase—with divided work areas for toolmaking and consumption located near a hearth. These are traits associated with our modern lifestyle and now are found over half a million years ago.*

How do you know Xhosa had headaches?

Well, I don't (of course—nothing 850,000 years old remains to indicate that) but recent research indicates there could be a gene variant that contributes to headaches that our ancestors could have had even as far back as 2 million years ago.

You often say these people squat. Don't they sit?

There is nominal physical evidence showing that early man squatted rather than sat. This includes tell-tale divots and scratches in the femur, tibia, and ankle bone of Neanderthals that would result from squatting a lot. Though Neanderthals are a more recent Homo *species than Xhosa's People, I make the assumption if they didn't sit much, neither did* Homo erectus. *Another reason we presume earliest man preferred to squat than sit is because it's far more natural for the body, even now, and it's quicker to get into and out of a squat should danger arrive. Try it—you'll agree.*

Were Big Heads smarter than Xhosa's species?

What Xhosa refers to as "Big Heads" were an archaic form of our species, Homo sapiens. *Morphologically and behaviorally, they fall between* Homo erectus *and modern* Homo sapiens. *They had higher foreheads and prominent chins. They were probably less violent than* Homo erectus *but based on the shape of their cranium, solved more problems with brains than brawn. If we define "smarter" as "cleverer", then yes, they were. The rise of multiple archaic forms of* Homo sapiens *contributed to the end of the long-thriving* Homo erectus.

Remember: Xhosa and Wind resulted from a mating between archaic Homo sapiens *and* Homo erectus *making them brighter than the average among Xhosa's People.*

Could primitive man build rafts as suggested in this story?

Yes, absolutely. They possessed the brainpower, and the required tools were available at the time. Because these rafts must have been made of wood and vines—-materials that don't preserve over time—no artifacts remain to prove this. Anthropologists speculate this earliest raft was more of a floating platform made from bamboo and tied together with vine. Scientists tested this hypothesis by building rafts using the prehistoric techniques Xhosa employed to cross the Straits of Gibraltar and then sailing the raft through Indonesia as the ancient people might have done.

What does "strong" and "weak" side mean?

Based on artifacts from 850,000 years ago (and longer), paleoscientists speculate that early man preferred their right hand. That made their right hand stronger than the left (though they didn't identify "right" and "left" at that time). Because of this, my characters call the right side their "strong side" and left the "weak side".

How did early man tell time?

Like today's most primitive communities, early man didn't care about hours or minutes. His metric was how much sunlight remained before he must find a safe place to sleep. Therefore, they indicated time in the future by pointing to a place in the sky where the sun would eventually reach. They might say, "Return by this point" and mean, "Return when Sun reaches this point in the sky."

What does a "hand of Sun's travel" mean?

A "hand" quantifies the amount of time it takes Sun to move the distance of a hand (the width of four fingers, together) held up to the sky. A finger is about fifteen minutes and four fingers—a hand—about an hour. This is one way the earliest People measured the passage of time. Test it yourself. Hold a finger up next to the Sun. It will take approximately fifteen minutes for the Sun to reach the far side of your finger.

What does the term "subadult" mean?

A subadult is a boy or girl older than a child but not an adult. Today, we might call him/her a teenager. In fact, in Xhosa's world, subadults—despite their immature bodies—performed much of what adults did save the duties of scouts, hunters, and warriors.

What is a "homebase"?

This is the name applied by many paleoanthropologists to a permanent space where these earliest people gathered, what we might call a home or a neighborhood. Groupmembers returned here after hunting and foraging to eat, sleep, knap tools, and care for those too young or old to care for themselves. It also affords a location where their injured could recover from wounds or sickness. Many scientists consider it a "place of origin" from which the populations foraged outward—up to about a hundred miles. It differs from the temporary sites that serve the People while they hunt or migrate. Homo habilis *and* Homo erectus *were the first species of man to establish this sort of central location.*

A note: Most paleoanthropologists write this as two words—'home base' but I use one word, reflective of how Xhosa's People thought of it.

Why are these characters so violent?

The answer to this question is simple: They had to be. If Homo erectus *hadn't been violent 850,000 years ago, he—and our genus—wouldn't have survived. With skin too thin, claws too short, and teeth useless for defense, man wasn't the era's apex predator. His only advantage over those who preyed on him was a thoughtful brain.*

It's hard to believe Xhosa walked from Africa to the Middle East to Spain.

Wilford Wolpoff of the University of Michigan says that Homo erectus *left Africa "because they wanted to, because they had to, and especially because they could."* Homo erectus *(Xhosa's species) is the first of our genus to inhabit Eurasia. Dozens of sites exist from Indonesia to Spain to Britain. We know— because of his tool-creation sophistication—that* Homo erectus *was smart enough to survive in varied environs. But why leave his homeland and go elsewhere? It could be to follow the herds or a reaction to changes in climate. They might have fled or chased enemies, or it could simply be our forebears suffered what many today do—wanderlust.*

Can early man really run down their prey?

That answer is a resounding Yes. Scientists call this the "Endurance Running Hypothesis". Early Man didn't run faster *than herd animals. They ran* harder—*all day or more. The* Homo *genus evolved a more stable head, looser hips, longer legs, shock-absorbing joints, and a springier foot formation. This made them—and us—well-suited to continuous running. Other changes in body makeup meant humans didn't tire or overheat from this activity. Most animals sprint only short distances before they must stop to catch their breath and let their bodies cool down. We didn't.*

Did early man live on the Iberian Peninsula?

Paleoanthropologists say that Homo antecessor—*the cannibals and Qu'tez's Cave Dwellers, kin to* Homo erectus—*showed up in Spain about 850,000 years ago. They vanished and then reappeared hundreds of thousands of years later. No one knows why but postulate the cannibalistic lifestyle caused the rise and decline of early man's presence there.*

Why didn't early man leave the Iberian Peninsula rather than die out?

The answer to whether early man left or became extinct in this area about 1 million years ago is lost in prehistory. Back then, water surrounded the Iberian Peninsula on three sides by water (except for a possible land bridge from Africa to Spain). Reaching it was not easy, even with the primitive raft technology they possessed. Frigid mountains blocked the fourth side. We see the difficulties Xhosa and her People endured crossing the Pyrenees. Who knows if Homo antecessor *was tough enough to replicate that? We still don't know why the Aztecs disappeared from the southwest USA.*

Spoiler alert: Wasn't Britain too cold for human habitation 850,000 years ago? How could the Islanders live there?

Paleoanthropologists agreed for a long time that human habitation in the area we now know of as the British Isles was impossible. Therefore, they pegged human settlement there at a much later date than current estimates. Recent evidence indicates that man has been there since about 900,000 BCE.

Spoiler alert: What star guided Seeker from the Iberian Peninsula to the British Isles?

The enormously bright star *Venus* is located directly above the horizon. This likely is what caught *Seeker's* attention, especially during this time of year. What he called a herd of stampeding stars was a meteor shower. He had seen what we today term "shooting stars" at times before in his life but not in this quantity and longevity. To him, it became a sign directing them to their next new home.

You made up the bird language—right?

Wrong. Imitating bird song to communicate over difficult-to-traverse expanses has been used throughout the world by different cultures. If you're curious, try this   link *https://www.npr.org/sections/parallels/2015/09/26/443434027/in-a-turkish-village-a-conversation-with-whistles-not-words*

I didn't read these books in order. Does it matter?

Each book in the trilogy is a stand-alone story and includes details to catch you up on what occurred in prior books but without most of the drama. They can be read out of order, but you may find the experience enhanced by reading the three books that make up each trilogy consecutively.

Foreword

No one told the heroes in the *Crossroads* trilogy—Xhosa, Pando, Nightshade, Wind, Zvi, Seeker, and Spirit—they represented the leading edge of man's dispersion across Eurasia. Their readiness to journey into the unknown marked our genus's flexibility, adaptability, fungibility, and wanderlust—hallmarks of an evolutionary fitness that 850,000 years ago challenged Nature for control of the world.

As you read the *Crossroads* trilogy, keep in mind these characters are 850,000 years old. They are pre-everything civilized. Their rudimentary culture fits broad definitions of this word because the People share behaviors, cognitive constructs, and memories, but it doesn't fit more detailed attributes. Many don't wear clothes (though Xhosa and her People wear pelts because of the brutal cold), don't marry (they do "pairmate"), and have no idea about religion, art, or music. They don't bury their dead—why would they? Other animals don't. They are without social norms, traditions, societal rules, and judgmental attitudes toward others. They don't have tattoos, jewelry, or adornments. They count to two (what some call the "one-two-many" approach to counting) but anything beyond that is described in different ways and prefer descriptions to proper nouns.

Their lives revolve around two simple goals: survive and procreate. To accomplish these, they became the cleverest creatures in the kingdom. How else could they endure in a violent world where an angry, disruptive creature called Nature ruled?

Chapter 1

The foothills of the Pyrenees

They came out of the mountains, hair frozen in sparkling strands, hands and feet wrapped in shredded pelts, ribs etched against their skin under ragged hides white with snow, faces haggard with fatigue. Blood crusted scrapes and gashes, many recent, others almost healed, reminders of the violent struggles endured on their journey.

Though their steps flagged, not one of these upright creatures exhibited a hint of defeat. All males and a few females carried at least one spear, some two, many with warclubs strapped to their backs. Despite the anxiety and fear of entering this foreign land, hope energized them today, that their migration might be at an end.

All of them—Xhosa and her tribe, Pan-do and his, Wind, Zvi, and Seeker—had been chased from their homes by enemies. In their flight, they found each other. It took time to work through their differences but now they traveled side by side, respected ideas not theirs, and called themselves the People.

Their charismatic Leaders—Xhosa, Wind, and Pan-do— were known as reliable friends to those who earned their trust and dangerous enemies to those who opposed them. Two wolves—Spirit and Black Wolf—journeyed with them. Though the People lacked the animals' sharp claws, dense fur, and piercing teeth, each considered the other "pack" and would defend them to death.

The exhausted group straggled down the gently sloping flank, feet shuffling carefully over the slippery scree. The ground changed from talus to stunted tufts of grass, sparse and brown which made walking easier. Optimism shone from their faces even as their tired eyes flicked side to side in search of unexpected movement, ears strained for out-of-place noises, and noses sniffed.

Rather than continue across the meadow, Xhosa led the People into the shade of the edging forest.

"Do you smell it, Wind?" Anticipation filled her gestures.

She and Wind, pairmates as well as Co-Leaders, stood quietly, absorbing their surroundings. Light filtered lazily through the canopy, the shadowed ground dappled with patches of warmth. She sniffed in the essence of wet earth and rotting leaves, the mustiness of moss, and something else much more enticing.

"It's there." She pointed and strode forward, lengthening her stride.

An icy gust whipped down the hillside through the shadows and raised bumps on her arms but she ignored it. The forest gave way to open sky and searing heat. It was too hot for her thin pelt but she didn't stop to remove it. Green stalks swayed as far as she could see, edged on one side by more mountains and the other by some sort of leaves and branches. Sunlight glinted off the rippled surface of a distant river as it curled over the terrain.

"Dung!" The scent overpowered every other odor.

Wind huffed to her side. "It's been a long time since we smelled dung that wasn't frozen."

"We did it, Wind." Her eyes glistened with relief.

For most of a Moon, dread gnawed at her courage and left her wondering if following the guidance of Seeker—a boy barely a man—was a mistake. But Seeker assured her in his ebullient way that once out of the hills, their new homebase would welcome them. Xhosa wanted to believe him because she wasn't sure what else to do. Nor did she know what to do if it didn't work.

Wind motioned, arms inclusive, "It's beautiful, Xhosa."

Siri, Pan-do, Ngili, the wolves Spirit and Black Wolf, and the rest of the People gathered around Xhosa and Wind, eyes locked on what lay in front of them.

Pan-do whispered, "We made it." His eyes were moist, mouth open.

Ngili, the People's Lead Hunter, motioned, hands close to his body. "With all this grass, Gazelle or Mammoth must be nearby."

Dust, the Lead Scout, trotted up, coming from a tall cliff far ahead on their forward path. "I think there are caves there."

The People hadn't slept in a cave since leaving Viper and the Mountain Dwellers. It would be a treat if true.

Xhosa looked behind. Shadows already stretched as far from the bottom of the rocky slopes as sunlight to the top. Daylight would soon end.

"We don't have much time. Let's rest and then see if those are caves."

Ngili, the People's Lead Hunter, motioned, fingers spaced out, palms up, "I'll go with Dust to check." He added a swift spread-fingered swipe with first one hand and then the other, followed by a quick bob of his head and a puff.

Xhosa brushed both hands down her sides. *Go.*

The People spoke with a complex combination of hand motions, facial expressions, body movements, and sounds augmented with chirrups, snaps, hisses, and whistles. By the time Ngili finished talking, Xhosa knew how many would join him, where they would go, and how long they'd be away. The People's communication was sophisticated but quiet, a precaution especially in unfamiliar areas. Unusual sounds— voices, for example—stood out. All animals made noises but few as varied as the People's. Why alert Others who lived here to their presence? Xhosa would do that in her own time, in her own way.

Dust, Ngili, and two scouts soon receded into the landscape, the only evidence of their passage a slight disturbance in the slender waving stalks. Despite the dung scents, the abundant plant food, and the glisten of a faraway river, Xhosa crossed her arms over her chest and paced.

Something is wrong.

She searched the forests and the rippling field that had swallowed up Dust and Ngili . Xhosa possessed the ability to see great distances in sufficient detail to find trails, footprints, movement, or the glitter of sun off eyes.

She saw none of those and that made her more uncomfortable.

With this wealth of food and water, Others should be here.

Wind motioned, palms flattened against his chest, "The mountains we crossed touched Sun. They're cold and barren. Few can do what we did to get here, Xhosa. We are safe."

Xhosa could hear in his voice, see in his gestures, that despite his bravado, Wind too felt uneasy about what they didn't see and hear.

But she grinned. "I don't know how I survived without someone being able to read my thoughts."

She trotted over to a stream that fed into the river she had noticed. She stretched out on her belly, flat on the soft grass at the water's edge, and took a long, satisfying drink of the sweet liquid. Thirst quenched, she collected handfuls of the tender shoots of new plants growing along the shore, ate what she wanted and tossed the rest into a communal food pile that would be shared with all the People. It was already filling up with fat fish speared from the slow-moving pools beside the river, tasty reeds and cattails, and even a handful of eggs plucked from nests not hidden well enough along the shore and in the roots of trees. The wolves snapped birds from the air and swallowed them almost whole, coughing up feathers.

Xhosa leaned back on her hands, sniffing the unique fragrance of each groupmember. Zvi was sweaty from wrestling with Spirit. Siri smelled sourly of hunger but she wouldn't eat until Honey's bleeding foot was wrapped in mulch and leaves. The females with new babies exuded the pleasant aroma of milk. Some scents jumbled together making them impossible to identify. When Xhosa became Leader of the People, before it merged with Pan-do's and Hawk's, the People had been small enough that she could recognize everyone by their odor. Now, she kept track of her tribe while Pan-do did the same with his. Wind helped everyone.

Done eating, the People sprawled on the warm ground, soaking up Sun's remaining rays, chatting contentedly with gestures and the occasional sigh. Water dripped from their thawing bodies, soaking into the thirsty ground, as the remaining ice and snow on their pelts and in their hair melted away.

Xhosa and Wind sat apart from the others, on a log long ago softened by rot. She uprooted handfuls of grass and wiped the sweat from Wind's body, as he did hers. The soft scratch felt good and the earthy fragrance reminded her of times long gone. When he finished, she harvested chunks of green moss from the log's decaying bark and stuffed them into her neck sack. All the People wore one of these around their necks. Even the wolves did when they were migrating.

Finished, she leaned against Wind and closed her eyes. In a group of Others, her pairmate stood out. A Big Head, the People's traditional enemy, the ones who drove Xhosa and her tribe from their long-established home, Wind had earned Xhosa's trust by saving her life more than once and then, as a member of her People, sharing Big Head spear tricks and warrior skills with her Leads. Before long, each of them individually told her that thanks to Wind they could now defeat an attack which they couldn't have done in the past. Whatever distrust her People harbored toward him faded away.

"Xhosa!" Dust panted up to her. "I found a cave. And we found trace of a herd. Ngili is tracking it."

By the time Sun settled into its night nest, the People were ensconced in the cave Dust found. They had to squeeze together to fit but all were thrilled to sleep without waking to frozen toes and numb fingers. Stone and Zvi—the burliest of the People—lugged rocks in and Siri built a fire that quickly warmed the interior. The subadults gathered kindling to feed it and arranged who would be responsible throughout the night for keeping it lit.

Usually, the wolves slept scattered among the People but with Black Wolf close to delivering her pups, she dug out an opening in the back and claimed it as her den. Then she settled to her belly, one leg forward, the other bent back, eyebrows twitching.

Xhosa strode toward the nest she would share with Wind but stopped at the sight of Seeker, weight on his bottom, legs crossed in front of his body in the uncomfortable position he preferred. His pairmate Lyta curled next to him with their best friend, Zvi.

Xhosa approached Seeker. "You are not outside."

Every night as long as Xhosa could remember, the enigmatic male lay on his back, gaze fixed steadily on the star-dotted sky, spouting what to Xhosa sounded like gibberish to whoever listened. Intermittently, he leapt to his feet and spun dizzying circles or bounced from one foot to the other, huffing and chirping. Lyta and Zvi would either join him or watch. He once explained to Xhosa that this was how he studied the changes in the night sky—the appearance and disappearance of particular stars or their movement in relation to each other—so he could guide the People accurately. This nightly process was how they had moved from the distant start of Endless Pond to this cave where Endless Pond seemed to end.

He didn't respond to her statement, didn't even acknowledge her. That worried Xhosa. She hadn't been able to shake the feeling that danger lurked around them, somewhere. Seeker's anxious look didn't help.

She squatted at his side and added a question to her declaration. "The stars aren't talking to you?"

To the side, Lyta wriggled, not comfortable in the seated position Seeker preferred but determined to try because Seeker liked it so much. Zvi crouched on the balls of her feet, the more traditional pose. She'd tried to sit on her bottom, legs crossed in front, but kept falling backward. Besides, it took her too long to rise from that position which meant if Lyta needed help, she couldn't respond quickly. Squatting, for her, made more sense. Seeker didn't care. He expected all to do what worked for them.

Both his best friend and his future pairmate were long accustomed to his eccentricities.

Finally, Seeker offered Xhosa only a confused frown.

That's not a "Yes they are," and that raised the hair on her neck. Before she could ask more, Ngili scrambled through the thistle barrier the youngsters had placed around the cave's mouth to prevent the entrance of intruders and hurried toward Xhosa.

He motioned, "I lost the herd's trace in the dark. I'll try again tomorrow," and then raced toward where the hunters had gathered. They were all tired. Some would mate before sleeping but not Ngili. He hadn't given up hope that his pairmate, Hecate, would come back.

After a final glance at Seeker, Xhosa joined Wind in their nest. She squatted behind him and teased the dirt and debris from his long head hair, occasionally focusing on a difficult tangle until her fingers could move easily through his hair. When she finished, he did the same for her.

As he groomed, he said, "I'll join Ngili tomorrow. If there are herds, we will find them."

"Pan-do and I will continue with the People."

They said nothing more, both enjoying the calming feel of nails scratching on their skin and the intimacy of someone they trusted implicitly. Done, both fell asleep.

The first rays of daylight filtered into the cave. Black Wolf was already outside, padding back and forth restlessly, huffing uncomfortably. Wind left with Ngili and a handful of scouts, knowing Xhosa would leave a trail to wherever they settled when Sun's light ran out. Though Spirit usually went with the hunters, today he stayed with Black Wolf.

Xhosa and Pan-do led. Dust copied their pace and direction but a distance away. With Ngili and Wind searching for meat, Xhosa focused on finding a cave large enough for the People. They strode onward, gaze sweeping the landscape, everyone grazing on berries, roots, and worms as they walked. Sporadically, Xhosa heard a faraway squawk or glimpsed a covey of birds as they exploded into flight, fleeing an unknown threat.

It was the direction Ngili and Wind had gone, and told her how far they'd gotten.

The People rested by a waterhole. They searched its shoreline for prints but found none. Wherever the herds lived, they didn't drink here so the People moved on, through copses of young saplings and around a bed of haphazardly-strewn boulders. The air tasted of flowers, warm earth, and the mild tang of salt, but the dung they found was hard and old.

Xhosa touched Pan-do's hand and both stopped, eyes forward. "Do you smell that? It reminds me of Endless Pond."

He pointed to his strong side and the direction they were walking. "From there and there. How can it be on two sides?"

Xhosa tingled. One of her People—Rainbow—had abandoned them long ago, taking many males and females with him. Others she and her People ran into while migrating here told her Rainbow traveled the same route she did but along the opposite shore of Endless Pond. For him, as for her, this was as far as he could go without folding back on himself.

If they got this far. If any survived.

She pushed aside those thoughts. Before searching for whatever remnants remained of Rainbow's group, the People must find a homebase. All they suffered to get here—the interminable walking, the loss of Hawk, the death of groupmembers, Nightshade's treachery—was for naught if they didn't establish a home.

Spirit bumped her leg. Black Wolf panted at her mate's side, her belly almost touching the ground.

Xhosa motioned, "Your mate's pups won't wait much longer. We will find a den for her."

Spirit took off, his movements graceful and fluid with Black Wolf lumbering after him.

Not much later, Pan-do squinted ahead. "I think Spirit found a cave."

Xhosa leaned forward, narrowing her gaze, and finally saw where Spirit stopped. He sat on his haunches at the base of a cliff, facing her, nose twitching, tail swishing the dirt behind him.

It took the rest of the day to cross over the craggy scrubland, up and down the deep ravines, and around the occasional spot of slippery ice. The cave proved too small for the People but not for Black Wolf's needs. With much scuffling and panting, she created a nest for her pups and disappeared into the cool dark hole. The People settled outside, under an overhang that would protect them from rain and predators, and far enough away to not bother the new mother. As soon as Ngili and Wind arrived, shaking their heads that they hadn't found a herd, they left again to search for signs of a trail left by former inhabitants of this cave.

Xhosa's chest squeezed and her stomach knotted. Spirit padded up to her side, hackles puffed, nostrils flaring. He agreed. Something about this area made her tingle but for now, until Black Wolf finished, they must stay.

Chapter 2

Black Wolf's pups arrived that night. Mother poked and nudged each bundle until a high-pitched mewl burst from their tiny muzzles. She bit the cord that connected them to her, ate the afterbirth, and placed the miniature creatures between her rear legs. Though blind, instinct guided them to the milk bursting from their mother's teats.

Black Wolf would nurse the pups until they grew old enough to venture outside. She would clean up their urine and feces and generally keep the den invisible to predators who would enjoy nothing more than feasting on baby wolves. Spirit's job was to provide their food.

The next day, while the pups sniffed and tasted their new world and the scouts explored it, Xhosa left to forage for the healing plants needed to treat the People's injuries. Some plants—moss and honey for example—could be found anywhere but others—a certain flower or grass—had to be replaced. It had become Xhosa's job to sort through new plants and find the ones to replace those she could no longer find.

This was a job Xhosa liked doing because for her, it was personal. Her chronic head pains could be controlled but the plant she required wasn't always where the People ended up. Today, she hoped that something she'd used in the past grew in this land, because she was almost out.

She stuffed her neck sack with throwing stones and gestured to a spot overhead, telling Pan-do she'd be back when Sun reached that spot. Spear in hand, she barked at Spirit and left. The wolf whimpered, head twisting from his pairmate to his departing Alpha, and sprinted after Xhosa. Honey chased both. The young female loved healing plants in the way warriors loved weapons. She never missed an opportunity to learn more about them.

Xhosa set a fast pace, enjoying the perfume of flowers, the tang of salt on her tongue, her head swiveling over the landscape. The Sun's hot rays made sweat drip down her chest and legs, the only coolness coming when air wafted over her clammy skin. A broad-winged eagle circled overhead, like others she'd seen but heftier. It spotted her and floated off in search of smaller prey. Not long after, it dove, something squealed, and it flew off, a shrew in its sharp claws.

Xhosa collected a rangy stalk, a yellow flower, and a handful of roots, one or all she hoped would treat the red fingers. If not, they might be useful to reduce inflammation, soak up blood, or suck poison from wounds.

A hand of Sun's travel overhead passed when Honey approached Xhosa, a straggly long-leafed plant with stiff ragged leaves in her hand. "I think this is what we use for red fingers."

Xhosa examined the roots, stem, leaves, and vein placement. "Rub it on a part—"

Honey stretched her arm forward. "The skin isn't inflamed, doesn't itch, and has no rash or bumps or discoloration."

"Did Spirit sniff it?"

"He licked it."

"Good. Take a small bite but don't swallow."

Honey rolled it around in her mouth and spit it out, fingers touching her lips. "It doesn't burn or numb."

Xhosa nodded, satisfied. "Collect it."

By the time their shadows dissolved beneath their bodies, they had filled the sacks they wore around their necks and were heading back to the encampment.

Honey hurried to El-ga as soon as she got back to the base. The child—nearly a subadult—had fallen into a chasm while chasing a hare and split his leg open. The blood crusted over but the wound was now hot to the touch and the perilous red fingers extended up his leg. Honey hoped the straggly stem she'd harvested would stop their growth.

Xhosa took a quick look around—everyone busy—and scrambled up the cliff behind the wolves' den. She settled on her haunches in a secluded area with an unobstructed view of the activities below.

She winced as the spike drove into her eyes, worse than the last one. She pressed against her temples and involuntarily sucked in a breath. The fire made her want to curl in a ball. The throb had started subtly, as she and Honey made their way back to the camp. By the time they reached the overhang, pain stabbed cruelly as though someone shoved a stick through her head. If she didn't stop it soon, she would start vomiting and be unable to keep the treatment down.

She hadn't found anything new so would use what she had. Light hurt so she fumbled blindly through the familiar roots, tubers, and seeds in her neck sack. She found what she needed, popped a leaf in her mouth along with a yellow flower, and chewed. The flower's sweet taste cut the leaf's rancidness. Her head drooped as relief washed over her.

This illness—she hid it from even Pan-do and Wind, but wouldn't be able to if her supply of treatments couldn't be replaced. That was a worry for another time. It was enough today that her head stopped pounding.

Every day, the People hoped Black Wolf would tell them the pups could travel but no one rushed her. El-ga's red fingers pulled back, now nothing more than soreness around the gash. Honey collected more of the plant, happy to again have a treatment for this deadly illness.

One day, as Xhosa pounded roots, softening them to eat, her mind drifted to Nightshade, the People's long-time Lead Warrior, the male she would have pairmated if he hadn't been expelled. By her. Nightshade had been savage in battle, so fierce all Others avoided him. Xhosa accepted his barbarism as what kept the People safe until he turned it on his own.

She first noticed there was a problem after she escaped the Others who held her captive. When she rejoined the People, Wind at her side, Nightshade seemed to fight with everyone, even the females who mated with him. Xhosa blamed it on Wind's presence but Wind said it was more than that. Yes, Nightshade hated the Big Head but he also resented Xhosa for stopping him from becoming the People's Leader.

Xhosa didn't believe him but didn't *not* believe him either. Whatever the reason, his barbarity resulted in the death of a young female with the callsign Deer. Nightshade said he did it to protect the People. He might have survived that but not when he admitted to slaying Hawk, a cherished Leader and Xhosa's future pairmate. That heinous act turned not just Hawk's People against him, but Xhosa's and Pan-do's. Xhosa worried Hawk's People would also condemn her because she once shared leadership with their Leader's killer. She asked Pan-do what he thought and he laughed.

"Xhosa, few liked Nightshade before he confessed. Afterwards, everyone—male and female—wanted to destroy him. But not you. Hawk respected you, took your counsel. The Hawk People haven't forgotten that."

Pan-do rolled back on his haunches without looking at her. "What you should ask is who will replace Nightshade. That I can help you with. Ngili. He was your father's Lead. All admire his ability."

Xhosa gestured, "Maybe, but there are other worthy warriors. Why not Sa-mo-ke? Nightshade trained him."

Pan-do ran his hand over the dirt at his feet, face suddenly tense. Sa-mo-ke had been his staunchest warrior since he became Leader of his People. Xhosa understood his reluctance to let Sa-mo-ke go but thought there might be something more. She watched Pan-do intently.

Eyes locked on the ground, he finally gestured, "Let's set that aside for the moment because it may solve itself. Hawk's former Lead Warriors, Talon and Water Buffalo, want the former-Hawk People to merge with your People. If that were to happen, it would make the choices clear."

Without saying more, he rose and left her to her thoughts.

Moon departed and reappeared as it always did. Hyaena ate one of Black Wolf's pups but the rest grew sturdy and rambunctious, clumsy on massive paws, alert to sounds with their oversized ears, and always aware of their pack's location.

Finally, the female Alpha trundled out of the wolves' den with her youngsters, the signal that the People could leave. Without wasting time, Xhosa set out. Black Wolf carried one pup in her mouth and Spirit's two-legged best friend, Zvi, tucked one under each of her muscular arms. She preferred to carry one between her jaws as Black Wolf did which would leave her spear hand free, but the People had encountered no Others since arriving so it seemed unnecessary.

Moving on lifted everyone's spirits. They walked in small groups, hands fluttering in spirited chatter, eyes roving hungrily across the terrain. Seeker reverted to his usual ebullient self and flitted from one plant to another, shadowed by Zvi and the wolf pups, and exclaimed over every color and insect and aroma.

The steep hills they had struggled to cross were now only a blur on their backtrail and the frozen wind that made them shiver constantly a welcome memory compared to Sun's intense heat. The males hung their pelts on warclubs strapped to their backs. Still, sweat matted their hair and their skin shone with moisture. Dust found many caves but always occupied. Though he could have driven the inhabitants away, Xhosa refused to trade one creature's home for hers.

Despite no herds, the People ate well, relying on the ample hare, ground birds, snakes, worms, caterpillars, ants as long as their hands, slugs, and eggs. Youngsters collected them from dead logs, scattered along the banks of waterways, and hidden in the abundant scrub of the plateaus. They became a welcome addition to meals.

One day, as the People gathered to eat, Spirit deposited a bloody, plump rat at Xhosa's feet, which made Wind laugh.

"Did I ever tell you about the first time Spirit shared a rat with me? I was tracking you and your captors and starving as I did so. One night, I was so miserably hungry, I couldn't sleep. Spirit showed up. I didn't know him then and thought he'd come to eat me but I was too wretched to care. Instead, he dropped a partially chewed hare in front of me and left. Another night, he brought eggs, and once, a still-warm rat. As I devoured the food, even sucking the marrow from the rat's bones, I explained to Spirit that I ate rats only as a last resort but thanked him for caring. He seemed to understand. Well, at least, he never again offered me a rat. Now that I know his eating habits, I recognize that he shared a valued meal with me."

His eyes clouded. "Those were bad times, Xhosa. You were captured. Nightshade had quit looking for you. That left me on my own and I would never quit. But I had to admit, even if I found you, I didn't know how to save you."

After a breath, and another, he motioned, "Spirit changed that. He helped me find you. For some reason I still don't understand, he wouldn't allow me to fail."

Xhosa looked at him. "I didn't know."

Wind's mouth moved into something between a smile and a grimace. "If you hadn't returned, your People would be far different than who they are now. As would I. I suspect Spirit, Zvi, and Seeker would have left, probably followed by Pan-do's People. Those who remained, I doubt your father would recognize as the tribe he gave his life to defend."

She gazed into the distance, a thread prickling through her brain, awed by what the unexpected partnership of Wind and Spirit had done for the People. She leaned against her pairmate, feeling his strength and warmth.

He rested his head on the top of hers. "I don't know why he trusted me, Xhosa, but I'm glad he did. My life is better with Spirit in it."

Some of the animals the People hoped to catch came out at night. Most nocturnal predators were no threat but that changed with the appearance of the owls. These birds were unlike every other owl Xhosa had ever seen, with bodies the size of a small child and a wingspan wider than Xhosa could stretch her arms. They flew soundlessly, the sole warning they stalked being the susurrus sound of rustling wings and then the panicked squawk of their unsuspecting prey.

The People slept in the open when they were unable to find a cave, which happened often. One night, they lost a child to Giant Owl. The next night, Water Buffalo and Snake suffered puncture wounds and deep scratches protecting a youngster from the massive bird. After that, if no cave was available, the children slept under overhangs protected by Spirit and Black Wolf. With the wolves there, Giant Owl stayed away.

Every day, as soon as Sun pushed the dark away, the People set out. Black Wolf scampered forward, a pup in her mouth, the other two carried by Zvi and Lyta. Spirit walked to the front or side but never far from his pack. He paused often, eyebrows bunched at a new scent, tongue tasting the air. If his hackles stiffened or he growled, it served as Xhosa's early danger warning.

So far, no growls, no raised hackles, no alerts.

The scouts were never farther away than they could return by daylight's end. Once a homebase was selected, they would go beyond that.

When Sun dipped below the horizon, turning the sky shades of pink and orange, the People gathered against a cliff or under a tree—in a cave if they were lucky. They ate from a communal pile of food and talked as a group. The adults explained to the subadults how to chop roots, remove termites from their mounds with a twig, and the differences among tracks that indicated size, speed, and whether they were prey or predator. When Sun slept, everyone else slept also.

One day, another like many before, Xhosa slowed down until Seeker caught up with her.

She motioned, "You are always happy here. Does that mean we are on the right forward path?"

Seeker turned to her, head tilted, youthful face smooth. A thatch of dark curly hair hung in a tangled web over his forehead. He seemed unbothered, even when it blocked his eyes.

"Yes, I am content. We are where we must be and going where we should. But the reason has changed."

Xhosa jerked to a stop and then forced herself to continue walking. This wasn't what she expected. She knotted her waist-length hair behind her neck to give herself time to think and then gestured, hands as fluid as she could manage, "What does that mean?"

"Be patient, Leader," Seeker motioned with the quiet authority of one much more experienced than a subadult should be. "I'll know soon and then, you will."

Without additional explanation, he joined Lyta and Zvi, prancing on his toes and moving his hands in circles which brought giggles to Lyta. Xhosa loosened her hair, forgetting she'd just tied it up. It fell down her back and swayed side to side as she hurried to catch Wind.

He motioned without turning, "The air tastes of Endless Pond."

Xhosa sniffed, finding the humidity and then the salt.

"We are close." She tried to keep the concern from her voice but realized the sharpness gave it away.

Wind turned toward her. He cocked his head as his mouth twitched and one eyebrow ticked up. "I see. We can talk tonight."

Chapter 3

Shadows deepened from blue to purple. The People found a small cave not far from a river. Xhosa hoped whoever showed up to drink would lead the hunters to herds. Guards patrolled the heights and would trade places throughout the night.

With most of the People asleep, Xhosa climbed a nearby tree. From here, she could see into the cave but still be hidden. A sharp-toothed crocodile was chewing inside her head and if she didn't stop it, she'd start screaming. That wouldn't be good.

She gripped a branch as the world spun, swallowing the bile that burst into her mouth, eyes watering as the pain flared. She dug through her neck sack for the root and then chewed. Gradually, the agony receded. She'd run out of her most effective treatment but this one muted it. Somewhat. At least better than nothing.

"I will have to tell Wind and Pan-do," she grumbled to herself. Her Co-Leaders had a right to know that she couldn't always be dependable. "Maybe I should step aside, let someone else lead."

As though he heard her thoughts, as he often did, Wind scrambled up the trunk, jostling the limb as he settled next to her, causing a hot spike to explode behind her eyes. Her hands shook but otherwise, she sat quietly, eyes panning the landscape. He did the same. Neither found anything of concern.

And then, he motioned, "You consumed those roots faster than usual."

How does he know that? "What?"

Without meaning to, she closed her eyes and rubbed the tender part of her temple, beating back nausea, trying to figure out if this was the time.

She sighed. "I suppose it is."

He touched her arm. "I already know. Pan-do does, too, but no one else."

"How could you?" The muted croak of her voice resembled more a sick frog than the Leader of a powerful People.

"That's what I do. I see things and draw conclusions." He touched her neck sack. "For example, that root you just ate is bitter. No one consumes it for pleasure. It didn't take much to figure out you ate it because you had no other choice."

She gulped.

"Xhosa, you can trust me. If I planned to turn on you, I wouldn't have saved your life once or again. My sole purpose as Co-Leader is to help you." He pulled something from his neck sack. "Try this."

He tossed her a lethargic yellowish plant, leaves drooping, but it was the root bundle with its smooth white bulbs that caught Xhosa's attention.

She gasped. "That's Fang's cure! Where did you get it?"

One good thing to come from being captured was learning of her abductor's highly effective treatment for her illness. She'd collected as many of the plants as possible when she escaped but hadn't seen it since.

He grinned. "There's a lot of it growing not far away."

She bit one of the bulbs and stuffed the rest into her neck sack as she wriggled deeper into the V of the limbs. Then, she twisted around to look into Wind's eyes.

"Why do you believe in me, Wind? I trusted a traitor. My last pairmate died at my command. I follow the advice of a boy-male who talks to stars. I can't find a new homebase. I am not the Leader you or my People deserve."

Her gestures came out stiff and unsure, her breaths forced and ragged with none of her usual confidence. Saying this to

Wind left her vulnerable, exposed in the way of an unhealed wound.

He cocked his head, eyes soft. "Because nothing stops you. I saw that when you challenged Nightshade, after your father's death."

Her brow furrowed, confused. "How—"

He raised a hand. "My entire tribe watched. We wanted to know who would lead in your father's place. We were riveted by your cleverness. Many of us cheered your win." He laughed. "Your methods were devious—we respected that."

A moan floated up from below. There, eyes shut, Spirit rolled, spreading his scent over the loose debris around the trunk. Done, he scratched himself with one hind foot and fell asleep. Taking ownership of where his Alphas slept, protecting them, let him sleep peacefully.

Xhosa pushed her face into the hollow of Wind's neck and breathed in the scent of his sweat-soaked body, the fragrance of the berries he'd eaten, and the tang of blood where he'd scraped himself. It was intoxicating.

The silence swelled to fill the space around them until Wind motioned, hands moving fluidly, "Seeker thinks we are here to find someone to guide us to our new homebase. He says you had to be enslaved by Fang so you could rescue Ngili and he could guide us here."

She laughed. "That's what Seeker meant. But what does 'but the reason changed' mean?"

"That I don't know."

"I'm afraid to find out."

They fell into a comfortable silence. Moon stared down, a slice of yellow against the black, masked by misty gray clouds that hid Seeker's precious stars. Xhosa wished this would never end.

"Pan-do, someone must challenge to become the former-Hawk People's Leader."

She knew her Co-Leader's answer because she'd asked him the same question a handful of times and his response never changed. Why she kept asking, she had no idea.

He answered immediately, "As I've said before, they want to join your People, Xhosa, which to them means they don't need new Leads."

She listened carefully to his response. He showed no resentment that merging the two tribes would increase her power, no tension that it might undermine him. In fact, the look on his face was relief. Pan-do had never wanted to Lead, did it because no one else would. Now, there was Xhosa. They had been involved in handfuls of dangerous events, many neither had ever before faced, and he often told her that her calm decisiveness and ability to make decisions assured him she would care for his People as her own if anything happened to him. He was right, of course, but her People would be weaker without Pan-do at her side. The combination of his patience and her forcefulness made both stronger and she dreaded the day he would push to blend his People into hers, retiring to be just another warrior or hunter.

She harrumphed. "Well, even if the two tribes merge, the former-Hawk males can challenge for Leads—Warrior, Hunter, or Scout. Some are highly skilled, maybe more than those who already hold the positions."

She stared at their forward trail. Somewhere ahead lay their future if they could overcome the challenges sure to arise over the next handful of Moons. All they needed was courage, hard work, and the right people making decisions.

"What about Talon? He is Lead Warrior of the former-Hawk People."

Pan-do picked a crawly creature from Xhosa's hair. She'd felt its tickle, tried to shake it off to no avail, and now reveled in its absence.

He tossed it aside and motioned, "He doesn't like making decisions and always goes to Wind with questions."

Her jaw twitched. Nightshade should have trained his Lead better. Talon shouldn't need to rely on Wind, or anyone.

"What about Snake or Water Buffalo?"

Pan-do laughed. "One loves power and the other is weak."

Xhosa didn't disagree. "Or Stone? From my People?"

"He is committed to Ngili."

She scratched her chest and looked away. "Who is one of the current Leads."

"Which brings us back to you."

Xhosa bit back her exasperation but couldn't hide the shadow that clouded her eyes. "It must be resolved—"

"It is. The Hawk People respect you, Wind, and your current Leads. Blend Hawk's People into yours. Keep the same Leads. No one will object."

With that, Pan-do left. He'd told her what he intended. Now, it was up to her.

Pan-do and Xhosa led, the warriors arrayed to the sides, the scouts along the forward path, Ngili, Stone, and Spirit on the backtrail. Lyta, Pan-do's unusual daughter, hobbled on her twisted feet as fast as most walked, entertaining everyone with a voice that mimicked the sounds around her. Beside Lyta strode Siri, talking to Honey and a group of females.

Wind caught up to her, energy sizzling from him like mist from a waterfall. It made her heart beat faster which Xhosa didn't understand. That hadn't happened with Nightshade or Hawk but she admitted to herself, it felt good. Feelings weren't important to the People so this too didn't make sense. Why did she care that it "felt good"?

This mystery would have to be solved another day.

Wind motioned, "No sign of Others," though his hands move cautiously, as though he didn't believe his senses. "How was your conversation with Pan-do?"

She gave him a quick summary, hands pressed against her body. He grumbled. "I won't lead the former-Hawk People—he knows that. Blend them into yours and I will continue to co-lead."

"Pan-do agrees. I wonder if others do."

Sun had drained most of the color from the landscape as the group—aside from a handful of scouts led by Wind—drew near a cave they hoped would provide shelter. A stocky short-haired cat-like creature with a feral scent that promised power blocked their way. Its fur was as black as Panther and its head reached

Xhosa's chest. Beside it stood a smaller mate and behind them, cubs, their overgrown paws assuring that they would grow to be at least Spirit's massive size.

Xhosa motioned them onward. "Big Panther requires this cave as much as we do."

Spirit stayed behind, hackles up, head dipped, tail stiff, eyes locked onto Big Panther, his message clear: Stay away and I will too.

Dust found another cave but it too was occupied so they settled for an overhang surrounded with thistles. No one complained, happy for the warmth that radiated from the rock, gratified they had not yet faced any threat, and optimistic that tomorrow would bring a homebase not claimed by Big Panther. A lone wolf howled from the ridge above them. Another answered down the canyon. Spirit raised his muzzle and wailed a greeting to his wild cousins. And then, silence, disrupted intermittently by the chirp of insects and the croak of frogs.

Dark clouds threatened. Just as the first big drops of rain spilled from the sky, the scouts pounded into camp, running hard to arrive before the last vestiges of light left. Wind joined Xhosa in their nest.

She cocked her head and he answered, "Nothing. No problems. No Others. No trace of anything worrisome."

He should have been pleased but he pursed his lips with frustration, fine lines etching the skin around his eyes and mouth. In elders, they spoke of wisdom, resilience, and excellence and all were proud to have them. These were the first Xhosa had seen on Wind. She'd tell him later. He'd be happy to hear it. She had some but not enough for a Leader. The elders assured her they would come at the right time.

Wind lay down at her side, eyes closed, his closeness soothing. She listened as his breathing steadied, trying to match it, but couldn't. Her brain was churning, trying to pull something out of memory that she'd forgotten, or seen and didn't recognize, into the open where she could examine it. It was long after Moon arrived before she finally drifted into an uneasy sleep.

The morning air warmed and the People again set out in quest of a cave while the hunters searched for tracks. Thick calluses shielded Xhosa's feet as the earth heated but unlike the furry coat of the wolves, her hairless skin provided no protection. As though to prove this, she winced when a bee stung her nose.

And then ignored it.

The People trudged along the soggy shores of yet another waterway. Their buoyant optimism had turned to fatigue by the time their shadows stretched across the debris-laden ground, the distant water's surface reflecting the beauty of Sun's dying light. The hunters again returned empty-handed to a camp haphazardly spread along the base of a cliff. The People ate the ground birds, hare, eggs, nuts, roots, and berries collected as they walked. Disappointment cloaked all at the idea of another night in the open.

To herself, she whispered, *We must find a homebase.*

The next day, before Sun even reached directly over Xhosa's head, Dust shouted, "A cave!"

Chapter 4

The Iberian Peninsula

Between Dust and where the People had stopped to rest stretched a valley of waist-high grass sprinkled with color and the occasional brown mound. Invisible wings swished through the stalks. Bees droned softly as they visited flowers and birds cawed in search of food. Saplings bordered one side, knee-high bushes the other. The bluff where Dust stood was scarred by deep fissures and dotted with thirsty scrub brush. One bent tree gamely maintained a precarious hold on what looked to be a crumbling wall of dirt. From a jutting ledge as far below Dust as above the ground, Eagle found Xhosa. She imagined its sharp eyes evaluating whether this unusual creature who walked on two legs and couldn't fly meant danger to its eaglets. Apparently satisfied, it lifted into the air, leaving behind a clutch of tiny wriggling bodies, mostly beaks and squawks.

Xhosa breathed in warm earth and sunlight, fragrant flowers and ripe berries, and water. As soon as Wind caught up to where she was, they sprinted down the gentle slope and across the valley, Spirit and Black Wolf keeping pace, leaving the rest of the People to descend at a rate suited to children and elders. Dust had disappeared, Xhosa assumed to take a trail on the opposite side of the rock face that would lead to the valley floor.

Snarls greeted Xhosa as she and Wind approached the first cave. A gray wolf blocked the entrance. Its fur was bushy, stance fierce, neck lowered, and hackles raised. It rolled black lips back to expose yellow fangs and red gums. Pale eyes glowed with intensity, fixed first on Spirit and then Black Wolf. The gray wolf might be smaller than Spirit but not by much. Spirit snarled and hissed, warning the wolf if they fought, it would lose. Head high though non-threatening, tail stiff but not aggressive, Spirit didn't move closer, nor did he back up. Black Wolf matched him.

The alpha males took turns growling at each other. To Xhosa, it sounded more like talk than threats. She imagined Spirit explaining that his pack needed a home and the gray wolf telling him to find one elsewhere. When it seemed to reach a stand-off, Spirit peed on a bush to demonstrate his dominance and padded away. The gray wolf moaned softly, licked the urine's odor from the air, and disappeared into the shadowy interior.

The next cave was too small as were the two after that but finally they found one that looked unoccupied. Inside, musty aged odors of mold, old feces, and decay assaulted Xhosa. She blinked until her eyes adjusted to the darkness. A grotto unfolded in front of her, tall enough for Wind and herself with sufficient space for all the People. An abandoned nest crowded into one corner, filled with a pile of bones from a long-dead creature.

The smell of rot wafted across her nose. Xhosa made a sharp downward stroke with her hand. "Something's dead."

From Wind, "Or dying."

The People hustled in, feet shuffling through the detritus of twigs and debris blown in by the wind. Siri pulled out fire stones while Xhosa and Wind tracked the fetid aroma deeper into the cave. With only dim light, they dragged their hands along the wall to find their way, feet scuffing through the layers of dirt. Xhosa swiveled her head side to side, watching for any shadows that stood out in the gloom.

They crept down the main tunnel, diverting occasionally into side tunnels. Some ended at a rough wall coated in dank algae or sticky dust. Others were blocked by a collapsed roof or a boulder. Where the primary shaft ended, a narrow fissure in the ceiling opened to the outside.

Wind motioned, fingers bent, hands loose, "Dust checked this from the hillside. It's well hidden and too small for predators."

Xhosa wrinkled her nose. "Whatever died is near." She turned into a passageway on her weak side.

She dodged rocky spikes that hung from the ceiling nearly to the floor, the rot more pronounced with each step. The passage ended in an alcove with enough light for her to see what lay in the back. There, curled around itself and pressed against the wall was the body of a wolf-like creature, grimy fur tattered, mouth open in a toothy snarl, eyes dark holes. One leg bent backward in a way no limb should.

"It must have been injured, crawled inside the cave to escape, and died."

Death that didn't bring food or security to the People was meaningless to Xhosa so she retraced her steps to the front, never giving the animal's death another thought. A fire crackled and the subadults had already layered bramble bushes around the mouth, high and deep enough that any who had once claimed this den would have to find another.

The People gathered around the blaze, hands fluttering in hushed conversation. Xhosa warmed herself before curling into the nest she would share with Wind. Lyta, and Seeker. Zvi followed, as did Pan-do and Siri.

Spirit and Black Wolf lay at the cave's mouth, each with one eye open, ears tweaked. At one point, a mournful howl floated on the night air. Spirit pushed to his feet and padded outside. He whimpered and then moaned a doleful wail. After a breath and another without a reply, he curled again by Black Wolf and slept.

Xhosa awoke, the pressure below her stomach telling her to release her water. She tiptoed between the bodies, nimbly jumped over the bramble barrier, and trundled outside. Moon unfurled its muted light over the landscape as it did most nights. It was the constant in her life, as her father had been in her childhood and Nightshade after that. Moon had come and gone, once and again, since the People left Viper. Here, in this land beyond the frigid mountains, she wanted to believe the People could settle, that it would be their new homebase.

The hoot of Owl and the scream of its food shattered the quiet before fading away. The night air was pleasantly cool on her skin as she entered the cave, moving past the glitter of Spirit's watchful eyes, his tail thumping once against the debris-laden floor, and made her way back to Wind. In no time, she fell asleep.

The next day, the Primary Female, Siri, arranged the homebase while Xhosa joined the scouts to explore the area. By the time daylight left, they had found nothing suspicious, nothing even of interest. Tomorrow and the days after that, they would venture farther.

Xhosa climbed the cliff that rose above the cave and, avoiding Seeker where he lay talking to the stars, squatted in the moonlight and listened to the sounds of night. So many she recognized and just as many she didn't. Moon arrived and she returned to the cave.

An odor assaulted her. Female blood, and new.

She followed the aroma down the dark rear tunnel to where a narrow passageway broke off. She peeked around the earthen entrance and saw Lyta, head down, red liquid dripping down her leg. She wiped it with a handful of damp moss and then swiped between her legs. Finished, she wandered off, oblivious to Xhosa's presence.

As Lyta's soft steps faded away, Xhosa sensed someone behind her. She sniffed and didn't have to turn to know who it was.

"She can now pairmate." Pan-do's voice was resigned but happy, knowing whom she'd pick. Lyta had no interest in anyone except Seeker, the strange gangly boy-male who twirled in circles, spoke in riddles, and guided the People by talking to stars.

Xhosa turned and moved to where Pan-do couldn't avoid her face.

His gaze caught hers and she motioned, "Nothing will change, Pan-do," but the look in his eyes told Xhosa it already had.

Most fathers saw themselves as protector, scavenger, food-provider, teacher, and one of many who watched over the child they had borne. Pan-do saw himself as more. He called it "love". When Xhosa didn't understand what that meant, he described it as caring for another beyond logic and reason. It meant he never took Lyta for granted, calmed just knowing where she was, and worried when he couldn't find her.

He offered a limp smile. "Yes, it will but I've expected it."

In fact, from the first day Lyta met Seeker, a bond formed between the two, different from the one with her father, not stronger and not in place of, but one Pan-do realized was oddly similar to the emotion called love. He'd thought it could only be between a father and child but now saw he was wrong. Over time, she was inexorably drawn into Seeker's ethereal world and his enthusiasm for topics that confused everyone but her. For example, once, long ago, Seeker spent most of a day evaluating how high a coconut must be to crack when it fell. He scampered up one tree after another, each taller than the one before, a coconut under his arm. He dropped it, listened for a thud, and then scooted down. Once that question was answered, he began chasing a butterfly to see how far it would go in search of flowers.

Lyta followed him, mimicking the sounds of the coconut hitting the ground and the butterfly's wings in flight.

Pan-do's forehead puckered. His lips spread into a thin smile and then he left, striding toward the main cavern.

Sun glowed orange, chasing the cold away and awakening the People to a new day, this one without nonstop walking.

Lyta twirled up to Xhosa. "The pups opened their eyes. They are blue, like Spirit's," and she cavorted away, prepared to spend the day watching Black Wolf and her children.

Ngili trotted up. "Sa-mo-ke, Snake, Talon and I will be gone until here." He pointed at a spot on Sun's overhead journey close to the horizon. "Dust found the tracks of Short-tail Cat."

This wily creature with its squatty limbs and sharp ears was as smart as Sabertooth but without its lethal fangs. It had shoulders wider than most of its cousins and its head reached taller than Dust's chest. The People often hunted with Short-tail because they stalked the same prey.

"Wind and I will come with you."

They tracked the cat to a pool of clear water edged by reeds and cattails. Wildflowers dotted its muddy banks. Green algae coated stony protrusions poking up from below. Fallen leaves and dying insects layered the black water. Waterlogged branches floated lazily on its gentle current, bumping off the banks to head nowhere. Water birds chased the snakes that slithered along the surface while ducks paddled away, eyes locked on the depths.

Judging by the hardness of its dung, Short-tail passed here long ago. Still, a waterhole attracted many animals so the males and Xhosa slathered mud over their bodies to hide from would-be predators and prevent bites from the flying insects. Then, they slogged through the shallows to a dense sedge bed where they hid and waited.

Xhosa nibbled berries and the sweet inner center of the cattails, listened to the croak of frogs from the round flowered pads that floated on the water, and tried to ignore the incessant insects. The sole predator that approached the waterhole was an odd-looking red Eagle with a notched tail and narrow wings. It snatched up a water snake and flew off, the serpentine creature wriggling in a futile effort to free itself.

The hunters finally gave up and returned to the cave.

On the next day's hunt, they ran across a burly creature taller than any of them that Viper called Bear. It sniffed, turned their way, roared, and then scampered away before anyone could get close. A few pigs also escaped. The lone success was a bison they slaughtered, divided amongst themselves, and then resumed the hunt.

It wasn't until Sun hovered a hand past overhead that the hunters stumbled on a herd, creatures Xhosa had never before seen. They were tall, thick-bodied, with long slender legs, flowing manes, broad backs, and intelligent eyes. They covered the meadow from one end to the other, munching on the abundant grass, tails swishing, ears perking to sounds.

Wind motioned, "I know these animals. They run fast and never slow. I have never been able to catch them."

Xhosa believed it. Their burly shoulders and ropey hind legs promised they could outdistance most predators.

She motioned, "If we could kill one, are they edible?"

Her stomach grumbled. Berries and roots couldn't quiet her insides the way fresh meat rich with blood and fat could.

Wind extended his hands, brow furrowed. "The first time I hunted these, it took a hand—maybe more—of Sun's movement to separate one from the rest. We surrounded her but she fought tirelessly. Her hooves are lethal, like rocks. She charged two of our males and kicked one in the head, the other in the chest. When that didn't dissuade us, she bit two more. That long neck of hers stretches further than you'd expect and her teeth are like slamming rocks together.

"When she began to tire, the herd's leader charged up, placing his body between us and the female."

Xhosa's eyes popped open. "That never happens, Wind. Leaders of every herd I know leave each member to take care of themselves."

"Not this one. He fought for her. Between the two, they injured a handful of our males, many seriously. We finally stabbed the female and she collapsed but the male still didn't leave her. He rose to his hind legs roaring at us, some hoarse sound I've never heard before or since, intent on giving her time to recover. She tried to get up, whinnied, and then gave up. He snorted, flung his mane as though warning us, and galloped away.

"After all that considerable effort, her meat was too tough for elders and children to chew and had little fat. We never hunted them again."

Xhosa studied the graceful creatures, failing to find any that seemed wounded, making them easier prey. One raised her elegant head, mane shivering as water does in a stream, and found Xhosa. Her gaze was curious, without worry. She pawed the ground and whinnied, which drew the attention of a magnificent black animal who must be the Leader. He galloped over and tweaked his ears toward Xhosa, stamping a foot and flaring his nostrils as he decided if this upright creature meant trouble. He flung his tail, jaws open to reveal strong yellow teeth.

Xhosa neither advanced nor fled, staring into his eyes as she would a respected stranger. He pranced once more, neighed boisterously, and then galloped away, the female at his side, the rest behind her. They flew, faster than the People could run and never slowed. Soon, they vanished beyond the edge of the grassland.

This Leader has earned the respect of his flock. They never questioned his decision and followed immediately. If we stay here, I will learn his tactics.

Xhosa wrapped her sweat-soaked hair in a vine and tied it at her neck.

She motioned to Wind, "The male Leader—he was smart enough to stop out of range." She could see Wind draw the same conclusion—that these creatures understood spears. "He departed not out of fear but choice."

As they headed a new direction, one they hadn't yet searched, Xhosa put voice to the worries that had been bubbling inside her most of the day.

"Wind. We've been here long enough for Moon to disappear and reappear yet we've seen few of the carrion birds. I don't understand that. If Others live here, do they eat only small animals?"

Wind motioned, hands slow and hidden by his body, "You wonder why they aren't scavenging carrion as they have every other place we've lived. Give it more time, Xhosa. Seeker wouldn't bring us here to starve."

Worry twisted her stomach but she kept her face impassive, forcing her shoulders to relax. The People were too tired to leave this place anyway, and besides, she had no idea where to go. If there was any way to make this home, she would do that.

He tipped his head up at Sun. "Daylight remains. Let's continue looking."

They trotted onward, the hunters talking with subtle quiet hand motions. All seemed ready to try again another day except Ngili. His energy never lagged, his attitude always upbeat.

Xhosa was about to turn back when Ngili signaled, "Over here!" Excitement spilled from his hands.

Wind and Xhosa raced to the thicket where Ngili had stopped. Arm extended, he patted the air—*Quiet!* They snuck through the trunks until only tall undergrowth hid them from the sounds in the meadow beyond. There, on the far side of the field, a female Bear plodded, probably the one they'd seen earlier.

Ngili whispered, "She doesn't know we're here. I'll get closer!"

As he moved downwind, an odd panther-like creature trundled into the field, unknowingly placing itself between Bear and the People. It hissed. A squeal from beside Bear told Xhosa the mother was with a cub and Like-Panther wanted the smaller creature. Maybe Like-Panther thought Mother Bear would abandon her youngster but Xhosa already knew she wouldn't. Against Like-Panther, with no weapons other than claws and teeth, Mother would win.

Like-Panther slunk forward, maybe knowing Bear had notoriously poor eyesight, but it didn't work. Mother smelled him and roared, raising herself to a height taller by far than Wind or Xhosa. She clawed the air with her front paws as sharp yellow canines the length of Xhosa's forearm dripped saliva. Xhosa's hackles spiked. Even Spirit moaned. When Like-Panther leaped for the cub, Mother slashed. Claws as long as Xhosa's hand raked across the animal's ribs. Like-Panther flew to the side, yowling in agony, blood spurting from the deep gouges in his chest. He slammed to the ground, bounced once, and fell silent. Mother Bear leaped forward on all fours and stomped on the surely dead Like-Panther. Then, she took off at a speed far too fast for an animal of her bulk. Her cub struggled to stay at her side but really, it didn't matter. The predator was dead. The cub bawled occasionally, forcing Mother to slow, let it catch up, and then charge off again. Xhosa watched as the two melted into the foliage.

Wind motioned to Xhosa, "Let's add Bear to those we stalk only when too hungry to care it could end in death."

It wasn't until Sun rested only two hands above the horizon that they tracked down a small family of Gazelle, browsing idly, oblivious to the predators concealed upwind.

Xhosa panted up to Wind, hands moving quickly but low on her body. "These are part of a larger herd. I can see the tracks leading away," and swept her hand across the sky on her weak side.

Wind turned to Ngili and motioned, "Take the carcasses back to homebase. Xhosa and I will see where the tracks lead."

Without question, Ngili headed down the backtrail with the rest of the hunters while Xhosa and Wind followed the prints. The ground was hard which meant the only clues they could find were crushed twigs, pebbles turned over, or scratches on a rock.

Sun was close to its sleeping nest by the time Wind stopped, frozen in place, hand up. *Stop!* On the opposite side of a hill they'd been climbing, Xhosa heard it, too, contented munching sighs. It could only be the herd.

"Daylight's gone. They won't go farther today."

Xhosa tilted her head upward at a threatening wall of clouds. "Those will reach us soon."

As though confirming it, a tremendous explosion crashed overhead and fire lit the sky, its shape like the leafless branch of a tree. Within a breath, maybe two, chunks of ice the size of a fist pummeled the two as they sprinted to the protection of a small forest. There they sheltered, crouched forward, knees against their chests, drenched hair and pelts clinging to their bodies.

As fast as it started, the storm ended.

Xhosa motioned, "The rain erased the tracks but the herd won't go far. They need to wait for the rest."

"Let's get back to the cave. We'll find them tomorrow."

By the time they reached the homebase, Sun was long asleep. Ngili was helping Sa-mo-ke and Stone skin Bison while Snake worked on a pig.

Xhosa warmed herself by the fire and updated those around her on the next day's plan. All in all, it was a good day. They had plenty of meat and they'd found their first herd since arriving here. Hopefully, it would be one of many.

Chapter 5

The new homebase

The next day, as Sun lit the sky, Xhosa took the hunters to where she and Wind had tracked the prints and then they trailed the churned up rain-drenched soil left by the herd as well as the many piles of dung. Wind stuck a finger in one and it sunk up to his knuckle.

"It's soft. We will find them before Sun reaches," and he stabbed at a spot straight above.

As their shadows shortened, the animal tang in the air grew stronger as did the brine Xhosa had first tasted yesterday. Was it salt blocks? And was that what drew this herd here? She hadn't seen salt blocks anywhere since the People arrived but they must be somewhere. Animals needed them as much as the People did.

Xhosa continued, marking her steps with the bounce of her neck sack against her chest. The throwing stones caused a rhythmic scrape as they rubbed against each other, muted somewhat by the travel food mixed in. It reminded her of the many times she'd chased herds over vast expanses with the People. A breeze blew through her hair, cooling her body even as the sticky air promised another hot day.

Finally, the ground shook under her feet.

Hooves! The herd is close!

A short distance later, over the buzz of insects and the chatter of birds, she picked up the rumble of Gazelle voices.

Wind huffed to her side and moved his arm forward. "They're over this hill," and went to alert the rest.

Xhosa slumped to her hands and knees and crawled to the top of the incline and then scooted behind a shroud of bunchgrass. Her ears strained to create a picture of what lurked below. No terrified howls, no startled surprise at the intrusion of predators, the serene grazing of animals content in familiar surroundings.

Comfortable her hunters hadn't been spotted, Xhosa poked her head over the top of the grass. An unintentional sigh escaped her lips at the glut of Gazelle that filled the field below, enough to feed the People for a Moon, or more. Her chest pounded. Maybe it would work out here after all.

She wriggled deeper into the scratchy ground cover, ignoring the feathery feet that crawled over her legs and the snake that scurried out of her way. When the biting insects found her, she swathed herself with mud from a wet patch by her elbow. She slit her eyes to block the sparkle of Sun's light and tried to decide the best strategy to bring down the most animals. One Gazelle raised her head, examined the surroundings without seeing Xhosa, and then again buried her face in the rich grass.

A rustle announced Wind and he tucked in beside her, eyes fixed ahead, breathing steady. He smelled of the dung coat that hid his Other essence and the confidence that infused him before every hunt.

Head forward, hands against her body, she motioned, "Do you see the injured Gazelle?"

A smallish female, clustered with others too young to survive on their own, favored her rear leg.

Wind nodded, "But there, on the opposite side of the field— what is that?"

Xhosa refocused where Wind indicated. Her farsight allowed her to see details farther away than most of her People.

"I see it...," a dark creature, tall and narrow, long arms, longer legs, and little hair except fuzz on its head. The back of Xhosa's neck puckered.

"An Other." The muscles in her jaw bunched. "He is also after this herd."

Desperation clung to his gaunt frame, ribs etched starkly against his skin. Bringing down Gazelle would probably be the difference between life and death for him but that didn't affect his concentration. He was alert, agile, and carried two spears and a warclub with practiced ease.

A second Other popped up, this one toward the far end of the herd. "They both move fluidly, quietly, as though experienced hunters," Xhosa motioned, her hands low enough that the grass hid her movement.

The Other motioned to someone else who then slithered through the stalks until he was in front of the animals, all without them noticing.

"I wonder how many there are—" and then Xhosa's eyes narrowed and she wedged herself deeper into the scratchy earth. "These aren't males, Wind. They're females!"

Her thoughts spun, stunned, trying to make sense of it.

Wind glared at a spot well-away from the Gazelle. "Except that one. It's a male. Why doesn't he help?"

Xhosa studied the male. Sweat made his knotted, ungroomed hair soggy and his eyes darted everywhere, settled nowhere.

"He's tired. Maybe he's done his part and others do the rest?"

The unknown male rubbed a hand down his side and then crossed an arm over his chest, the other hand that should have gripped a spear, empty. He wore no warclub over his back.

Xhosa cocked her head, studied the shape of his head as he leaned back on his heels, watched his gait as he paced. She squinted, once and again before she could believe what stood in front of her.

"It's Rainbow!"

She growled without meaning to, disgusted by this deserter who long ago, rather than confront the enemies of the People, fled, making promises he could never deliver to those who joined him. Her eyes flitted over the hunters below but she didn't recognize any. Those who left with Rainbow must be somewhere else, maybe preparing to help with the cutting and carrying. At least, that's what she hoped.

Why did these talented females partner with Rainbow? Surely they recognize he is not a Leader.

That gave her an idea. She scanned below and quickly identified one female who studied the herd as Xhosa would, one who all others looked to for direction. She was easy to track because one side of her face was scarred. Xhosa waited until the Gazelle lowered their muzzles to eat and the female gazed across the field and then, Xhosa stood. She kept her spear down, shoulders back, head high, and didn't move. Her mud coating and downwind location kept the Gazelle from smelling her but the female Other latched onto Xhosa immediately. Her eyes smiled above the white of her scarred face.

She recognizes me! How is that possible?

Xhosa bobbed her head and ducked as the female motioned to those around her and they passed the message on.

Wind eyed Xhosa. "You know her? Because she knows you."

Xhosa's brow furrowed. Something about the female was familiar but at this distance, Xhosa couldn't be sure.

She finally shrugged. "She is either friendly or famished. Either way, she is willing to work with us."

As though these females knew how Xhosa hunted, they dispersed the same way the People did, trapping the Gazelle between their weapons with no way to escape. When everyone was in place, the scarred female looked at Xhosa as though awaiting her motion to begin. Xhosa leapt to her feet and sped forward, howling, followed quickly by the female Lead and her hunters. Gazelle bleated, necks stretched and ears perked, and took off. The male Xhosa suspected was Rainbow made no effort to participate. The two groups chased their prey with the ease of those accustomed to working together. Both launched their spears, one after the other, followed with a bombardment of throwing stones, expertly funneling the herd to the hunters ahead.

"They are well trained," Xhosa muttered to herself, excitement burning within her at the thought of such accomplished females as part of her People. "How did they end up with Rainbow?"

When this hunt ended, would Rainbow challenge Xhosa, supported by this capable collection of females? If they were loyal to him, they didn't show it. Not once did they look to him for guidance but, Xhosa had to admit, they didn't need it. They were skilled and aggressive and would be either a valuable addition to the People or a significant foe if they sided against her.

Xhosa would resolve that later.

Within a short time, the two groups brought down as many gazelle as could be eaten before the white worms took over and then, as though by prior agreement, stopped the killing. They must leave enough animals to replace—with babies—those slaughtered today. They would feed the People in the future. Xhosa was pleased these others avoided the pregnant and nursing females and the young, as the People did.

The surviving gazelle fled, leaving behind their broken, dead, and injured. Both groups set about cutting the carcasses into portable pieces.

Xhosa stopped at the edge of the carnage, bent forward and panted in ragged gasps that burned her throat. Her mouth hung open to gulp in the fresh air and still she couldn't help but grin. Then, she dragged herself into the carrion, not surprised to find the other Leader working beside her hunters.

She's not winded at all.

Rainbow still stood off to the side, arms flapping as though directing the females, which he didn't. In fact, as during the attack, no one paid any attention to him. He finally huffed his displeasure, bent and picked up his spear, and marched toward Xhosa.

Spirit padded to Xhosa's side, a quiet growl rolling from his muzzle. "You're suspicious, too."

Together, they scrutinized Rainbow as he approached. When he recognized her, he jerked, arms stiffening at his sides, and then pasted a grin on his lips. Xhosa hardened her face and flattened her eyes to hide the revulsion that rose in her throat. Spirit suffered no such inhibitions. The closer Rainbow got, the louder the wolf's snarl. Rainbow's steps stuttered when he noticed the fangs, glistening with blood, malevolent blue eyes slitted.

He motioned, hands shaking. "Do you know there's a wolf at your side?"

"And he doesn't trust you."

Spirit sniffed and then sneezed, hackles now straight up, and fixed the slender male who smelled of fear with the look usually reserved for prey. Rainbow sidestepped, trying to put Xhosa between himself and Spirit. The wolf mimicked his steps making sure he could leap on this foul-smelling antagonist at the slightest signal from the pack leader. Rainbow's legs trembled and sweat prickled his upper lip but he managed to tighten his grip on his spear, something warriors did to look threatening.

Spirit's growl deepened.

Xhosa didn't even try to hide her contempt. "Take your hand from your weapon, Rainbow. It makes Spirit angrier."

Rainbow dropped the shaft and crossed his arms over his chest, never removing his gaze from the wolf.

Wait until he finds there is another like Spirit, and pups. Maybe he'll leave.

Xhosa hid the grin. "Spirit is of the People. He protects his friends."

Rainbow took a deep breath, keeping both hands away from Spirit. After a moment, he addressed Xhosa as though it was his efforts that had triggered this reunion.

"Thank you for the assistance. I will have my hunters carry it to our site. It has been a long time."

He rattled on, telling about his bravery in the face of unimaginable risks, his unmitigated success against impossible odds, and the glory he'd achieved on the far side of Endless Pond. Xhosa didn't listen, her thoughts on how his betrayal had caused the death of many among her People. The hair stood up down the length of her neck and she clenched her hands.

She cut him off. "How many are left?" That confused him so she slapped him on the cheek. "Of my People. What else would I mean? The ones you lied to because the truth—that you knew nothing about where they would migrate—would have discouraged them from joining you. Those People—how many did you kill?"

Spirit growled and Rainbow gulped, his expression strangled. His mouth opened but nothing came out.

"Never mind. I wouldn't believe any answer you gave. You told nothing but lies before you left the People and I can already tell that hasn't changed."

He visibly shook, face pale, telling her she was right. Finally, he pressed his palms to his sides and forced the corners of his mouth up. "Xhosa, that is in the past. We can help each other—"

"I don't need your help. You're a worm I want to step on."

Whatever Rainbow planned to say next, he swallowed and chose instead to simply stand silently, arms hanging, eyes down. Spirit leaned into Xhosa's side as if to absorb her anger. Her hand touched his head and the soft fur relaxed her as it always did. She knocked a chunk of dirt from the bottom of her foot and then pulled a thorn out that had been bothering her.

"Anyone can tell these aren't your people, Rainbow. They're hers."

Xhosa indicated the young female with the shiny white cheek. Though she looked no older than a subadult, her bulging muscles rippled as sweat poured down her smooth neck and back. Luckily, no one had told her females couldn't penetrate hide and crack bone with a chopper or lift a haunch one-armed because as Xhosa watched, she did all of that.

Xhosa studied her graceful movements, the way she attacked her work, and the intensity of her concentration. A memory niggled of a subadult, long ago, but she couldn't place it. The female must have felt Xhosa's eyes on her because a smile lit her face with unexpected joy. That's when Xhosa saw it—the shiny white skin stretched snugly across most of one cheek, a burn so vicious it pulled her mouth up slightly at the corner and left part of her head hairless. This sort of damage happened to those caught in a firestorm. None of Xhosa's plants relieved the anguish. Only healing did that, which took many Moons. This female had suffered badly.

Xhosa turned the image around in her head, tipping and pulling until it snapped into place. She remembered a subadult racing into a fire to save the life of a child while others fled.

"Mbasa."

The shiny-cheeked female flicked a glance at her, nodded once, and slashed open the side of the carcass. With a powerful tug, she yanked out a handful of ribs and then reached in for the rest.

Rainbow drooped like a cattail in a heat wave.

Quiet intensity burned in Xhosa's fierce eyes, her muscles tense. "She's the one who risked her life when the Big Heads chased us from our home. She suffered much for it but survived. No surprise she flourished on your poorly considered journey."

Rainbow poked his nose in the air. "Our males were all killed. I trained the females to do the work—"

"There's no way you taught Mbasa or anyone to hunt with such prowess. The Rainbow I knew always chose the easiest path, the safest option. Here's what I think happened. You played Leader until problems developed, and then quit. Maybe you offered yourselves—my People—as slaves to a local tribe."

She paused when he twitched at the word "slave." That concept was unknown in their original homebase, before the People were driven away from it. Rainbow could only recognize it because he ran into them on his migration, as Xhosa did.

Her eyes hooded and her movements took on a bite. "Mbasa wouldn't allow it and then she did what you couldn't. How close am I?"

He blinked once, and again. He didn't answer but when he avoided her eyes, Xhosa could tell she was right. She turned to the females working alongside her males, just as hard and with the same level of talent. It took a breath to identify Hecate, Ngili's pairmate. At her side, a subadult matched Hecate chop for chop.

"Starlight."

She and Nightshade mated frequently and Starlight once asked him to train her as a warrior. He laughed at her so she left with Rainbow. Watching her, Xhosa never would have guessed that the mild-mannered creature who never fought back against

Nightshade could now slash the entire hind leg from a gazelle in one stroke.

Starlight reminded her of Viper.

Xhosa gestured to Rainbow, "I suspect Hecate, Mbasa, and Starlight are the ones responsible for saving the lives of my People."

Rainbow's head drooped even more. "Well, we ran into problems."

But Xhosa walked away, too disgusted with Rainbow to listen to one more word.

Mbasa raised her head at the sound of Xhosa's steps, hands red with blood, face splattered with muck, joy filling her eyes.

Xhosa gestured, "I am glad we found you and the rest of the People."

Mbasa motioned, hands low, "I heard you with Rainbow. Starlight left not because she didn't trust you but because I needed her. I had a feeling we would face difficult challenges and Starlight's strength would help us survive."

Xhosa breathed out, releasing the worry that her People wouldn't want to return to her. "Finish here, Leader, and join our meal. Bring your People."

Mbasa's eyes locked onto Xhosa and her brow wrinkled. "Leader? My People?"

Xhosa ignored her shock. "Mine missed you. Ngili especially."

Mbasa jerked toward Hecate, too far away to see Xhosa's gestures. "Ngili is alive?" Then she whispered, eyes wet, "Hecate never stopped believing they would reunite."

"Ant will guide you."

She turned to leave and realized Spirit was missing. Her throat tightened and her temples started to throb. A huff and a soft growl came from somewhere close. She snapped her head around and found him, rolling in a ripe carcass—not eating it, just drenching his fur in the fluids so his senses could feast on the aroma and taste later. He hadn't been able to do that in a long time. With everyone focused on him, Xhosa popped a root bundle into her mouth.

When Spirit finished, the two of them trotted back to the People's cave. Carrion birds circled overhead on great wide wings, waiting for the two-legged creatures to leave the carcasses. They would clean up what remained.

Ngili hurried up to Xhosa, face tense, hands lurching through the question on his mind. "Did you see Hecate? Is she alive? Is she still with Rainbow?"

Xhosa stuttered and hurried off.

So much for a surprise!

Ngili's grin warmed her like a soft breeze on her back.

Chapter 6

The small cave

"They're coming!"

The scouts atop the precipice by the People's cave shouted to those below. The excitement was palpable. Hands flew with the joy of being with those they had given up hope of ever seeing again. Black Wolf's pups sprinted from one pack member to the other, bouncing on their oversized paws, barking their high-pitched calls, and wagging their entire backends. They didn't know what was going on but recognized their pack was happy.

Mbasa's and Xhosa's Leads strode in together, steps light and quick, all heavily burdened with meat. The rest trailed behind, carrion slung over their shoulders, nibbling on ribs or internal organs as they walked. Though the two groups had been apart for as many Moons as fingers on both hands, chatter was non-stop as though talking with trusted friends. To Xhosa's surprise, Mbasa's People brought all the carcasses, leaving none for Rainbow's campsite. The only reason Xhosa could come up with for that was a good one.

She couldn't find Rainbow at first but finally saw him off to the side. In this time of great excitement, no one paid him any attention or looked to him for counsel. He shrank with each step, body curling in around itself, head drooping until it touched his chest. Whatever he had gone through changed him from a formidable disruption to an insignificant presence among those who knew him best. The arrogant male, so sure of his opinions that he disdained Xhosa's, no longer existed.

Not Mbasa, though. Her face glowed with excitement, her muscles bunched, surrounded by all her Leads. Each carried the bulky carcasses with a fluid grace that said it was routine, their eyes roaming the meadow, the cliff, and the scrubland around the cave in search of shifting shadows or unexplained movements.

Xhosa recognized most, often by their scent, and turned her attention to anyone she didn't know. One boy, not yet a subadult, shadowed Mbasa, carrying a slab of ribs without complaint. His long strides, clear gaze, loose arms, and cocked head mimicked her. He carried himself with the same power and authority manifested by her Leads. Toward the back of the crowd was an unfamiliar male-female pair who carried no spears or warclubs. The male dragged his feet as he walked and the female looked frightened. Xhosa frowned and scratched at a biting bug crawling through her hair. The People had no place for those who didn't contribute. She'd ask Mbasa about these two later.

A howl disrupted her thoughts. Ngili had found Hecate. He took his pairmate's face in his hands and dipped his head until their foreheads touched. Neither cared that everyone watched. Ngili never gave up hope that he and Hecate would be reunited, not when he was captured by Big Heads, not when he learned Hecate had joined Rainbow, and not when it seemed this migration would never end.

Everyone set to work skinning the animals, disarticulating the joints, defleshing the bones, and removing the tendons that would serve a myriad of purposes. No one asked about those not there. Death was part of life. When Starlight inquired about Nightshade, no one responded and she didn't bring it up again.

Mbasa walked up to Xhosa, the young boy from earlier at her side.

"This is Shaga. His parents are with us but he insists on shadowing me. Leave, Shaga," she motioned, kindly but firmly. "I'll talk with you soon."

Shaga turned to face Xhosa. "I hear you are a great warrior and Leader. Before I leave, you should know that Mbasa saved my life. Because of that, it is my responsibility to do what I can to ensure she lives. When I am older, if she hasn't picked a pairmate, it will be me."

Mbasa flushed and her eyes softened. "Shaga finds plants I need to treat the injured. When I lead, he joins me, not caring that such a position places us first to face a threat. Few subadults are as brave as Shaga."

Shaga seemed satisfied and scooted back, stopping far enough away to give them privacy but close enough if called.

Xhosa couldn't help but see that the female she once knew had changed. This older Mbasa radiated a fierceness that spoke of decisions made under difficult circumstances and a confidence in her own abilities grown from having the right answers more often than not. She exuded a dangerous quality Xhosa found in few, male or female. It warned those around that weakness would not be tolerated and threats would be challenged. She had become one Xhosa could rely on.

Mbasa turned to Xhosa, a question in her eyes. "The entire time we have been gone, Leader, we fought to get back to you. That is what kept each of Rainbow's People—"

Xhosa interrupted. "Mbasa's People. Not Rainbow's. Surely you notice everyone looks to you for direction. Even Rainbow. Ask what you want but as a fellow Leader, not the youngster you once were."

Mbasa colored. "But—"

"If I am wrong, Rainbow must ask what you are about to."

Xhosa could see understanding flush Mbasa's face. She breathed deeply and bobbed her head once.

"Bird saw you, Leader Xhosa, skylined at the top of the white-tipped mountains but didn't recognize the People. They have grown since we left. And the ones you call Spirit and Black Wolf confused us. What People travel with wolves? Bird thought it unwise to get any closer, that you must be formidable Others."

Something clicked in Xhosa's head. When they had crested the peaks long ago, exhausted but excited, Spirit had alerted. He must have picked up Mbasa's scent.

Mbasa continued, "I have only one request, to again be part of the People."

Xhosa intended to grant that but first, there was the issue of Rainbow. "How is it that you survived, Mbasa?"

"Without a reputation, we were at the mercy of strangers who wanted our tiny bits of food and mouthfuls of water. Others who called that area home recognized Rainbow's abysmal weakness and spread the word. Soon, no matter where we went, the natives tried to take advantage of us. It made me realize the importance of your strength—Nightshade's strength—to the People's security. It is as much about fighting Others as frightening them, forcing enemies to think carefully before they challenge you.

"So, we claimed to be separated from you, that if we didn't find you, you would search for us. They all recognized the callsign of the mighty female warrior and the vicious Nightshade. All feared you until too much time passed without anyone ever seeing you."

She glanced around, face worried. "Where is he— Nightshade?"

Xhosa never wavered as she motioned, "He is no longer with us."

Mbasa crouched, rested her forearms on her thighs, and dipped her head but not before Xhosa caught the flush of relief.

"Mbasa. Do your Leads also wish to rejoin the People? And do they understand what that means?"

Normally, Xhosa didn't care what Leads wanted but Mbasa's were different. Their confidence and independence likely fed their power. Xhosa didn't want to interfere with that. On the contrary, their attitudes could add a new dimension to the People's ability to defend themselves.

Mbasa nodded. "Hecate, Bird, Starlight, Tor—myself—we left for reasons unrelated to you. Mostly, it was because of Nightshade and that appears resolved."

Xhosa didn't want to explain what had happened to Nightshade tonight so ignored the questions in Mbasa's eyes, and instead motioned, "I heard a mention of someone called the 'Shore Dwellers.' Who are they?"

"They were a prosperous group until cannibals arrived at their homebase. Many were killed, others died from Fire Mountain's fury as we fled the cannibals. Almost all those who remained drowned as we attempted to sail a raft across the violent waters of Endless Sea, to this land."

Mbasa paused to search those gathered around her and pointed out the brawny older male and his frightened pairmate whom Xhosa had noticed earlier. Now, she could see the female was younger than she first appeared despite streaks of gray in her head hair.

"Only Acto, his pairmate Qaj, and their son Shaga remain."

Shaga perked at his callsign, ready to sprint to Mbasa. She patted the air with her hand. "Wait."

Xhosa turned to Pan-do. "This Endless Sea, could it be the same one you spoke of?"

Pan-do shook his head and frowned, "I don't think we're near my former homeland. There, we had more foliage, interminable herds, and rampant Big Heads. We've seen none of those here."

Mbasa gestured to Acto, Qaj, and Shaga. "They hope if you accept my People, you will also allow them to join you."

Xhosa carefully studied the family. All members of the People must work for the benefit of everyone. No one took without giving. Acto's intimidating size and muscular limbs couldn't hide the bruises to his spirit, probably because as Leader, almost all of his People died.

Mbasa seemed to read Xhosa's thoughts. "When I first met Acto, it was he who organized his People to build rafts and inspired them to cross a violent waterway which they'd never done before. When so many perished doing as he suggested, something inside of him broke.

"His pairmate, Qaj, was the sturdy backbone of the Shore Dwellers. She never gave up regardless of the problems and continues to do so. And Shaga—it's easy to see he will grow into a valuable adult."

Without warning, fire shot through Xhosa's eye, the pain exploding and then fading. She gritted her teeth as she pressed her palms against her forehead, trying to stop the thump. Pan-do looked away, ignoring it, but Mbasa stared, curious without pity, confused without judgment.

She must hear the thud in my head, but Xhosa said nothing. She didn't share this weakness—or any—with others and wouldn't start today with this young Leader.

Before Mbasa could ask any questions, Xhosa gestured, "We missed you, Mbasa. You saved at least one life when the People fled the Big Heads, probably more I don't know about."

Mbasa colored. "There is one other we haven't talked about, a subadult with the callsign Vaya."

While Mbasa searched for One-called-Vaya, Xhosa popped a root bundle into her mouth along with a handful of meat and chewed.

"There," and Mbasa pointed out a young male with wild eyes, unruly hair, and fidgety hands. He twisted his head their way at the sound of his callsign and then back to where Seeker was prancing in front of Zvi and Lyta, eyes closed, arms flying. Zvi lumbered to her feet and then Vaya, both stumbling through a faltering rendition of Seeker's elegant dance. They spun in a woozy circle, feet shuffling through the dirt, heads thrown back, arms straight. Seeker ignored both but not rudely.

Mbasa turned back to Xhosa. If she noticed Xhosa chewing, she said nothing. "Vaya was what is called a slave for Others. When we defeated them in battle, they offered Vaya as payment for the damage they caused. He guided us to the end of Endless Pond. We released him from slavery when we got there but he begged to stay with us." Mbasa shrugged. "I allowed it, to thank him for guiding us, but… "

Xhosa cocked her head, her head already feeling better. The glossy swath of straight black hair swayed against her back. "You're unsure of his value to the People."

Mbasa's eyes clouded, conflicted. "Yes, no—I'm not sure, Leader, but what are his chances without us?"

Spirit padded up to Mbasa and licked the air, tail swishing side to side. She patted his head and he rejoined Black Wolf in the tunnel at the back of the cavern that served as their den. The tiny balls of fluff perked their floppy ears at the pack leader's entrance and then chased each other, growling and biting at their packmates' faces and legs. Tired, they lay down, paws up, and slept.

Xhosa waved Mbasa's unease away. "Spirit is right. Vaya and Acto must either do their part or they cannot be part of the People. It will be your responsibility to make that happen. If you don't believe you can do this, I will tell them they must leave."

The remains of the fiery spike that impaled Xhosa's head still throbbed but nothing Xhosa wasn't accustomed to tolerating.

She turned back to the People, not interested in Mbasa's response, and raised her arms, palms skyward. "We welcome back Mbasa's People." A cheer went up. "For those who have been away and don't know of the changes to the People, we are now a partnership of myself, Pan-do, and Wind. The Mbasa People, the Shore Dwellers, and Vaya must select where they best contribute."

Vaya looked confused but Zvi leaned toward him, hands moving, seemingly explaining what that meant. After a short time, his face relaxed. Everyone else understood this requirement and chatter resumed as did grooming.

As soon as Mbasa left to rejoin her old groupmates, Rainbow strode toward Xhosa, face happy, head high, confidence filling his being as it had the day he left, with so many of her People.

That would change when she told him the rest of her decision. She turned to the male who tried to destroy her People.

"Thank you, for giving me a second chance—"

Xhosa chopped her hands down, her eyes cold. "You misunderstand, Rainbow. Mbasa's People are again part of the People. That doesn't include you."

Chapter 7

The small cave

Rainbow froze in place, mouth open, attention bouncing anywhere but at the figure in front of him, frantic for help that wasn't there.

Xhosa relished his terror, enjoying every bit of discomfort he surely felt, but she kept her face neutral, shoulders relaxed. Instinct warned her to denounce this traitor. Given the chance, he would certainly try again to crush her People.

She motioned, hands smooth and fluid, "My People despise you, Rainbow, and Mbasa's reject you. What do you offer?"

The old Rainbow would have shouted and argued but this one surprisingly took the best course of action: silence. His arms hung stiff at his sides, fists clenched, body swaying from one foot to the other.

When he didn't respond, she gestured, "Your poor decisions resulted in the deaths of many." She bit her lip hard enough to draw blood and then continued, "You can remain under the following conditions. You have no say in what happens. You do what you're told. You never question anyone, never offer suggestions."

Rainbow began to sputter but Xhosa stopped him, her voice hard and angry. "And, if Mbasa disagrees, you leave. I don't care either way. No one else will either. I suspect most of my People who still survive will stay here."

Xhosa's head began again to throb, hard and sharp which made her as angry as she must look. Blackness crept into the edges of her vision. Her knees shook as though soon, they would no longer hold her. She ignored it all. Spirit appeared at her side, hair up the full length of his back. He leaned against her but his blue eyes burned into Rainbow as a fiery stick pokes a wound.

Rainbow's eyes skittered between Xhosa and Spirit. Sweat prickled his forehead and drenched his face though the night was cool. He took one measured breath and another as he tried and failed to bury the panic that swelled within him.

After a deep breath, he motioned, "Yes—I accept your terms and thank you." His lower lip trembled and his eyes glistened. "I learned my lesson. Leading is challenging—"

Xhosa interrupted. "I don't care about challenges you faced. It's your betrayal that makes me sure you aren't worth the trouble."

He held his hands out, patting the air. "I know, I know. I just want to tell you I recognize my failures. I'm not clever or smart and we stand here, alive, because of Mbasa. I—we were lucky to have her. I gift her to you—"

"She is not yours to give."

He harrumphed. "I release her to you—"

"She has already agreed to rejoin my People, bringing with her any she chooses. Except you. That will require more conversation between her and me. She must accept responsibility for your actions if you remain. If she isn't willing to, you are out. If she comes to me later and says you broke the arrangement, you are out."

This time, he said nothing. She studied him. He had remained apart from everyone since reaching the People's homebase and no one included him in their groups. Mbasa's People seemed to pity him while Xhosa's were distrusting.

He tried to pull up the corners of his mouth into a fleeting smile but she didn't return it.

Finally, he motioned, "I have learned humility."

Most children discovered humility through failure. She'd grown up with Rainbow and knew how often he failed but always blamed others. He never understood that failure required two. So, what made her think he'd finally learned?

"I say again, Rainbow, what use are you to the People?"

It wasn't a question because she wouldn't trust his answer. Instead of waiting for whatever lie he would offer, she turned away, dismissing him. He scurried off, she hoped to think about what she'd said.

Tor approached her, carrying a Giant Shrew-like creature with teeth as red as blood. He frowned at Rainbow as the male hurried away, head down, shoulders so tense they almost touched his ears.

Xhosa motioned to Tor, fingers spread, "You've grown into an adult."

He stood as tall as most males but broader, more muscular in his chest and legs, no doubt because he had performed the work of a handful of adults since separating from the People. Little remained of the youth Xhosa once knew, the one with bright curious eyes who wanted to grow up in the image of the great Nightshade.

The shadow of a smile crossed Tor's lips. "I'm surprised you remember me. I didn't stand out."

"Nor did anyone around Nightshade," Xhosa gestured, hands brushing her sides as she spoke. "Mbasa's People speak highly of you."

At the sound of her callsign, Mbasa jogged over to Tor, Shaga with her but at a distance. Mbasa bumped against Tor and felt the familiar tingle. This simple act of touching him, without a word or gesture, told her his mood, how relaxed he was, and enabled them to share their strength. It was as though they spoke through their skin. That didn't happen with anyone else, including Nightshade when they had mated, but she knew it did happen for other females. Xhosa flushed when she found Wind in a crowd and Siri's eyes glistened when Pan-do touched her. Qaj, though, never reacted to Acto that way or any way. Mbasa pondered that and then dismissed it.

How Xhosa ended up with a Big Head, especially the one who drove the People from their homebase, was a story Mbasa wanted to hear.

"Tor is Lead Warrior," Mbasa motioned. "We are here in large part because of him."

Tor tossed the Red-eyed Shrew carcass toward the communal food pile. It fell short and Shaga sped over. He tried to lift it, found it too heavy for his young body, and kicked it until it rolled into the pile. After that, he scurried back to his spot where he again watched Mbasa.

Tor focused on Xhosa, brow puckered. "Someone followed us as we hunted. Subadults I think, based on the lightness and small size of the prints. They aren't well trained. They scuffed through the grass and didn't shade the glint from their eyes."

He couldn't keep the disdain from his gestures.

Xhosa gestured, "Are you sure they were young?"

"Maybe females? Or the adults here are small and stupid."

Mbasa added, "Or they could be emaciated from hunger." She smiled at Tor. "We know that look."

Tor continued, "I tried to follow but lost their tracks on a talus slope."

He scratched a swollen bite on his arm. When that did no good, he licked it.

Xhosa motioned, "That's the first Others we've seen. I sensed their presence before but never saw any trace."

Tor waved toward the Red-eyed Shrew. "I think they were also after this animal but didn't know how to bring it down. If they're youngsters, why didn't the adults help them?"

"Tor—you and Shaga eat. Mbasa, come with me."

Xhosa walked far enough from the group to hide her gestures and then motioned, "I told Rainbow he could remain with the People, if you agreed, but can never question anyone, never offer suggestions. Decisions about his compliance are up to you. If you tell me he didn't abide by the agreement, he is out."

Mbasa was shocked. "Why? What if I don't know if he complied?"

Xhosa huffed at her reticence. "You must figure it out. Mbasa, you led these People. You made decisions that protected them for many Moons. You know Rainbow better even than I. If you are the Leader I'm sure you are, that means making difficult decisions. I could banish him from the People but he would die. If you no longer consider him a threat and think he can serve the People, tell me he deserves another chance."

"How will I know?"

"Trust your instinct but I must know now."

Mbasa mulled that over for a handful of slow breaths. Xhosa waited patiently. Mbasa knew the answer. What she didn't know was what Xhosa wanted to hear. In the end, she decided on truth.

"You always told us to be either strong like Mammoth, patient as Eagle, leery like Gazelle, cunning as Wolf, or lacking that, wise enough to mimic someone who is. Rainbow is none of those but I believe he has learned wisdom. If I'm wrong, I will solve it when the time comes."

Xhosa thinned her lips and jutted out the bump under her mouth. "You will make a good Leader."

They joined Tor in the cave and he handed them ribs. As they ate, Siri crouched by a debris pile just outside a circle of rocks Mbasa had seen the males drag inside. Siri smacked two stones together over and over until suddenly, a fire exploded from them. Mbasa's legs tensed, prepared to spring to Siri's assistance, but the Primary Female didn't back away from the flames and no one else seemed worried. Bewildered, Mbasa nudged Tor but his focus was elsewhere.

He shouted Sa-mo-ke's callsign. "I'll go with you," and they headed out with Bird and Wind to check the boundaries.

Mbasa edged toward Xhosa. "The fire, by Siri—it came from stones. How is that possible?"

"Because of the boy-male, Seeker, and his large friend, Zvi," and Xhosa nodded toward the two. "We didn't need fire where you and I lived, Mbasa, but here, the air is often cold and fire provides welcome warmth. I don't believe we could live here without it."

Siri shoved a log into the fire. It sparked and a few blazing cinders struck Siri but she ignored them.

Tor, Bird, Wind, and Sa-mo-ke returned. Xhosa beckoned Mbasa and Tor to take a position by the fire at her one side while Wind and Pan-do moved to her other side. No surprise, Shaga settled behind Mbasa's elbow and the wolf, Spirit, squeezed between Wind and Xhosa.

Everyone ate from the communal pile. No one took more than they could eat or less than they required. As the fire crackled, the People pressed closer to the blaze, stretched their hands forward, palms open, skin flushed red. Mbasa stayed back at first, cautious of the flames. When no one burned themselves, actually smiled, she pushed toward it also. As her body thawed, she scanned the group for the enigmatic Seeker and found him bobbing through the dark recesses, exclaiming over discoveries that made no sense to Mbasa or anyone else as far as Mbasa could see with the exception of Lyta and Zvi.

She motioned to Xhosa, "How did you find Seeker? And Spirit with his pack? All are ... unusual."

Spirit perked up at the sound of his callsign and wagged his bushy tail once before snuggling his muzzle again between his paws and closing his eyes.

Xhosa finished what she wanted of the ribs and tossed the rest to Spirit's pups before answering. "They arrived at Hawk's homebase the same time we did."

Her hands slowed, wilting under the weight of her memories. She drew a deep breath and then continued, "It is because of Seeker we are here, with you. He saw our path in the stars."

Mbasa wanted to know more about that—how he guided the migration of the mighty People—but had a more pressing question first, a name she'd heard about from almost every one of her groupmates.

"Who is this Hawk everyone talks about?"

Xhosa stiffened. "Long after you left, Hawk's People took us in when we were desperate. He was a talented and fair Leader but perished when invaders forced us to flee." She rubbed her eyes, voice now muted but harsh, an arm fluttering over those gathered. "Most of those you don't know are from Hawk's People."

Chapter 8

The small cave

Mbasa fell silent, knowing she shouldn't have asked that. She struggled to come up with a way to move on but Tor did it for her.

"Xhosa. Can you demonstrate the stones that make fire?"

As he leaned in front of Mbasa, his hand brushed her arm. She felt it in her fingers. Regardless of what she had lost getting here, she gained Tor.

Xhosa pulled two stones from her neck sack. "I hit these together until the sparks set fire to dry kindle."

Xhosa smacked one against the other, repeatedly, her hands moving with the sureness of having done this frequently. Many of the strikes created tiny sparks but it took a long time before one burst into a flame. Mbasa and Tor jolted backwards, ready to slap the fire away with their callused hands but Xhosa stopped them.

"This is fire. I can keep it safe. Once lit, the subadults must keep it burning."

Mbasa shot a look at Tor, his face as pale as hers felt. "Where do we find these stones?"

"Some are buried in caves or scattered in riverbeds. Others are hidden inside another stone."

The flames danced. Cinders leapt out of the rock-lined pit, settling on pelts, the ground, sometimes arms or legs, but died before they did any harm.

Xhosa addressed the group gathered around the warmth. "Let's share stories of how all of us got here. Mbasa. You and your People go first."

Everyone had noticed the many white scars carved into the chests, arms, legs, faces of Mbasa's group. Some also had crooked limbs—breaks that hadn't healed properly. Others had round enlarged knuckles likely earned from violent fights. These were warriors' injuries from fighting hard every day and winning. The tribe wanted to hear what caused them and how these who had joined Rainbow ended up winning so often.

Mbasa hunched toward the fire's warmth, her shadow flickering on the cave's walls, and told how her People—which she now called the Xhosa People—found out that the easy migration promised by Rainbow to a new homebase wasn't. The danger didn't come from Big Heads. It was Others like them who picked their males off one by one until all the scouts, warriors, and hunters were gone.

Xhosa asked, "Gone? Or dead?"

Mbasa stopped, confused. *Why didn't I think of that?* "We didn't see their bodies."

Xhosa motioned, "Did you follow the prints, see if maybe they had been captured and kept as slaves in the way Ngili and I were?"

Mbasa gasped, stricken that she might have abandoned her People. "No—I never even thought of that—"

Xhosa stopped her. "I'm not criticizing. If they're alive, they will try to escape. If successful, they will follow your backtrail here. If that is possible, we will watch for them."

Mbasa's throat closed and she croaked, "How do you know they will try to escape?"

Xhosa rubbed her neck, causing her wealth of dark hair to glisten in the firelight. "They are of the People, Mbasa. That is what we do. Our enemies know—or find out—that we are too much trouble as captives. Take our lives or let us go, those are the only choices."

"Then we should help them, as Wind helped you. Shouldn't we?"

Xhosa studied Mbasa before answering. "Think about this as a Leader, Mbasa, balance the needs of the few against the requirements of the many." She raised a hand and ticked the reasons off. "The terrain you crossed is unforgiving. There was little food and less water. You were constantly attacked by Others." She dropped her hands but continued, "Mbasa, if your males *were* captured and *can't* escape, they will pairmate and use their talents for the good of their new tribe. That is what you did with Rainbow, what Pan-do and Wind did with us. What more is necessary? Learn this: When calm prevails over chaos, don't do anything."

Tor touched Mbasa's hand. Warmth seeped into her body, like jumping into a hot pond. The cavern was quiet, everyone breathless to hear more about how their groupmates survived.

Hecate picked up the story. "As you say, we are of the People. We survive. Mbasa treated the loss of our warriors as but another problem to be solved. She called the females together and reminded them that you—Xhosa—never succumbed to adversity. How could we do differently? She asked everyone willing to defend the People to stand. One after another, they all did, even though they had never done anything like it."

Now Bird spoke. "Mbasa, Hecate, Starlight, and I started training them. It was slow at first with many mistakes but no one quit. When the first battle came, with an Other tribe, everyone was frightened except Mbasa and Tor. They told us to do as we were trained and we would win. And we did!"

Bird's face flushed with pride though she tried to hide it. "It turned out our adversaries rarely fought so their skills were weak."

Pop! Something exploded, followed by a loud crack. Rainbow screeched.

Shaga spoke up over the giggles of the children, hands calm, body relaxed. "That was hot sap, Rainbow, from a log, and the other was a wet rock that overheated."

Shaga bounced on his knees, not nervous—excited. It didn't bother him to have all eyes turned to him. Rainbow hung his head as he flushed red.

Starlight picked up the story. "This success inspired the males to join us. Tor turned out to be a good teacher—relentless, unforgiving, demanding—and focused on our goal to rejoin the People."

Xhosa blinked back the smoke that clouded her eyes. "Starlight, Mbasa, Hecate, Bird, Tor. You all have defeated death not once but repeatedly. You have trained those around you to do the same. Those are valuable skills—"

"It's more than that, Leader Xhosa."

Xhosa turned toward the voice and gestured, hands soft but quick. "Come forward where we can see you more easily, Shaga, and say what you mean."

"Most of my People—the Shore Dwellers—died because they didn't know how to do what Mbasa and the rest accomplish easily."

Shaga spoke quietly as though inside his young body was an elder who had seen too much, suffered too often, and could no longer be shocked by what life threw at him.

"If Mbasa hadn't survived our crossing, Leader Xhosa, I would have had to lead. My father was too shaken to do more than trail behind. I would have done it, of course, but Mbasa did it better."

His father nodded in agreement but otherwise, showed no interest in what was happening, maybe not realizing that based on the stories, decisions would be made about his future. He simply crouched, outside the circle of People, head down as his finger swiped through the dirt at his feet. Xhosa's gaze hardened. Acto must recover or he had no place among the People. Shaga, though, impressed her, his ability to thrive despite the loss of his People and the weakness of his father.

She rolled forward on the balls of her feet, elbows on her knees, and focused on Mbasa. "Can the cannibals traverse Endless Pond as you did?"

Qaj, Acto's pairmate, answered for Mbasa. "No. Violent waves fill the crossing, Leader Xhosa. We, my People, know how to guide rafts. The cannibals don't."

Acto opened his mouth as though to say more but instead stuffed it with a handful of ribs.

Pan-do motioned, "I know of such crossings, Qaj. The waves thrash you with sticks made of water and the blasting wind stings harder than a hailstorm. It feels like maneuvering through a waterfall that moves *across* a lake instead of *down* a cliff."

Xhosa turned to Tor and Mbasa. "We are looking for a new cave. Have you seen any?"

Tor furrowed his brow and looked around the cozy confines stuffed with the People. "What is wrong with this one?"

"It is too far from herds, though we still have no idea where those are."

He shrugged. "There are none where we came from. That's why we kept moving."

Xhosa directed her next question to Acto. "One-called-Acto, tell us your story. How is it that all of your People are gone?"

Her words were sharper than necessary but exactly as she intended. She had no patience for a coward. Acto must explain to the People why and how he had failed so abysmally. In that way, everyone learned how not to make the same mistakes.

The finger dragging across the dirt stopped. Acto's nose twitched as he lifted his head. A smile limped across his face and he sucked air through the gap of a broken tooth. It should hurt but if it did, she couldn't tell by looking at him.

Acto's voice was soft forcing everyone to concentrate on his story. "We lived peaceably along Endless Sea as my father and his father did, in caves like this one. We caught fish, collected eggs, and scavenged the occasional carcass abandoned by a predator. Others like us had caves down the shoreline. We didn't notice they had disappeared until the time came to trade mates. This we did when the weather warmed and the water calmed. Everyone enjoyed traveling to see other tribes. We would share stories, discuss problems we had faced, and then swap females that hadn't pairmated."

His hands moved without emotion. Inside his body, where passion once burned, it was now as empty as an abandoned snail's shell.

"When we got to the first cave, no one was there. We thought maybe they had gone down the shore to the next camp for the same reason as us, so continued along Endless Sea. But the next and the next were also abandoned so we returned to our homebase. It wasn't long afterwards that the cannibals started to prey on us."

Acto sighed a long breath. "We knew we must leave so started building the rafts but didn't know how to plan our escape. When Mbasa arrived, she solved that and so much more. In fact, we survive because of your People—Mbasa, Hecate, Bird, Starlight, Tor, and the rest. Not me. I appreciate Mbasa allowing us to be part of her tribe and now yours, Leader Xhosa."

Xhosa hooded her eyes to hide the disdain she felt for this weak male and then crossed her arms to keep from snapping that she had given no such agreement. Why would she welcome one who had no idea how to care for himself or his People, and then dismissively handed the future of his pairmate and child over first to a subadult he barely knew, and now, to a stranger he had just met?

Bile burned her throat at the thought of Acto as one of her People but she wasn't sure about Qaj. Siri had spent most of the storytelling with the Shore Dweller female, leaning over now and then to speak to her or explain something she didn't understand. Qaj had somehow made a friend of one of the most influential females among the People, a female who didn't suffer incompetence any better than Xhosa tolerated weakness.

She harrumphed. If Siri saw value in the female, Xhosa would welcome her. As she worked through decisions to reject Acto, accept Qaj, and discuss Shaga further with Mbasa, Pan-do slipped to Acto's side. The former-Cave Dweller Leader halted his finger's travel through the dirt and swiveled his head toward Pan-do until their eyes met.

Pan-do touched Acto. "My People's story is like yours, Acto. Enemies chased us from our homebase. We fled, never stopping until we found Xhosa's People. We lost many but found a tribe we admired and who respected us. Problems shared are lighter to carry. And easier to solve."

Xhosa grunted, almost a whine. If Pan-do saw value in the exhausted male, she'd give Acto a chance, but only if he could prove himself valuable. That left the boy, Shaga.

She forced her lips together and motioned, hands high so all could see, "The last story comes from Wind. Listen carefully, former-Mbasa-People, because you may decide not to partner with us after hearing what he has to say."

A shadow darkened Wind's face and he focused beyond the group, on the emptiness outside of the cave. Mbasa searched the darkness but saw nothing disturbing there.

Before he could start, she motioned, hands firm but without anger, "I remember you, One-called-Wind. You drove the People from our homebase, slayed many of us, and empowered Rainbow to rise against Xhosa." Her eyes flattened, her face hard, and she did nothing to soften her words. "You slaughtered us for no reason."

Wind shook his head. "Not me." His eyes rested on Mbasa without judgment. "My brother, Thunder, did that. He looks like me except for a scar across his cheek."

He went on to explain how Thunder expelled him from their tribe when Wind refused to support an assault on the People, how Wind then freed Xhosa from her captors—with Spirit's help, and how he accepted Xhosa's offer to be part of the People.

Ngili gestured, movements strong and comfortable, "He rescued me also. I am indebted to him."

Wind accepted the compliment with a faint smile. "Thunder intended that I should die when he ejected me. He thought no one could survive alone. But I did. In his eye, that makes me a lethal challenge to his authority. Because Xhosa is the most formidable female known to anyone, he wants to possess her. He will never quit chasing us." He turned to face Mbasa, his eyes pinning hers. "That means any who travel with us are in mortal danger."

He moved his hand, palm forward, stiff with resolve. "But I promise you and everyone here, I will stop my brother. My father was fair and honest. I can't help but think the warriors he trained, males I fought alongside my entire life, whose lives I saved more than once as they did mine, must have tired of Thunder's purposeless brutality and personal vendetta. I will take advantage of that and turn it in our favor."

Wind finished, his body sure, his expression calm, knowing that whatever Mbasa's decision, it wouldn't change what he or Xhosa did.

Tension vibrated through the cave. For long breaths, the only sound was the crackle of the fire and the tiny snores of the wolf pups, punctuated occasionally by sleepy yips and mewls.

Out of the quiet, something from among Mbasa's former-Leads crunched, like knuckles cracking but louder. Then a slurp and another snap as though someone crunched bones to reach the marrow inside followed by a rhythmic patter of hands hitting the dirt floor.

Mbasa finally asked, "That's it?"

When Wind scratched his arm, gaze sliding to Xhosa and back, laughter burbled from Mbasa and Hecate, and then giggles from Bird and Starlight, followed by a yowl from Tor. Shaga's high-pitched youthful joy chimed in. Even Vaya snorted, eyes down, shaking his head as though Wind had said something silly.

Wind and Xhosa looked at each other, then Pan-do.

Mbasa bit back her laughter long enough to gesture, "You don't frighten us, One-called-Wind. I can't tell you how many treacherous enemies we faced, the countless desperate battles we fought and won. We are good at doing the impossible. We will help you defeat this Big Head who ended the life of our former Leader. In fact, we will do it for you. You have my promise in exchange for yours."

Wind cocked his head. "And what would that be?"

"Teach us to make those stone tips I see on your spears."

When everyone again settled, Xhosa rose with athletic grace and faced the assembled People. "The issue of Leads must be resolved. All former-Hawk and former-Mbasa People are welcome to challenge for those positions."

Hands fluttered but no one stood. Xhosa let it go. She would speak privately with those who should challenge.

With stories over, Siri and Pan-do paired up, as did Lyta, Zvi, and Seeker, Ngili and Hecate, Mbasa and Tor, and everyone else. Hands worked efficiently to pick debris and insects from hair, smoothing away tangles, scratching skin. Conversation centered around whether Mbasa's group would challenge the existing Leads.

Xhosa left the cave as she often did before sleeping and found a secluded spot where she could reflect on Tor's sighting of the small Others. Maybe this tribe hid because they were intimidated by the People's large size and powerful weapons. But if they lived here, more of the Others must also, which suggested another worry. What if they planned to pick off her hunters and scouts one by one, as the cannibals did the Shore Dwellers and the Others across Endless Pond did to Mbasa's People? If it hadn't been clear before, it was now, that the People needed a way to communicate when they were out of sight of the rest of the tribe.

In Xhosa's former homeland, and again in Hawk's, the People controlled everything around the homebase including where they hunted and foraged. From oversight positions, her People saw all who entered their terrain and responded before they became a threat. But that wasn't the case here. Yet. Until it was, they needed a robust way to communicate beyond a simple callsign saying only *"I am of the People"*. Other animals had this—like chimpanzees, birds, and wolves. Why couldn't the People?

I will bring this up to Pan-do and Wind.

She shivered and returned to her nest. Wind was already asleep. She tucked against his body, relaxed as the pounding in his chest assured her that she and her Co-Leaders could solve any problem.

Chapter 9

Small cave

Xhosa sucked a mouthful of water from the river, enjoyed the cool flavor as it rolled down her throat, and then stood. She wiped the wet drops from her mouth as she squinted into the bright morning sun. It would be a good day to hunt.

Hecate waylaid her on her way back to the cave. "He's not coming with me, Xhosa. He's always trouble."

Rainbow caught up with Hecate, huffing, mouth hanging open, sweat dotting his forehead though it wasn't yet hot.

"No—not this time, Hecate," he motioned, hands in front, shaking. "I promised Xhosa I could work with everyone. If I don't, she—or Mbasa—or you can ban me from the People. I've learned I am not a Leader. No—all I want to do is contribute."

Xhosa said nothing, waiting to see Hecate's next move.

She harrumphed. "He lies when it suits him. I don't believe what he's saying."

He crossed his arms over his chest and clenched his fists. "I've changed, Hecate. I promise. I'll do what you say... "

And then he fell silent as though realizing Hecate was not listening.

The female motioned, "If it is my decision, I will toss him out before he has a chance to hurt one more person with his lies—"

Xhosa stopped her. "It *is* your decision so consider what you do next carefully, especially if you have any thought to challenging Ngili for Lead—or Co-Lead. Prove right now you can make decisions that serve the People."

Something changed in Hecate, as though this responsibility connected pieces she hadn't realized fit. Her face relaxed and the anger that had tightened her muscles evaporated. She crossed her arms in front of her body, moved them to her side, and then smoothed her hair out of her face.

"What does that mean?"

Xhosa never changed her calm, implacable expression. "Figure it out."

Xhosa had no doubt Hecate would make the right decision, even if Hecate didn't yet know that.

Hecate's jaw clenched and then relaxed. Without looking at Rainbow, she motioned, "I expect failure. Prove me wrong," and caught up with the hunters.

They were going to follow the tracks Dust had located the day before which would give Ngili, Tor, Wind, and her the opportunity to observe the skills of the young hunters. The group spread out as they advanced, eyes swiveling over the surroundings in the manner they were taught, arms cocked, feet light. Rainbow trailed behind and to the side as though watching the backtrail though no less ready and observant.

They didn't return until Sun touched the horizon, and then without meat. Hecate's hand clutched her spear so tightly her knuckles whitened. Her face was red and sweat stiffened her hair. Tor stomped after her, Wind frowned, and Ngili uncharacteristically grumbled.

Pan-do called out to Hecate but she didn't respond and didn't make eye contact so he caught up to her.

Without being asked, she growled, "We found the prints but they disappeared into a waterway. That's not why I'm angry." After a breath, she added, "And it's not Rainbow either."

She and Wind beckoned the hunters to a field that stretched longer than a spear throw and had proven a good place to practice. Though everyone looked ready to drop, Hecate didn't care. To her, exhausted and dispirited was the perfect time to train.

As Xhosa and Pan-do watched, the Leads—Hecate, Wind, Tor, and Ngili—took turns drilling the hunters in spear work while walking or running, crouched or lying down, and with no rest or water. Rainbow looked the most tired but never quit or slowed. His shaft traveled as far as some but well short of Hecate, Ngili, and Tor. And Wind.

"Good. He sees he doesn't measure up."

They finished as Moon arrived and returned to the cave. Rainbow slathered a salve over his hand and wrapped it in a leaf. He was the only hunter with blisters and they must have broken.

Hecate crouched on her heels, calmer than when she had arrived at the camp. She picked at the carcass that was her meal and marveled at the diversity that now made up the People. She knew Pan-do's People, but the former-Hawk People, Wind, Zvi, Seeker, and Spirit's wolf pack had all joined after she left. Tribes merging was unusual. None of the Others Mbasa ran into along the shore of Endless Pond invited her People into their tribe. Hecate had ascribed that to the severe lack of food, water, plants, and everything in between but seeing the People's group, now she thought those Others simply didn't have a Leader like Xhosa, one open to new ideas and tolerant of differences. To Xhosa, those who contributed to the People's health and security were welcome. She never backed away from unusual problems, always invited discussion and disagreement, and embraced decisions that made a demonstrable difference in the lives of the People.

From what she'd seen of Wind, he was similar. He neutralized the reticence many felt for trusting a Big Head with liberally applied patience. Like now. Though he must be exhausted, he was demonstrating to Ant how to perfect his hold on the spear, position it properly above his shoulder, and step into the throw.

Odd how much alike Wind and Xhosa looked, especially that bump under their mouths and the smoothness of their hair.

As Hecate fell asleep that night, it was with happy thoughts to again be part of the People.

This was Xhosa's first break all day. She'd planned to talk to Mbasa's Leads about challenging for the positions, couldn't find the time, and now that she did, couldn't find them. She wound her way through the People and finally saw Mbasa on the edge of the camp talking with her group. Xhosa headed that way but diverted when she saw Acto sitting by himself, languidly watching Qaj and Siri chop tubers. If Acto had nothing to do, he must look harder. She would explain that more firmly.

"Former-Shore Leader! Have you decided what task you are best suited to?"

Without a flicker of emotion, he scratched the air and said, "Foraging."

When he said nothing more, she pointed toward a gathering of females sauntering toward the field adjacent to the cave. They had gathered around Lyta as she sang some sort of beautiful bird song that no one had ever heard before and Xhosa was sure even the birds couldn't improve on.

Xhosa motioned, *Go,* to Acto and he lumbered off. Despite his size, Hecate said Acto lacked the aggression to fight or the instinct to hunt and Bird complained he made too much noise to be a scout. Foraging might be the sole option.

The former Leader caught up with the group and slowed to walk beside Zvi. From the back, with their similar height, both with broad sturdy bodies and brawny limbs, if not for Acto's thinner head hair, it would be impossible to tell them apart.

Zvi was a valuable addition to the People. She could do all tasks equally well because she and Seeker had spent many Moons traveling alone before finding the People. They joined not to be part of a tribe but because the stars told Seeker he would find Lyta here. Now, Seeker and Lyta spent most of their time together, often with Zvi. When Lyta became the target of assaults, Zvi committed her considerable strength, attention, and courage to keeping the fragile but brilliantly clever female alive. Once, a snake fell from an overhead branch and would have wrapped itself around the youngster except Zvi slapped it away.

Another time, a panicked pig plunged through the group. With a vigorous swing of her foot, Zvi sent it rolling through the stubble and it bounced off a boulder with a squeal. When Pando suggested to Zvi that his daughter no longer faced danger, especially with Nightshade gone, Zvi merely smiled and carried on shadowing Lyta exactly as before.

Vaya, too, hurried after the foragers. Usually, he walked with Zvi but Acto had claimed that privilege today so Vaya joined Spirit at the front, both of their shorter bodies well-hidden by the tall green stalks. A lifetime as a slave taught Vaya to move quietly, speak minimally, and look for clues others missed. Dust called him a natural scout but Vaya preferred foraging because Zvi did. Evenings, Vaya groomed the big female while Lyta groomed Seeker. The two could be mating but Xhosa had seen no evidence of that.

Xhosa finally approached Mbasa and her Leads, and of course, Shaga. They heard her approach and all turned expectantly.

"Shaga," she motioned, and the boy sprinted to her side. "Go with El-ga and Gadi. Learn what children of the People do. Become useful."

He scrunched his face, annoyed, but a nod from Mbasa sent him away without a backward glance.

El-ga scowled when he approached as only a child can do. "Gadi left but I waited for you."

With no other comment, she jogged after the youngsters tasked to collect eggs, roots, nuts, and other ground food they found.

Xhosa took a moment to appreciate the aura of competence that surrounded these Leads. Each radiated a relaxed assurance and a promise that they were ready for anything, especially surprises. Intelligence glowed from their eyes as Moon did on a dark night. What struck Xhosa also was the easy way they worked together. All had proven themselves in battle, trusted each other, and relied on Mbasa only for guidance, not decisions.

"You are an unusual group. I am reluctant to change that." When no one said anything, she asked, "How did you work with Rainbow?"

Scowls flashed. Tor gestured, hands stiff. "We stopped calling him Leader after he lost the last of the warriors. Mbasa suggested replacing the males with trained females—the idea inspired by you, Xhosa—and it worked better than we ever imagined. We would not like to change it."

When no one added more, Xhosa motioned, "All know what you accomplished in dire circumstances and everyone agrees your qualities make us stronger. I encourage every one of you to challenge for Lead."

They exchanged glances and this time, Hecate spoke for them. "We have a better idea."

The next day, Xhosa sent Bird with the scouts, Hecate with the hunters, and Mbasa and Tor with the warriors. Shaga tried to follow Mbasa but El-ga dragged him with her to forage. Xhosa swallowed a laugh, admiring the way El-ga controlled the boy. She was forceful in her kindness, pushy but with a smile. Shaga didn't know how to handle her and finally just did what she wanted.

To herself, Xhosa mumbled, "There's our next Primary Female."

When the groups returned at the end of the day, Dust reported that rarely did one as young as Bird have such mature instincts. He suggested she Co-Lead with him. Wind said Hecate moved with a natural smoothness and grace but could remain motionless for long periods of time when necessary. Her strides always matched those of the male in front of her and if she had to step out of sync, she hid it behind a bird's call or an insect's burr. In short, when hunting, she was invisible. Wind suggested Ngili and Hecate co-lead.

With no enemies to battle, Tor and Mbasa demonstrated their skill on the People's warriors. Sa-mo-ke beat them once. The best of the rest—Snake, Water Buffalo, Talon, and the giant Stone—lost regularly.

Talon suggested Mbasa and Tor Co-Lead but Xhosa shook her head. "They must challenge you."

Xhosa curled against Wind that night, feeling good about the day. With the Leads mostly resolved, it was time to figure out how the People could communicate with each other when away from the homebase. She let her mind drift, lulled by the soft buzz of the children, the snores of the wolves, and the rhythmic beat within Wind's chest. Often, the answer would float forward out of the miasma of her thoughts but this time, as she slid into darkness, what popped to mind was that the People must find a larger cave. Solve that first before the rest.

Chapter 10

Small cave

Xhosa squatted on her heels, her hands in her armpits. The wind blew cold with the taste of water. Despite the chilly nighttime air, Xhosa felt sure this was the area's warm time. Wolves were finding dens where they would care for their pups as Black Wolf did. Fruit and berries bloomed in abundance, and new grass poked up through the dead brown stubble in the meadows.

Where are they?

She looked up at the sky. The hunters were a full hand past when they should have returned. Now, Sun rested on the ground, its dying light turning the rocks red and orange. Darkness owned the distant valley where the hunters had gone. Xhosa crossed her arms, then uncrossed them and paced.

They're late—too late.

Again, she would have to organize a search. Because the scouts were still exploring this land, there was no way to know what the hunters might have run into out there. She couldn't risk waiting if they were injured or dying.

She took one last glance, called to Bird, but when she turned back, finally, there they were, far away but headed for the cave. One carried a gazelle, the rest ribs and long bones scavenged from some predator's kill. They stopped to drink at the river, dumped the cool water over their heads, and then hurried into the camp, dropping the meat in the communal pile. The partial carcass was missing the meaty parts and vaguely rancid but would feed the People tonight. That and one gazelle wasn't enough for a full day of hunting but at least they'd found that. Every day, the hunters searched farther. Soon, they would have nowhere to go.

Darkness drove the People inside and they bunched together in their nests, the wolves mixed in for warmth. Wind and Xhosa headed toward their nest, picking their way through the bodies, avoiding haphazard arms and legs while sniffing for each groupmember. Xhosa had mentally ticked everyone off by the time she approached her nest when Tor called from behind her.

"Xhosa. Wind. There is a problem."

They both turned. Spirit scrambled to his feet, ears flapping, and trotted to their side. His tail waved low on his body, hackles as flat as his ears, eyes moving through the gathering in front of him. Behind Tor, in the flickering shadows of the fire, crowded Mbasa, Sa-mo-ke, Talon, Water Buffalo, Snake, Stone, and Pan-do.

Xhosa dipped her head, hiding a yawn.

Pan-do looked to Talon, raised an eyebrow, but the Lead Warrior remained silent. Pan-do shrugged and motioned, fingers stiff but away from his chest, "Talon wants someone to challenge him."

Xhosa turned deliberately toward Talon as did Spirit, her mouth now a tight line, eyes dark pools. She had no patience for one unwilling to do his job. He withered under her glare and cringed when Spirit growled. She held a hand out to the wolf and he quieted.

Pan-do harrumphed. "One look intimidates him. That should tell you enough." Xhosa glared at Pan-do but it didn't stop him. He was used to working through issues with Xhosa. Keeping his hands obvious to everyone, he continued, "We all agree Talon is a deadly warrior. We've seen him in battle but he is also kind. The question is whether his skills better suit a warrior or the Lead?"

Xhosa's stomach turned. *Hawk was a blend of harsh and kind, as are Wind and Pan-do. Why can't Talon do that?*

But she knew why. *Talon's kindness distracts from his toughness rather than enhances it.*

Pan-do watched her evaluate his question. Finally, involuntarily, one corner of her mouth raised slightly—what he told her she did when she'd untangled a problem.

He continued, "Talon knows Nightshade chose him because he performs as ordered. He made no decisions without Nightshade's approval. He also knows you want an independent thinker, a clever problem-solver, someone inclined to act rather than wait. You respect the confidence Mbasa and Tor have to take quick and aggressive action without additional direction."

Xhosa chopped her answer, directing it at Pan-do but her eyes on Talon. "He has always performed his job well. Why do I care what he'd prefer?"

"Because Sa-mo-ke, Mbasa, or Tor might be a better choice. Talon planned to bring up a challenge at the time you resolved the Lead Scout and Hunter but you skipped Lead Warrior. Now, no one will challenge him."

"Talon should steer this conversation, not you, Pan-do," which proved Pan-do's argument. She wanted to slap Talon, or glare, but settled for deep breaths. Anger would not fix this problem.

Pan-do turned to the gathering. "Xhosa and I don't pick Leads. That hasn't changed." Xhosa nodded at him, one quick up and down. Pan-do concluded, "Decide and let us know."

Pan-do, Wind, and Xhosa didn't get far before Sa-mo-ke stopped them.

"We have reached a decision. Tor regales us with stories of Mbasa's effectiveness against the enemies her People encountered while migrating here. Talon admits to having none of that experience nor does he believe himself to be as crafty as Mbasa."

Talon breathed a sigh, as though relieved it had finally been said.

Xhosa's eyes flicked from one face to another. "So Mbasa will Lead and Talon will be her Second?"

Sa-mo-ke shook his head, face flushing. "Water Buffalo insists I am as skilled as Nightshade without his... issues... and reminds me that I beat Mbasa. Me, I am not sure how and want never to face her again. She is more deadly than Cat, cleverer than Owl. Woe to enemies who raise her ire. What she lacks in physical power becomes irrelevant next to her cleverness."

"So, you will Lead and Mbasa will be Second... " Xhosa peeked at Pan-do and Wind out of the corner of her eye, hoping this made sense to him, but both frowned, attention bounding between her, Sa-mo-ke, and each other.

"Not quite." Sa-mo-ke accepted the subtle approval around him. "Mbasa and I will co-lead with Tor and Talon Seconds."

Xhosa leaned back on her heels and scratched her arm. "We didn't want warrior Co-Leads."

Both Pan-do and Wind motioned, "But they do."

Xhosa made the announcement the next night, confirming that she, Wind, and Pan-do were co-Leads for the People who now included not just the former-Hawk People but the former-Mbasa People and the former-Shore Dwellers.

Leads resolved, Xhosa's next concern was how the People could stay in touch in this vastness of rolling hills, forests, and steep gullies. Hunters must have a way to ask for help or tell Xhosa they would return late. Otherwise, Xhosa would have to send warriors to find them, even if it was dark, which endangered those males as much as the missing ones.

As though to emphasize the importance of this issue, hunters again didn't return when they should have. This was barely a handful of days after the last time which wasn't even a handful of days following the prior one. Sun sat on the horizon, steadily sinking. Soon, it would be too late to help them. Thankfully, this time—like each time before—the males finally appeared. They had blundered into an unknown ravine, its sides lose talus making them almost impossible to climb. It took longer than expected to escape and by then, it was too dark to quickly travel over the unfamiliar terrain.

This had become an ongoing problem, one none of the Leaders had any idea how to solve.

A solution came from an unlikely source. After watching her father pace and frown too many times, eyes glued to the distance while his jaw twitched, Lyta finally worked up the courage to tell him her simple solution. At first, he said nothing, barely looking at her as she spoke, but then questions gushed. She always had answers and each compelling. To her, this was obvious. Finally convinced, Pan-do shared it with Wind who agreed immediately. Now, they must discuss it with Xhosa.

Pan-do padded from the cave, Lyta to his side, Wind and Xhosa behind. He continued until he reached the shadows beyond the fire's glow. He didn't trust Rainbow and wasn't comfortable with Vaya. Nor did he know enough about Acto and Qaj to judge them.

The cool night air wicked the sweat from the back of his neck, left over from the day's intense heat, and sent shivers down his body. He turned to Xhosa.

"We have had many conversations about how to communicate with scouts or hunters that are far from the homebase, at least to find out if they are safe. We've both thought it unsolvable until we control a larger area which will take a long time, maybe too long for some of our males. Lyta has a different solution, one we could implement immediately. She can explain."

Lyta's eyes shone with excitement and her hands moved deliberately and confidently.

"What you consider my birdsong isn't just pretty singing. The sounds are the verbal equivalent of what the People communicate with gestures, facial expressions, and body movements. I sing whatever I want to—a story, directions to a fruit tree, even landmarks I can follow should I need to reach a location a second time. Those who hear them either know it's me or think it's birds chirping. But if they understood the sounds, they listen to a story or directions or something else."

Pan-do rubbed his chest with an open palm. "My first objection when Lyta proposed this was its noise."

Lyta nodded. "I reminded my father that our world bursts with sound. We hear only what doesn't fit. Birdsong is invisible. No one will ever suspect it's us talking to each other."

Xhosa cocked her head, confused. "No one except you can make those calls."

Lyta smiled. "I can teach everyone. It's easy. You form birdsong with a simple arrangement of tongue placement against the lips and the roof of the mouth and then unfurl or narrow your lips. If you shape a tunnel around your mouth with your hands, it makes the call louder and it travels farther. When you roll your lower lip, it changes the sound and pitch."

The more Lyta talked, the more energized her gestures. Her body sparked as though struck by sky fire, alive with energy. Xhosa had never seen the mild, quiet young adult talk this much and with such enthusiasm. And why not? If this worked, Lyta would solve a critical problem. The question was, could the People replicate it?

Xhosa tried to follow Lyta's directions but her birdsong came out a hiss. After a handful of attempts, her whole body sagged.

Lyta bestowed a brilliant smile. "You're doing fine, Leader. It doesn't have to be perfect. We will all come to recognize your bird sounds. You're not trying to replicate a particular bird, just its song."

Xhosa scowled and Pan-do laughed so hard, his shoulders shook. "You look the way I felt the first time. I told her even if it was effective, no one could learn it but then, I did," and he chirped out a bird call, "as did Wind."

Wind emitted a beautiful tweet and held his hands up, palms out. "That's all I know but I'm convinced this is possible."

Xhosa scratched her arm and tugged on a generous strand of hair that had worked its way loose of the vine. She avoided Wind's eyes, not wanting him to see how flummoxed she was, and motioned to Lyta, "Is there a way to make it easier to learn?"

"Yes, of course." Lyta pressed her palms together, gaze rolling over the night sky as she considered how better to explain what to her seemed simple. She ended up repeating her instructions but with slower hand motions. "Do you see now?"

No, I don't! But all Xhosa said was, "How does anyone know who you talk to?"

Lyta bounced on the balls of her feet, a movement Seeker did when excited. "Each communication starts with the speaker's callsign and then the message."

That made sense

Lyta swayed forward and back, toes to heels. "Let me demonstrate."

She whistled a glorious birdsong. "That's Seeker's callsign," and Seeker's head popped out of the cave. Lyta waved and he went back inside.

Another short collection of sounds and this time, Zvi appeared. She yawned. "Why do you need me, Lyta?"

Xhosa answered for her. "Why do you think, Zvi?"

Zvi shrugged, "She said *find Lyta*," and Zvi trudged back into the shadows, yawning again, more loudly.

Lyta motioned, "Seeker and Zvi know their callsign and basic commands but Spirit learned much faster. I will tell him to bring me a particular root."

Lyta sang a beautiful series of sounds with the addition of curious whistles and chirrups. Spirit trundled to his feet, sniffed around the communal food pile, and snapped something up which he delivered to Lyta. Then, he laid down at her side, tail sweeping the dirt as though happy he'd pleased her.

Xhosa motioned. "Is this the root you asked him to bring?" Lyta nodded and Xhosa asked, more excited, "Can birdsong be heard from a remote hill?"

Lyta jolted to her feet and hustled away, her gait awkward but fast on her bent feet. Spirit sprinted after her, tail wagging at the joy of running with his pack. Zvi started to chase, noticed Spirit with Lyta, and returned to the cave. The Moon moved a finger before Xhosa heard the next birdsong. Pan-do leaped to his feet and chased after her.

"I guess she asked him to find her."

Again and again, the calls of night birds reached the gathering, softer each time but still clear. Finally, on a faraway hill, an upright two-legged figure limned itself against the moonlight. Soon, two others emerged at its side, one taller, the other the shape of a wolf. Everyone could clearly hear the birdsong.

As though to prove it, Seeker popped his head out of the cave. "Why does she keep calling me?"

Xhosa laughed. "I think she's proving a point."

Seeker nodded tiredly and went back inside, his shape silhouetted for a breath in front of the flickering fire before he disappeared. Moon had nearly finished its journey by the time Pan-do, Lyta, and Spirit returned.

Pan-do motioned, "If we know birdsong, hunters can call to each other. Scouts can tell us where Others live, and we will know where our People are."

Xhosa motioned to Lyta, "And you can teach it?"

Lyta looked confused. "You already asked that. My answer didn't change."

The next day, the air resounded with whistles, chirps, buzzes, warbles, and trebles as everyone practiced birdsong while they worked. A few times, the birds answered but no one—not even Lyta—understood what they said.

Chapter 11

The small cave

Wind crouched next to Xhosa as they knapped spear tips. A handful of Suns had come and gone since groupmembers took up the challenge to replicate Lyta's beautiful bird sounds. He and Xhosa had mastered it quickly but too many others—well, their calls made Wind cringe.

"That was the strangled chirp of a frog being stepped on."

Xhosa grinned. "You step on frogs a lot, do you?"

Wind scratched his arm and wondered about frogs. Usually, waterholes burst with them but not here. Was it possible whoever inhabited this place ate the frogs because they couldn't find herds?

Wind slashed one stone against the other. "My brother is close, Xhosa. I feel him. He is chasing us."

Xhosa looked toward the frozen mountains, almost invisible so far had they traveled. "Would Thunder cross that ice and snow just for revenge?"

"Without a second thought."

His hands stilled. How best to explain? Xhosa deserved an honest response. "I've known him my entire life. He grew from an eager and skilled youth to an angry opinionated adult after my father's death. Now, once his mind is made up, it doesn't change."

Xhosa rolled the cobble around in her hand. "What should we do?"

That, Wind couldn't answer. What could anyone do to avoid chaos and destruction?

He slammed the hammerstone with more power than necessary and hit his thumb. He sucked in sharply and shook his hand. That did nothing to stop the throb so he clenched a fist around the swollen digit and waited, lips pressed together and thin face pale. The discomfort peaked and receded.

One handed, he managed to gesture, "He'll never quit, Xhosa. Since we were subadults, he carried grudges in the way others carry weapons. Let me tell you a story. One day, Thunder's best friend decided to taunt a wolf. The poor creature was starving so Thunder's friend offered it food and then snatched it away, over and over. The frustrated wolf finally ran killed the boy, snatched the morsel from his hand, and scurried away. Thunder vowed to destroy the wolf and left.

"Moon came and went and one day, Thunder stumbled into our camp. Though covered in dirt with crusted blood congealed on his hands and a festering bite in his leg, he glowed with excitement. In his hands were a rotting paw, a long gray tail, and a small ear. He had killed every member of the wolf's pack. He didn't care some were innocent, and the other merely did what instinct drove it to.

"That's when I realized he'd changed. Killing had become more than justice meted out to a rival. Thunder now enjoyed it. I've never seen that before."

Wind shivered despite the heat. Xhosa started to respond but Wind stopped her. "There's more, Xhosa, and this is why I know he's coming. As children, Thunder and I could sense each other, even far away. He was a whisper inside my head, a spider's tickle on my mind. If one of us was confronted, the other would be there instantly. Everyone knew a battle with one would end up with both. I found it reassuring as a youngster. Now, it keeps me awake.

"I hear his voice in my sleep, Xhosa, calling me, laughing."

He breathed deeply before continuing and then motioned, "Like air, Thunder is invisible. Like fire, he can't be stopped."

Wind closed his eyes but saw Thunder in his mind, as clear as though he stood in front of him. His brother was trudging up the steep flanks of Viper's mountains, his mouth a scowl, arms gripping his weapons, his stride long and sure. Following him were a slew of well-armed Big Heads, many Wind recognized. Nothing, not frozen water, slippery slopes, or icy snow slowed them on their quest.

Wind tried to smile but failed. "He comes for us, Xhosa."

Xhosa stared at her pairmate, hands still and concern shading her face.

She placed a dry hand on his sweaty cheek and said, "You are as lethal as Thunder, and smarter. You fight with passion, he with anger. They are equally powerful weapons but you have another he doesn't: the loyalty of your warriors. I don't think Thunder can say that about his followers."

Wind nodded but Xhosa wasn't done.

"I will stop him, Wind. He destroyed my father. I won't let him do that to my People. If the only way is Thunder's death, that's what will happen."

Any males not busy, no matter their experience, trained all day and into the night, hungry or thirsty, whether or not Moon revealed itself. They fought with their eyes shut or one-armed or hopping on one leg.

"You must continue even when you've lost, you're exhausted or injured. If you break a limb, use the other. If you have no spear, use your club, no club, use rocks. If those run out, use your body. I promise, Thunder will. We will turn my brother's strategies against him in ways he never imagined."

His most ardent student was Mbasa. She fought as though defeat was akin to death. The day inevitably came when no one would face her. She glared at the assembled warriors, sturdy males, many with youthful exuberance, others with confidence born of experience, but no one came forward.

"Tor?"

When Mbasa and Tor sparred, a crowd always gathered, knowing whoever won would do so by using some trick no one had ever seen before. Once they started, it didn't matter that their shadows dissolved into darkness, that they could only find their opponent by listening for movement or smelling their blood. Neither would quit. Only exhaustion stopped them but both always left in good humor, jabbering about a particular incident and how the other defended and what the defense or offense should have been.

Tor guffawed. "I am still recovering from our last battle. Give me more time."

Wind sighed. "I guess it's up to me to put this youngster in her place."

Water Buffalo stopped him. "I will do it."

Scars marked his many victories, layered one over the other on his brawny chest and arms, but gray streaked his black hair and his clear-eyed stare once filled with confidence now carried a hint of doubt. He was desperate to restore the respect he'd long ago lost. Beating the most-talented among them would do that.

Everyone formed a circle around the two, a mix of worry and excitement on their faces but not Mbasa's. She should be intimidated by Water Buffalo's strength, experience, and quickness but she reeked of something Water Buffalo had long lost: passion. That, every warrior knew, could win where loss was assured.

Within a breath of beginning, Water Buffalo charged. To his surprise, he was able to immediately hit Mbasa. That made him cocky. Wind watched the transition in his face—*She is tiny and weak, no challenge to my size and strength. I am better than those she beat in the past.* Wind cringed. He had warned Water Buffalo she was devious, that she would use his overt physicality against him. He didn't understand what Wind meant so ignored him with a smirk.

After taking that first hit from her opponent and then one more, Mbasa engaged. First, she slammed her head into Water Buffalo's which opened a bloody cut on his forehead. While he stood, dazed, she pummeled his temples cruelly. He finally roared and grabbed her arm savagely, yanking it behind her back with one hand and then wrenched it upward. When he let go, an evil grin on his face, Wind bit back a warning—to Water Buffalo. Mbasa cradled her arm, feigning misery, seemingly a breath or two from capitulating. Wind knew she wasn't but Water Buffalo couldn't resist going in for the kill. He darted forward, surprised that the end was so close and excited to so easily defeat this intractable opponent with the colossal reputation.

He grinned as she lurched backwards, distress shining brightly from her eyes. He rushed forward again and grabbed her uninjured arm. Rather than resist, Mbasa jabbed her two stiff fingers—from the arm that was supposed to be injured—at his eyes. He snapped his head back to avoid her thrust. Her hand shot out with the speed of a rattlesnake and crushed his gonads. To his credit, he made no sound, but when he batted her hand away, she smashed his knee with her foot hard enough to make him forgot about his penis.

His legs shook and he staggered. Wind willed him to find the strength to continue. If he quit now, he would lose the respect of his fellow warriors, but he crumpled. Mbasa kicked his head, yelling at him to get up, that she wasn't done, once and again but he didn't move.

He'd passed out.

Mbasa wasn't even breathing hard. "I barely began and it's over. Who's next?"

Wind growled. He had wanted Water Buffalo to prove himself a better fighter than the one who lost miserably to Nightshade and then Wind himself had easily defeated. All that anger from those battles should have been turned against Mbasa.

She reminded Wind of Viper.

Water Buffalo lay on the ground, a neglected heap, unconscious and abandoned. After forcing herself not to kick or spit on the still body at her feet, Xhosa left. Today, she had an important promise to keep, one she made when the People crashed on the shore of Endless Pond. Many had perished before help reached them. Xhosa had resolved to teach her People to care for wounds.

Xhosa gathered everyone not hunting, scouting, or foraging and started by describing each plant she carried in her neck sack, its purpose, and where it could be found. Then, she demonstrated how to select the stems, leaves, bulbs, roots, and flowers to treat common injuries.

"Let's say you are cut."

She walked into a nearby grove, slumped to her knees, and then dug under a particular trunk, its roots thick cords spreading away from the base until she found yellow-green nodes.

"Use these to stop the poison that often accompanies cuts. Keep the root for mulches."

As they walked through the surrounding terrain, she had everyone collect a variety of healing treatments from under logs and bark as well as the lumpy brown fungus from trunks and mushrooms that sprouted in shady places.

"The bark of this trunk has a soft underside that can be scraped off and chewed. The bark itself can be used to stiffen injured legs, arms, or ankles. Keep it in place by wrapping it with vines...." "The stem of this flower—the one with bulbs on its roots—works on snakebite." ... "This one, toss away the root." ... "This flower with leaves that are dark on top and pale beneath helps the joint ache of elders..." ... "A flower's sweet fragrance could mean it is poisonous..."

When the group finally returned to the camp, someone had propped Water Buffalo against a bush where he now sat, his knee red and swollen, his penis bloated as though prepared for mating, and his face pale. Xhosa gave him a plant for the swelling but he refused one for pain. Everyone else avoided him. No one respected weakness.

He had aged drastically since confronting Mbasa. Xhosa doubted he would ever again join the People's warriors, would instead stay with the elders who did what they could without much being expected of them.

Chapter 12

The small cave

"Xhosa." Ngili approached her moments after she awoke as though he'd been waiting. "We are out of the hard stones for choppers, cutters, and handaxes. Come with Dust and I today as we hunt. With your farsight, maybe you'll see something."

She grunted acknowledgement, motioned to Wind, and then trotted after Ngili. Spirit and Black Wolf caught up, the pups chasing their alphas but soon turning back. Sun swiftly burned away the day's early mist and the air warmed. The group followed a path into a valley that seemed to cut a swath through the terrain and then shadowed a stream that burbled along its floor. Xhosa wiped an arm over her forehead, eyes bleary from the constant surveilling, and then splashed the refreshing liquid on her face. No signs of the hard stones or herds. She slumped but quickly straightened. It was too early to give up hope.

They finally stopped to rest. The water teamed with fish but Ngili couldn't manage to stab even one.

He scowled. "They are speedy!"

Wind motioned ahead. "You and Xhosa wait for me in that shallow cove," and then waded into the shoals of fish, Spirit and Black Wolf with him.

He and the wolves shuttled the writhing creatures toward Ngili and Xhosa who easily scooped them from the shallow water with their hands while the wolves snapped them right out of the water. They ate in the shade and wrapped the leftovers in leaves which were stuffed into neck sacks.

Refreshed by the cool water and filling food, they set out again. Not far from where they'd eaten, Black Wolf and Spirit huffed once and sprinted up the stream's bank, through a wide spider's web built between two trees, and out of sight. Xhosa could hear them crash through the underbrush and then, only silence. She raced forward along their trail and found them sitting on their haunches at the edge of a small copse, obscured from whatever lay ahead by a screen of tall foliage. Their heads swiveled to acknowledge her, fangs exposed, and then turned back.

Hackles up, nose twitching, Xhosa motioned to those behind her, "Down!"

When she parted the stalks, she saw Others, subadults, gathered in front of a cave that was well-hidden in the shadow of a massive hill. The youngsters were stripping bloody shreds from a partly-chewed gazelle, scavenge from another predator, and smashing the long bones with rocks to expose the marrow. Their eyes flitted nervously over their surroundings but still, they missed the obvious scent of Others not from their tribe.

The skinny bodies and the craving in their eyes told Xhosa that today, here, hunger outweighed caution, though she had seen nothing that would frighten them like this.

What are they afraid of? And why are youngsters doing the work of hunters? Where are the adults?

It didn't take long for Xhosa to satisfy herself that this gathering presented no risk. She sang a birdsong "leave" and backed away. The Others froze at the beautiful sound but relaxed, apparently thinking it a native bird.

Surely by now, they should know the voice of every bird here.

When Xhosa, Wind and the rest returned to the People's base, Pan-do was working with a handful of males on stone throwing.

He took one look at her face and caught up with her. "You look worried."

Xhosa told him about the subadult Others, bending each finger to tick them off while saying *"here is one, here is another, here is another"*. It took only one hand.

"More might have hidden in the cave, too frightened to come out, but I couldn't tell."

Pan-do rubbed his arms. "They could be youngsters left behind while the adults hunt or scout."

Wind motioned, "If that's true, why are they hungry? The scavenged carcass I saw would feed few."

Xhosa motioned, "We can bring them food tomorrow. If we see adults, we leave."

Sometime later, with everyone settled for the night, Seeker beckoned Xhosa. "Come watch the stars with me."

Without questioning, Xhosa followed. He hadn't talked about the stars since they arrived here so Xhosa couldn't help but wonder why now? She had planned to discuss the subadult Others with Wind but that would wait.

The boy-male nimbly scaled the rock wall behind their homebase and flopped down, Xhosa beside him. She stared upward, the night sky shimmering with the beautiful spots of light that must have been cast across the darkness by a giant hand. Xhosa first located Always-there Star and then the identifiable patterns of those that always hovered around it. Beyond these were the stars that had moved to different positions or new ones Xhosa didn't recognize. It was these that Seeker focused on. They were the ones that talked to him.

As Moon slipped in and out of the clouds, Xhosa ignored the chilly air, enjoying Seeker's gasps of excitement. Right now, a crocodile could gnaw his leg and it wouldn't distract him. Spirit padded up and licked his cheeks and mouth, something Seeker usually enjoyed, but he didn't even notice. The wolf whimpered and returned to where Zvi and Lyta crouched, in a friendly argument about something, waiting for Xhosa to leave.

After long breaths, Seeker sighed, "Do you see the new ones, Xhosa? To the side of Always-there? They tell us who we must rescue."

"Rescue?"

He continued as though she hadn't spoken. "It may be the ones you found today—what Wind calls the Cave Dwellers—but I don't think so."

Xhosa squirmed, heart pounding. "Maybe Mbasa's People."

"No. These stars are new."

A lump formed in Xhosa's throat and her stomach tightened. Regardless of the stars' lack of interest, she had to help the Cave Dwellers or they would starve. It reminded her of fleeing the Big Heads, when Hawk came to their rescue.

Seeker said nothing more, now lost in his world of stars and messages, so Xhosa left. Zvi, Lyta, and a reluctant Vaya scampered past her and joined Seeker. Anticipation filled Lyta's and Zvi's faces, frustration Vaya's. The boy rubbed his arms and glanced longingly at the fire dancing and leaping in the cave. Little did Vaya know the group he'd attached himself to spent many nights staring at the sparkling dots that dappled the darkness.

Xhosa found Wind and told him what Seeker said about their mission here, concluding, "We want a new homebase, not a rescue mission."

He pulled her toward himself and they fell asleep.

The next day, she, Wind, Ngili, and a handful of warriors loaded their arms with food and again visited the Others' cave. Spirit accompanied them but Black Wolf stayed with the People. If this was a trap, the female wolf would lead Pan-do to the subadults' homebase.

Xhosa and the rest gathered at the edge of the clearing, again well hidden, and observed the Others. The females pounded roots and tubers. The males crouched over a carcass even older than the one yesterday, scraping dry meat from almost-bare bones. Such a paucity of food, Xhosa couldn't imagine they would bother with it except that they were starving. The subadults sniffed the air and stiffened. They must have caught the People's scent—or Spirit's feral one. Fear leaked from their bodies but they continued, movements now jerky as they tried to hurry. Someone jabbered a loud order and they settled, maybe deciding whatever they smelled couldn't be worse than abandoning the only food they'd find all day.

Xhosa motioned, touching her wrist and back, "No weapons. Maybe they're in the cave."

Wind replied, "That's too far away for defense if they're attacked."

Ngili moved to the side for a better view and accidently flushed a small flock of birds from the grass. The youngsters jerked and again babbled to each other.

No sense hiding anymore, and Xhosa strode into the open, Wind at her side, the rest of her assemblage an arm's distance apart and a pace behind her. All spears pointed down and warclubs remained strung over their backs. The young Others froze, gawking. Their legs began to shake but still, no one made a move to defend themselves.

Xhosa motioned to Wind, "I recognize some from yesterday."

One of them barked and a subadult male stepped out of the cave closely followed by a female. His forehead prickled with sweat but otherwise, he managed to hide the alarm he must feel toward well-equipped warriors who entered his camp uninvited. As Wind and Xhosa approached the boy, the subadult's eyes darted between them and then latched onto Spirit. Xhosa didn't have to look to know the wolf's startling blue eyes rested on the subadult. That would intimidate the bravest adult much less these children. It was something about his fangs.

Still, the boy held his ground. Maybe he hoped the wolf, who was nearer to the strangers, would attack them first. Spirit lowered his head and took one step toward the subadults making it clear which side he fought for.

Wind cocked his head and Boy-who-must-be-Leader snapped toward him. Wind imagined what the boy saw—a physically imposing male, taller than all others with a full regimen of weapons—so he tilted his head and offered a slight smile, hoping to soften his appearance. The youngster responded with his own, though shaky and brief.

"We mean you no harm," Wind motioned with generic gestures most Others understood.

Boy-who-must-be-Leader remained expressionless, eyes hooded. The rest of his tribe wriggled uncomfortably. Xhosa studied them as they studied Wind. She searched for threats and found only worry, and a brittle resolve to confront an enemy who might end their lives. They stood shorter than Wind but taller than Ngili. Their broad flat faces had a delicate look with sunken cheeks, prominent noses, and narrow foreheads above subtle brow ridges that would never keep water out of their eyes. In some ways, they resembled Wind but with a smaller face set in a flatter head, their bodies with stockier chests, longer arms, shorter legs, and no necks.

Wind extended a hand palm up toward the cutter in the subadults hand. The youngster retreated but not far, confusion and worry flashing across his face.

Wind dug a cutter—a small stone that was beveled on all sides—from his neck sack and offered it to the boy.

"Let's swap."

He reluctantly exchanged his cutter for Wind's and then again backed away. His young group clustered around as he ran his finger along the edge and then gasped when blood beaded on the tip. He jabbered with hand gestures foreign to Xhosa.

Wind motioned to Xhosa, "These tools remind me of the crude ones Pan-do described used by the Hairy Ones." He extended the boy-male's cutter toward her. "See. There are no marks that they resharpen the edges when they dull."

Wind slid his thumb over the edge. Barely a crease appeared, certainly no blood.

"These are made without planning or attention. Pan-do described the Hairy Ones' toolmaking as rushed without concern for details. And these are all pond pebbles. I don't see any of the hard stones we need."

Hard stones didn't break when slammed into rock or bone which made them perfect for spear tips and handaxes. Pond pebbles broke easily and were used only if nothing else was available which would happen soon.

Xhosa frowned and crossed one arm over her chest. "Maybe there aren't any here, Wind. I'm not sure what we would do—"

Wind interrupted, "No, that's not true," and pawed through a pile of rocks near Boy-who-could-be-Leader. "See? This one was knapped from a hard stone."

That these Others could find hard stones thrilled Xhosa but she hid her excitement, instead gazed blankly at them as they did her, probably wondering why Wind was digging through their stones.

She motioned quietly to Wind, hands below her waist, "Did you notice that each of the Others holds a tool suited to the task they perform—cutting, pounding, or crushing. They understand that the right tool makes the job easier. Either they don't realize the value of hard stones or no longer have access to where they live."

As she thought about that, Spirit trotted up to Boy-who-must-be-Leader, sniffed, sneezed, flapping his ears violently, and then backed away. Rather than frightened, the boy seemed excited to be so close to a wolf without being eaten.

Xhosa dipped her head to hide a grin and whispered, "Spirit smells the rot in their pelts. They are poorly made and unpreserved. No one wastes skins in this way. I don't think they know any better."

The primitive tools, the rotting pelts—it made no sense.

She peeked into the cave's darkness. "And no fire pits. How do they stay warm at night? Or keep predators away?"

Wind handed the tool back to Boy-who-must-be-Leader who did the same, his eyes remaining on the wolf. Spirit's hackles flattened and he panted, muzzle open in a grin, tail waving side to side. He sensed no threat and the boy showed no fear of Spirit. Somehow, he seemed to accept that a wolf would travel with these strange new Others with the mighty weapons. Not so his groupmates. They chattered worriedly and flapped their hands nonstop. At first, it was a string of nonsense but slowly, Xhosa recognized gestures. She concentrated on the fluttering hands, bobbing heads, and started to understand what they were saying.

She motioned to Wind, "They use the same gestures Viper did and talk the way she does."

Viper always spoke with specifics, never generalizing. She referred to Xhosa as "the two-legged upright creature with too-long and too-straight hair" rather than "female Other". She explained to Xhosa that with this description, none of Viper's People would ever confuse Xhosa with a different Other. Viper had learned Xhosa's callsigns for each of the People but said they made no sense so created new ones when talking to her Mountain Dweller tribe. Hers relied on a prominent characteristic of the individual. For example, the one who captured her—Fang—became "Fang-the-Ugly-One." Nightshade morphed from "Nightshade-fearsome-warrior" when they first met to "Nightshade-the-Evil-One" when she got to know him.

Xhosa's People used the same approach when migrating or hunting, to identify markers. It enabled anyone to find a spot, even in an unknown area.

Wind motioned to Boy-who-must-be-Leader using Viper's Mountain Dweller gestures, "I am Wind. This is Xhosa. Behind us, our warriors. The wolf, Spirit, won't hurt you if you present no threat to him or us."

The young boy squared to Wind, head up, eyes clear.

"I am Qu'tez. This is Re'ez." He elbowed the female at his side, also a subadult.

Qu'tez displayed the confidence gained by surviving a toxic life and making impossible decisions most avoided. He reminded Xhosa of Mbasa. This close, Xhosa could see what Wind called a chin pushed out from beneath the boy's mouth. Wind said just his kind—and those a mix of his and hers—had chins so how did it make sense that this boy, far from Wind's People, had one?

She stored that away for a later discussion and motioned, "You are the only Others we have come across since arriving here." The term *Others* confused him so she clarified, "Creatures who walk upright. You are an Other. Spirit," and indicated the wolf, "only thinks he is."

"No. We are Cave Dwellers. We are different from Those-who-eat-Others. They are killers."

Chapter 13

Cave Dwellers' cave

Xhosa scrunched her forehead to hide her surprise. "Where do Those-who-eat-Others live? And how many are there?"

Qu'tez's eyes smoldered. "It is too late to stop them. They surely know of your presence. You, like us, have become their prey."

Spirit pounced on a ground squirrel and the noise made Qu'tez jump. He waved frantically to his People, motioning them to the cave, while scouring the surroundings in search of the sound. He didn't see Spirit, already collapsed amidst the hip-high scrub brush, enjoying his catch.

He took two strides toward Xhosa, leaned forward, and barked, "Did they follow you here?"

Xhosa had to force herself not to gag at the smell of stale blood on his breath. Rather than withdraw, she moved closer, now a hand's width away and towering over his head, her muscular shoulders wider than his entire body. He had no choice but to back up just to look into her face. When she saw his eyes, they held a small amount of alarm and a lot of desperation.

"No, Qu'tez. That will never happen. What you heard was the wolf Spirit catching a squirrel. You must calm down. You can't win a battle if you are too frantic to think."

He flushed, chastened, and nodded.

She tied her hair back behind her neck, something she always did when preparing for a fight. "If they are here, Qu'tez, it's because they followed you. I promise, if they assault you while we are here, it will be their last."

Qu'tez's scrutiny flicked from Xhosa to her muscled warriors and back. Spirit padded to Xhosa's side. His blue eyes fixed on the boy, the carcass of a dead squirrel hanging from his mouth, blood coloring his fangs. He sniffed and his hackles raised and ears twitched. Xhosa's hand on his neck told him there was no threat so he plopped down at her side to devour his food.

Qu'tez once more scanned his surroundings. "They—Those-who-eat-Others—are sneaky, sly, and treacherous. Don't underestimate them."

Xhosa forced her annoyance aside and took his face between her fingers. Then, she turned it until he met her eyes, smoldering with barely contained impatience. "You don't know us well but believe this: We are worse."

Qu'tez twitched to the cry of a squirrel, maybe calling its dead mate, and then relaxed. "We would leave but there's nowhere to go. Those-who-eat-Others over there," and stabbed toward Endless Pond, "are like those here."

Wind motioned, "He must mean the cannibals Mbasa told us about."

Xhosa motioned to the boy-male, "They are no longer a problem, Qu'tez. They angered Fire Mountain."

"You are wrong. A few survived. We saw them. They remind me of you. Well, not you, him," and Qu'tez indicated Ngili.

Re'ez edged toward Qu'tez, hands clamped together, and motioned, "Maybe they are you."

Xhosa gestured, "Those you saw are my People. They escaped the cannibals who live across the channel by sailing rafts from that shore to this one. The cannibals don't know how to do that."

Re'ez shuffled her feet and motioned one handed. "Can you prove you aren't Those-who-eat-Others?"

Xhosa motioned calmly, "You can do that yourself, One-called-Re'ez. Sniff. Do we have the sweet stench?" Re'ez and

Qu'tez inhaled and shook their heads. "We disdain them also. They hurt one of our People."

Quick hand motions passed between Qu'tez and Re'ez—*"Do you believe her?" "Yes, but even if she lies, what choice do we have? Her People—they are well-armed. If they confront us, we will lose!" "For some reason, I trust her."*

"Enough of this! Tell us, we will leave. You are nothing to us."

Qu'tez stiffened, shuffled, and motioned quietly, "We do need help." He pointed to the mountains Xhosa and the People crossed to get here. "We can't go there because of the cold," and then turned to his weak side. "A lake with no shores covers the entire horizon that direction. And Those-who-eat-Others live where Sun sleeps. We are stuck here with no way to escape."

Xhosa motioned. "Are Others here that aren't what we call cannibals—what you call Those-who-eat-Others?"

Re'ez shook her head and Qu'tez nodded. Qu'tez clarified, "We are both right. There are Others held captive by Those-who-eat-Others, kept alive until needed for food. Soon, they will all be gone."

When he finished, his tongue poked around in his cheek and he winced.

Xhosa rummaged through her neck sack and pulled a root bundle out. "Chew this, Qu'tez. It will help."

He chewed, swallowed, and his face brightened as the throbbing stabs melted away.

His head dipped. "It has been so long… I never thought… " He raised his head, face now dark, eyes intense and focused. "Leave if you can, Ones-called-Xhosa-and-Wind. Go back to where you came from. No one survives here."

Xhosa cocked her head. "If that's true, how do you?"

He motioned, "We were part of Those-who-eat-Others but fled when they began to eat the young, weak, and sick, many of them our friends. We'll survive," but Qu'tez's face said he lied and his body said he was tired of the fight.

Without another word, Qu'tez left, Re'ez with him but not before she cast a pleading glance at Xhosa. Their eyes never separated until Re'ez disappeared into the shadows. Then, Xhosa and the rest of her People dumped the food they had brought in front of the cave and left.

That night, she asked Seeker if the Cave Dwellers required rescuing, according to the stars.

He wriggled and fluffed his hair which told her he was thinking.

Finally, he replied, "This journey and its detour have served a purpose. You will not be disappointed."

The next day, Xhosa, Wind, and Mbasa again visited the Cave Dwellers, carrying as much food as they could, and this time, bringing Shaga and El-ga. Xhosa hoped meeting the children would reinforce to the Cave Dwellers that the People were committed to make this their home.

Qu'tez and Re'ez met them outside the cavern.

Xhosa motioned, "We will trade meat for the hard stones."

When both looked confused, Wind dug through the pile outside the mouth of the cave and dug two of the hard stones out. Xhosa slammed them together, once and again, and they scarcely chipped.

"Strong stones, like these."

Qu'tez scratched the hair on his chest, confused. "No one cares about those stones. We have many. Take what you want. They are too difficult for us to knap."

Re'ez motioned to Qu'tez, "Show them. I'll play with the children."

Xhosa nodded. "Their callsigns are Shaga and El-ga. They will teach you a favorite game our adults enjoy playing."

Once inside the Cave Dwellers' cave, the tiny size and extreme hunger of Qu'tez's community appalled Xhosa. Drool dripped from their mouths when they saw the food the People carried.

She shrugged her carcass to the ground as did Wind and she motioned to Qu'tez, "Can we leave this here? It is for your group."

He managed a nod and headed down a narrow tunnel at the back of the cave. After many turns and twists, they reached a pile of stones amidst the rubble of a roof cave-in. Xhosa dug through the pile and held up several old, worn tools made from the hard stones.

"Who made these?"

Qu'tez's chin trembled. "Our fathers. We don't know how to smooth the surfaces and sharpen the edges as they did."

Xhosa slammed two of them together and grinned. "These are perfect."

"But how can you knap them?"

"We'll teach you. They take time to shape but last longer once completed."

He turned and guided them back toward the front but stopped at a nook. Inside, scattered around the floor were piles of tools—cutters, choppers, flakes, and hammer stones. Many had been knapped from common stones but others from antlers or large bones.

Xhosa motioned, "What do you use the shoulder blades for?"

"Our fathers and mothers used them for digging, the antlers for punctures."

Qu'tez perked up, eyes now bright, face flushed. "Take these also if you like. We'd like to learn to hunt."

Xhosa motioned, "Show us where to find the herds and we'll teach you to knap strong tools as your fathers did."

Qu'tez slumped. "We have old spears and no warclubs." He looked away, his face flushing.

Xhosa nodded. *No wonder they scavenge another predator's food. How did they survive this long?*

Xhosa motioned to Wind with Big Head gestures, got a nod in response, and turned back to Qu'tez. "Be prepared tomorrow."

On the way back to the homebase, El-ga and Shaga gushed about the huge spaces within the cave where they had played their game with Re'ez. They asked if there was room in the People's cave for that.

Which made Xhosa think.

Chapter 14

Cave Dwellers' cave

The next day, Xhosa, Wind, Mbasa, and Dust delivered armloads of tubers, roots, berries, corms, sprouts, and fruit to the Cave Dwellers. Qu'tez greeted them, his hand gripping a poorly made spear, tension radiating like heat from his body.

Xhosa asked what happened and he motioned, palms touching lightly, "Those-who-eat-Others captured two groupmembers last night. Only Cucu'tez escaped," and indicated a scrawny subadult with close set shifty eyes.

Xhosa wrinkled her nose. Wind did the same. The putrid sweetness of cannibals oozed like mist from Cucu'tez.

Xhosa approached the subadult. "It is good you saved yourself. How did you manage that?" His answer could explain his stink.

He gestured nervously about how they captured his friends before he could do anything and he wanted to help but couldn't without getting caught himself and he couldn't let that happen because his People needed him. As his explanation gushed out, his feet shuffled through the dirt, eyes anywhere but on Xhosa, *as though afraid I'll see the lie*, but she kept her face passive, listening to his answer.

Finally, she interrupted, "How?"

He stopped mid-explanation, eyes rolling over the gathering, and finally asked, "How what?"

"How did you escape when they couldn't?"

"No. You don't understand. I was protecting the backtrail. Those-who-eat-Others came from the *front* and surrounded our scouts."

But his body said he'd hid.

"Somehow, even though they didn't capture you, they forced you to roll around on the ground with them?" *Or eat one of your friends?*

"What?"

She touched her nose. "You stink of them."

Wind nudged her and shook his head.

Qu'tez glanced between Xhosa and Cucu'tez but didn't defend the boy. Instead, he motioned, "This loss is lethal for us."

Xhosa waved his words away. "It's done, Qu'tez. You will survive but not if you starve. Let's go hunting as planned."

He bobbed his head. "I will come but Zak'ez and Asal'rez must remain at the cave, to protect the females."

"And Cucu'tez?"

"He is recovering. He doesn't feel up to hunting."

Xhosa turned away, disgusted.

It took most of a hand of Sun's travel overhead to find the herd Qu'tez had seen a handful of days before. Gazelle munched happily on a dense field of green and yellow grass, oblivious to danger. Xhosa crouched, hidden in a thick stand of stalks, careful not to step on the dry thatch that covered the ground. Finger-length bees buzzed here and there while ants moved in busy columns through the grass and spiders built their webs near the base of the stems. Clouds drifted across the sky and shafts of yellow lit the meadow in mottled patches. Somewhere, a stream bubbled.

Without warning, Qu'tez took off, yelling to her rather than using quiet hands. Almost as one, the gazelle jerked their heads up, found the charging predator with the loud voice and flailing arms, and fled. A flock of ground birds exploded into the air, gone before anyone could unleash their stones. Qu'tez pulled to a stop, panting heavily, and then trotted back to Xhosa and the rest of her hunters. His face flushed with excitement.

"I almost got close enough!"

Mbasa stomped over to Xhosa, Qu'tez trailing but scurrying to keep up. "We just lost the largest herd we've seen here! These Cave Dwellers—or maybe just Qu'tez—don't know anything. I want him away from my hunt!"

Xhosa silenced her with a raised hand. "We discovered this meat because of him," and then turned to Qu'tez. "You don't have the basic hunting skills every subadult possesses. You should have told me that."

The joy drained from Qu'tez's face and he hung his head, arms loose at his sides. Without looking at either Xhosa or Mbasa, he motioned, "I know where another is. I will do better. I promise."

"When we find them, stay downwind, out of sight, and motionless. Watch what Mbasa and I do."

He nodded and took off, across the meadow where Gazelle had been eating, down one side of a steep valley and up the other. He suggested pausing to rest but Xhosa scowled so he continued, mouth open as he gulped in air. After descending and climbing another gully and diverting around a bed of boulders, Qu'tez pulled up to the edge of a field that seemed to go on forever. He looked over his shoulder at Xhosa, wheezing. Xhosa stepped past him, not waiting for him to cough out whatever he wanted to say.

And stopped, awed. Covering one end of the field to the other was an endless herd of the biggest gazelle Xhosa had ever seen. They were burly creatures with muscular shoulders as though willing and capable of fighting if assaulted, nothing like the graceful, slender gazelle Xhosa had seen earlier. These had long thick necks, their tails almost touching the ground, and their eyes wise as though they knew more about surviving than Xhosa. They must have smelled the hunters because they began to prance, ears forward, nostrils flared, necks arched, but they didn't run. Gazelle always ran.

Qu'tez approached Xhosa as Mbasa caught up. "This isn't the herd I planned to show you. This one, we don't eat. It is called Equiis."

She motioned, "I know these animals. We ran into them before we met you. Wind said they aren't good food."

She stared, at one in particular, a proud, long-legged creature with a shock of long hair that ran down its neck, an elegant tail that could sweep flies from its entire body, and a beautiful voice filled with whinnies, neighs, nickers, and the occasional blow of air. She remembered the light-colored stripe that ran from its mane to its tail, offset against the darker shade on the rest of its body.

Qu'tez grumped, breathing almost normal. "He's right. They are more gristle than meat with little of the fat found in Bison or Bear. And they are challenging to bring down. My People never managed to funnel them over a bluff as we do Gazelle. They seem too smart to be tricked in that way."

The sweat on Equiis glowed in Sun's light, mane and tail soft and clean. Several pricked their ears toward the two-legged Others, curious but not afraid. Xhosa searched for the Leader and finally found him, positioned on the edge of the herd between her hunters and his herd.

His gaze rested on Xhosa.

"I know this Leader, too."

The noble male watched her, without fear, as though asking if she was friend or foe. Xhosa placed her spear on the ground, shook her hands loose, and stepped toward him. He didn't back up, let her approach, one stride after another. She tried to look friendly but wasn't sure what that would be to Equiis. Finally, she was close enough to touch his forehead. It was warm and soft and she saw no fear or aggression in his eyes.

Qu'tez shouted behind her, a harsh sound that put Xhosa on edge as much as the Equiis Leader. He snorted, flipped his elegant head high, and galloped away, the rest of his flock close behind, like a swarm of bees chases their queen. Xhosa remained where she stood, watching them go, clenching her fists in anger at Qu'tez. When the herd was almost out of sight, the Leader turned, legs spread, beautiful tail swishing, and called to her. A loud neigh as though inviting her to join him, and then turned and disappeared.

Xhosa walked softly back to her People, breathing slowly to calm herself.

When she rejoined them, Qu'tez motioned, "This field goes on a long way. Gazelle graze here if Equiis isn't around but the trip isn't wasted. Not far from here are a lot of caves if you're still looking for a new one."

Xhosa nodded and they jogged forward. The first few they reached looked as though they could serve the People but Qu'tez said no.

"Cave-dwelling Hyaena live there. They prey on Equiis, Bison, Gazelle, and us. Normally, they hunt in packs but if we come to one by itself, we can sometimes intimidate him enough to grab the carcass of his prey."

The remaining caves were too small. Qu'tez didn't have a good understanding of the size of Xhosa's tribe.

When Sun's round orb began to sink below the ground, the group headed back to the Cave Dwellers' homebase, empty handed. When they got there, the food left earlier by the People was gone. No one greeted them but they no longer looked afraid, just busy.

As Xhosa's group began the trek back to her People's cave, she sensed Qu'tez wanted to ask her something. She slowed, giving him a chance to catch up, but he didn't and soon, his homebase was hidden beyond a turn on the trail.

That night, Xhosa, Wind, and Pan-do discussed the Cave Dwellers. "Qu'tez lacks simple knowledge but is eager to learn. Whoever should have trained him didn't. He tried to teach himself but had no skills to do that."

Wind nodded. "He is a risk-taker and will grow into a valuable adult."

Pan-do added, "If he survives."

Xhosa wriggled, wrapping her arms around her knees. "I have an idea."

When she finished explaining it, Pan-do and Wind suggested they bring it up to Qu'tez the next day.

Xhosa, Pan-do, and Wind arrived at the Cave Dwellers' homebase soon after Sun awoke. Re'ez and Qu'tez greeted them, the boy again looking like he had a question, but Xhosa held her hand up, palm forward.

"I know you're worried about the small size of your group, your inability to defeat Those-who-eat-Others should they find your cave. I have a solution. Move in with us. It is crowded but we will make room. With such a large group, you will be more secure. Repay this protection with your knowledge of this area."

A smile played at the corners of Re'ez's lips and she nudged Qu'tez. He fingered his chin—something Wind did—and motioned, "We are grateful for the offer," though rather than pleased, he sounded uncertain which made no sense. This boy's group couldn't survive much longer on their own.

She waited, not knowing what would come next.

Finally, he gestured, "Xhosa, you've only seen part of our cave. Let me show you the rest. It's big. Maybe when you've seen it, you'll decide that you should move in with us."

With a nod from Xhosa as well as Wind, Qu'tez led them beyond the main space, through tunnels so dark only dragging her hand along the cold, rough walls kept her oriented, past an underground waterhole she could hear but not see, deftly dodging rocky growths from the ceiling and cracks in the floor that seemed to have no bottom. Intermittently, water dripped from the ceiling and plopped onto them or the dusty floor.

They had progressed well beyond where Qu'tez stored the hard stones before he stopped.

"This is as far as we've gone but it seems to continue a long way. We thought if Those-who-eat-Others invaded, we would escape down this tunnel and they would eventually stop chasing us. You can see there is ample room for both of our People. What do you think?"

Without giving her a chance to answer, he made his way back to the front.

When they arrived at the main cavern, Xhosa gestured, "We'll bring our People tomorrow."

On the way back to her camp, Wind motioned to Xhosa, "I don't trust Cucu'tez."

Xhosa responded, not slowing, "That's why we're moving in."

Qu'tez and his small community of Cave Dwellers gaped in disbelief at the long line of Others that poured into the clearing by their cave. Qu'tez couldn't find Xhosa anywhere, nor did he recognize any of those from the earlier visits. Finally, just as he thought he must confront the aggressive female at the front of the group who carried two spears and a warclub, Xhosa strode toward him, a smiling female at her side, and Qu'tez relaxed.

Xhosa joined him but Smiling Female continued, stopping when she reached the Cave Dwellers, clustered together, faces puckered, arms tight across their chests.

Xhosa motioned, hand waving in front of her body, "That is Siri. She's our Primary Female and will organize your cave to accommodate the larger tribe."

Qu'tez wanted to ask what she meant by Primary Female but remembered his mistakes with hunting and decided to watch, wondering what One-called-Siri would do differently than Re'ez had.

Siri smiled at the Cave Dwellers, a gathering of less than would be ticked off on a hand, and scrutinized one after the other. When she reached Re'ez, she stepped closer to her.

"You must be One-called-Re'ez. Xhosa called you Primary Female."

Re'ez shook her head, her wide-eyed look jumping between dread and determination. "No—I don't know what that is."

Siri smiled. "I'll help you," and set about to locate sleeping spots, a communal food pile, an area to knap tools, and more. As she and Re'ez worked, the rest of the Cave Dwellers watched Xhosa's People take over their cave, marveling at their confidence, staring at Lyta's hobbled but efficient gait, enjoying Seeker's flamboyance and the rambunctious children, but more than anything else, they whispered among themselves about how wolves treated this tribe as pack.

When Siri and Re'ez finished, Siri took Black Wolf and Spirit around to meet each Cave Dweller by licking their hands and mouths. She encouraged the subadults to rub the rough fur on their backs and bellies, pointed out their flat hackles which she explained meant they felt no threat from the Cave Dwellers. Something about Spirit's panting grin and Black Wolf's wagging plumy tail relaxed everyone.

When she led the wolves toward Cucu'tez, they started to sneeze violently and flap their ears. Siri tried to encourage them onward but they dug their paws in and growled, low but menacing, their bottomless eyes fixed on the isolated Cave Dweller.

Cucu'tez screamed a high-pitched howl. "Keep them away from me!" Sweat dotted his forehead and his hands shook.

"Spirit! Black Wolf!" From Xhosa. "Leave him," and they did. Xhosa motioned to Wind, "They don't trust Cucu'tez either."

Siri gathered the Cave Dwellers and described how the People shared tasks.

She concluded with, "Until you determine what task is best suited to your skill, try all."

As she talked, the Cave Dwellers watched her, mouths open, eyes glazed. No one asked questions or nodded and to an individual, they looked frightened rather than excited.

Siri turned to Qu'tez. "What did I say wrong?"

Qu'tez explained, hands quivering, "It's not your fault. We were always told what to do. We don't know how to pick a task."

Siri crossed her arms, paced with her head down, and finally motioned to Pan-do. At his agreement, she turned back to the Cave Dwellers.

"Each of you will partner with one of the Leads. The two of you will decide if that particular task suits you." She made eye contact with each Cave Dweller individually, moving on only when they nodded agreement.

While the two-legged Others organized themselves, Black Wolf claimed an alcove at the end of a short tunnel as a den, snapping once at Cucu'tez but otherwise, leaving him alone.

Pan-do pulled Xhosa aside. "The Cave Dwellers ask why you and Wind are taller than everyone else."

Xhosa smiled. Her People no longer noticed. She could explain it was her complicated parentage but wouldn't.

Instead, she asked, "Pan-do. Do they remind you of the Hairy Ones?"

Pan-do stared through Xhosa, his face softening as though seeing the long-gone people he once relied on for life itself. The Hairy Ones' childlike trust of Pan-do's People destroyed them when the Big Heads attacked. That still hurt Pan-do like a deep festering wound.

He cocked his head. "Where we run smoothly and effortlessly, the Hairy Ones were jerky and slow. In a battle, their strength and power would have allowed them to overpower most anyone—like Zvi can—but they didn't even try. Their spears were sharpened sticks, like the Cave Dwellers, and their skill about as poor.

"But the Cave Dwellers seem smarter than the Hairy Ones. I think we can train them to overcome their failings before they are obliterated."

The next day, Asal'rez, Cucu'tez, Zak'ez, and Qu'tez joined the People's Leads. Before they even started, Cucu'tez whined about the long walk and the danger from predators. When Xhosa ignored his complaints, he began to limp, grumbling about a sprained ankle. The Leads left him with Lyta and the rest of the Cave Dwellers to learn birdsong.

Qu'tez stepped carefully into Ngili's footprints, keeping his arms at his sides and his breathing quiet, as the Lead had told him to do. He failed the first time with One-called-Wind but committed himself today to do better.

I will convince Lead Hunter Ngili I am worth his time to teach.

Ngili disrupted his thoughts. "Wind said despite your many mistakes, you did one thing right, Qu'tez: You didn't quit. Today, we build on that."

Qu'tez nodded, thankful for another chance.

Ngili speared a shrew, by himself because Qu'tez's shaft fell short.

As Qu'tez helped him cut the carcass into pieces, he motioned, "Even our adults don't hunt the Giant Shrew, Ngili. Their size makes them a tempting target, like Bison, and their meat tastes salty—which we like—but if you are bitten, you will probably die."

Ngili's legs wobbled. "Next time, tell me that first."

They were the last ones back to the cave. Asal'rez and Zak'ez glowed with excitement, babbling about their new skills and how they wanted to learn more. Despite his failures, Qu'tez admitted he too, for the first time in a long time, felt optimistic about the future.

Xhosa huddled with Ngili, Mbasa, and Bird and then beckoned the Cave People to her. Qu'tez trotted up, eager for feedback on the day. He didn't have to wait long.

Xhosa motioned, hands abrupt but without anger. "None of you did well today but all show promise. You're new to the People and we are patient but understand: Simply being here isn't good enough." She glanced at Cucu'tez, still nursing his sprained ankle. "You must contribute or leave."

No one had ever drawn that line for them. Qu'tez shuddered. *What if I fail? Where will I go?*

At least he was now convinced Xhosa and her People wouldn't eat him. Why train him if he didn't have a future?

While everyone gathered around the fire pit and devoured the meat of the shrew—after assuring the Cave Dwellers no one would be burned, Ngili described hunting tactics used to kill the Giant Shrew, Dust how he and Zak'ez tracked a bison they later lost, and Mbasa demonstrated the correct way to hold the shaft to throw a spear with accuracy. When the People's subadults giggled—because they had learned this before being given weapons—Xhosa glowered at them.

"They will learn. Qu'tez will soon be better than most of you—"

Dust interrupted, "As will Zak'ez—"

Mbasa added, "And Asal'rez."

The gigglers blanched and each motioned their willingness to help the Cave Dwellers.

Ant turned to Qu'tez. "What snakes live here, Qu'tez?"

Qu'tez cocked his head, mouth dropping open. "Snake? What is that?"

Ant pulled a squirming serpentine creature from his neck sack about the length of his arm and tossed it into the clearing.

Qu'tez jumped back and motioned, "That's a Red Viper. You are lucky to be alive. See the bright spot on its neck? That is one of the most dangerous kind here. Be happy it slithered away."

Xhosa motioned, "Now I understand Viper's callsign. She is tricky, toxic, and treacherous—like this viper."

Qu'tez motioned, "Viper?"

Xhosa explained how Viper had been captured and enslaved, how she escaped and learned to be a warrior so she could defend her People. Qu'tez crossed his arms over his thin chest and clenched his fists. "I need to learn. Fast."

Ngili motioned, "You did well today, Qu'tez. It's a start."

"There is much I don't understand."

Xhosa faced him, hands chopping and quick, "Tell me how you hunt."

Qu'tez thought a moment, eyes rolling over the cave's ceiling, and finally motioned, "We chase the weak or injured. If we get close enough—which is unusual—we stab the neck or eye, not the chest or flanks because our shafts often break trying to penetrate the tough hide. If we slay one, we eat at the site and then carry what we can, leave the rest to scavengers. We simply don't have the strength to transport a heavy carcass back to our cave.

"If the animals flee, we chase until they are out of sight."

Xhosa motioned, "Why don't you throw your spears?"

"We aren't accurate and they don't go straight."

Xhosa motioned, "Give me your spear, Qu'tez," which he did, though reluctantly.

She balanced it on her hand, revealing a pronounced curve along its shaft. "This is made from a bent trunk. A well-made shaft means the spear will fly straight. A curved one—like this—goes somewhere else."

She placed her hands to either side of the middle and snapped it in two. Qu'tez gulped down whatever he wanted to say. Surely, she realized he had no replacement.

Xhosa laughed at his shock, not unkindly. "This was worthless, Qu'tez. To make a useful shaft, the wood must be hard, the bark smoothed until the nodes are removed, and the tip sharp enough to draw blood. It takes most of the daylight." She gestured dismissively to the broken shaft. "You made this swiftly and wrong. There are saplings not far from here. One of us will help you pick the right one and then turn it into a weapon."

Xhosa turned to Lyta, done with that discussion. "How did the birdsong lessons go?"

The young female began to hum, eyes shuttered.

Siri put down the roots she'd been pounding and motioned, "The Cave Dwellers can't shape their mouths correctly. The sounds they make—well, no one can confuse them with birds."

Cucu'tez jumped in. "No—that's not true! I can do it!" He launched into a screeched noise that could be a bird's agonizing death or a small child snatched in Owl's ruthless claws.

Xhosa cut him off. "If you need help, sing like that. We'll know it's you, Cucu'tez."

Re'ez and Zak'ez laughed with Qu'tez.

Xhosa stopped them with a glare and pointed to her neck sack. "Where are yours?"

Qu'tez frowned. "I—we—don't have one. Why do you wear that?"

That night, around the firepit, Qu'tez and Zak'ez got the bladder and stomach of Giant Shrew, Cucu'tez, Rul'ez, Re'ez, and Asal'rez large leaves which wouldn't last long but would serve the purpose of learning to make neck sacks. Xhosa demonstrated how to clean and smooth the inside with sand and water, rub it with salt, and poke small holes along the edge with a chopper. She softened a vine by running it through the span of her hand, then fed it through the holes and looped the completed sack around her neck.

"These, made from animal stomachs and bladders, are waterproof and strong. They carry food, throwing stones, choppers, plants—anything needed for your day's tasks. Wear it always."

Cucu'tez fell asleep right after starting his.

Xhosa found Wind in their nest. She loosed her hair from its vine so it could warm them through the night and motioned, "I don't trust him either. It's more than his stink. It's his eagerness to learn about us."

Chapter 15

Cave Dwellers' cave

The next day, Xhosa, Hecate, Ngili, and Spirit left to hunt as soon as Sun awoke. Qu'tez insisted he join them and promised to stay out of the way.

Xhosa prepared to say no but Ngili stopped her. "He practiced with Ant's spear long into the night, in the back tunnels."

"He needs practice, not experience, Ngili," and sighed as she realized what she'd said. "Good enough. He comes."

Not long after they started, a giant sow with a line of piglets crossed in front of them, tails and manes whisking as they rooted in the soft earth. The sow screamed her displeasure at the two-legged interlopers and hurried away, piglets scurrying behind.

Xhosa explained to Qu'tez, "If we slaughter the sow, those babies will die and with them, our future meat. Why risk that for one meal?"

Sun moved another hand, the trail winding its way around boulders and through rugged terrain. Xhosa's throat was dry, her tongue sticking to the roof of her mouth, before finally, she smelled water. Not only could she drink but the hunters always found herds at a waterhole.

The People reached what turned out to be a small shallow pond, drank their fill, and then skirted to the opposite side where they settled into the silt along the shore to wait. After a hand of Sun's travel overhead and no animals, they wandered farther down the forward trail. It wasn't long before they heard a whimper, softened by distance, but clearly an animal in distress.

"An injured animal!" Qu'tez motioned excitedly and began to run.

Not far ahead, a wolf pup huddled in the middle of the trail, crying, tail tucked, short legs shaking. Qu'tez called it a Red Wolf. Its coat was dull and the fur stood up in places it shouldn't clearly showing the pup's ribs through thin skin. There wasn't enough meat on its bones to feed one of the People much less the entire tribe

She motioned, "Not hurt. Hungry."

"The last time I passed through here, the male wolf guarded the den, probably while the female took care of their pups. Now, they're gone."

The youngster panted, its gaze locked on Spirit, and then gamely wagged its tail though its legs continued to shake. Spirit snarled quietly but with enough aggression to tell the youngster it talked to an alpha and should do so with respect. The red ball of fur rolled over, exposing its stomach, telling Spirit it was no threat.

Xhosa stifled a grin but Qu'tez motioned, "I know we're supposed to spare babies but without protection from an adult, this one will die and we are hungry."

Spirit's hackles stiffened and he curled his lips back as he edged between Qu'tez and the ball of mangy fluff, then issued a low, guttural growl. The Red Wolf crouched and licked Spirit's chin, lips, nose, and muzzle.

Xhosa motioned, "We must go. Leave it. Its mother will return."

As they left, the pup snorted and bounded after them. Spirit peered back and whined an order to hurry but the youngster couldn't keep up. Soon, the bouncing furry shape faded into the distance.

Qu'tez took the group to where a Horned Beast usually rooted for food. "It is too big for me but with you, we can do it."

Xhosa frowned. "What's a 'horned beast'?"

Qu'tez described the colossal thick-skinned beast with squatty legs, massive blocky head, and two long deadly tusks. To Xhosa, it sounded like what her People called a rhino but with two horns instead of one.

After squatting in the shade of a grove long enough for their shadows to switch sides, Xhosa motioned. "Let's try again tomorrow. It's time to go back."

They didn't get far on the backtrail when carrion birds appeared. A chill ran down Xhosa's back and Spirit whined.

"We should have claimed the Red Wolf ourselves, as Qu'tez suggested, even though it wouldn't have been much meat."

But the carrion bird's prize turned out to be the carcass of a young antelope brought down by a pack of snapping Hyaena. Unfortunately, the scent also attracted Red Wolf. It slunk toward the carrion, hungry drool dripping from its mouth. Its legs shook with either fatigue or fear—maybe both—but starvation won out over caution. Its vulnerability drew the attention of the Hyaena. One of them padded toward the Red Wolf, slowly and cautiously. Spirit sauntered toward it and growled, continuing until he had placed his massive fanged and clawed body between Hyaena and the Red Wolf. The pup now yipped boldly, convinced it had a protector.

Spirit was gigantic even by wolf standards, and far outsized and outweighed Hyaena but the smaller animal's pack was many.

Xhosa's face hardened. "Spirit needs our help," and she strode to Spirit's side.

The rest of the hunters followed her. The magnitude of Spirit's pack persuaded Hyaena to abandon the carrion and find easier prey. The group divided up the antelope's remains giving everyone a load to carry back to the cave, munching as they worked. Spirit and the Red Wolf circled each other as wolves do when they become acquainted.

As the People left, Ngili tossed a chunk of ribs to the Red Wolf. "That will give it enough food until its pack rejoins it."

Xhosa motioned, "It also has the carcass," and then turned to the Red Wolf and added, "Better eat fast. The carrion birds are preparing to drive you away."

The Red Wolf snapped the leg up and raced after Spirit, short legs churning. Her mouth opened to pant and the food fell. She skidded to a stop, snatched it, and again chased the wolf she had decided was her Alpha, floppy ears blinding her at times. The massive wolf huffed at her—*Stay back*—and slapped his paws against the ground but the Red Wolf didn't listen. Again and again, she dropped the meaty leg, snatched it back into her jaws, and sped after the departing cluster of hairless, upright creatures, a little more behind them with each of their long-strided steps but no less enthusiastic about joining them.

Spirit turned his blue eyes on Xhosa, his message clear: *"It will die if we leave it."* Xhosa ignored his plea and the wolf turned his back on the youngster, which didn't stop her. She forged onward, her high-pitched bark a constant reminder of her presence, to the People and any predators around.

With a huff, Spirit stopped which stopped Xhosa and the rest of his pack. The pup tripped over her outsized feet in her eagerness to reach Spirit. Once she did, she bobbed in front of him while trying to lick his muzzle and cheeks.

Xhosa motioned, "She can't keep up, Spirit."

Spirit whined. The pup wound her way between the large wolf's legs.

Xhosa sighed. "Then you carry her." Xhosa strung a neck sack around Spirit's neck, stuffed the tiny pup into it, and couldn't help but smile when it licked her palm.

As they trotted homeward, she grumbled, "There isn't enough food for us and now you, Red Wolf, but we'll make it work."

Sun dipped toward the horizon which meant darkness would soon arrive. That's when Dust shouted, "Tracks! And a lot of them!"

Xhosa sprinted across the uneven ground, through a dry river, and into a dense stand of trees. It reeked of smoke and flashes of yellow and orange light lit the sky. They broke out of the forest to a sea of fire that was racing toward them.

Chapter 16

Cave Dwellers' cave

Pan-do paced, more worried with each breath. Heavy smoke saturated the air where Xhosa and the hunters had gone. The crackle of fire in the distance frightened him but the endless reverberation of hooves under his feet—animals fleeing for their lives—bothered him even more.

Wind sped past, heading toward the billowing black clouds. "Gather everyone in the cave, Pan-do! I'll be back with the hunters!"

Pan-do shouted after him but Wind didn't acknowledge him, didn't slow. Fires had burned everywhere the People lived. It was part of life and they had prepared for this by moving boulders around the mouth of their new homebase, ready to be rolled over the opening to block the People from assailants, floods, or in this case, fire. What they couldn't plan for was how to save those caught by a conflagration.

Pan-do yelled behind himself, "Zvi—push the boulders into place!"

But the huge female also sprinted toward the flames, almost knocking him over in her rush. He yanked at her pelt as she raced by and dragged her to a stop.

Jaw set, he leaned forward, nose against hers. "We need you here. They will be fine!"

"Stone—talk to Stone!" Wild eyed, Zvi wrenched herself loose and chased Wind.

Pan-do sucked in a long ragged breath, not surprised. Zvi would never forgive herself if she failed to be there when Spirit needed help. The wolf was her packmate more than the People. Each had nearly died several times protecting the other and would do so again.

Stone was already rolling the monstrous rocks, taller than the cave's mouth, over the opening so Pan-do bellowed to El-ga and Nak-re, "Clean away the stalks—"

Siri interrupted, "We're on it. You stay out here and watch for the hunters, in case they're close and need help."

He tried to smile but it faded instantly and he returned to pacing, back and forth along the bluff. At some point, Black Wolf joined him. She moaned, once and again, her muzzle aimed the same place as Pan-do's. She wanted to be with Zvi, helping her mate, but her first responsibility now was her pups. She would have to trust her two-legged packmates.

Re'ez appeared at Pan-do's side, hands clammy, face wet with tears, eyes searching the miasma. Pan-do didn't bother to tell her she should be inside.

She took a moment to calm herself and then motioned, evenly and deliberately, "Qu'tez lost his sister to a fire storm."

Pan-do rubbed between Black Wolf's ears, eyes on the orange glow that lit the distance. "They know what to do, Re'ez. Qu'tez will be fine."

If it wasn't a flash fire, or too pervasive, or they weren't injured.

Re'ez nodded, said something lost in the fire's roar, and wandered back to the cave. Pan-do and Black Wolf stayed, watching, ears perked, mesmerized by the mushrooming smoke that gave way intermittently to leaping orange flames. Black Wolf tipped her head up to Pan-do, eyes overflowing with trust. Hidden by the billowing gray clouds that shrouded the ground, Pan-do heard the crackle of fire and the explosion of sap as entire forests were engulfed. Worse than that were the cries of animals, wailing their death song. Tongues of orange fire had already crested the hill, eating everything they could reach.

Pan-do didn't know how long they stood there, he and the wolf. The sky was a murky gray mist with barely a hint of light coming through but the bumps on his arms told him Sun must be close to her sleeping nest. The distant dark smoke had become an impenetrable wall, nothing visible within, but Pan-do refused to leave his position. He was afraid if he did, Xhosa and the rest would be lost.

And then figures appeared out of the gloom, at first simply shapes darker than the surroundings, gliding forward. They grew, taller and slenderer with each of Pan-do's ragged breaths. A hand waved—Wind or Xhosa, whoever led. The blur dissolved into bodies and Pan-do ticked off the figures. Zvi carried a body, as did everyone. At first, he thought it was Others caught in the inferno, but the chunky forms turned into carcasses charred black by flames.

A lot of them.

"The fire storm rushed through the valley like stampeding Mammoth. The animals fled faster than any thought they could but really, there was nowhere to go but forward. They're only hope was to outrun the flames. We were ahead, safely out of the way, but Qu'tez shrieked—"

Qu'tez laughed. "That there was a cliff ahead! If we didn't change directions, we'd fall over it right before the animals did!"

Xhosa sat up straighter and grinned at a soot-covered Ngili, eyes white spots on his grimy face. He was grinning back. "To us, that was great news. I explained to Qu'tez that we've discussed using fire to chase herds over a cliff. No time like now to try it."

Qu'tez picked up the story, energized by his part in the successful hunt. "I showed them a route to the base of the bluff, one I use often and had dug steps into so it's easier to climb."

Ngili nodded. "We descended and waited, planning to harvest the animals as they tumbled over."

The People were gathered around the fire pit, chewing on charred meat as they listened to Xhosa, Ngili, and Qu'tez tell the story. For reasons no one understood, being blackened by flames made meat easier to chew. Even Qu'tez with a sore tooth had no trouble eating, nor did the elders who'd lost many of their teeth. Charred pieces of wood and fresh dry limbs burned merrily, the smoke bringing tears to their eyes but not like it did outside. A short rain had stopped the fire from going any further but not the dark clouds filled with embers and debris.

"We didn't have to wait long. First, the air around us darkened and thickened. Each blink stung our eyes and breathing burned our throats. A tree exploded and showered us in sparks.

"That's when Wind and Zvi yelled from above, limned against the light from the flames, asking how we got down. By the time they descended, a steady stream of animals was pouring over the bluff, the air bursting with their desperate cries. Even those who tried to stop were pushed over the edge by the mob.

"We harvested what meat we could carry and then headed back here. Much remains."

Qu'tez turned an awed face to Zvi. "You carried more carcasses than all of us put together," and his arms encompassed the entire gathering of Cave Dwellers.

After an embarrassed silence from Zvi, Qu'tez explained, "I shook with fear. I was sure we would die but I learned a valuable lesson today. Xhosa, Ngili—Spirit—no one lost courage. I want to be that brave by the time I'm an adult."

Ngili smiled at the subadult, the boy's face layered with dirt and ash, hair matted with gore from scavenging, but eyes alight with the fire of a job well done. "You did well. It turns out you are as crazy as us, Qu'tez."

Re'ez edged toward her future pairmate and began to pick the twigs and debris from his hair, lick the blood from his face.

Pan-do waved toward the back of the cave, where Red Wolf contentedly slept buried in a pile of fur and muzzles.

"Who is this Red Wolf who persuaded you to save her life and then made friends so quickly with Black Wolf's pups?"

The wolf perked her floppy ears at what she must think was her callsign, squeaked once, and then rolled over on her back, ears flat, eyes closed, legs dangling inelegantly, tongue licking the fragrance of her pack. One pup butted its head against her soft belly and sighed as its tail wagged to the thrum of Red Wolf's heart.

Qu'tez and Ngili took turns explaining how they found the pup abandoned by her parents, how Hyaena threatened her and Spirit saved her life by adopting her. That was endorsement enough for Black Wolf who no doubt remembered how Spirit took her as his mate when she was orphaned, that she wouldn't have survived if not for him and his two-legged pack.

Ngili motioned, gestures expansive so all could see, "Red Wolf demonstrated great courage, standing against the Hyaena."

Qu'tez wagged his head. "After Spirit did."

"I think even without him, Red Wolf wouldn't have backed off. She will grow into a formidable pack member, you'll see."

Stories ended and grooming was completed in silence. Hecate and Wind pulled and pinched the fire debris from Ngili and Xhosa's hair. Qu'tez's dense hair required both Re'ez and Rul'ez to clean.

Xhosa rose and started for the mouth of the cave. "I must go back for the rest of the carcasses," but Wind stopped her.

"Do it tomorrow. We'll all help."

She didn't argue. It had been a long day.

The youngsters who would watch the fire all night slipped through the narrow gap beside the boulder, collected twigs and debris to feed the fire, and then wriggled back inside with their largess. Everyone else lay down with whoever would keep them warm that night. Soon, the only sounds were the burr of insects, the rustle of small creatures drawn to the crackling fire, and the soft snores signaling the People's contented rest.

Chapter 17

People's Cave

By the time Sun yawned itself awake the next day, the mixed scents of blood, burst entrails, feces, and the sweaty smell of work overwhelmed the cave. Some of the People had gone to harvest the remaining charred meat while others cleaned the bladders, stomachs, and pelts of animals killed the prior night, preparing them to be turned into neck sacks and warm skins. It would take an entire day, or longer, with everyone working to clean them.

Tired but happy, the males were back with the final load of carcasses by the time Sun reached its height. Xhosa's spirits lifted. Maybe there was enough food here after all.

The day had become unusually chilly and raw so they kept the fire burning. As Xhosa worked, she took the opportunity to evaluate Re'ez's and Qu'tez's clumsy but enthusiastic efforts to clean pelts. Their desperate lack of skills bothered her but their eagerness to learn could compensate for that. It was Xhosa's job to determine if these Cave Dwellers enhanced the People or burdened them.

She motioned one-handed to Qu'tez, continuing their discussion about the paucity of meat in this area.

"My People—we have been to more areas than I can tick off on both hands. If we can't find food somewhere, we move on. I don't understand why your former tribe preyed on Others rather than leave."

Qu'tez bit into a charred chunk of meat and then chewed while he answered. "We moved here long ago. I don't know when it happened but at some point, food became scarce. We first tried to escape through the mountains but they were too cold, and then over the water but no one could swim. Someone suggested we eat our dead." He shrugged. "They weren't groupmembers anymore so no one objected. And the females with babies needed the internal parts. Then, when we didn't have enough dead, we targeted living Others. They were plentiful and easy to stalk though not as filling as other animals."

Xhosa shook her head. She couldn't imagine hunger ever becoming so severe, her People would consider eating Others. Despite the chronic food shortage of Mbasa and her People, they didn't eat their dead, or living.

She forced her face to remain neutral, her hands to continue scraping the pelt in front of her and asked, "Qu'tez, Why do you trust us?"

Re'ez laughed, wiping her forehead with her palm and leaving a streak of blood from the carcass she worked on. "The only Others we don't trust are our own People. You and Wind are too tall. The rest—it was easy to tell they didn't belong to our tribe."

Xhosa turned to Re'ez. "How did you know we weren't of your People? Maybe we were new members?"

Qu'tez answered, "Your footprints. They're not like any of ours."

That surprised Xhosa. She looked down at the faint shape of her print in the dirt by Qu'tez's but saw no obvious difference.

"What do you mean?"

"Put your foot next to mine."

Xhosa and Qu'tez pressed their feet into the dirt on the cave floor. If their prints differed, she didn't notice.

Qu'tez shook his head. "How can you miss it? Your toes are longer, the ball wider, and our heel is deeper than yours. Your prints are from strangers."

Qu'tez motioned to Re'ez. "Step next to me," and then, "Do you see, Xhosa? Re'ez and I have similar prints but even they are different."

Again, nothing caught Xhosa's attention. She glanced discreetly at Ngili and he shook his head.

Qu'tez smoothed the dirt around the print. "Re'ez's is lighter at the largest toe and the heel. And the bridge between front and back is narrower. If I see this print, I know Re'ez has been here. Rul'ez's print," and he nodded toward the other Cave Dweller female, "is even shallower, Asal'rez's shorter, and Cucu'tez's lighter. We know the print of every member of our People. They are unique, like your callsigns I think. We would never confuse any of them with a stranger or even with Others like us.

"Besides that, I smell the scent of each individual in the print. If they aren't fresh, you have to brush them clean but then, it's unmistakable. Go ahead, try it."

Xhosa bent forward and sniffed Ngili's print and snapped backward. "You're right. I smell him."

Xhosa reassessed her opinion of Qu'tez and his People.

As Xhosa cut tendons from bones, chopped the meat into pieces, and removed the remaining shreds from the skins with scrapers and sand, she described the process for the Cave Dwellers.

"Once the pelts are clean, they must be rubbed with salt."

With all bent over their work, trying to replicate what she'd done, Xhosa quietly ate one of her pain plants.

As the People worked, the wolf pups rolled around, banging into the carcasses, the rock walls, and each other. One stole a bone from Pan-do and carried it around as though a prize, until another pup snatched it away.

And the chase started over.

Siri motioned, "We are out of salt. Re'ez. Can you bring more?"

"That was the last of it. We don't use much because we never harvest more meat than we can eat in a day. Or two."

Xhosa motioned, fingers together, "Where do you gather it?"

"There's a salt lake on the edge of Endless Pond. The journey takes longer than a Moon but is an easy trip. Well, it's hot, but few predators."

Mbasa frowned. "We came from there. I saw no sign of a salt lake, just Endless Sea."

Qu'tez shook his head. "Not there. On the side where Sun awakens. That's where you'll find more of Endless Pond."

Wind became pensive, hands moving slowly as he asked, "Do herds live there, Qu'tez? Maybe we find so few here because they live by the salt blocks." ·

Qu'tez shook his head. "No more than here because there is less grassland for grazing and fewer waterholes."

Xhosa gestured, "How many times have you made the trip, Qu'tez? Can you take us there?"

He cocked his head, mouth slightly open as though confused. "Never. Of course."

Xhosa paused a breath, considered what he had said, and decided she believed him. Besides, how hard could it be? According to Qu'tez, they would walk toward Sun's waking place, following the increasing taste of salt in the air.

She nodded to Wind and he turned back to Qu'tez. "We go tomorrow—Ngili, Xhosa and I, and you, Qu'tez, will lead."

Qu'tez preened, unable to keep a grin from his face.

Zvi called out, "Stone and I will join you, to carry the blocks."

Mbasa added, "And I. For protection. In case, despite what Qu'tez says, there is danger."

Xhosa turned to Ngili, "Decide who else should go. The rest stay here, find out where Those-who-eat-Others camp, practice birdsong with Lyta until everyone is proficient."

Wind nudged sideways so only Xhosa and Pan-do could see his gestures. "I too am worried."

She nodded. "Not about us, about the ones staying behind. Those-who-eat-Others—I feel their eyes on us as we hunt and forage. They never approach, never want to share, just watch."

Pan-do gestured, "While you're gone, I'll follow some of their hunting parties, see where they go and what they do."

Xhosa turned to Qu'tez. "Before we go, can you tell Pan-do where your old homebase was, with Those-who-eat-Others live?"

Qu'tez shook his head. "They have moved. We can't find their new location."

She motioned, "Is there any chance they'll know many of us left and strike those who remain?"

Qu'tez again shook his head. "I don't think so. The People—you appear powerful, with weapons no one else has. No, I doubt they'll even try to pick you off one by one as they do us. I think they'll wait until they are much larger in size and then attack as a group."

Xhosa turned to Wind. "Should we find them first and then get the salt?"

Wind and Mbasa both motioned, "No. We can't wait. We are out of salt."

Pan-do motioned, moving his hand broadly through the air. "We will scout them and report how dangerous they might be when you return."

Everyone left to sleep. It would be a long day tomorrow. Spirit curled against Xhosa, soft fur pressed against her legs. Hearing Spirit's deep steady breaths, feeling Wind's heart on her body, she soon drifted off.

Until a noise awoke her, outside, one not from a groupmember releasing their water.

Wind murmured. "It's Cucu'tez. He left when he thought we all slept and now returns."

Odd. No one travels alone at night.

She tried to get back to sleep, turned over, wriggled into Wind's body, but there seemed no comfortable position for her thoughts.

The next day, clouds muted Sun and the air threatened rain. Ngili, Sa-mo-ke, Mbasa, Dust, Zvi, Stone, and Spirit departed with Xhosa, Wind, and Qu'tez, each carrying extra neck sacks. Somewhere a squirrel chattered, telling them his life was normal with no unexpected threats. Qu'tez warned Tor not to underestimate the adversary. What they lacked in skill, they made up for with treachery.

Seeker stood on the bluff above the cave, eyes fixed on the oversized round head that bobbed next to Spirit. Seeker and Zvi had not been separated since they found each other. Where one went, the other did. He imagined her kind eyes, squatty muscular neck, and the Mammoth pelt that easily wrapped her broad shoulders and pendulous breasts that had never fed a child. The two of them, with Spirit, killed this Mammoth somewhere between their home and Hawk's base. The pelt, luxurious and thick at first, had grown ragged with holes where they hadn't been when Mammoth wore it but finding another large enough for Zvi had proven difficult.

At Seeker's other side stood Tor and Shaga. As was his habit, the boy mimicked Tor's strong posture and emotionless face, his gaze never leaving Mbasa until her image faded away. She turned back once, and again, but made no gesture to either. Nor they to her. This was not goodbye. Today, they collected memories in case the future included nothing else.

Spirit stopped frequently to look back. His ears flattened and tail drooped, and he whined before focusing again on the forward trail. It was not just for Seeker—the young boy-male knew that—but also his mate, Black Wolf, next to Seeker. It wasn't long before Spirit's squatty shape was swallowed up by the distant blurry stalks, and then Zvi's, and finally the tallest of the group, Xhosa and Wind. A clutch of ground birds exploded into the air, screaming about the intrusion on their territory as they evaporated into the distance.

Lyta asked Seeker, "Will you be alright, pairmate?"

"Well, yes, no, I think so—but Zvi has never been on her own, without me, since she saved my life. I—she will be lonely."

"Spirit is with her." Seeker nodded forlornly and Lyta added, "And I am with you."

Seeker stammered and shuffled his feet as he tried to come up with a response. He didn't need to because Red Wolf distracted him. She had trailed behind those who left but apparently, they got too far ahead of her so she abandoned the effort and padded back to the rest of her pack. Her steps were slow, tail drooping and tongue hanging. Spirit was her Alpha and no one else could fill that spot. Black Wolf seemed to understand and huffed to tell Red Wolf to join her above the cave. Together, they watched those departing until even their dust vanished.

Pan-do spent much of each day in the salt hunters' absence working with the Cave Dwellers on weapon skills. Most of the subadults' shafts broke under the stress of his non-stop practice so the Leader taught them how to turn narrow trunks and strong straight branches into shafts and secure carefully knapped tools to their tips.

Siri carried on with Xhosa's lessons on healing injuries. Cucu'tez proved excellent at finding healing leaves and root bundles. He claimed to know how to avoid his former tribe while regularly returning with information about where Those-who-eat-Others camped and how they had grown.

With many gone, the white worms arrived in the burnt carcasses before the People could finish though they did last much longer than fresh ones. They tossed what was left to the wolves. What they didn't consume was dumped far from the cave for the scavengers. Now, they must hunt more meat.

Chapter 18

Leaving Snake in charge of the homebase, Pan-do asked Cucu'tez to take him with Hecate, Tor, Zak'ez, and several others to where the subadult remembered seeing a herd. Black Wolf accompanied them which meant Red Wolf did also. If they separated the pup from her Alpha, she howled piteous high-pitched screams that would draw predators like Those-who-eat-Others.

"If anything happens, Snake, block the cave's mouth with boulders. If you must escape, use birdsong to tell me where you are."

Cucu'tez led, trotting up and down steep hills and across shallow rivers, most of them unfamiliar to Pan-do. The farther away from the homebase the group went, the more Zak'ez's gaze darted over the landscape and the tighter he gripped his spear, as though he were expecting danger. Pan-do kept a wary eye but saw nothing unusual. Maybe this had something to do with Cucu'tez. The subadult had left the cave late last night, alone and after everyone else fell asleep, and didn't return until just before Sun awoke. He took care to not awaken anyone but Black Wolf had noticed. She growled a low quiet sound that was meant to alert Pan-do to danger. When he looked for what bothered the wolf, he heard another growl, further into the cave, and then saw Cucu'tez slip into his nest at the back of the cavern.

Could Zak'ez be worried about that? Pan-do didn't think he even knew about it because the subadult had slept through both the departure and return.

Maybe we are entering areas Cucu'tez and Zak'ez hunted as part of their former tribe and that's what worries him.

He was about to ask Zak'ez when Hecate nudged him and pointed to a clearing beyond the tiny woods they were currently moving through. Pan-do's hair stiffened the length of his back.

Not a herd, a large group of Those-who-eat-Others' hunters, some milling around, others bent over a carcass. If Hecate hadn't been scouting ahead and apart from Cucu'tez, the People's hunters would have stumbled on the cannibals unaware.

Pan-do motioned, "Down!" Everyone dropped and then silently crawled backward, slinking deep into the shadows. So far, Those-who-eat-Others seemed oblivious to the People's presence.

Cucu'tez knew his old tribe would be here and led us right to them.

Pan-do controlled his fury but barely, wondering how he'd allowed himself to be tricked.

No, even if Cucu'tez wanted to, how could he tell them we'd be here now? But he knew. *That's why he snuck out the night before the salt hunters left.*

Something zoomed by Pan-do.

Red Wolf!

The pup smelled the carrion. In her short life, no Others had ever tried to hurt her. As a result, she deemed two-legged predators to be friends who would share their food. Hecate tried to snag the pup's tail but missed.

The cannibals turned toward Red Wolf as she cleared the thicket, watched wide-eyed as she sprinted across the clearing and dove into the carcass, rear end wagging with happiness, muzzle buried to her eyes in the bloody gore. Those-who-eat-Others might have thought this simply an orphaned wolf pup except that Cucu'tez screamed, yelling at the pup to stop.

Pan-do winced. *He just told them we are here, and that wasn't a mistake!*

Hecate solved the question of what to do.

"Go!" She sang out in birdsong as she lurched to her feet and charged across a corner of the clearing. Every cannibal jerked toward her, forgetting Red Wolf in their eagerness to capture an Other. She sprinted away, leading the enemy the opposite direction of where the People hid, quickly outdistancing them before they could even get started. Still they hurried after her.

She birdsonged to Pan-do as she rushed past him, her eyes nowhere near where he hid. "Rescue Red Wolf while I outsmart these slow, noisy, stupid creatures who can't even throw a spear!"

She sprinted up and over the hill they'd crossed to get here, Those-who-eat-Others already huffing as they fell further behind with each of her long strides. Once on the other side and out of sight, she tumbled into a ravine she remembered on the journey here and banged to a stop when she rolled into Tor. Other than a huff when she slammed into his chest, he made no noise. Then, it was her turn to be shoved aside when a stout furry body flung itself to her side, filling the gulley to capacity.

"Black Wolf!" she exulted but quietly.

As they lay there, inhaling shallow breaths, eyes slit, she heard Pan-do whoop, followed by the pounding of feet going away from the ravine. But not all of them. Some got louder, finally wheezing to a stop close enough that Hecate could impale the runners with her spear. Voices jabbered loudly—cannibal voices in between gasping for breath. They asked each other where such a noisy Other could have gone and why weren't they told she could run so fast.

A whimper filtered through their boisterous voices though they didn't seem to hear it. Hecate stared across the field, at one bush that shook as though blown by a strong wind. When she leaned forward, she could see dark red feet pawing at the ground beneath it.

Black Wolf hissed and the paws stilled but not the whimpers.

"Red Wolf! Calm!" she called in birdsong.

The cannibals twitched at the birdsong but nothing else, finally leaving to chase Pan-do. If they had turned for one last look, they would see a shivering spot of red fur, maybe put it together with the red wolf they'd seen earlier, but they didn't. Once out of sight, Black Wolf sprinted across the glade, snatched the youngster by the nape of her neck, and dove back into the now overcrowded gully.

Hecate was about to stand when Tor slammed his hand down on the ground and hissed, "Shhh!" Zak'ez sprinted by, oblivious to their presence, eyes wild with fright. Hecate started to call out when again, Tor's palm hit the ground as a handful of Those-who-eat-Others flew by, eyes fixed on the young Cave Dweller.

Hecate motioned to Tor, "Let's go. They have to catch up with Zak'ez to stab him. All we have to do is get within throwing distance."

The two leapt to their feet and gave chase. Those-who-eat-Others should have heard them but were too intent on Zak'ez, maybe thinking the steps behind them were their own tribe. One of them was faster than the rest and much faster than the young Zak'ez. He closed on the subadult and raised his arm to skewer him. Hecate screamed and threw her spear, accurately but not soon enough. Both Zak'ez and his attacker fell, their blood mixing as it spilled over the ground. Tor and Hecate both flung spears and impaled more of the enemy while Black Wolf ripped the throat out of one more.

Two of those remaining sprang at Hecate. She unleashed her warclub from the sling on her back and swung it two-handed with all her strength. The hard wood struck one cannibal with a sickening thwack. He fell but she kept swinging and caved in the head of the other. Tor and Black Wolf each killed one more and the last fled, the air reverberating with his high-pitched squeals.

Red Wolf crouched, well away from the bedlam, ears flat on her head, tail tucked, a string of drool oozing from her muzzle. Exhaustion swamped Hecate, her breath no more than gulps, but her body remained alert for any lingering cannibals. Steps pounded behind her and an odor assaulted her, sweat with a tinge of blood and a familiar scent.

She slumped, relieved. "Pan-do!"

Tor bent over the young Cave Dweller, for just a breath, and then stood. "He's dead."

Pan-do considered Zak'ez and then Tor and finally the foe's backtrail. "We must go."

Hecate stared along the backtrail. "Not yet. You must hear it. The one who escaped brings reinforcements."

Tor clutched her arm and glared. "Don't do it. We have time to leave!"

She let his words wash over her, clarifying her thoughts as rain cleaned dirt from her skin. Zak'ez's broken body, young, hopeful for a chance at a good life.

"Zak'ez was betrayed. He deserves revenge."

She yanked a spear from a dead Those-who-eat-Others. Tor grabbed for her arm but she pushed him away. "Go. I will catch up," and she turned to greet her assailants.

Tor sighed, loudly. "I'm behind you."

Another sigh beyond Tor. "And I'm behind you."

Those-who-eat-Others appeared, a handful, walking tentatively, weapons raised beside frightened faces. Confusion spilled from their bodies that only a single Other—a female— stood against their many. They rolled their shoulders back, tiny smiles playing on their lips. Even seeing Tor and Pan-do didn't warn them of the trouble they were in.

Hecate growled, eyes latched onto theirs, dark pools of anger. "Don't worry about my fellow warriors. They're taking a break. Focus on me, an angry female. You made a mistake taking the life of a friend," and she bared her teeth.

The lead male blanched.

Her first spear penetrated his chest and her last impaled the chunky square-faced warrior next to him. The small black eyes stared in disbelief as he gave a strangled cry and fell forward, dead before he hit the ground.

The rest froze in place, unable to figure out what to do without someone telling them. Hecate burned, like an uncontrolled firestorm, fury undimmed by the deaths. She started toward them and they fled, leaving behind the dead and almost-dead bodies of their groupmembers. Hecate spit on all of them and left.

Tor caught up, yawning. "You fight like a crowd. It gave me time to rest."

As daylight drained and the dark Moonless night descended, the small group huddled inside a cavern, happy to have found it, and treated their wounds. They didn't start a fire, choosing caution over warmth. They didn't want the cannibals to find them.

Sun woke everyone, bringing not only light but oppressive heat. Hecate, Pan-do, and the rest of the hunters took a circuitous route homeward, over dry ground and gravelly surfaces that left no trail. They avoided the waterholes, to avoid the cannibals but also not wanting to waste the time. Hecate killed two cannibals, their corpses thrown into a cave to hide them from carrion birds. When they finally reached homebase, Re'ez met them outside the cave. Pan-do held his hands out as though to block her questions and explained what had happened while filling his belly with water from the cave's pond.

When he stopped talking, Re'ez motioned, "Zak'ez? And Cucu'tez?"

Pan-do was dumping water over his steaming body, as were the rest of the hunters, so Hecate motioned, "Zak'ez died defending us and Cucu'tez is missing," thinking, *though we all know where he is.*

Tears rolled down Re'ez's cheeks. "Those-who-eat-Others— they played with Zak'ez as a child."

Hecate watched Re'ez out of the corner of her eye while throwing handfuls of water on her head and chest. Black Wolf and Red Wolf had leaped into the pond, paddled around, and now shook violently to get rid of the excess water.

Hecate motioned to Re'ez, "Many more of them died than us. They now see what fighting us will cost. They won't be so quick to engage."

Re'ez stiffened. "Death doesn't matter to them, Hecate. It means food."

Hecate nodded, heading to the cave. *She is right.* "When will they come at us again?"

"Not until they finish the food they have."

Hecate bit back what she wanted to say, that the People should leave.

Pan-do must have been thinking the same thing. "We are no longer safe here. We will try to wait for Xhosa but she knows where we'll be if we must leave."

Bird trotted past them. "I am going to scout her backtrail—" "I'll join you." "And I." Tor and Bone motioned together.

Cucu'tez dragged into the cave a day later. Scrapes coated his body as did the stench of the cannibals. Black Wolf charged him, stopping short of biting his arm. Red Wolf howled.

Without being asked, Cucu'tez motioned, "They captured me. I escaped."

Hecate glared. "The wolves smell the stink on you."

He bobbed his head but turned away. "They forced me to eat Zak'ez," not quite hiding his satisfaction.

Re'ez threw up.

Pan-do imagined Xhosa and her group gathering the salt and hurrying back.

The sooner the better.

Chapter 19

Going to the salt lake

Xhosa breathed a sigh of relief when Red Wolf turned back. It was a long way and the youngster would never keep up.

She set a quick pace, slower than a run but faster than a walk. When Xhosa's shadow moved from in front where she could see it to behind, she slowed to a trot. When it grew longer than she was tall, she started an earnest search for a sleeping cave and settled for a wide-trunked tree. Some clustered around it while others built nests in its limbs by interleaving branches, leaves, and grass.

Sun awoke and the People trekked on. Xhosa asked Qu'tez how he was so sure he could find this salt lake when he'd never been there.

He explained, "My tribe's Lead Scout provided a detailed explanation of how he got there including all the markers I would need to make the trip, names like 'branch-without-leaves' or 'flattop-mountain-with-ridged-sides'."

It turned out, the Lead Scout was thorough. As soon as one landmark passed out of sight, another appeared. The People were never without guidance. Only once did Qu'tez stop in his tracks, eye the forward trail, veer one direction and then the other, and then sprint into a small forest. Everyone took a break, nibbling on roots and leaves drenched in water. Shortly, Qu'tez returned, grinning, and proceeded, strides long, head high.

The most serious problem those early days was the heat. Sun blazed overhead in a cloudless sky with no shade and not even a warm breeze. Xhosa's former home was at least this hot which made it easy to ignore the sweat that dripped down her back and between her breasts. Not Zvi, Sa-mo-ke, or Qu'tez. They panted and huffed, cheeks bright red and feet dragging.

The group walked on through lifeless terrain, past endless scrub and spindly saplings, headed always toward where Sun awoke, in silence except for the occasional insect chirp or a pant from Spirit as he fought to cool himself under his heavy pelt. Everyone ate while they walked, a desultory meal of roots and wilted greens augmented with worms, slugs, and scorpions. Once, they slew a deer, another time Giant Shrew, and then, to their surprise, a Bison pair whose meat fed them for a handful of days. Mbasa tracked each animal's prints but they always faded away before leading to a herd.

Moon had grown to full size and begun to shrink since the start of this journey. All adjusted to the heat but the problem now was water, or liquid of any sort. Sun had come and gone a handful of times since the last waterhole. Xhosa's tongue stuck to the roof her mouth. Swallowing proved almost impossible without saliva. Mbasa told her to suck on a pebble. It worked for a while and then didn't.

Despite the lack of water and the extreme heat, Mbasa looked fresh.

"I've been through worse," she motioned. "I once chased a snake so I could drink its blood."

Xhosa thought that wasn't a bad idea. If she could find a snake, and if she could catch it.

Qu'tez huffed up to her side, eyes bright with excitement. "We're not far from a waterhole."

But what should have been a stream ended up a dried out river bed. All Qu'tez could do was shrug. There was nothing to do but force one foot in front of the other, again and again. This Xhosa did, avoiding a stream of the massive ants that lived in the hills, the angry scuttle of a scorpion when she tried to smash it with a rock, and stones that seemed intent on tripping her. She sighed heavily, well beyond worrying that the latest promised pond hadn't materialized. She drew strength from her conversations with Mbasa. The indomitable female had fought long after food and water ran out on the far side of Endless Pond. Grit—nothing else—kept her going.

"I can do that," Xhosa mumbled.

She crested another of the many hills and the aroma hit her, making her want to cry. They'd found water. She croaked a call to those behind and stumbled forward. Usually, she cautiously searched the shores of a waterhole but today, no amount of danger would stop her from drinking. Spirit sprinted by and buried his muzzle in the water up to his perked ears. Maybe because the surface was not slimy and green with no fecal scent, or maybe the wolf's internal sense said it was drinkable. Whatever the reason, he wasted no time filling his belly, though he coughed occasionally when he swallowed a fly.

Seeing Spirit drink heartily, everyone submerged themselves in the cool water and gulped down as much as they could. Steam rose from their overheated skin and sighs of pleasure from their mouths.

Qu'tez motioned, gestures rigid, decisive, "Finish up. Daylight runs out soon and there is still a long way to go."

They loaded their neck sacks with moss doused in water and wrapped in leaves and left.

This part of the journey, with its gently rolling hills, strangled shrubs, and scrubby thistle bushes, reminded Xhosa of home. Sandy trails and cracked waterless rivers cut across the dust-blown landscape. To the side sprang flat-topped plateaus with barren faces and thin rocky spires that rose like cactus spines into the sky. As the People passed, brown hares and skinny Small-shrews sprinted from one bush to another while ground-burrowing birds dove into their earthy dens. A squirmy creature with gristly scales, resembling a four-legged snake, skittered away as the People advanced. Gravel crunched underfoot and prickly scrub scratched their legs and arms.

The blue sky was cloudless though occasionally streaked with white. Heat rippled up from the striated expanse. Spirit caught giant rats, once even a small shrew, and shared it with the People.

Xhosa chewed through a particularly rancid gift from Spirit and motioned to Wind, "Next time, we bring more travel food."

She slapped another of the biting insects and popped the squashed body into her mouth. A streak of blood stained her arm. She and Wind took turns licking the salty sweat from each other's skin while both committed to memory the details around them so they could find the salt lake at a future time, without Qu'tez.

"The last waterhole is ahead," Qu'tez motioned. "We must drink as much as possible. There are no more until we reach the salt lake."

His throat was so parched, he didn't think he could swallow. Xhosa snorted, clearly suspicious this one too was little more than a memory.

"I hope so, Qu'tez, because we are at our limit."

It took another hand of Sun's overhead passage before a delicate familiar aroma wafted across his nose and moistened his mouth. He charged up the hill—more of a gentle rise—and stopped. The waterhole! It was a narrow but long expanse of deep blue, its shore lined with thirsty drinkers. If he had tears to spare, he would cry with pleasure.

"We found it!"

His craving for water had become visceral but he waved everyone past him, smiling at their excitement. Finally, the last of the People headed toward the water, Qu'tez tumbled his way down the hill and wriggled into the shoreline with the Wild Beasts, Short-tooth Cats, a lone Mammoth, and the graceful Equiis. He immersed his face up to his ears in the cool liquid and drank his fill, without thought for the Two-horned Rhino who eyed him suspiciously or the Hippo who splashed a stone's throw away.

Done, Qu'tez went with Mbasa to fish, the slithery scaled creatures so abundant, he easily caught them with his hands. He devoured one with gusto and stuffed more in his neck sack beside the water-drenched moss. When he motioned to continue, Xhosa handed him a bleached skull overflowing with water.

It didn't take long for the waterhole to be lost over the horizon and the scrubby flats they now traveled to become a narrow passage between steep cliffs.

Xhosa eyed it suspiciously and licked the air. "I taste water."

Qu'tez tipped his head up to study a cloudless heat-soaked sky and raised his palms. "This is the only way."

Xhosa set a grueling pace through the gorge, intent on reaching the opposite side before the storm Qu'tez couldn't see but she knew was coming. He panted and then wheezed, too tired to shut his mouth, and then turned back to see how the rest of the group were doing.

Black billowing clouds had appeared since the last time he checked. Before he could gasp in surprise, the rain started. At first, Qu'tez enjoyed the pleasant drizzle, cool on his sizzling body and filling his throat, but soon, the light sprinkle hardened to a downpour with a gusting wind that whistled through the canyon, whipping it into slashing sheets that battered Qu'tez's arms and legs.

He shivered, wishing for Sun and its warmth, even if that included heat.

"Faster!" Xhosa shouted. "As fast as you can run!"

Sky fire lit the air, followed by a thunderous explosion that shook the ground, and then more webs of sky fire and more rolling explosions.

Xhosa screamed above the howling storm, "We won't make it! We have to climb!"

What could she possibly mean? The cliffs were too steep and with all this rain would be too slippery to climb. But Qu'tez had been around Xhosa long enough to understand that "impossible" meant nothing to her and this, no matter how improbable, was the only choice.

So, he ran, feet slapping through the growing puddles already reaching his ankles, as booming explosions spun across the sky. The desiccated ground couldn't absorb the onslaught. The water that had started as rivulets soon became a thunderous river climbing well up the canyon's sides, surging directly for the People.

Everyone sprinted, arms churning, faces stiff with worry. Qu'tez wheezed, mouth open, drawing whatever air he could into his burning lungs. These People—his groupmates—had stamina he couldn't begin to match. Ngili and Sa-mo-ke quickly overtook him, as did Mbasa and Stone. Each screamed he must speed up or die. His throat throbbed as though he'd swallowed sand and a cramp ran up his side but he didn't stop. The sky fire crashed and the rain turned into a cascade of needles. Footsteps pounded up behind him. He expected another shout, trying to hurry him when he was already going as fast as he could, but instead, a rough hand attached to an arm the size of a tree limb caught him around the waist and hurtled forward.

"Zvi—put me down! You can't carry me!"

Zvi grunted what could have been, "Why not?"

Qu'tez tried to insist but the crash of the storm and the boom of the sky explosions blew his words away. He started to repeat himself when Zvi flung him roughly over her broad shoulder.

"Hang on to my pelt!" and then, as though he weighed nothing, she scrambled upward faster than Qu'tez could have done alone. Once above the peril, she stopped, hanging on to a protrusion by one hand, toes gripping a narrow crevice, chest heaving but face calm. The roar below increased as though a massive herd pounded past. Qu'tez imagined the flood as it pushed every piece of debris that had accumulated in the dry riverbed toward Zvi—and him. Logs, debris, gravel—all driven down the canyon by the irresistible force of the water. Qu'tez's butt pressed against the cold damp rocks and his feet dangled between the mounds of Zvi's breasts while his mumbled thanks were buried in her back. Her breathing evened out and the thump in her body became even slower than the one in Qu'tez's.

The deafening roar disappeared and the river of rain ended as fast as it started. Zvi descended and flopped Qu'tez to the ground in a heap.

"You alright?" Zvi's voice soft, the only evidence that the physical rigors of escaping the storm had tired her.

Qu'tez didn't trust himself to answer so nodded, a vigorous up-down movement of his head, while he crawled to his knees and then his feet. Zvi scurried over to Stone. Scratches etched the warrior's chest and back where Spirit had clawed for a hold. Qu'tez joined Xhosa to lap up the rain collected in puddles and rewet the moss in their neck sacks. She, Zvi, and Stone grunted agreement that the risk was worth the abundance of water.

Day turned to night once, again, over and over, each hotter than the one before. Xhosa and the hunters crossed over piles of sand and dirt, hiding from Sun's sizzling rays when possible in the shady side of a gully.

A surprised yelp broke the monotony. Xhosa turned and spied a dark crack in the ground that hadn't been there when she passed. She crawled up to the edge and peeked over. There, far down, Dust's head canted up and his face lit at the sight of Xhosa. He smiled calmly as he clung to an ancient root that poked out of the moist earth, his toes dug into the dirt wall.

Qu'tez panted up to her side, a flush growing up his neck and face. "I forgot to mention the crevices. They appear out of nowhere but I know what to do," and he sprinted away at a ground-eating pace.

Xhosa stared after him until he faded away, wondering where he thought he'd find anything to help. Rather than wait, Dust began to claw his way up the sheer wall, muscles hard with strain, body slick with sweat. The root gave way and he plummeted. His fingernails tore at the earth until he managed to snag another root. With an oof, he jerked to a stop. There he hung by one arm, breath coming in gulps, body dark with muddy soil that was wet with his sweat, but he was of the People. He ignored adversity. All life ended with death and Xhosa doubted that was today.

She motioned to one side. "There are more roots over there."

He muttered about digging more handholds but did as suggested and began another slow ascent.

Qu'tez pounded toward them, panting heavily. He held a vine in his hand.

Xhosa looked around, seeing nowhere this should grow. *I'll ask about that after Dust is rescued.*

Qu'tez held one end of the vine and tossed the other to Dust.

Zvi elbowed Qu'tez aside. "Stone and I will pull him up."

The two gripped the vine and walked it backward until Dust breached the lip of the crevasse, grasped Mbasa's and Ngili's hands, and they yanked him onto the flat land.

He nodded his thanks to all, a smile playing on his lips. "I didn't expect it to be that easy."

Sa-mo-ke barked a laugh, without humor but teeming with happiness. "If you'd missed that root, you'd not be saying that, or anything," and he tossed a rock down the crevice. It clattered once against the side and then vanished into the darkness without a sound.

Qu'tez motioned, "I forgot to mention, if the ground becomes soft or dark and crumbly, avoid it."

Xhosa motioned, "Where did you find the vine?"

"Our Lead Scout buried it when one of our People almost fell into a crack like this one. I must return it in case it's needed by someone else on the next trip," and loped off, catching up only after everyone was settled for the night.

The farther they journeyed, the more uneasy Xhosa became. It wasn't the potential danger. Wind, Mbasa, Ngili, Stone, Zvi, Sa-mo-ke, Spirit, and she could handle anything that came up. It was something in her stomach telling her—screaming—that those left behind were in trouble. They must finish this task quickly so she could return and solve whatever problem they had encountered.

When she asked Wind, he motioned, "Our People have faced worse. They are smart and well trained, Xhosa, and meaner than Cat. No one will beat them." He smiled. "First, we get salt. Then, we deal with that."

She shrugged, telling him she was satisfied if not content.

Qu'tez puffed up to her side. Sweat turned his copious chest hair into a soggy tangle. "Enjoy the cool air, Xhosa. At the salt lake, it becomes hot."

With a grin, he hurried off to join the scouts on their way to explore the brown rounded hills, more barren dirt than scrub.

As the People settled for the night, looking forward to reaching the salt lake in the next handfuls of Suns, Others appeared on their forward trail. They bore the defeated look that Qu'tez's People once had. Xhosa sniffed but didn't find the cannibal stink. When they reached the People, Xhosa offered food and then both shared their stories. Xhosa told how her People crossed the mountains with the intention of making this their new homebase. The new Others squirmed silently.

Xhosa took another bite and between chews, asked of no one in particular, "Why do you leave?"

A female with bright hair that glistened in Sun's dying light caught Xhosa's eye and then each of the People, stopping at Qu'tez.

"Because of cannibals who look like him," and she spit in the direction of the Cave Dweller. "There are too many and more all the time."

Xhosa started to respond but Qu'tez held his hand up. "She's right. You're right, but I left for the same reasons you do. They planned to eat me." He looked at Xhosa and then back to the New-Others. "They never hunt this far out."

Sun-bright-hair refused to look at him but the New-Other-Leader shrugged. "I believe you, because you don't stink." He took a deep breath, his long tangled hair shrouding a beleaguered face. "Leader Xhosa, you waste your time. There are no animals, no berries or nuts, and few plants here. The salt lake—its surface is salt, not water, and savagely hot. The Endless Pond beyond— the water can't be drunk though the fish are easy to catch. We must leave or die."

Xhosa motioned, "Go to the mountains. You will find plenty of food and little risk, just extreme cold. We—I have come to believe that may be a good choice for us, too."

Sun-bright-hair gave Xhosa a tired but thankful smile. "We will do as you suggest. I see no other option."

The next morning, as the new Others prepared to leave, the Leader waylaid Wind and Xhosa. "Come with us," and his hands fluttered to a stop.

Desperation seeped from every part of him, twisting his face and making his hands stiff and choppy. She wanted to help him but not his way.

She shook her head. "You may join us but we go first to harvest salt, and then we go back to our homebase, where you came from, to rejoin the rest of our People."

He drooped. "No, we can't do that," and trundled away.

The new Others left shortly after that, heading toward the mountains, away from the home of Those-who-eat-Others, their steps crunching over the crumbling rock, the Leader tripping over a rock. Sun sparkled off the female's white-yellow hair, reminding Xhosa of a sunny, burbling stream until the glistening streak sunk below a rise and out of sight.

Chapter 20

To the salt lake

Xhosa and her group trotted along a dry riverbed. Qu'tez assured her it never flooded and would take them to the salt lake. Brutal heat rose from the baked earth. The ground burned through Xhosa's thickly calloused feet so she tied pelts around them and did the same for Spirit.

About the time Xhosa decided they must find shade, they crested another rise, like many before, but this time, a vast expanse of smooth sparkling white greeted her, without hills, gullies, bushes, or boulders to break its surface. The brightness blinded her so she had to look through slitted eyes.

"Is it snow?" Wind motioned.

Qu'tez shook his head. "Smell—it's salt, more than anyone could use their entire life."

Xhosa flung herself down the hill.

Qu'tez shouted, "Be careful!" but too late. She strode onto the smooth surface and her foot slipped out from under her. She skidded forward, throwing her arms out. Hands snatched her from behind and yanked upward.

"I've got you," from Wind.

They both wobbled, flailed for balance, and found it.

She motioned, "It's as slippery as the ice on the frozen waterholes."

She and Wind stood still, staring, while the rest of the People gathered around. Choking heat washed over them, worse than Fire Mountain's anger or the firestorm they'd faced. It rippled up from the white surface in a wave, as suffocating as dense reeds around a lake on a hot, sticky day.

Xhosa scrutinized the dull dry area around the white salt lake. "There's no life here, not even scorpions. Why aren't animals licking the salt or Others chopping away blocks of it to carry back to their homebases?"

Qu'tez shook his head. "My father said Others were here most times he and the hunters came. They'd trade females, share stories, swap food. Coming to the salt lake was a prized journey despite the treacherous heat. But the last time they made the journey, my father said it was like this, empty."

Xhosa listened and then shook herself. "Alright. Let's get started. The sooner we finish, the faster we get away from this stifling heat."

And back to our homebase. Xhosa not only couldn't shake the worry that preyed on her, it grew worse each day that passed.

She wrapped her long hair in a vine and chopped ferociously at the rough glistening surface. Salt sprayed up with each strike. Soon, granules coated her hands and face, a thick layer that cracked if she smiled or frowned. She rubbed an arm over her forehead, wiping away the sweat but leaving behind a white, crusty streak.

"This is harder than I expected," but no one answered, all focused on their own efforts.

She hurled her first block toward the edge of the lake and started again. Soon, another chunk thudded atop hers, and then more. No one said a word, just worked. Salt-laden sweat covered Xhosa, cutting into her hands as she worked. She wrapped the bottom of the chopper in vines which slowed her but at least she could work. The others did the same.

Xhosa wiped the moisture from her face, winced as the salty liquid got in her eyes, and chiseled out another block. In some places, the salt was so compact, it required a handaxe to break apart but in others, a chopper easily penetrated the surface.

She worked nonstop, her shadow shrinking on one side and growing on the other. She wanted to harvest enough to last the People through the hot time so they wouldn't have to make this trip again until the cold time. She panted, wiped an arm over her forehead, and continued. Every inhale burned her chest and throat as though she breathed in a firestorm but the People needed salt so she kept digging.

Exhausted, her throat raw, thirst tormented Xhosa, blurring her vision and making her dizzy. How long had it been since she started? She looked up at Sun's position and then down at her shadow. When she glanced upward at the horizon, tears filled her eyes.

"A lake—there!"

Sunlight sparkled off its wet surface. Xhosa let go of her tools and hurried forward though she could barely lift her feet.

Qu'tez grabbed her. "There's nothing there, Xhosa. My People chased what you see, desperate for water, and no matter how far they walked, it was always out of reach."

She shook off his hand but he seized her again. "One of our groupmembers—we found him face down in the dirt, still clawing his way forward until the moment he stopped breathing."

He handed her damp moss and she sucked greedily. The sand in her throat dissolved. This time, when she looked at the pond, something about it was odd. The leaves once shivering in a cool wind, now hung limp, frozen in place, and some—were they upside down? How did she miss that?

She picked up the abandoned tools and resumed her work.

Xhosa swiped a hand over her neck and licked the sweat. Without doubt, this was the most brutal place she had ever been, worse than the green bubbling miasma the People encountered on the journey from their homebase. Salt stuck to her feet and between her toes in the same way ice did to Spirit's pads when they tromped through snow. She cracked it away as she did for the wolf. Blisters covered her hands, many oozing clear mucus and some bleeding. When salt got in the open wounds, the sting made her eyes water. None of that mattered to Xhosa because the faster and harder she worked, the sooner they could leave.

Something *chunked* to her side. Xhosa swayed her head toward the sound, sweat flying from straggles of hair that escaped the vine. There, Qu'tez lay, body flat against the sweltering salt.

"Qu'tez—get up! You'll burn." Xhosa jabbed at him with her spear but he didn't move. "Zvi, help him to the shade—and take Spirit." The wolf panted so hard that one breath started before the other ended.

Zvi motioned, "I think Spirit wishes he could remove his fur as we do the pelts," and wobbled away.

Dust went next, his skin dry and red. He jabbered words that made no sense. Mbasa staggered over to help him.

Xhosa motioned, "Take him to Zvi, Spirit, and Qu'tez and stay with them."

The heat worsened. Sa-mo-ke flushed red and his eyes rolled into his head.

Xhosa grabbed his arm. "We'll finish tonight."

With Wind's help, they dragged Sa-mo-ke and Ngili off the salt.

Moon's glow reflected off the salty surface making it bright enough for them to continue without problem. To Xhosa's surprise, a lone gazelle crept out onto the salt. It licked diligently, ignoring the odor of Others. Its ribs stuck out of its young body. When Ngili approached, it didn't run, as though it knew what would come next and didn't care. They ate the stringy, fatless meat as they worked, the first they'd eaten since arriving.

That night, they collected as much salt as they could carry and returned to their base. Xhosa didn't sleep well, now worried not only about those left behind but how she and her group would get back. She had expected to eat from the land but the outbound journey proved her wrong. Then she assumed herds would be here, licking the salt, but the People were alone.

Where would they find enough food to get home?

Sun awoke, spreading its orange and yellow rays across the terrain, and Xhosa had an idea.

"Qu'tez. Is Endless Pond near?" When he nodded, she beckoned everyone to follow her. "We are going fishing."

Endless Pond turned out to be a turbulent blue-black waterway, the surface flecked with gray foam. Qu'tez assured her this was the same Endless Pond that touched Hawk's homebase. At least, that's what he'd been told.

A narrow white beach edged the shoreline, sparkling with the heavy salt that filled the water. Beyond the shore head-high grass bent in the breeze and beyond that, a small forest. The People waded into the water, Spirit with them. Steam rose from their overheated bodies as they immersed themselves. Those unable to swim, which included Qu'tez, strode in no deeper than their thighs and shoveled water over their chests and head hair.

Once cool, many caught fish, devouring their flesh for the water it contained, while others searched for eggs and ground-nesting birds. Some moved to the shallow pools and caught the hard-shelled beasts they'd first seen at Hawk's homebase.

The problem now became how to transport all that they had collected. Between the fish, the reeds, handfuls of eggs, and the salt, their neck sacks overflowed.

Zvi motioned, "My former-People wrapped what we couldn't carry in bark and dragged it behind us. Stone and I can do that."

Sa-mo-ke motioned, "Spirit and I can haul a load, too."

Once that was completed, they set out for home, keeping Sun in the same position on the backtrail as it had been on the forward trail. Unlike the outbound journey, water wasn't a problem because they knew the locations of wet waterholes.

"If we move here, Spirit, we'll have plenty of salt and fish, enough water if we're careful, and no enemies."

Spirit and Xhosa walked together, the wolf at his Alpha's side, his sensitive ears tweaking to every sound, his feral scent comforting to Xhosa.

"Or we can follow the shore of Endless Pond and go back toward Hawk's homebase. Several of our camps had plenty of food and water. We would have stayed if not for Seeker and his stars assuring us our destination remained ahead."

Spirit huffed and Xhosa nodded, "No, it doesn't matter if Qu'tez and the Cave Dwellers don't come with us. They'll make decisions that work for them, as we must for ourselves."

Spirit whined, tail tucked, liquid blue eyes fixed on her. "I don't know, Spirit. If Seeker insists on staying here, well, we can't if it's dangerous for the People. My obligation is different than Seeker's, which I frankly don't understand. And before you ask, I don't know if Pan-do would stay with Seeker—and his daughter—or leave with us."

Spirit moaned and tucked his tail even deeper between his legs.

"Well, could you tolerate this heat?" When Spirit didn't respond, she continued, "I do realize you would want to stay with Zvi and the rest. I hope that time, when you must choose, never comes but if it does, you too must make the decision that works for you, just as we do.

She lightly touched between his ears. "To answer the rest of your question, yes, I can find the way without Seeker."

Spirit interrupted her with a pant and she stiffened. "Oh. I see what you mean. Yes, I promise we won't move anywhere that's too hot for you. Does that mean you'll come with me?"

That, she didn't expect the wolf to answer. Maybe at some future time. The two trotted in companionable quiet, each secure in the comfort of being with a friend.

Wind's chest heaved as he sprinted up to Xhosa. Sweat poured from his hair and a smile cut his face. "We've reached our outbound markers. We'll be back in two handfuls of Suns."

From then on, no one spoke but all wondered what awaited them. After another hand of Sun's movement, Xhosa froze midstride, the hair rising the length of her back. A visceral dread wafted over her as chilling as a cold breeze. Wind too stopped.

"Down!" They both raised their hands and then dropped them, palm down. Within a breath, it was as though they had never been there.

Wind edged toward her. She motioned, "That's Tor warning us. And something else I missed."

Someone called another birdsong, telling them again to continue with care.

A shiver went through Xhosa's body, from her ears to her toes. "Wind. Something's happened. We always move cautiously. He's warning us that danger could be close."

Wind grunted. "I've heard only two voices. They might be here to guide us into the mountains."

That was the plan they had made with Pan-do. If the People had to leave the cave, they would go to the mountains.

Before Sun slept that day, Tor, Bone, and Shaga appeared, greeting the salt hunters with grins.

Tor motioned, "I can't tell you how good it is to see you."

Xhosa swirled her arm overhead and Sa-mo-ke, Stone, Ngili, Spirit, Dust, and Qu'tez trotted up.

Tor motioned, "Mbasa?"

"She covers the backtrail, with Spirit," and then paused, gaze locked on Tor, asking what happened in her absence. He explained briefly how Those-who-eat-Others assaulted the People's hunters, injured Red Wolf and killed Zak'ez.

Xhosa nodded. Death was life. "You know who is responsible."

Tor glanced at Qu'tez and the subadult stepped toward him, legs spread, hands fisted. "If it's one of my tribe, I will help you kill them. My loyalty is with you, the People."

Xhosa nodded and Tor shrugged. "We think Cucu'tez is a traitor."

Chapter 21

Xhosa tipped her head up but saw nothing. Still, the loud cawing and the muted flap of heavy wings said carrion birds were circling somewhere, waiting their turn at a feast. Her first thought was the People had been attacked, slaughtered, but Tor said it couldn't be. They remained at the cave with Pan-do. When Tor reported the salt hunters were close, Pan-do had decided to wait for their arrival so they could leave as a group.

Then why the huge flock of carrion eaters?

She motioned to Wind, "They aren't settling. The predator must still be there."

Xhosa increased their pace, up and down one rise and another, through a copse of lonely trees, and then around a rock formation as big as a family of elephants. That's when the stench hit her, like a slap across the face. They continued but now stooped, hiding below the waist-high stalks of brown grass. As they got closer to the carnage, the stench included not only blood but the acrid scents of feces and urine, an odor Xhosa associated with a slaughter.

It wasn't one carcass. It was many.

It didn't take much longer to find it, a pile of furless limbs and narrow chests surrounded by the largest group of Others Xhosa had ever seen, all chopping the carcasses into chunks, butchering them as Xhosa and the People had done when the herds died in a heap after the firestorm.

These are the bodies of Others, massacred by the cannibals.

She shivered, resentment welling, her vision blurring.

Wind touched her. "These could be the Others Qu'tez said left his group. It doesn't have to be who you're thinking, Xhosa."

Her brow furrowed. "If they survived this long, why not return to the Cave Dwellers? And this is many more than Qu'tez said had disappeared. No. This is an entire tribe, even children, wiped out by the cannibals."

It had to be her People. No other non-cannibals lived here. She swallowed hard to force back the bile that rose in her throat. Her mind raced trying to figure out how they caught Pan-do— and her People—so unaware. What caused her Co-Leader to come this far from the cave? Was he trying to warn her or simply desperate to escape an attack on the homebase by too many cannibals, following the plan they had made knowing she would understand?

Her head pounded. She fumbled in her neck sack for her pain plant, shoved it into her mouth and chewed, eyes closed.

Wind nudged her. "I don't recognize any of the dead—"

Xhosa opened her eyes, hopeful for a moment, and then gasped. A flash of yellow, buried in the bloody pile, slender strands of hair fluttered in the slight breeze.

"Sun bright hair… "

Her face twisted in anger. She barely stopped herself from charging, screaming into the group of gluttonous Those-who-eat-Others, knowing she didn't serve her People by trading her life for revenge.

"Wind," she whispered after a deep breath. "These are the ones we met traveling to the salt lake. They planned to go into the mountains. Why are they here?"

She didn't expect an answer. Even knowing why would do nothing for this tiny tribe Xhosa had shared a meal with.

As the People backed away, one cannibal stopped his work and scanned the surroundings. He snuffled, shouted to the rest of the massive group, and a large group padded slowly toward the People, hands clutching the choppers they'd been using on the carcasses. Xhosa and her group had just enough time to coat themselves in mud and curl into the roots of a giant tree, weapons ready, eyes alert but slit. With barely a handful of fighters, they wouldn't survive the encounter but they would take many with them.

The cannibals got within a spear throw, moving cautiously, peering into the shadows and the clumped scrub, clearly unsure of what they would find and how dangerous it would be. A carrion bird saved the People's lives. The huge bird, its wingspan wider than Xhosa could stretch her arms, saw the carcasses undefended and landed, tearing into the meat and calling the rest of its flock to eat. When the cacophony became deafening, the cannibals abandoned the hunt for uncertain prey in favor of food they'd already slaughtered. Once they were out of sight, the People slipped away.

Chapter 22

Back from the salt lake

Darkness shrouded the landscape by the time they reached
the cave but instead of entering, they sniffed and listened, tasting
the air. Xhosa kept one eye on the entrance and the other on
Spirit. He would alert to danger before she did but right now, his
hackles were flat. He huffed once but so quietly she would have
missed it if she hadn't been watching him.

Xhosa and her group remained silent and motionless long
enough for the insect sounds in the area to return, and still, no
one left the cave to relieve themselves or for any reason.

Mbasa whispered to Xhosa, "I'm going to sneak in through
the tunnel at the back," and without another word, slipped away.

Too much time passed and Xhosa was about to follow
Mbasa's trail when a wail echoed from inside the cave and then,
a red ball of fur tumbled—well, hobbled—out. It was Red Wolf.
She skidded to a stop, panted loudly, ears tweaking in all
direction, nose twitching to the thin night air. Mid-pant, her
whole body jerked toward Spirit and then she sat back on her
haunches and howled, head back, snout raised, the mournful call
of a wolf to its pack.

Spirit answered.

With a moan, the young wolf plunged toward her Alpha and
leapt on him, licking his face and biting at his muzzle, touching

noses to get reacquainted. Within a breath, Mbasa appeared at the cave's mouth with the rest of the People, some almost knocked over by Black Wolf and the pups as they too raced toward Spirit. The pups had grown considerably, now reaching Black Wolf's chest. Judging by their paws and ears, they would reach Spirit's gargantuan size.

The hunters unloaded the salt and the fish they hadn't eaten inside the cave and then answered the group's endless questions. *"Yes, we faced no threats the entire journey." "Yes, there is more salt than we'll ever use." "No, we found no herds and fewer Others. But we did find fish."*

Pan-do stopped them. "They are tired. Let them rest."

As Xhosa and Wind went to their nest, Mbasa to Tor's, Zvi to Seeker and Lyta's, and Sa-mo-ke to where the warriors slept, Qu'tez joined Re'ez, Rul'ez, and Asal'rez.

Qu'tez motioned, "I don't see Cucu'tez."

Re'ez answered. "Scouting. Bird joins him if he tells her he's going. I don't trust him anymore. No one does," and told Qu'tez her suspicions about the part Cucu'tez played in Zak'ez's death.

Qu'tez thought about that for a moment and motioned, "Do you get along with these strangers?"

Asal'rez motioned, hands low and tense, "I—we—respect them but they are different, Qu'tez. Surely you notice. They ... " He tilted his head down and struggled for a word, settling on, "...insist we do things their way."

Qu'tez grinned. "Yes, you're right. They expect us to do what we can to serve the needs of everyone and in return, they provide what we require—food, pelts, tools, healing plants, or anything."

"We are not used to that—"

Qu'tez interrupted, "Become used to it," his gestures firm enough to leave no doubt he meant what he said. "Our fathers would approve."

Hands still raised, he eyed each of the Cave Dwellers individually until all responded, "I will."

Re'ez motioned, "It feels good to work hard and care for others." Rul'ez nodded.

Qu'tez made his voice and gestures inflexible and stern in a way the rest usually heard only from adults. His time away taught him the importance of leading, that he must protect these few of his People who remained. Before traveling with Xhosa and Wind, he'd included everyone in decisions. Now, he saw the wisdom of listening but then making his own decision.

"Do not doubt they will reject us if we fail to do our part."

Asal'rez motioned, "But Qu'tez, we are poor hunters, weak fighters, and unobservant scouts. What can we offer?"

Qu'tez smiled at the memory of Spirit, trotting in front of the traveling group, tail waving, tongue out. The wolf was proud to provide security for his pack, keep them from danger.

"Look for opportunities, Asal'rez. For example, I know the area of the salt lake more intimately than they. This freed everyone else to do the tasks they excelled at. All of us know this area better than they." When no one spoke, he added, "A division of duties works well. I see why the People live this way."

Re'ez motioned, "Siri treats me as the males treat Leads."

Rul'ez gestured, hands calm and sure, "I'm happy to do as they require but for different reasons. Without them, we will die."

Qu'tez sighed, relieved that, regardless of why, all agreed with his conclusion. He started to compliment them but stopped when Cucu'tez entered the cave. An uncomfortable silence fell over the gathering.

Cucu'tez vaguely greeted Qu'tez but ignored the rest. Qu'tez forced a neutral tone and asked, "Where have you been?"

Cucu'tez's body tensed. His hands fisted, and his eyes darted through the gathering of Cave Dwellers. "Trying to find meat! What Asal'rez should be doing."

Qu'tez bit his tongue to keep from blurting out that Cucu'tez's lie was obvious in his stance and his gestures.

Asal'rez motioned, his face pinched with anger, "Why didn't you ask me to join you? Never mind—we know why," and his hands fluttered to a stop.

Qu'tez let that sink in and then asked, "What did you catch?"

Cucu'tez exploded, "I tried—you know that!"

Qu'tez stood, hand gripping his spear—the way Wind and Pan-do did when they wanted to intimidate others. He scrutinized Cucu'tez and allowed a frown to crease his forehead.

"Things have changed, Cucu'tez. We are now part of the People. We contribute or are rejected. Trying counts for nothing."

Cucu'tez grimaced and stomped off to the back of the cave. Black Wolf snarled and bared her fangs as the subadult got too close to her den. Cucu'tez jerked away and moved deeper into the rear tunnels, as far as he could get from the wolves and everyone else.

Qu'tez pulled a chunk of fish from his neck sack, took a bit, and then handed it to Re'ez to share with the rest. Between chews, he motioned, "Black Wolf doesn't trust him. I have learned to rely on the wolves' instincts. You should, too."

The treatment for her head pains sometimes made Xhosa groggy so she would talk to Hecate before taking it. She found the Lead Hunter with Ngili and Sa-mo-ke, answering their endless questions.

"No, soon." With a glance at Cucu'tez, added, "But I might be wrong."

Her expression said she didn't believe that. Xhosa didn't either. She couldn't think of a time Hecate had been mistaken about a person.

Xhosa motioned to Hecate, "Why are you so sure Cucu'tez is the traitor?"

Hecate wasted no time answering. "From what Re'ez and Asal'rez tell me, Cucu'tez was always weak, even as a child. He never stood out for his skill at anything and most of his groupmates didn't like him or his whining. He joined the small group of subadults who decided to escape because he had nothing to lose and they were willing to take anyone.

"No surprise, escaping didn't solve his problems. Soon, once again, he had no friends and no one trusted him. He became tired of hiding and running for his life and convinced himself his new tribe couldn't win. Personally, I don't blame him. His entire time as a child and a subadult, he had seen Those-who-eat-

Others win because they overran every other tribe. Weapons skills and cleverness never played a part. Why would he ever think a group as small as the Cave Dwellers could win? To his twisted thinking, it was just a matter of time before his new tribe was discovered so he decided to change loyalties."

"We arrived but he underestimated how much that changed things. We think group size is secondary to skill, cleverness, and a passion to survive. He thought learning our skills, saying they would help the Cave Dwellers to save themselves, was a waste of time. He probably didn't even bother to mention the neck sacks and the stone spear tips to Those-who-eat-Others because he couldn't explain their importance or how to make them which would make him look stupid."

That made sense to Xhosa but didn't explain the most important question. "One reason I've held back on calling Cucu'tez the traitor is because I don't understand why he wouldn't bring Those-who-eat-Others to our cave."

Hecate grinned. "That's easy. He and Rul'ez planned to pairmate but now that she bleeds, she spends her time with Asal'rez. Cucu'tez hopes she'll change her mind. When he realizes that won't happen, he will want to hurt her. And us."

"Which puts a deadline on this."

Xhosa glanced around, realizing someone was missing. "Where's Bird?" Her aroma was faint. She'd been gone a while.

Snake motioned, "Scouting with Dust and Bone. They like going at night."

"And Rainbow?"

"Where he always is at night. Practicing with his spear in the back tunnels."

The next morning, Xhosa spotted Red Wolf buried in a pile of ears and muzzles. As though she felt Xhosa's gaze, Red Wolf jerked awake, leaped over Seeker, past Lyta, and around Zvi in a mad dash to lick Xhosa's face, yipping her joy at the sight of the two-legged Alpha who had saved her. Xhosa gently held her in place with one hand while the other felt her nose. It was warm.

"What happened to your leg, Red Wolf?"

There were deep tears in the young wolf's flank where a creature had bitten savagely and then ripped. Red streaks already stretched well outside of the slash. If the pup were an Other, she would be dead. As Xhosa studied the wounds, Black Wolf padded up, licked them, and lay down, head between her paws, eyebrows twitching.

Seeker motioned, "Black Wolf cleans the gashes constantly."

Lyta motioned, "She's a good mother. I learn a lot from her."

Zvi added, "Siri applied mulches but Black Wolf licks them off."

"I have a new salve, from a flower I found by the salt lake." As she dug through her neck sack, Spirit trotted over carrying a fetid smelling chunk of meat. White worms covered it but that mattered little to the wolves. They considered the wriggling creatures as simply more food.

Xhosa slathered mulch on the laceration and wrapped it with leaves. "Black Wolf will find this much more difficult to lick off because of the taste. Keep Red Wolf inside and quiet until the wound begins to heal."

She rolled back on her haunches and motioned, "What happened to her?"

Lyta motioned, "Hyaena snatched one of the pups while they played outside. Red Wolf chased them. Hyaena abandoned the pup and launched itself at Red Wolf, probably seeing a larger meal. It might have killed her except that Zvi slammed it with a tree limb."

Zvi paled and staggered out of the cave. Seeker remained seated, face impassive, his gaze tracking the retreating figure. No part of him moved except for his eyes and his hand, fingers running through Red Wolf's fur from neck to tail over and over. Finally, mercifully, Zvi's snuffles and gulps faded away.

Xhosa motioned, "What upset Zvi?"

Seeker spoke, his voice hollow, "When Zvi saved Spirit's life, when Spirit was a new pup, she also rescued his brother. She took them to her tribe's cave, where she thought they'd be safe, and her mother bashed his head in for food. She tried to do the same to Spirit but Zvi fled and never went back. Shortly after that, we found each other.

"For me to meet my best friend, Spirit's brother had to die."

Never had Seeker said so much with such honesty. When he finished, he rose unsteadily and followed Zvi's trail into the brush.

Xhosa and Wind spent the next day patrolling the terrain. Pan-do said Those-who-eat-Others tried to pick the People off who hunted or scouted in small groups but so far, had failed. Still, where the scouts normally marked the boundaries of their territory with urine to warn off predators, they didn't, not wanting the cannibals to know the camp's boundaries.

That night, Seeker joined Xhosa as she prepared to patrol. "The last time we watched the stars, I think I confused you, Xhosa. Rescuing the Cave Dwellers is part of why we're here, necessary to the bigger plan but inconsequential to our future."

Xhosa crossed her arms, her brain trying to unravel what he'd said, knowing she needed to ask questions but had no idea what those should be. So, she sat, waiting for Seeker to explain.

And he did. "Befriending the Cave Dwellers will lead us to those who know the location of our new homebase but we must find them quickly or it will be too late."

Xhosa hugged her chest to stop her hands from shaking. "How?"

Seeker shrugged and left.

Xhosa called Bird over. "Have you found any Others who won't eat us given a chance?"

Bird gave her a funny look but shook her head. "We've searched toward Sun's nest and the area by Endless Pond. We haven't yet investigated the other side of the mountains, across from Viper's homebase."

Xhosa turned to the distant peaks, green flanks that gave way to dirt brown and then the stark white that stretched upward to the gleaming tips.

"Then we go there."

The next day, Wind, Mbasa, Hecate, Qu'tez, and several warriors left to explore the mountains. Wind shivered at memories of his last journey through these hills, of frozen toes, hair stiff with ice, and many mornings awakening unable to move. He hoped finding the new homebase wouldn't require they cross these spires again.

After a full day of exploring, they found a cave, ate, groomed, and settled in to sleep. The plan was to continue into the mountains farther each day, never quitting until they found the Others both Viper and Seeker mentioned. Xhosa and Wind were sure they existed. They just had to find and then befriend them.

That all changed when Wind went outside to the next day to relieve his morning water, and the wind almost knocked him over. He grinned as he stretched, soaking in the glorious land around him, the briskness invigorating though infused with the smell of rain.

"Over there."

Hecate hurried up to his side and pointed, frowning. When he followed her gaze, he saw dark clouds shooting fire to the ground. A roar echoed beyond the fire, as loud as any explosion from Fire Mountain.

Qu'tez bounded out of the surrounding brush, arms laden with kindling, racing for the cave. Behind him came Mbasa dragging a massive log.

She motioned, "We'll be stuck inside at least all day, maybe longer. Moisture already collects on my skin."

The rain started as soon as they ducked through the mouth of the cave. Instead of blowing itself out by nighttime as Wind hoped, it worsened, the rain turning to what Viper called "hail"—tiny balls of ice the size of Wind's thumb and sharper than cactus spines. Everyone huddled around the fire, shivering despite pelts, eating from their travel food. The next day was colder and the hail became snow, something Mbasa and Hecate had never seen. Wind regaled them with stories of the incessant storms the People experienced coming through the mountains.

Snow battered them all day. Wind paced the length of the cave, kicked at dirt clods and the occasional pebble, and tried to stay calm. Which didn't work. He must either find the Others Seeker talked about or get back to Xhosa. Right now, the storm prevented both.

He shuffled outside and scrutinized what he could see, feeling more desperate with each breath. Then, his skin prickled.

Strangers!

He searched the snowfall but saw no one and nothing strange. Somewhere, water dripped. The ground crunched what could be cautious steps over ice but in cold air, sounds were louder than normal and carried greater distances. Wind couldn't tell how close these were but his instincts bristled. The open space in front of the cave was the distance of a spear throw. His People could make that throw every day, with accuracy, but Wind had yet to meet an Other who could.

Besides, why would they stand in the frozen darkness to spy on him? He'd done nothing threatening.

He spun around, rubbing his arms for warmth, and hurried back into the cave.

"Mbasa, Hecate. Tomorrow we go back regardless of this storm."

Many sets of eyes noted when Tall-one came outside and searched without seeing them. It confused them he carried no weapon. He must know they watched. Did he think himself safe?

He wasn't, especially if he brought trouble.

Chapter 23

Cave Dwellers' cave

A scream woke Xhosa. Sun streamed through the mouth of the cavern as she jolted upright. A sniff told her the scouts weren't back. Despite the warmth, a shiver passed through her body. She rushed outside and Qaj grabbed her. The female shook with fear, eyes so wide Xhosa could see the white all around the black center.

"Shaga! He disappeared!"

Her son. Xhosa gestured, making sure her hands were slow with the right amount of urgency, "Tell me what happened."

Qaj shook uncontrollably. Even her lips trembled. "He went to release his water. I fell back to sleep and now, he isn't here! The cannibals—did they take him?"

Lyta hurried to Xhosa, shoulders dipping as her feet moved faster than their odd deformities allowed.

"Black Wolf is gone also, and one of her pups. Spirit went to look for them."

Xhosa didn't worry about the adult wolves. They would survive on their own but none of the pups had ever known fear. Always their Alphas protected them.

The subadult—Rul'ez—responsible for tending the fire motioned, "Black Wolf's pup ran into the brush and she and Shaga chased it."

Before Xhosa could send anyone to track them, Black Wolf trotted into camp, Shaga's hand in her mouth, the boy giggling. The wolf delivered him to Qaj and sprinted back into the undergrowth. Qaj hugged her child, happy, relieved, and angry in equal measures.

She shook him. "Why leave and not tell me?"

Shaga scrunched his face. "Black Wolf and I went to release our water. Her pup sprinted away. She chased but I couldn't keep up and then couldn't find my way back."

Xhosa touched a deep gash in the boy's arm. "What happened?"

Shaga hugged the wounded limb against his chest. "I fell," he motioned one-handed with no sign of the agony he must be suffering.

Xhosa motioned to Honey, "Bring moss, honey, and leaves."

Qaj's mother shook her head. "I'll do it."

Xhosa moved out of the way. Another catastrophe averted. Black Wolf would find Spirit and together, they would find the pup. Her thoughts moved back to the People's missing scouts.

Where is Wind? He should have come back yesterday.

Bird touched her arm, startling her. "I'll look for them, Leader."

"I'll go too," Zvi added, her hands quivering.

Bird thought about what Rul'ez said. *No, he is wrong.* Black Wolf hadn't chased after her pup. Both had smelled the scouts. Bird figured if she followed Black Wolf's prints, she'd find the scouts.

She and Zvi tracked the wolf through the forest opposite the cave and then along the stream the People drank from. The prints were faint, often dipping into the water, but Bird didn't succeed as a scout by quitting. Dust called her the People's best scout and Wind told her she should challenge for Lead. She wouldn't, though. It was the land that intrigued her, not being Lead. Dust still had much to teach her. Maybe she'd consider it when he ran out of answers to her questions.

A faint print stopped her. Zvi was so close behind that her hot breath washed over Bird's neck.

"Others' tracks, Zvi. Black Wolf's prints are over them."

She hadn't brought weapons but touched her neck sack, felt the bulge of many rocks. Though she smelled nothing unusual, she crouched, her shape now well below the top of the grass. Without looking, she knew Zvi did the same. The two had never scouted together but Zvi and Seeker had survived handfuls of Moons traveling unknown lands by themselves, without a tribe. Bird trusted Zvi's instincts.

The two stilled, barely breathing, until finally, the grasshoppers again cried, birds began to sing, and a sound like Cousin Chimp calling its mate told Bird all was back to normal. She poked her head up, studied the area, and found nothing that raised the hair on her neck.

"Let's go," and hurried along Black Wolf's trail.

As they toiled up the flank of a steep, scree-strewn hill, Bird stopped Zvi. A light breeze drifted by carrying a faint sweetness. It could be a skunk, frightened by a predator, but Bird didn't think so.

"Cannibals are on the opposite side of the hill."

The two dropped to the ground and then crawled to the crest, keeping a tangled scrubby bush between them and whatever was on the other side. Bird fingered the twigs aside and smiled.

There, partway down the hill, Spirit and Black Wolf hunkered, bellies on the ground, motionless except for Spirit's quick peek back at Zvi. Between Black Wolf's paws snuggled her pup. Bird couldn't tell if it was asleep or dead.

Bird followed the wolf's gaze and froze. A cluster of Others crouched in the undergrowth, hiding from whatever was below them. Each carried weapons. Bird doubted they knew anyone was watching them.

Zvi motioned, "They're hunting."

Bird's vision narrowed and she stiffened. "Look who their prey is."

Just coming into view a handful of stone throws farther down the hill, moving toward the People's homebase was Wind, followed by Mbasa, Hecate, Qu'tez, and the rest of the missing scouts.

Bird motioned, "They don't know Those-who-eat-Others
are there. Why don't the cannibals strike?"

"I think they're hiding, planning to strike only if our People
let their guard down. Which they won't."

"Spirit and Black Wolf smelled them. That's why Black Wolf
left the camp—to help."

Zvi nodded. "And so will we."

"I have only throwing stones."

Zvi grinned. "You have me and we have Spirit. We don't
need more."

Bird, Zvi, the wolves—the pup in Black Wolf's mouth—and
the lost scouts straggled into the camp. Every one of them
looked rested and well-fed, most carrying the partially-eaten
carcasses of several goats and a pig. Wind was the last to enter
the camp, a smile on his face after assuring himself all was well
on their backtrail.

The tension drained from Xhosa and the blistering head pain
eased. She approached Zvi and Bird and asked, "What
happened?" Her voice cracked but no one seemed to notice.

The two, talking in tandem, told how they found Spirit and
Black Wolf hidden within sight of the cannibals who were
watching the People.

Bird motioned, face lit with excitement, "When our People
passed them, Those-who-eat-Others crawled away."

Satisfied, the scouts were safe, Xhosa must now make sure
Those-who-eat-Others never again got so close to the homebase
without being noticed. If not for the wolves, an attack on Wind's
unsuspecting group wouldn't have ended this happily.

"Dust!" Her hand was quick and abrupt, as frozen as the
mountain air they had migrated through to get here.

The scout's eyes widened at her tone. She ignored his
reaction and walked briskly to the edge of the clearing.

When she smelled his scent of sweat mixed with confusion,
she asked, "Where were those that should have seen the
cannibals?"

Dust's face paled, eyes shifting over the distance before settling back on Xhosa. His light-hearted attitude evaporated at the quiet anger in her words.

"You're right, Leader Xhosa. Bird and Bone have been watching the other side, where we thought Those-who-eat-Others would strike. I'll fix that."

Xhosa wanted to yell but his reasoning was good. She crossed her arms over her chest and breathed in, calming herself.

The next day, Xhosa gathered the People and said what was on everyone's minds. "We must leave. Wind, can we move to the cave you sheltered in?"

"It's too small, and because of the storm, we didn't explore the area."

Xhosa motioned to Seeker, "Is the guide we seek up there?"

He cocked his head, thinking, and finally answered, "Yes. Maybe."

She scowled at his answer but turned to Wind. "You and I will go there tomorrow while Pan-do and Siri prepare the People to migrate."

"Xhosa!" Dust sprinted toward her from the waterway side, panting hard. "Viper—she's coming, and at a ground-eating pace!"

Xhosa unfurled her warclub from her back. "Is she by herself?"

"Yes."

No one would travel alone without a good reason especially so fast and from as far away as where Viper lived.

"She must be in trouble."

Before Xhosa could say more, the young female stumbled into the camp. Her chest heaved with the struggle to breathe, her hair soggy with sweat, legs shaking from fatigue.

She lurched to a halt in front of Xhosa and croaked, "Xhosa—my People—they need help!" and then bent forward and threw up.

Xhosa crouched at her side, pressed a water-soaked leaf into her hand, aghast at the distraught state of one of the strongest females Xhosa knew. When the two last parted, Viper had been confident she could lead her People, the Mountain People. Now, she smelled of defeat, panic, and desperation.

Viper sucked in water and tried to catch her breath enough to speak. Xhosa waited, not patiently, and finally huffed. "Tell me, Viper."

"Scarred One and Fang—please—come with me! They're slaughtering my People!"

Xhosa recognized the callsigns of the two thuggish Others who had once captured her.

She forced her face to remain calm, her hands soft, and motioned, "How many are with them?"

"More than my People but not as many as we saw in the camp where they held us. Scarred One probably thought he could easily defeat us, as he did the last time, but we will never again be enslaved. We are killing one of them for each they kill of us but we can't last much longer."

Xhosa looked at Pan-do and then Wind. Both offered subtle nods. "We will help you, of course."

Xhosa's nostrils flared as she gestured to Ngili, "Decide who should come with us."

Pan-do motioned, "Wind and I will stay here with enough warriors to handle whatever Those-who-eat-Others plan. We will also prepare the People to leave, when you return."

Viper placed a hand on Xhosa's chest. "I have worse news. In the chaos, Nightshade escaped."

Anger welled in Xhosa's throat. In the past, she had relied on Nightshade's enormous strength, brilliant cleverness, and love of fighting to protect the People. Now that would be thrown against her.

Viper seemed to read her thoughts and motioned, "My father says Nightshade can't survive the cold."

It will take a lot more than cold air to kill Nightshade. But Xhosa dipped her head, not wanting Viper to see her doubt or hear her thoughts.

"We leave tomorrow, Viper, with daylight."

Xhosa sighed to herself. Sun was not even overhead and already, she was tired. One more problem that must be handled immediately, another she'd never before faced. And then, as though Sun lit the landscape of her mind, assurance flowed within her. They would win because they couldn't lose.

Lyta tugged on Xhosa's arm. "You must teach Viper bird language."

Viper stiffened.

Xhosa motioned, hands moving with renewed strength, "We use it to communicate over distances. It is like a callsign but more involved."

Viper's head moved from Xhosa to Lyta. "How much more?"

Lyta motioned, "Spread your lips or narrow them while you blow air out. Place your hands around your mouth to call louder or softer. That's all."

Viper paled and sweat prickled her forehead.

Lyta beamed a brilliant smile. "It's easy, Viper. All of us have managed. Well, except for the Cave Dwellers. You'll see. Xhosa can teach you as you travel," and she hobbled away.

Viper still looked doubtful so Xhosa motioned, "Nightshade doesn't know these calls."

That made Viper grin.

The next day, Ngili, Stone, Snake, Spirit, Xhosa, Viper, and a handful of warriors set off for Viper's homebase, leaving behind the same amount of males to defend the People. They moved at a ground-eating pace and by the time Moon shrank to nothing in the night sky, arrived at the outskirts of the Mountain Dwellers' territory. Viper sang the call that identified her as one of the People but silence answered it. They slipped up to the edge of the Mountain Dweller's homebase, remaining well hidden behind a shroud of stubble. Fang and his thugs hunched around a bloody pile on the ground. A heavily muscled male elbowed his way past Fang for a better look, his chest from nipples to waist marked by wide white scars.

Scarred One.

Sometime in the past, cat viciously clawed this warrior, scars Scarred One wore with pride, shouting out to all that his power could beat the mighty Cat.

A dangerous stillness wrapped Xhosa's throat, strangling her more with each breath. She and Viper must beat Scarred One with such finality, that he never returned.

Xhosa had an idea how to make that happen.

"Stay here," she motioned and walked into the clearing. Within a handful of steps, she saw what held their attention.

Leopard's ruined body.

Chapter 24

Viper's camp

Scarred One didn't notice Xhosa at first, too intent on poking Leopard's carcass. Even from here, Xhosa could see the blood red gouges that slashed her chest and face, and her grotesquely contorted head, like someone had squeezed it tight enough to collapse the bones. The beautiful young female's life had ended in misery.

"You killed Leopard, Scarred One." Xhosa's gestures controlled but stiff with anger. "Why? Did she refuse to be your slave again?"

He spun around and locked his rat-like eyes onto hers. Xhosa kept her spear down, the shaft lightly gripped. She wanted him to make the first move, let those around him see the coward that lived within his cat-clawed chest.

His face turned red and he blurted out, "You!"

Xhosa cocked her head, hid her seething fury behind a complacency designed to make Scarred One frantic. Then, he would make a mistake.

He searched behind her. "Where's the tall male, the one who calls you slave? Did you escape again? I was almost executed when you disappeared. It won't happen again."

He flicked a finger. A ruffian yanked Xhosa's arm but she didn't budge. Her nose wrinkled at the stench from his open mouth. She turned just her head toward him, offered a sweet smile, and then stomped on his foot with her considerable strength. Stink Breath squealed. When he lifted his injured foot, she kicked his kneecap so ferociously, his leg folded back and he toppled over, face white, mouth open in a silent howl.

Scarred One's snarl couldn't hide the worry that flashed through his eyes, there and gone in less than a blink.

She turned to him. "I told you to leave us alone. You didn't listen."

He motioned toward Leopard keeping his gaze on Xhosa, respect showing that hadn't been there before. And hate. "This one disobeyed. I have no use for slaves who don't follow orders. The same will happen to your friend Viper. And you."

Two more thugs tried to seize her. The first, she buried her foot so far into his groin, she felt it hit something hard. The other, her elbow slammed his temple and he went limp. Both fell. Stink Breath struggled to his hands and one good knee and crawled toward his spear. Xhosa twisted her fist through his hair and dragged him up until his face was level with hers.

"Don't do that," and then kicked him across the clearing where he bounced at Scarred One's feet. This time, he stayed down.

Scarred One's face turned cold, emotion draining as water would from a damaged gourd.

He studied her. "On the way here, stories were told of a great female whose warriors are undefeatable, who is protected by a wolf that will tear the throat from any who threaten her. Those who told the stories were awestruck, filled with not only fear for her power but admiration for what she accomplished.

"That's you, isn't it?"

Xhosa's gaze flickered past him, beyond his languid warriors with their ragged pelts who gawked at her with dull, sullen eyes, to Spirit's low form, barely hidden at the edge of the clearing. Blue eyes blinked and yellow canines glistened, waiting for her command.

Scarred One reached Xhosa in two quick strides and slapped her, a stinging blow that cut her cheek. He wanted her to wince—screech—but she merely cocked her head, bored.

She motioned, "Where's the Fire Tender, Dreg's friend—Ork was it? Oh, I remember. He escaped with us. He's back with his People."

Scarred One's face reddened and loathing flashed through his eyes.

He spit at her and then motioned, "I'd end your existence but my Leader insists on meeting the powerful female with the huge reputation. Tell your warriors to reveal themselves. I will teach them how to handle a female who won't listen."

He leered at her and she lowered her eyes, shifting from one foot to the other as though nervous. Her entire time as a captive, she had made herself invisible so she could evaluate her enemy without being noticed. Most of the warriors were captives, slaves, with no loyalty to the Leaders. They obeyed not out of respect but fear and since no one trained them how to fight, didn't do that well.

Scarred One was the lone exception but Xhosa didn't worry about him. He wouldn't realize his warriors were out-skilled until it was too late.

She raised her head, lifting her hand, palm forward, a sign to Stone as she ticked off each male in mock surprise. "Only two handfuls? Again, you underestimate me, One-with-Cat-scars."

He laughed. "You once offered to trade yourself for a life with my People. I can still arrange that, One-called—"

As he shut his eyes, searching for a suitable callsign, the males on both sides of him collapsed as did the two behind them. Stone and Snake stepped into the clearing and charged their next victims, this time with warclubs. The focus forward, Spirit launched his assault from behind, his fangs and claws more deadly than any warrior's weapons, and ended the life of another.

In the melee, Scarred One fled which left Fang to fend for himself.

He screamed, "Wait—where are you going?" and scuttled backwards but didn't get far before Viper stopped him.

"This is for Leopard!" And her warclub smacked into his head, the sound like a melon thrown to the ground from a great height.

Xhosa glanced around and then motioned to Viper, "I guess Scarred One fled—"

"Not fled. Just went for reinforcements."

Xhosa pulled in a shallow breath, trying to hide her surprise at who Scarred One had pinned to his side.

Fighting for calm, she motioned, "Leader Davos won't last long with a spear in his side. When he dies, will you then hide behind Dreg?" She gestured to the subadult at Scarred One's side.

Davos laughed at her boldness, nodding agreement and then spit on Scarred One. "It's not deep, Xhosa. Talk to Dreg first. He remembers you and Viper. I think we can help him."

No one ever called Davos weak but the seriousness of his injury belied the Leader's brave words.

Xhosa motioned to Viper in Cave Dweller gestures, "Watch Davos while I talk to Dreg, as your father suggests."

Scarred One snarled at them, "Don't use gestures I don't understand or I'll chop off your hands!"

Xhosa dipped her head and offered a tiny smile—reasonable and friendly. "Alright. That's fair," and then turned to Dreg who looked more frightened than frightening. His jaw had been broken some time ago and hadn't healed properly. That left a lump in the back and teeth that probably couldn't even chew food.

"Dreg, your jaw, is that punishment for my escape? Despite that it wasn't your fault? It must hurt."

In fact, it must be agonizing, all day, the only respite being sleep if Dreg was so tired, he could sleep through the pain.

Scarred One motioned to Viper, still standing by Fang's body, "I free your father after I escape."

His use of "I" wasn't lost on Dreg. The warrior jerked, face pale. "Wha agga ma?"

Xhosa took a step toward the subadult, eyes soft, head cocked, "He doesn't care about you, Dreg. He never did. I'll help you with your broken jaw after I stop him."

She turned back to Scarred One, eyes smoldering. "Beg for mercy or die right here in this dirt, failed-Leader."

He laughed as he stabbed the spear deeper into Davos' side. The Mountain Dweller Leader's eyes widened and he stiffened.

Scarred One continued, "One-called-Davos doesn't have much time. Let me go, return to the rest of my group. I'll leave him. You'll have time to save him—"

With a nasty snarl, Spirit leaped, slamming a massive paw into Scarred One's chest. The warrior toppled over, taking Dreg down with him. The subadult let out an *oomph*, smacked his head against a rock, and stilled. One glance told Xhosa his pain was gone and he felt only peace.

Scarred one thought he could use Dreg's death as a distraction but when he tried to sit up, Spirit stepped on him with the full weight of his massive body. Xhosa could hear the bones collapse, and dung flowed from Scarred One's body. Viper rushed past the motionless Scarred One and dropped to her father's side.

Face covered in sweat, each breath filled with frothy red bubbles, he waved her away. "I am dead, daughter. Don't waste time fixing what you can't. Hear me! Scarred One doesn't intend to take us away. He wants to make this his new homebase."

He coughed, spraying blood over his hands. After a tortured gargled breath, he beckoned Xhosa. "He has partnered with those you call Big Heads. He is after you and Wind. You must stop them before reinforcements arrive. If you can't … take Viper and her Mountain Dwellers… to your homebase." His powerful voice was now a whisper and he struggled to pull in enough air to speak. "Viper trained the males. They are … not as good as your warriors … but will help you."

A cold shudder ran through Xhosa's body. Something Davos said bothered her. "Davos. No one would stumble over your homebase in these hills. How does Scarred One know where it is?"

His eyes closed but his hands spoke for him. "My fault… Nightshade—he escaped … found Scarred One… led him to us."

Viper stuttered, "No. That's not right. Why would the Big Heads trust the one who slaughtered their best fighters?"

Xhosa muttered, more to herself than the young female, "At the battle that killed my father, Nightshade's prowess stunned Thunder. He invited him to join the Big Heads. Nightshade didn't answer. Now, he has."

For the first time since this battle with Thunder started, fear clutched Xhosa. Whoever remained of Scarred One's tribe didn't worry her but the combination of Nightshade and Thunder was like Mammoth aligning with Bear. That alliance might be unbeatable.

Xhosa clutched her hands behind her back and squeezed until they stopped shaking. Only once they were steady did she motion to Viper, "Your tribe is welcome at my homebase."

"No. We stay here. I will train my People better. If we lose, I will find you."

"My People—we're moving but I don't know where."

"I'll find you if I must."

Xhosa and her warriors left before Sun rose from its sleeping nest. Once out of the cool air, the sticky heat smothered them and the flying insects bit relentlessly. She ignored both, eager to get back to her People. At no point did she reach out with birdsong. The risk of alerting Cucu'tez was too great. No doubt, the People's scouts had seen her arrival and would signal when they could. If not, it meant she would lead her group to the mountains.

It wasn't until she reached the cave that she heard, "Welcome back!"

She spun and saw Pan-do's grinning face. A weight lifted from her chest when Wind and Sa-mo-ke appeared also.

"We are glad to be back."

Xhosa and her warriors wiped their faces with the damp moss Wind handed them and she told how the People—with Viper—stopped Scarred One but not before he ended the life of Davos.

Her brow furrowed. "What's left of Scarred One's warriors are now allied with Thunder. If Viper can't stop them, she and her warriors will join us."

Wind's forehead puckered and he looked away. "Hate drives my brother. He will lose but maybe not to Viper." Then, his gaze fixed on Xhosa. "Seeker has been worried since you left. He says something's not right with the stars. He thinks Nightshade isn't dead."

Oddly, this comforted Xhosa. *It must be part of the plan.*

She shook her head. "He escaped and also partnered with Thunder."

She expected Wind to pale at the massive power this coalition brought against the People but instead, he guffawed, loud and long. She waited and waited more but it took an endless amount of time before Wind could control his mirth enough to explain.

"Don't you see, Xhosa? Those two—they're like fire and tinder. They are both egomaniacs, obsessed with their own power, with no respect for anyone. They will destroy each other, one at a time or both at once, without doubt and probably soon. You couldn't have brought better news."

That cheered Xhosa as much as Seeker's prognostication.

As they trotted back to the cave, Wind relayed the events that transpired in her absence. "The cannibals come closer each day. Pan-do and I believe if not for their fear of us, we would be overrun. We must leave before there are more of them than we can defeat."

"You have a plan?"

He nodded, the corners of his mouth pulling up and his eyes sparkling.

Xhosa yawned. "Do I have time to sleep?"

He flashed a grin. "Yes. We leave tomorrow when Sun sleeps. They won't expect us to travel in the dark."

Xhosa was happy to be home, with Wind, Pan-do, and a plan. Whatever was wrong, and that seemed to be a lot, they could solve together.

Even in a deep dreamless sleep, part of Xhosa's brain remained alert, ready should the cannibals find the People, but the night passed peacefully. For that, Xhosa was thankful. She needed her rest.

The next day, in case Those-who-eat-Others watched, everyone knapped tools, cleaned pelts, and engaged in normal activities. Qu'tez never let Cucu'tez go anywhere by himself. Wind and Pan-do's plan was dangerous but after spending time with Xhosa's People, Qu'tez had come to accept that victory went to those who earned it.

When Sun dipped below the horizon and before Moon arrived, the People snuck out of the cave in small clusters, each going a different direction as scouts might to confuse any who saw them. They reunited at a predetermined point down the forward path and continued together, detouring around all Those-who-eat-Others' hunting locations.

Xhosa set a quick pace, not slowing even after a spine burrowed deep into her foot. Her message: Tolerate discomfort. Adults carried the youngest, the People's future. Without them, the People would cease to exist. The elders understood this, knew they must keep up or be left behind. They had done the same as younger adults.

Qu'tez caught up to Xhosa. "Rul'ez and Asal'rez want to know when we are stopping."

Xhosa squinted up at Sun. After a moment, she answered, "When I say."

That wouldn't be for a very long time.

The grass gave way to glorious canyons with soaring sides. Sun shone warm but not hot. Ground birds pecked around the seedlings and chased crickets. A family of birds chased some noisy squirrels out of a nearby thicket but they resumed their barking from the shelter of another canopy. The subadults hit many of both with throwing stones and ate while walking, sharing with each other. Scouts checked the front- and backtrail and always found them empty. Still, carcasses and the People's own waste were buried, hiding their presence from scavengers and carrion birds. The People splashed through waterways rather than leave prints along the shores. They stopped occasionally to rest or drink, often continuing their journey under Moon's light.

Days passed and Moon shrank away to a sliver. The farther they went, the better Xhosa felt. The worry about Those-who-eat-Others, the Big Heads, and Nightshade melted away, replaced by an intangible feeling that life would be fine.

They entered the foothills as Sun slipped behind the clouds, highlighting the brilliance of the foliage, the reds and yellows reflecting off the boulders on the hillsides. Dust and Bird found a cave large enough to be a permanent homebase and everyone happily settled in, hoping it marked the end of migrating.

Around the fire one evening, after everyone had eaten well from a mountain gazelle, tubers, berries, and fruit, Xhosa motioned to the scouts. "Tell us about this area."

Dust began. "The slopes on Sun's sleeping side are not tall or steep. The other side drops to Endless Sea with only a narrow strip of shore between the rocks and the water. Bird and I stayed for more than a day and never saw Others anywhere on the shore."

Acto looked around, pawing at the dirt until he finally caught Qaj's eye. "It reminds me of our former homebase along another shore of Endless Sea. Food was plentiful between reeds, tubers, fish, birds, and the hard-shelled creatures."

Acto's hands drifted to a stop. When no one said anything, Dust continued, "The mountains to the front are treacherous. Bird and I trekked into them for over a day and still they ascended with no end in sight."

Xhosa motioned, gestures stiff, "Viper says none of her tribe ever reached the other side."

Wind added, "Before we consider that route, we must find out what is further up the mountains and on the other side. It may be no better than here."

Xhosa nodded. "If we can find Viper's friendly Others, they might know."

Dust gestured. "Bone and I did find the occasional sign of Others but few and well hidden."

Xhosa didn't respond for a breath, wanting to give Seeker an opportunity to voice his opinion, but he seemed distracted by the swirling dirt at his feet.

Acto stood, "My People—we will settle on the shore of Endless Sea. We invite any of you to come with us."

Qaj paled and Shaga stiffened.

Vaya edged toward Shaga and motioned to Acto, "I lived by the shoreline before being captured. I will go with you. Maybe I'll find my People there."

Shaga leapt to his feet. "No, we can't leave the People! We-we are too few—how will we survive?"

His father ignored the boy's concern. "The decision is made."

The People discussed both options—staying where they were or joining Acto—until no one could keep their eyes open. In the end, only Vaya would leave with Acto while the balance of the People would remain at this cave where they would try to find the Others Viper had talked about.

Everyone chose what worked best for them.

The next day, the two groups parted ways. Vaya's steps faltered and he turned back, searching, stopped when he found Zvi's sad face fixed on him. Neither said anything, simply stared and then Vaya hurried to catch up with Qaj and Acto. The boy's choice solved a problem for Xhosa. Vaya had yet to find a job that interested him that he did well. He couldn't understand the People's central concept that he shouldn't wait to be told what to do, that he must find what needed doing and do it. Xhosa had hoped that associating with Zvi, Seeker, and Lyta would show him how to contribute but when they worked, he switched to digging in the dirt with Acto, foraging only when told to do so. Both lived off the work of others, and that couldn't continue. Xhosa had talked to Mbasa who understood this was her responsibility because she had invited them into the People.

Acto and Vaya's leaving solved the problem but Shaga's departure was a loss for the People. He had learned to do most jobs well and made a lot of friends. In that way, she was glad he went with the Shore Dwellers. They would need his energy and leadership to survive.

As his father and mother walked toward the mountains, he stopped between the two clusters, head down, immobilized. Qaj shouted his callsign but the boy seemed unable to respond, his eyes now latched onto Mbasa, begging her to make this right.

She crouched in front of him, took his small hands in hers. "You are a skilled warrior and hunter, young friend. With practice, you will be better than me. Your tribe needs that expertise and knowledge. I count on you to keep them safe. I will see you again."

"I know that's not true, Mbasa. Seeker already told Vaya you won't be staying here. You will soon be too far away for me to find."

Mbasa smiled. "That may be true but look at Xhosa and Viper. They found each other though separated by many Moons of travel. We all go where we're needed, not where we choose. Remember the birdsong. If you call and I can hear you, I will answer."

The boy nodded and trudged toward his People. He didn't look back. Soon, the small cluster of Shore Dwellers became lost in the foothills.

Chapter 25

People's cave

The cave proved easily accessible to forests, grass, lakes, and plains. Herds of gazelle, elephant, Equiis, and many beasts they didn't recognize browsed the foothills. The females picked berries and fruit and with the children, dug roots and tubers, and collected more slugs, snakes, and ants than the People could eat. The males found slender saplings for new spears and located the area's boundaries and oversight positions.

The air cooled more each day, especially at night. The snow that coated the soaring peaks crept down the flanks toward the spike-leafed trees and the scree slopes at the base. Hunters searched for animals with warm pelts to replace the People's tattered skins.

Always, their senses tested the air for Others.

Morning dawned bright and cold. Today, Xhosa, Wind, and Spirit would search for the Others Viper had told them lived here, as well as a replacement for Xhosa's head pain treatment. She'd run out days ago and last night, as pain savaged her head and the world spun, all she could do was pant.

The two set a moderate pace though too slow for Spirit. The pups tried to follow but Spirit's growl sent them scurrying back to the den. Xhosa's wealth of hair glistened and swayed to her steps, warm against her back. As they traveled, they explored the foliage and shadows for movement, the ground for prints, their noses searching for unusual scents—especially the sweet smell of cannibals—but they found no sign of Others.

Xhosa pulled to a stop by a small copse of trees, head pounding but not as bad as last night.

"Those trees, Wind, with the gnarled bark, I think they're the ones Viper told me about."

Using her cutter, she chopped away a strip of bark and then separated the white inner layer from the rough exterior.

"She says I should eat the pulp."

The birds fell silent and a shiver went down her back. She kept her hands scraping at the bark and her head down. Spirit had disappeared, probably to check out whatever was watching them. Her spear lay on the ground at her side, close enough to grab, and her warclub rested on her back.

She wasn't worrying, just preparing.

The air around her changed and Wind stepped closer to her side. "We have company."

Xhosa gently picked up her spear and then raised her head as a handful of Others stepped out of the shadows. They stood quietly, spears pointed down, and stared at Xhosa and Wind. Xhosa sniffed. Their skins, though new, were rotting but nothing stunk of cannibal.

Behind them, a squirrel screamed, probably because of Spirit, and then scampered up a tree out of sight. A strange brown furry creature—maybe an oversized mouse—bounced away from the two-legged creatures.

Xhosa tilted her mouth up at the corners to communicate that she represented no threat to these Others. Wind did the same. After a quick survey of the gathering in front of her, she approached an older male. A white streak ran through his otherwise dark hair but his green eyes sparkled with energy and authority.

She motioned with Qu'tez's gestures, "I am Xhosa. This is Wind. We seek a new home."

The Others whispered to each other with sounds like Qu'tez's. Green-eyes dismissed her and turned to Wind, scrutinizing his knobby chin, long straight hair, over-long legs, and then everything else.

Finally, the male gestured, "I am Kasiika of the Islanders." His tone was flat and steady but bursting with resolve. The stubborn set of his jaw said he would be dangerous to cross. "We know of you from Ones-called-Mountain-Dwellers who live over there," and turned toward Viper's homebase. "We tried to greet you on your last visit but the storm forced you to leave." Xhosa detected no anxiety but more than a little curiosity.

That was good.

As he spoke, Spirit slipped to Xhosa's side, head raised, ears pricked forward. The hair on his neck bristled as his blue eyes fixed on Kasiika. After a huff, and another, his tail whooshed side to side. Kasiika mistook this friendly acceptance for a threat and stiffened, hand fisting his spear.

"Spirit is pack. Assault him, you assault us," Xhosa growled. "He greets you as a friend. That means a lot to Wind and me."

Kasiika raised his hands. "We have never seen a wolf befriend Others but this too, the Mountain Dwellers mentioned."

Wind gestured to the flatlands below the hills. "You are like those down there?"

Kasiika laughed, chuckling deep in his chest. "The ones that eat Others? No. We live up here. The cold keeps them away."

He reached out for Xhosa's hand, the one holding the pulp she hoped would fix her head pains. "If you eat that, you will get sick, maybe die."

Xhosa narrowed her eyes. "The Mountain Dwellers said it would help my illness. Their Lead Warrior now Leader—we helped each other escape those who captured us. Viper has no reason to wish me ill."

He motioned, "What you want looks almost the same. We lost several to this poisonous look-alike when we first settled here."

She sniffed the pulp. "It smells fine."

He patted his temples. "You have discomfort in your head?" Xhosa nodded, unhappy he'd announced her weakness to all. With a small, noncommittal gesture of one hand, Kasiika motioned, "Come," and left the way he had arrived, his warriors with him.

Before following, Wind whistled birdsong to those on the backtrail, explaining they had met friendly Others and were going to their base. The message would be relayed until it reached Pan-do. In the event Xhosa and Wind failed to return, Pan-do would start the search here.

The Islanders exited the forest and stopped immediately. A step further would have put them over the edge of a precipice. Kasiika trotted along the ridge and then turned onto a well-hidden trail that wound its way downward through gray rocky slabs bulkier than Mammoth. To Xhosa's eye, they seemed to have been tossed as Xhosa would scatter stalks of dry grass but what creature was big and strong enough to do that? The Islanders paid them no attention, descending quickly and without thought. Spirit instinctively picked areas with less loose gravel but whined when the People had to slide down on their bottoms. Xhosa tied a vine around him and then to her waist, motioned him down until his belly rubbed the ground, and then dragged him behind her. He yelped, clawing deep ruts in the soft earth as he slid. If he went too fast, his front legs wrapped around her and she slowed him. Both sighed with relief when their feet touched flat ground.

Kasiika motioned toward the distance. "This was a shortcut. You'll find the return trip longer but easier."

It took over a hand of Sun's movement overhead before they reached a narrow valley, flanked by steep rock faces and terminating at a waterfall. Its powerful spray drenched the surrounding cliffs until they glistened in the sunlight.

Kasiika continued through the valley, toward the waterfall. Xhosa didn't ask but wondered where he was going. The rocks would be too slippery to climb. Maybe there was some path around that she couldn't see. When Kasiika reached the cascading water, he and his group walked right into it so Wind, Spirit, and Xhosa followed. The heavy spray drenched them but sooner than expected, the deluge became only a mist. To Xhosa's surprise, behind the falls was a trail that led to another towering cliff, this one with steps dug into the side. Kasiika and his warriors ascended with impressive dexterity.

"You go first, Wind, with Spirit. I'll catch you two if something goes wrong."

Wind draped Spirit's front paws over his neck and back ones around his hips, secured the wolf with a vine, and started up. Spirit had been carried before so relaxed into the arrangement with only an occasional quiet moan. Xhosa scampered after them with the skill of the mountain goats who had taught her to climb, never looking down, copying where Wind put his hands and feet.

They finally breached the top and were greeted by a rugged landscape edged with barren hills and ragged gorges. A flat plateau stretched into the distance.

Kasiika dropped back and approached a shaggy-barked tree like the earlier one except this one had leaves tipped red. "This is the plant you need. You see the difference."

Xhosa flushed. "Viper didn't mention the color."

"The poisonous one doesn't grow on her side of the mountains."

While Xhosa stuffed it into her neck sack, Kasiika gestured, "There is a better treatment for what you suffer."

Without waiting for her response, he continued forward. Xhosa noted the location of these trees and hurried after him, knowing she could return if the new treatment didn't work. Soon, she made out caves ahead with handfuls of Others scurrying around in front. A burly red-haired male trotted toward them, his forehead creased with a frown. He had Kasiika's green eyes but instead of welcoming, his were stormy. They bounced from Xhosa to Wind, paused at Spirit, and then jerked back to Kasiika.

"Who are these you bring to our homebase?"

His gestures carried more irritation than she would expect when greeting strangers who you expected to be friendly. He was comfortable with authority but not with being challenged.

This must be the Leader.

Kasiika clarified, "These are the strangers we heard of from the Mountain Dwellers," and explained when this happened, the

Mountain Dwellers' description of the strangers, their background—on and on.

Impatient at Kasiika's rambling explanation and tired of being ignored, Xhosa interrupted. "I am Xhosa. This is Wind. The wolf is Spirit. We mean you no harm. We come in search of a new homebase." She mixed Kasiika's gestures with those from the Cave Dwellers and the Mountain Dwellers.

One-who-must-be-Leader cocked his head and motioned, "I am Betaaka, Leader of the Islanders. How do you know our gestures?"

"We live with Others like you."

Betaaka stiffened, eyes now fierce, mouth an angry line. Spirit's hackles rose and a soft growl rolled from his jaws. Xhosa touched Spirit's head without taking her eyes off Betaaka.

"You live with cannibals?"

"No," she corrected. "A small group of subadults escaped rather than join them. Like you, they look like the cannibals but don't consume the flesh of Others. We protect them because the cannibals, what they call Those-who-eat-Others, become increasingly hostile to Others. We found a cave up here, nearby, and hope to live amicably with the Others who call these foothills home. Like you."

He nodded, calmer, and Kasiika explained that Xhosa required a treatment for the ache in her head.

Betaaka called to a stout, green-eyed female. "Tuuka!"

She hurried over, taking in the Islander Leader as well as the newcomers. Gray streaked her thin hair and her body carried as many scars as most males. She stooped while walking, her fingers bent as so many elders were, but her green eyes were awash in the energy of youth.

Without a word, Tuuka squatted in front of Spirit, hand out, palm up. He panted his pleasure and she motioned to Xhosa, eyes still on Spirit, "I am Tuuka. I heal my People. You have someone like that?"

Xhosa nodded with a smile and placed her hand, palm open, on her chest. "I do that as well as lead. We are new to this area and I don't know the plants yet."

When Betaaka described what Xhosa needed, Tuuka patted her temples with her palms.

"Here?" Xhosa nodded and Tuuka motioned, "Come."

Xhosa followed the green-eyed female as she marched into a grove of tall thick-trunked trees. Xhosa glanced back when Spirit whined. At a subtle hand movement from Xhosa, he stayed with Wind, already deep in conversation with Betaaka and Kasiika.

Tuuka waved her hand in front of a tree that grew as tall as some hills. "The leaves are difficult to reach but you want what grows on the bark."

She approached one trunk and chipped away a lumpy, dark-colored fungus growing on the Sun side.

"Watch how I prepare it," and she headed back to the camp.

Tuuka settled in front of a flat rock, scraped it clean of debris and then pounded the fungus with the dull edge of her chopper until it became as smooth as a leaf and as crumbly as dry dirt.

"Eat as much as you want."

Xhosa rubbed it against the inside of her wrist. When that didn't turn red or bumpy, she placed a piece the size of her fingertip in her mouth. The flavor was mellow and earthy and the chunk dissolved on her tongue. By the time Betaaka motioned her toward the caves, her head tingled and the ache in her temples had receded.

Chapter 26

Islanders' camp

Betaaka welcomed Xhosa, Wind, and Spirit into the Islander cave. They shared a meal of nuts, berries, eggs, roots and something he called goat. Spirit's enthusiastic panting and dense warm fur brought shrieks of glee from children and adults. Satisfied he'd made new friends and could expect attention from any of them on demand, he rolled against Xhosa's leg and fell asleep, ear twitching occasionally to the unusual noises.

Wind and Xhosa squatted by Betaaka as they ate. Between bites, Wind asked about the area while Xhosa observed the Islanders. Like Qu'tez, they were small and slender with smooth, flat faces and Wind's jutting chin below their mouths. Many had green eyes and all had copious body hair. Red head hair seemed common and added a cheerfulness to the gathering, like flowers do in a meadow. It reminded Xhosa of Red Wolf. Overall, every one of them, male and female, looked well fed and sure of themselves. Despite that, when Xhosa managed to catch one of their eyes, the expression included hope, as though they'd been waiting for some solution to a problem and wanted it to be Xhosa.

She turned her attention to the group's Leaders, starting with Betaaka. He exuded power and a pride in his People that Xhosa respected. That sense of assurance was probably why the sudden appearance of tall, muscular, and well-armed strangers—with a wolf—didn't threaten him.

Tuuka wove her way through the crowd and crouched by Xhosa. Spirit lifted an eyelid, fixing a blue eye on the ground bird in her hand. Without removing the choice internal meats, she tossed it to him. The wolf swallowed it in two bites and fell back to sleep with a contented huff.

At Xhosa's surprise, Tuuka motioned, "Food is not a problem. This in front of you is a normal meal. Even when the earth freezes and animals tuck into underground burrows, we eat well from supplies gathered during the warm times."

Her hands fumbled to a stop and her eyes stared over her People, at nothing.

Xhosa wriggled around to hide their conversation and motioned, hands cupped, "What worries you, Tuuka, and your People?"

Tuuka's head dipped once and she rubbed her arm. "The cannibals—those who live where you did. They're the reason you left the flatlands?"

Xhosa considered Tuuka's question. If the Islanders and the People were to align, Tuuka had a right to know that the cannibals represented not even the worst of the People's problems. In her position, Xhosa would want to know.

She decided to ask her own question first. "Tell me about yourself."

Betaaka's attention swiveled from Wind to Xhosa's conversation.

Before Tuuka could respond, he motioned, "We are from a frigid island far away, much of it layered in ice so thick you can walk on it and snow that reaches our thighs for Moons before finally melting away."

Xhosa placed her palms together in front of her chest. "I don't understand 'island.'"

"It is land surrounded by water. Long ago, our fathers' fathers' fathers left in search of a warmer place to live."

Wind's joined the conversation. "You left on rafts?"

"Rafts?" Betaaka looked at Kasiika and then Tuuka but both shrugged. "We crossed Endless Sea on a narrow bridge that connected our island to an unending plateau. I am told that it was no wider than I am tall."

Xhosa motioned, "We know these bridges made of dirt. One once separated Endless Pond from Endless Sea but became submerged."

Betaaka waved her away. "I can't answer whether it still spans the water. None of us have ever gone back. Once across, we migrated until we reached here. This place with its many caves and plentiful food was all we needed until recently. For many of the reasons Wind has told me you seek a new homebase, we too want to leave."

"Have you always lived up here, where it's so cold?"

"We originally established our homebase below, on the flatlands. It overflowed with herds and friendly Others. We moved into the mountains when we realized down there was too hot for us. Remember, we are accustomed to cold worse than any here. After that, we visited only to trade mates which is how we missed the changes below.

"Gradually, between our occasional visits, the herds left and the plants dried up. By then, Those-who-eat-Others had arrived and many of those familiar to us disappeared. We assumed they left until the cannibals came after us. Then, we understood."

Betaaka's breath spun whitely in front of him, vanishing into the chill. Xhosa spread her hair over her arms for warmth and looked for the firepit. Was it possible, they like the Cave Dwellers, didn't know how to make fire?

When Betaaka said nothing more, Xhosa and Wind went outside to collect kindling and rocks and then placed them in the middle of the cave, the rocks in a circle and the kindling in a pile.

Betaaka watched and finally huffed. "What are you doing?"

Xhosa pulled fire stones from her neck sack and motioned, "Your People are shivering."

He looked around at Tuuka's blue lips, the children with their arms wrapped around their knees, and barked what might have been a laugh. "It is warm compared to the cold time."

Xhosa gathered a pile of kindling and motioned, "I'll build a fire. They'll appreciate the warmth. You won't survive the higher mountains without fire."

"That's impossible—"

Tuuka broke in, "Warmth would be nice."

Xhosa smacked the stones together above the kindling. It took many tries before a spark leaped to the tinder and ignited. Xhosa cupped the minuscule fire in her palms and placed it in the pit where it began to feed on the lavish supply of twigs and debris.

Betaaka's eyes popped open and a gasp came from Tuuka. Once the fire roared, everyone huddled around it, basking in the unexpected warmth.

When Xhosa noticed the Islander warriors staring into the bright light, she gestured to Betaaka, hands wide enough all could see, "Your warriors should be careful. If they look too long at the flames, they will not be able to see in the night. Before they leave the cave's interior, they should fix their gaze somewhere else until their eyes adjust to the dark."

The warriors looked around at each other and a few jumped up and ran outside, probably to confirm what she'd said. When they returned, they nodded.

Betaaka asked about the fire stones, prodding her for details which she freely gave. When she finished, he asked about her People.

Wind took over, describing the blend of groups within the People, including the wolves who joined after losing their packs. Wind described how each brought skills the others hadn't known, making the tribe a formidable force.

Finally, Xhosa motioned, "Betaaka. We've shared why we are here. Now tell me what worries your People and how you think we can help."

Betaaka's eyes hardened, maybe at her abruptness, and then his shoulders drooped. He waved a hand toward the fire pit. "As you just did. We respect fire's power to burn fields and forests but never did we think it could work with us rather than against us. With its warmth, we can live anywhere, even our island."

He said no more as though that was everything necessary.

Without a glance at Wind, Xhosa knew he had reached the same decision as she.

She motioned, "Betaaka. We must get back to our People. They will soon think we're in trouble and send warriors to find us. Come with us. Meet our People before you make any other decisions."

He motioned, "I trust you, One-called-Xhosa, but I have never met a cannibal who didn't try to eat me."

Xhosa smiled. "These are subadults and call themselves Cave Dwellers."

Except for one. Should she mention her doubts about Cucu'tez? A touch from Wind answered that. It was instinct, hers and Wind's, that told her not to trust Cucu'tez but nothing definitive. The Islander Leader should make his own decision. If he felt the same way she did, that would be proof enough.

Wind added, "I promise not to let them eat you."

Betaaka guffawed and made eye contact with each of his Leads.

"What if you stayed here with us? Our combined strength would surely persuade the cannibals to leave us alone."

Xhosa appreciated the offer but he might rescind it once he knew the entire truth.

She motioned to him, "There's more I haven't told you. Enemies pursue us. If they catch up, they will slaughter us and any with us."

"The cannibals?"

"No. Wind's former tribe. They are smart and have proven themselves more treacherous than any adversary we have ever faced."

Wind jumped in. "They are led by my brother. When our father died, Thunder drove me out. Without my presence to control him, he uses the tribe's power for his own purposes. Not all agree with that and he fears I will return and challenge his leadership. Rather than allow that to happen, he plans to destroy me.

"Xhosa has different reasons. Thunder killed her father and she seeks retribution."

Xhosa motioned, "If you align with us, you must fight with us, as we will with you against Those-who-eat-Others. We will understand if you choose not to." Her hands moved without apology as she stated these truths.

Betaaka roared with laughter. "Xhosa and Wind. My warriors and I relish a good confrontation."

Chapter 27

Islanders' camp

Something woke Xhosa. She shivered, moved closer to Wind, and then cracked an eye open. Toward the mouth of the cave were sparks of light and muted shadows—the fire was dying. She lurched to her feet, kicked the sleeping subadult tasked with feeding the blaze, and then tossed enough tinder in the flames to make it burn merrily.

Done, Xhosa padded outside and immediately wrinkled her nose. *The waste needs to be buried or it will attract predators.* She released her water and then stared up at Bright Star. It rested on the horizon where it always did but sparkled as though talking to her.

She yawned. *I don't understand, Bright Star,* and turned back to the cave.

Brush rustled behind her, too quick for the movements of the night hunters. Instinct threw her sideways as a warclub zinged over her head. Her weapons were inside so she snatched a rock and flung it at the dark male shape looming over her. He slapped it away as though it were nothing.

Xhosa glared at the dusky face framed in ragged hair with Wind's chin and a spear aimed at her "Who are you?" Instead of fear, fury saturated her voice.

Confused, he froze. Xhosa didn't. She seized the shaft of his spear in both hands and yanked downward with strength born of climbing rock walls chasing her next meal. It should have forced him to let go but he didn't even loosen his grip. Pulled two different directions, the shaft splintered, leaving her assailant with a broken stick and Xhosa a stone tip. Without releasing the damaged weapon, the warrior swung his warclub, one-handed. Xhosa dodged out of the way but not far enough and it slammed into her shoulder. The arm went numb and she curled inward, pretending to protect her injury. His eyes lit with the fervor of victory and he raised the splintered shaft, intending to thrust it through her neck. To do that required Xhosa remain still but she had piles of dead enemies who would attest that she rarely did the expected. In this case, she flung herself at her assailant and thrust the spear tip into his exposed armpit with such power, her fist slammed into his ribs as the stone tip penetrated deep into his chest.

He winced, and then blinked in surprise that this inferior was about to win. As he fell, she wrenched the shattered shaft from his body, tearing a ragged hole that allowed his life blood to pour out. Death claimed him quickly.

Wind huffed to her side, hand on Spirit's neck while the wolf sat complacently on his haunches, satisfied his packmate was secure.

Betaaka gaped, awed. "You won with nothing more than a broken stick, Leader Xhosa." He had never before called her Leader. "Where did you learn that trick?"

"The shaft? It was all I had. Well, and a rock."

Betaaka harrumphed. "Your Big Head enemies may be smart but you are clever. I am happy to fight with you."

Xhosa cocked her head, scrutinizing the oddity of the dead body at her feet. "This is a Big Head warrior, Wind. You see the healed wounds and old scars? He has been in more battles than me."

Wind bent over and stiffened.

Her eyes widened. "You know him?"

He nodded, one small movement. "He was my tribe's most notorious warrior. If I'd recognized him, I would have helped. No one beats him, Xhosa."

She huffed. "He can't say that anymore. Did Thunder send him?"

"Thunder won't relegate you to any of his warriors. He'll do it himself. This male came for me. You were simply in the way."

Xhosa shuddered. "He knew our location—"

"No, I think he stumbled on us."

"Where are the others that should be with him?"

"This one always preys alone. I doubt anyone knows his whereabouts." After a breath, he said to no one, "But if he's here, that means my brother is close."

Betaaka's gaze darted from Wind to Xhosa and back. "Is this one of the enemies you mentioned?"

Xhosa nodded. "I will understand if you no longer wish to partner with us."

He guffawed. "You mistake my question. This makes me even more eager to align with you!"

Xhosa motioned to Wind, "Sun will soon light the sky. Let's get ready to go."

By the time Sun's first rays lit the land, Wind and Xhosa's neck sacks overflowed with travel food, throwing stones, and healing plants. As they prepared to leave, Kasiika and Betaaka joined them as did two handfuls of Islanders, Betaaka's pairmate Zooka, their unnamed baby, and the healer Tuuka.

Xhosa cocked her head, allowed one corner of her mouth to rise, but said nothing.

Betaaka grinned. "We all wish to meet your People and these Others-that-aren't-cannibals. Isaalka will remain with my People."

As they traveled, Tuuka told Xhosa everything she knew about the plants they passed. When the Islander female left to talk with Zooka, Betaaka joined Xhosa and she asked him about his former homebase.

"Ice Mountains cover most of the area in cold times."

Xhosa's heart pounded. "Ice Mountains. We know these."

"Then you know the snow and ice makes them colder than other mountains. Every cold time, they encroached further into our home. Mornings, always someone had frozen to death. Finally, we had no choice but to leave."

He paused, a smile flitting across his lips, his thoughts far away. "But during warm times, grass grows as tall as children. Rain is abundant and herds overrun the area—great fat Gazelle with massive antlers, fur-covered Bison, and more ground food than we could eat. By our homebase along Endless Sea, we caught fish with our hands whenever we were hungry."

He grinned. "With your fire, we can survive the cold, Xhosa."

They finally arrived where Xhosa, Wind, and Spirit first met the Islanders. Xhosa chirped a birdsong greeting and Ngili immediately responded, *We hear you.*

Betaaka motioned, "What is that? You talk to birds?"

"To each other, with the language of birds. You will learn it."

Shortly after, two males rose out of the waist-high grass. Betaaka jerked, poised for battle, but Xhosa greeted them.

"Ngili. Tor. All is good?"

They nodded and she presented Betaaka, Kasiika, Tuuka, and the rest of the Islanders.

Xhosa motioned to Ngili. "We must hurry. It isn't safe here," and told him briefly of the Big Head whom she killed and what it meant about how much closer Thunder was than they had thought.

When they reached the People's cave, the Leads went off together while Tuuka and Zooka explored the cave with Siri.

Betaaka waved a hand over the People. "They don't look like you and Wind."

Xhosa didn't want to explain that she and Wind resulted from a mating between her People and Big Heads so responded simply, "We are a collection of People. You'll find we are all different."

She started to ask Pan-do where the Cave Dwellers were when they entered the cavern. Qu'tez led, Re'ez, Asal'rez and Rul'ez with him, all chattering about something Xhosa couldn't make out. At the back was Cucu'tez, alone, sullen, and angry, as usual. Betaaka bristled.

"You!" His eyes darted from Cucu'tez to Xhosa. "He is one of those who attacked my People! Why is he here?"

Cucu'tez's legs almost buckled and he grabbed Re'ez for support, then pushed her between himself and the Islander. Qu'tez moved toward Betaaka. His body shook but his eyes remained steady.

"No, friend-of-Xhosa, not us but I know who you mean."

Betaaka shoved his face close enough to Qu'tez's, spittle spattered the boy's cheeks as he spoke. "That one—he captured one of my People and chopped him apart piece by piece, for food. He pled for his own death. I lost this trying to rescue him!"

He held up his hand, showing the missing tip of his middle finger.

Qu'tez extended his hands, palms down. "That is why we left our former tribe. Eating Others changed them. Groupmembers we grew up with, we didn't even know anymore. We are no longer one of Those-who-eat-Others. Now, we are of the People."

Betaaka's face reddened and his breathing became more strangled with each word from Qu'tez. Finally, Tuuka plodded over to where Qu'tez stood, sniffed once and again, and then smiled.

"Betaaka," she motioned. "This boy does not stink as those do who eat flesh."

He inhaled and wrinkled his nose. "Something does," and peered beyond Qu'tez. Cucu'tez shuffled behind Asal'rez, the lone Cave Dweller taller than Cucu'tez.

Xhosa strode forward. "We call Qu'tez friend," and explained how the subadult invited her People to share his cave, helped them find hard stones for tools, and took them to the salt lake.

Betaaka listened but her words made him no less angry. Shoulders like rocks, jaw so tight, his teeth must hurt, he walked past Qu'tez, sniffed the next Cave Dwellers, but didn't stop until he reached Cucu'tez.

He snorted. "You're right, Leader Xhosa. One-called-Qu'tez doesn't smell of cannibal, nor those behind him, but this one, hiding behind One-called-Asal'rez as though I won't see him— he reeks!"

"If you have concerns about Cucu'tez, I am happy to talk about that later."

Her gestures said one thing but she hoped he grasped her true meaning. He breathed in deeply, thinned his cracked lips, and nodded.

When everyone left, he and Xhosa stayed behind. "I talked at length with Wind on the journey here. It is no coincidence your cannibal problems started with these Cave Dwellers. Most are innocent but one is a traitor. He must be dealt with before we proceed."

A menacing growl made them turn. Black Wolf stood by her den, legs spread, hackles stiff, facing where one of the large back tunnels bled into the main cavern. Feral eyes were locked on Cucu'tez. The subadult's panicked gaze jumped from Black Wolf to Xhosa and then calmed, taking on an evilness Xhosa hadn't seen in them before. Another growl, this one louder, from deep in Black Wolf's chest, and Cucu'tez left.

Chapter 28

People's cave

Each day, the cannibals ranged closer to the talus slopes that edged the People's homebase. Qu'tez proved instrumental in finding and observing his old tribe but Betaaka continued to growl at the anxious young male, asking why he didn't do something *this* way instead of *that* way and how he ever expected to become a valued member of the People. Qu'tez took it in stride. He admitted to Re'ez who told Siri who passed it along to Xhosa that in most cases, Betaaka was right. The boy instinctively understood that criticism from Betaaka meant he cared.

Or maybe Tuuka told him. She would know.

But Betaaka's treatment of Cucu'tez was different. On a good day, he greeted the subadult with frigid silence. On a bad day, he drove Cucu'tez from the cave. In fact, no one wanted Cucu'tez around. The scouts refused to include him when they explored the area even though he repeatedly said he could guide them around Those-who-eat-Others. When he adopted the deliberate slightly hunched posture of a warrior, caused by the warclubs strapped to their backs, everyone laughed at him, even the females. When he tried to mate with Rul'ez, she was always busy learning new skills or committed to grooming Asal'rez.

Qu'tez claimed Cucu'tez would learn to appreciate the People but Betaaka believed the subadult was there to spy for Those-who-eat-Others.

The time was fast approaching when the People had to do something about the cannibals which meant Betaaka must decide if he trusted the Cave Dwellers. If he couldn't, or could everyone but Cucu'tez, Xhosa would do what she should have done long ago.

She found Betaaka alone one day, slamming a rock into what would have become the tip to a shaft except it shattered under his anger.

"Leader," she interrupted as he searched for a replacement stone. She lowered her hands to make their conversation private. "You have spent sufficient time with the Cave Dwellers. I need your decision."

His body stilled for a long breath, only his eyes flashing from his Islander People to the Cave Dwellers and finally to Xhosa. His face gave away nothing until two deep lines formed in his forehead and his head dipped to the side.

"Before you disagree, let me explain why I'm right.

"My entire life, what I call instinct has always warned me of danger. It is why I took my People away from these flatlands long ago, even before the cannibals took over. My father was the same. I think Seeker has a version of this, as do you. It warned you Cucu'tez is trouble but you wanted proof, which became me."

Xhosa hid a smile. Betaaka was as smart as she'd hoped. "And what have you decided?"

He took a deep breath. "I'm sure you agree he's not here to escape the cannibals or protect his groupmates."

Xhosa glanced around to be sure they were alone and then motioned, hands quick, "I haven't changed my mind."

Betaaka thinned his lips and nodded. "And I have seen nothing to change mine, either. Are you willing to deal with him before we leave?"

Xhosa pushed her palms together in front of her body and then pressed her fingertips against each other. "Let me tell you a story. You've met Ant, the scout who walks with a limp. That is what remains of a massive boil that took over most of his lower leg. No matter what I did, it grew larger. It became apparent if I couldn't stop its growth, he'd lose his leg—or his life—so I did something I'd never before contemplated. I cut it out. It hurt him terribly though he never complained. Moons passed before it healed, leaving him with the limp he still has. But he lived, the boil was gone, and the People are stronger for having Ant's skills as a scout.

"It seems I have another boil to excise."

Nothing more needed saying.

The issue of the Cave Dwellers solved, Betaaka now ignored Cucu'tez and treated Asal'rez like any other warrior, but for some reason, he continued to snipe and growl at Qu'tez, challenging him any time the two were in the cave. It made everyone uncomfortable and finally, Xhosa had enough.

Qu'tez was resharpening the edges of a palm-sized handaxe he'd used to crack the long bones of a pig. Asal'rez was doing the same for a cleaver while Re'ez and Rul'ez worked on choppers required to cut roots and tubers.

Xhosa motioned to Betaaka, "You had a question for Qu'tez, didn't you?"

Betaaka grumped and then barked, "Qu'tez," his voice clipped.

When Qu'tez looked his way, Betaaka asked, "If your former People threaten your new People, whose side are you on?"

Xhosa froze. *That's what's bothering him.* She thought she knew but wanted to hear Qu'tez's answer.

The subadult stopped his work and looked at Betaaka, confused. "The People's, of course."

"But you were raised with Those-who-eat-Others. They have been your People longer than this new tribe."

Qu'tez's eyes filled with sadness. "Who I grew up with doesn't matter, Betaaka. These," and his gesture swept over not just the remnants of the Cave Dwellers but the People of Pando, Xhosa, the wolves, and the Islanders, "are my People. I appreciate contributing, to eating because of my efforts, to saving lives. No one taught me the skills your subadults learn as children. The Leads promised to once I—all of us—were older but never did. Our parents died so we could escape. I won't waste that."

His hands slowed and his eyes focused on the distance. When he couldn't continue, Re'ez did. "We fled the night Those-who-eat-Others killed our parents. No one noticed our escape because they were too busy with the slaughter."

Her voice shook with misery. A tear rolled down her cheek.

Rul'ez now took up the story. "We hid, always moving. We were a much larger group back then but our former groupmembers picked us off one after another."

When she stopped, Asal'rez started. "The last to die was Qu'tez's closest friend, Zak'ez. Those you see here," and he waved a hand over the few remaining Cave Dwellers, "are all that survive. We would be dead if not for Xhosa and her People."

After a breath, and another, Betaaka slapped the ground. "I believe you, One-called-Qu'tez, Re'ez, Rul'ez, and Asal'rez, former-Those-who-eats-Others. Joining forces will not only fend off assailants but find justice for you."

Betaaka didn't mention Cucu'tez. None of the Cave Dwellers corrected him.

A day later, Qu'tez approached Xhosa. "Dust and I found prints of Those-who-eat-Others. They are closer than ever before."

Xhosa shared this with Wind and Pan-do. "It's possible they are braver than we thought."

Wind motioned, "Or hungrier."

Pan-do rubbed a hand up his arm. "We all agree we must leave but aren't sure where to go. Betaaka wants to return to his Ice Mountains but we could also go to Viper's homebase. It's no colder there than where the Islanders live now and Viper never finds traces of Those-who-eat-Others anywhere around it. Betaaka might prefer it."

Wind nodded. "I'll talk to him."

A wail roused Wind. "My baby! Someone took him!"

He scrambled to his feet. Could it be Those-who-eat-Others? He had told Betaaka about the prints Qu'tez and Dust found and the need to leave soon, suggesting Viper's homebase might be an alternative to the Ice Mountains. After talking for a while, Betaaka had grunted. Not a yes or no but enough to indicate he considered it possible. They didn't have to decide until after the tribes agreed they could hunt together as one People. The Leads had planned to test that over time but if Those-who-eat-Others had stolen a child right out of the People's homebase, time was up.

And then there was Thunder. Wind could feel his brother, still at a distance but closer every day.

Wind raced out of the cave. Puffy pink clouds floated across the sky in golden streaks that faded to white as Sun revealed its face. The morning smelled humid but fear filled the air as did the pungent odor of diarrhea.

It didn't take long to find the female attached to the screech. Zooka was spiraling in crazed circles, eyes wild, arms flailing. Wind timed his movements and grabbed her by the shoulders, holding on until she stopped wailing.

"Zooka. Tell me what happened."

She bobbed her head while struggling to free herself from his grasp. "I came outside to relieve my night water, set him down over there to do the same."

She indicated a spot far enough from the refuse pit that the child wouldn't fall in but where she could watch him.

"When I turned back, he was gone!"

She fell silent, panting heavily, eyes rolling in a delirium of panic. Wind needed to let her go so he could track the child's footprints but he couldn't do that until she'd calmed enough to not damage herself. He looked around for someone to watch her while he was gone and found Tuuka. She was across the clearing, smiling, crouching in front of Black Wolf who was carrying Zooka's child by the scruff of his neck. The boy giggled.

At the sound, Zooka screamed louder. "Black Wolf eats my child!"

Spirit growled, blue eyes on the terrified female, hackles beginning to rise.

"Zooka—stop!" Betaaka ordered.

She immediately fell silent, raced toward the boy and clutched him to her chest as she pitched forward and back.

Betaaka seemed speechless, eyes wavering from his pairmate to the anomaly of a wolf rescuing a child. Wind figured he'd better explain.

"Black Wolf has done this before, Betaaka. Once, a former-groupmember's child disappeared and Black Wolf brought him back to us. I don't understand why but she seems to consider the People's children her responsibility."

When Zooka had calmed, Tuuka approached Wind. "You have Black Wolf's callsign wrong, Leader. She is Ocha—savior. No wolf has ever saved the life of an Other, yet this one has done it twice."

Seeker wandered over from whatever he had been doing at the edge of the clearing, head back, scanning the sky, seemingly oblivious to the lost child or Black Wolf's rescue or the healer's statement until a smile swept his face.

"Ocha. Yes, you're right, Tuuka. Thank you."

Betaaka scratched his chest, plucked a tiny bug from the hair and popped it in his mouth. "Ocha?"

Zvi explained, "We learned Spirit's true callsign from a stranger, too."

Black Wolf—now Ocha—huffed, head cocked, message clear to any who understood wolf, *What took you this long to find my callsign?*

For the next days, Wind, Ngili, Xhosa, Hecate, Betaaka, Kasiika, and a mixed collection of People and Islanders hunted together, to establish whether their methods were compatible. To the Islanders—as it originally had been to the Cave Dwellers—hunting meant stabbing an animal to death. Betaaka bristled at Wind's suggestion they throw the spear from a distance, waved aside Qu'tez's protests that his People had come to realize how well it worked.

"My People are brave. Hooves and horns don't frighten us, and close means accurate."

Wind asked, "How many are injured trying to bring down Gazelle or Bison?"

"Many, of course. It is part of hunting."

"No, it isn't, not the way we do it."

Betaaka snorted. "We will show you."

They tracked a herd of gazelle, the People behind Betaaka's hunters so as not to interfere with their regimen. Though the Islander males moved quietly, the prey smelled them and fled. His hunters boldly gave chase but quit when the animals disappeared over a rise. Two healthy bisons escaped in the same way, though Betaaka did get close enough to spear another.

After a family of wild pigs eluded the Islander spears, prey Hecate and Ngili could have brought down by themselves, Wind gathered the males and motioned with strong expansive hands, his facial expressions open, "I've rarely experienced such daring and bravery as from your group. I am proud to hunt with them."

Betaaka's chest puffed with pride. "They did well today."

His males nudged each other and spread their feet.

Wind continued, "You act with the courage of Cat," and Betaaka stomped his feet, thinking this a compliment.

Until Wind explained, "Cat sneaks close enough to pounce. If her target flees, she chases a short time and then moves on, as you do. But you don't have Cat's speed, tearing claws, or deadly fangs which means you aren't as effective. I wonder, why do you hunt this way?"

No one spoke. Wind didn't expect them to. He motioned, eyes intent, hands open, "I can answer that. When the animal you chase pulls away, you assume it'll continue forever so you quit. But it must stop eventually to fill its lungs and cool off. While it rests, you could catch up."

Betaaka bristled. "When we did, it would run again."

"And you would again catch up."

Betaaka stamped his feet, fists so tight he could barely gesture. "But they would run again. We would never get close enough to stab them!"

There were nods but also anger.

Wind motioned to Hecate. "Tell us how often you slay quarry by stabbing it?"

Hecate scoffed. "It's almost impossible. Betaaka did well today to kill the one bison. Even with a dung pelt, the sway of grass or a covey of startled birds gives us away. And getting that close to their horns, claws, hooves, and teeth is dangerous. No, if we can't spear them from a distance, we chase. They invariably tire before we do."

Ngili nodded agreement but Betaaka frowned. "That isn't true. They always outrun us."

Wind motioned to Betaaka, "Because you quit. My hunters never quit, whether it takes a hand of Sun's travel overhead or all the daylight. Eventually, always, the animals become too exhausted to run. They stand unmoving, legs shaking. We slay them without imperiling any of our People.

"It is how Hyaena kills. It is what I did with the Big Heads."

Ngili shrugged. "Thanks to Wind, we lose few males and bring back more meat."

Betaaka opened his mouth but said nothing, his mind busy.

The Islander Leader was smart so it didn't surprise Wind when he motioned with one sharp chop, "Show me."

The next day, the People demonstrated how they hunted. No matter how many times their targets fled, the hunters always caught up when the animals stopped to rest. Finally, the weary animals couldn't run anymore, not even to dodge the weapons. The males slayed as many as they could carry and with no injuries.

On the backtrail to the cave, Wind stopped at a grove of slender saplings so the males who required a new spear could harvest a trunk or limb That night, by the fire's light, while the females and subadults skinned the carcasses, Wind taught the Islanders who had lost their spears how to shape and smooth the shafts so they would glide straight.

When Sun awoke the next day, Wind joined Betaaka for this day's hunt, Spirit and Ocha at the Big Head's side, panting their excitement, eyes alert, and ears tweaked.

Wind gestured, "Today, Spirit and Black Wolf—Ocha—join us. You will appreciate them so much you'll never want to hunt without wolves."

Doubt darkened Betaaka's eyes, as though sure the wolves would claim the dead prey as their own, but he pressed his lips together and remained silent. By the time their shadows shrank to a dark pool at their feet, Spirit had routed a pig from hiding. Ocha had driven a bison into the males' spears, and both wolves had protected two birds brought down with throwing stones until they could be retrieved.

As daylight waned and they prepared to return to the cave, Spirit froze in place, hackles up and tail straight back. A stench wafted across Wind's nose, wet animal mixed with decaying carrion. He found the source across the clearing.

"Bear," Wind motioned to Betaaka. "Is that a cub or adult?"

Neither male would end the life of a youngster. They wanted it to live long enough to have cubs of its own.

Betaaka motioned, hands quick and sure, "A cub's stomach wouldn't bounce off the ground as he walks. Nor do cubs have such small ears. Like their paws, they are huge until the cub grows into them. And if it is a cub, the mother should be here to protect it."

Wind focused on Ocha and Spirit. "The wolves smell only one feral scent. This must be a new adult trying to prove itself."

Betaaka huffed. "Not today."

Later, as the hunters divided up Bear's carcass, Betaaka tossed a limb to Spirit and Ocha.

"They earned it."

The wolves snapped it up and trotted toward the homebase where they would share it with the pups.

Ant hobbled toward the cave favoring his foot, which put him far behind everyone else. His mouth salivated at the earthy, grass scent of Bear. Its taste resembled Gazelle but sweeter and chewier, with a feral tang Ant found irresistible. The fat and blood in its tissues, what kept it alive during the cold time, would instead fill Ant with energy only drawn from meat. The last time Ant ate Bear, there was so much fat along its back—balls of it stuffed in every corner of the carcass—it lasted for days.

Ant sucked in his breath and winced but didn't slow. His swollen hand, already the size of his arm, throbbed so badly, he switched his spear to his weak hand.

I'll ask Siri to look at it before eating.

He wanted to slip in unnoticed but Bird saw him, mouth set in a grimace as she looked at his mutilated hand and gimped foot.

"What happened?" she asked as she joined him.

"Nothing, but I would like Siri to look at it." When Bird huffed, he added, "Well, maybe more than nothing... "

He wriggled into position where Dust wanted him, far away from where the main part of the hunt would be and downwind. If Mother Bear charged in to save her cub, Ant would warn the hunters.

The plan fell apart as soon as it started. Bear roared and that terrorized an Okapi herd Ant had smelled not far from Bear. The frantic animals thundered toward him, their only goal to escape Bear. If it had been a gazelle herd, he could have scuttled out of their way but Okapi were bigger and faster, and with their lethal hooves and head of many horns, aggressive when threatened. Ant had no intention of challenging them. All he wanted to do was scurry out of their way.

He breathed a sigh of relief as Okapi roared past at a safe distance but then, Bear bellowed again. This caused one frenzied creature to dart away from the main group and toward Ant. When the young male dodged, he tripped in a rut, threw his hand out for balance, and the Okapi trounced it. Ant swallowed a scream and lost hold of his spear. By the time he fumbled around with his good hand, found the weapon, and prepared to launch it, Okapi had escaped.

Ant huffed in frustration and started to rise but collapsed with a gasp, pain shooting up his leg and down to his toes. Awkwardly, one-handed, he wrapped his swollen ankle and his mangled hand in leaves, and then limped and hissed his way back into position. The hunters finished cutting Bear into totable pieces and headed back to the camp.

Ant started to follow but Dust motioned, "Watch the backtrail."

Dust didn't see his bloody hand or gimp foot and Ant kept quiet, wishing he'd remembered to refill his neck sack with pain plants. Not until everyone was well on their way to the cave did Ant head back, hoping to sneak in undetected.

But Bird was waiting.

"So, you see, I'm fine," but then he stubbed his injured foot on a buried rock. With a yelp, he unconsciously leaned against Bird and hobbled to where Siri stood. Scouting was not risky work but Ant found perils where no one else did. Once, a boil ate through his calf. Another time, he'd stepped into molten lava while crossing a volcano.

Siri got started. "We'll try to save your hand, Ant."

"You must. I am worthless without it."

Never would he be a burden to the People. He refused to scream as she ground the bones against each other, trying to shove the pieces into place and finally harrumphed, unable to hide her disgust.

"What comes next will hurt."

And she chopped the finger off with a handaxe. His eyes popped open and he gritted his teeth so hard his jaw ached but managed to block the horrified scream in his throat.

She stuffed the bloody stump with honey and moss, tied it in a leaf, and rolled back on her haunches.

"I saved your hand. You won't climb boulders as well but you'll scout fine. Now go eat. Do you want a stick?"

He waved it away, fists clenched. "My foot doesn't hurt." At least, not compared to his hand.

Thankfully, Bird didn't believe him and surreptitiously palmed a root bundle into his hand. He chewed hurriedly and swallowed. By the time they reached the communal food pile, the misery had become background noise rather than claws tearing into his hand. His belly grumbled. He was about to snatch a leg when Xhosa blocked him, gazing at his injury.

"Can you work?"

Her motions carried neither sympathy nor irritation but he knew at some point, she would tire of his constant injuries. He didn't want it to be today.

He pasted a fake smile on his lips and motioned, "It's one finger, Leader. I have many."

Chapter 29

People's cave

Besides the bear, the hunters also slayed two pigs, an okapi, and a massive bison. The bear and bison pelts would keep Zvi and Stone warm through the cold time though only just. Both were pleased to have the pelts because the cold would soon be upon them. The bees had left, animal fur had thickened, and many critters spent all daylight building nests and dens to protect against the coming frigid air.

The People, including the Islanders, gathered in the cave to clean and preserve the skins. They shivered, their breath white clouds in front of their mouths, and edged as close to the fire as possible. Most days, a crisp coolness replaced Sun's warmth, driven by a chilly wind blowing out of the hills. On a bad day, it thrashed the trees, whipping their bare branches in a frenzy. Most of the People still remembered crossing Viper's mountains, the wind gusting through the snow-laden passes freezing their hair and swathing their thin pelts in ice. Even during the day, their bodies had shivered so much that the simple act of walking turned into a stumbling trudge forward using their spears as walking sticks.

Those who stopped shivering died.

This homebase in the foothills, though colder than the flatlands below, would be remembered as a warm haven.

That night, everyone worked. Some scrubbed pelts and applied salt to make them last longer. Others sharpened stone tips, shaped antlers and horns into diggers, and smoothed warclubs. And everyone ate—legs, ribs, internal meats, even the paws and hooves. The snapping and crackling fire was pleasant and the smoky scent calming.

As fatigue overtook them, many settled into their nests. The youngsters Kiska and El-ga crouched by the pit, their task to feed the voracious appetite of the flames. Wind, Kasiika, Bird, and Dust left to patrol the perimeter. Qu'tez and Asal'rez joined them. It had been decided they would leave this good cave as soon as the scouts verified travel was safe. There would be little if any notice but the People were used to that. Everyone was determined to be prepared.

"Xhosa."

Seeker sidled up to Xhosa and stared into the darkness. She tried to see what caught his attention but found nothing.

Whatever he had to tell her she hoped would be quick. The hot spikes from the head pains had become worse than usual and she hadn't had time to collect the plants that treated them. The throbbing faded when she slept but reappeared slowly after daylight, adequately controlled if she kept busy. But today, they ground into her temples and pounded at the back of her head.

Seeker motioned, hands firm but eyes distant, "The stars talk to us. Come." A slight frown creased his placid face and he ascended to the precipice behind the People's cave.

She rubbed her temples. "What worries you?" She mumbled too quietly for him to hear, turning slowly so she didn't jostle her head more than needed.

Ignoring the numbing fatigue from the long day hunting and then the night cleaning pelts, she trudged after him, clumsily ascending to the bluff. From this high point, dots of light sparkled in the blackness with nothing to block their brilliance. Seeker flopped onto his back, arms stretched out, eyes locked overhead. He wriggled into the cold ground, his thin pelt scarcely covering his dangling parts. A smile crept over his face.

Xhosa collapsed next to him. The warm ground felt good despite the poke of tiny pebbles and the tickle of grass on her legs. The air smelled clean as though scrubbed by the darkness. She stared at the miasma above, the stars and their placement as familiar as the hills and waterways that cut the land. Seeker had explained the movements of these tiny balls of light, when they nudged together or drifted apart, which arrived or departed.

One star caught her attention. "Always-there Star is brighter than usual, isn't it?"

This one always graced the night sky, no matter where they migrated. Pan-do said that wasn't true in his former homebase which sent Seeker into a tizzy of excitement to go where Pan-do came from. And Seeker might have if the stars hadn't begun again to speak with him.

"Look to its side, above Scooping Hand."

A faint smile pulled at the corners of her mouth. "I see it."

"Scooping Hand never moves from a position opposite Butterfly." He pointed to a collection of stars that could look like a butterfly if you tilted your head and squinted. "They both rotate around Always-there Star…"

He droned on. Xhosa bit back a yawn, forcing herself to listen. He always had a point but must first provide background. Usually she enjoyed that but tonight, it threatened to put her to sleep.

She jerked awake when Seeker said, voice so calm she almost missed its importance. "Watch."

A herd of stars appeared on the far side of Endless Pond—over her former homebase—and stampeded across the night sky, charging through everything in its path. Along its backtrail flowed a serpentine tail longer than the assemblage itself, pulsing with colors.

"I've never seen that before, Seeker."

Seeker motioned serenely, "Nor I. Look—it is going to disappear over the horizon, by Bright-star-that-doesn't-twinkle. I have never seen it with those-that-stampede."

Xhosa studied it. "The one that almost touches the ground—it dwarfs every other star."

He smiled. "So you understand."

"Hunh?"

He heaved a sigh. "Bright-star-that-doesn't-twinkle and its herd want us to leave, Xhosa. Immediately."

"No. The scouts will tell us when the cannibals are too close. It's getting cold. Those-who-eat-Others don't like cold. Wind and I have been discussing the possibility of waiting until the warm air returns."

Seeker looked at her as he might a child who can't see the truth. "You didn't notice where the tail points? It's not warning about cannibals. Your scouts can't help you with this."

Xhosa crossed her arms over her chest, hugging her body. "Do they tell you whether we should go to Viper's homebase or the Ice Mountains?"

Seeker scratched his head. "They will send a guide."

When Seeker said no more, Xhosa yawned and returned to the cave, hair bouncing against her muscular back, blowing in the cold breeze. Misty raindrops splattered against her arms making her shiver.

The next day, Xhosa awoke, reveled momentarily in the pain-free morning and then told Wind, Pan-do, and Betaaka what the stars told Seeker.

Betaaka motioned, "They're right—he's right. The cannibals won't attack this close to the cold time unless they're starving, which they aren't."

Pan-do motioned, "So it must mean Thunder, that he's close."

Wind stopped him, hands rough and quick, "When I lived with my father's tribe, Thunder and I knew where each was even if we weren't close. The stars are right. Thunder is too close. You must go, all of you, but not me. I will wait here for Thunder. I'll kill him if the opportunity presents itself. His warriors won't continue without him. Most of them don't understand his vengeance toward me or Xhosa and those that do don't agree. When I finish, I will catch up."

Wind was about to say more when Qu'tez entered the cave carrying two ground birds. Betaaka raised his arm and summoned the boy. He trotted toward them, eyes flicking from one to the other, clearly wondering if he was in trouble. The nearer he got, the slower his steps, and the thinner his lips.

Betaaka grinned at his discomfort. "Don't worry, Qu'tez. You are among friends. We respect your courage. When we leave, which will be soon, you join us."

Relief washed over Qu'tez's face. "We are ready. If we go into the mountains now, Those-who-eat-Others will stay here, no matter how hungry they are. They detest the cold air."

Betaaka held a hand up. "Not all of you can come. Asal'rez, the females, and of course you, but not Cucu'tez. And you mustn't tell him."

Chapter 30

People's cave

It was decided. They would leave in two Suns. The day prior to departure was a frenzy of preparation that stopped abruptly when Viper sprinted into camp trailed by a handful of warriors, each with unhealed gashes on their bodies and dried blood clinging to their spears. Many among the People knew the Mountain Dwellers and acknowledged them with a wave but Viper never paused until she found Xhosa, with Wind.

"Xhosa!" Viper lurched toward her, face gray with exhaustion. "My People—they are being slaughtered!"

Wind caught her as she collapsed, pulled water-soaked leaves from his neck sack and pushed them into her hands. She sucked greedily, her color slowly returning to a healthy dark sheen. Siri and Honey did the same for the rest of the Mountain Dwellers.

Viper took a deep shuddering breath. Her left eye was green and watering, her right, black and swollen, the cheekbone below it shades of purple, blue and yellow.

"Others—they hide—pick us off. I can't stop them, Xhosa—I barely escaped. Please—help us!"

Xhosa motioned, her cupped hands emphasizing her confusion, "But Scarred One and Fang are dead. No one else in that tribe has enough skill—"

Viper shook her head. "Not them. Yes, they are there but following orders," and her tired red eyes rested on Wind. "From Big Heads. They are vicious and the scouts say more are coming, a Moon away, maybe two. If I don't get help, my People will disappear!"

Wind blinked, mind racing, and then gazed into the distance. "It is Thunder, Xhosa. He doesn't want Viper's homebase. He wants to destroy her People so they can't help us."

Xhosa rose with athletic grace, already reaching for her spear but Wind stopped her.

"It's my brother. He attacks Viper because of me. I'll stop him."

He smelled the anger that swept her body, saw it in the stiff set of her shoulders, and blocked it with his hand, palm forward.

"Don't argue, Xhosa. I must do this. I know him better than anyone else in his life. I can figure out how to stop him. If he weren't so crazed by anger and power, he'd know this is a mistake. I will make him see that."

He caught Xhosa's eye and wouldn't let it go until she agreed. "Wait if you can until I return. If the cannibals attack, leave. I know where to find you."

When she said nothing, he left to prepare.

Xhosa's head spun and pain stabbed deep into her temple. She closed her eyes, ignoring the shouts of warriors and the scrapes of weapons being gathered, focusing inside her head, behind her eyes, waiting for what Betaaka called instinct. He told her to trust it, that it never guided him wrong. Without expecting to, she found calm, like a pool of clear water, where chaos was moments before.

Why didn't I see this before?

Everything the People had survived the last handfuls of handfuls of Moons—traveling across unknown lands, defeating enemies, solving problems they had no idea existed, Hawk's death and Nightshade's treachery—all brought them to this day. She considered what the stars told Seeker, that change was coming and they would send a guide. Despite what often seemed bedlam, Seeker's guidance had always been true.

It took a long quiet moment, willing the facts to come to her, and then they did.

The solution—it's simple.

Her People were being stalked by two enemies, two tribes with nothing in common except their battles against the People. She must persuade them to turn their fury on each other rather than her, but how?

And then she saw how.

When she opened her eyes, her head pain was gone. Purpose had replaced confusion. Wind's plan was a good one, probably the smart move, but it was predictable. This strategy wasn't, and it would work.

She smelled Viper at her side, not the scent of fear anymore, but trust. When Xhosa looked at her, the undamaged eye burst open and a smile spread across her face.

Xhosa motioned, "Of course I'll help."

Pan-do shook his head with a grin, as though he'd expected it.

Wind dropped to Xhosa's side. "No, you can't—I know you, Xhosa—Don't even think about it—never mind. *We* will do this. Pan-do and Betaaka can prepare the People to leave when we return."

"No—"

"Xhosa," he interrupted, abruptly. "My father knew Thunder's mind was broken. As he died, he made me vow to take care of his People, no matter the cost. It's time I fulfilled that promise."

Xhosa grimaced which made Wind smile. "Not lead them. This, with you, is my home, but I must confront my brother. He won't quit, ever, but I can end it by winning."

Xhosa cocked her head. "Have you ever beaten him?"

Wind chuckled. "Never. Which means he will underestimate me."

She shook her head. "I too made a promise, to my father, to protect his People—"

He interrupted, "He always understood that to protect those important to you sometimes requires a fight."

Viper grinned which made Xhosa smile. If anyone knew her better than Wind, it was Viper. That's what happened when you spent Moons together as slaves to tyrants, surviving because of each other.

Xhosa gestured to Viper, hands wide enough for all to see, "Thunder has no idea our impatience with him is as deadly a weapon as his need for revenge. Wind and I will rescue your People and then together, we will leave for a new homebase."

Betaaka shouldered his way to her side. "I come with you. Kasiika can guide everyone to our homebase if need be—"

Xhosa stopped Betaaka, her eyes grim, mouth turned down at the corners. "This isn't your battle, Betaaka. I release you from your promise. I need to leave knowing you and Pan-do will make sure our People are safe. Wind and I will find you when we finish." She paused a breath, placed a hand on Betaaka's chest. "We all know some day we will die but that instinct you told me about, it tells me that won't be today."

"I'm coming," Betaaka said, as though she hadn't spoken, an edge in his voice.

Xhosa scowled. "Why does no one listen to me anymore?"

Pan-do laughed. "That's how you wanted it, Xhosa. *Allow everyone to voice their thoughts.* Well they are."

When Pan-do paused, Betaaka continued, "No more discussion!"

A rumble of agreement rolled from his warriors.

When Xhosa waved a hand through the air, Betaaka continued, "Here's my plan. It's simple and will work. We overwhelm those at Viper's homebase. They won't expect so many skilled fighters. We rescue the Mountain Dwellers, return here. Qu'tez believes the cannibals won't attack until Moon disappears. We will be back by then. With our full force back together, we extinguish the Big Heads, leave their bodies for the cannibals. Then they won't follow us."

Xhosa cocked her head, sifting through the details, and finally blinked. "This could work with one change. I know how to get rid of Thunder and the cannibals without costing us a single life."

Wind and Betaaka looked at her expectantly but instead of explaining, she patted Viper. "If this works, you will be doing us a favor."

The next morning, Xhosa strapped her warclub to her back, grabbed her spears, and hurried out of the cave. Tor, Mbasa, Ngili, Bone, Viper with her warriors, and Betaaka with his, stood ready to leave. Pan-do, Sa-mo-ke, Stone, Talon, Zvi, Snake, and Ocha would remain to protect the People should Those-who-eat-Others show up.

Before they could leave, Bird raced in, body slick with sweat. "Those-who-eat-Others are coming! They have a large group, all with weapons, and headed for this homebase."

Xhosa sniffed once and again. "Where's Cucu'tez?"

Qu'tez hurried up, distraught. "Gone. I told him we would leave him unless he proved his trustworthiness. I thought I was helping but I made it worse—this is my fault." His voice cracked but his face distorted with rage.

Pan-do motioned to Xhosa, "Go. I can handle this but it would help if you told me your plan."

Xhosa placed her hand on his arm. "Prepare for a battle like no other, Pan-do. That is all you need to know."

"But—"

Xhosa stopped him. "I'll explain more when we return."

Pan-do paused a breath and then smiled, a sparkle in his eye. "Take as many warriors as you need. I too have a plan and it will work with whomever you leave."

Warmth flowed from Xhosa. Pan-do was cleverer than any male she knew. Whatever his plan, the cannibals would never again underestimate the will of her People.

Qu'tez moved forward. "Asal'rez and I know how Those-who-eat-Others think. We'll stay with Pan-do. They won't be able to trick us."

Without another word, Xhosa and her assemblage left. Going at a ground-eating pace, they faded into the foothills.

Pan-do beckoned Qu'tez. "They haven't attacked. What are they doing?"

Qu'tez motioned, gestures low and in front of his body, "Watching. If not for Isaalka and the Islander warriors, they probably would have attacked by now. When I was part of Those-who-eat-Others, before they became cannibals, stories abounded about the mighty Islanders who defeated Bear, swam flooded rivers like fish, and hunted in the coldest air with no pelts. We feared them and now Those-who-eat-Others probably fear you because they align with you."

"When will they confront us?"

"When they're done watching," and Qu'tez left to sharpen a handaxe.

Before the day ended, the People had slain two cannibal scouts and the next day, two more. They left the bodies where they died. Shortly, they disappeared.

Qu'tez motioned to Pan-do, "The scouts we killed were sent to spy on us, poke at our boundaries, see how close they could get and how we would respond. We should strike first, before they're fully prepared."

Pan-do was standing on the bluff, watching for movement, listening to the silence of the insects, both revealing where his opponent hid.

"I need them closer."

In fact, he needed them in the talus slopes at the base of the hill.

"Pan-do! They are at the hill!"

Pan-do turned to his warriors. "It is time."

Each knew exactly what he must do and all were eager to start.

One behind the other, they sprinted to a canyon a short distance from the cave. It was the only way to reach their homebase so once the cannibals descended the hill, they must pass through it on their way to the cave. The People took up assigned positions—Talon, Snake, and Starlight hidden by the entrance, Kasiika and Zvi concealed at the exit. Pan-do, Sa-mo-ke, Stone, Hecate and the rest unfurled along the bluffs, eyes fixed below.

Sun was at its highest when a flurry of ground birds exploded from a scrub-filled fissure. Beneath Pan-do's feet, the earth rumbled.

Pan-do grinned to himself. He had hoped for overwhelming forces. It seemed that would happen.

At his side, Stone nodded. Excitement lit the burly male's face, his body taut but not rigid, his attention riveted to the expanding dust cloud.

Those-who-eat-Others entered the gorge without a glance at the crest. Hecate lit her shaft but didn't throw it. Not yet. She waited until the final male was well within the walls. He tipped his head up, saw her with the fiery stick but dismissed both, probably wondering what one female could do.

When this last male was too far into the gorge to escape, Hecate revealed the power of one. She hurried along the line of warriors, touching their lances with her fire. Once lit, they moved to the edge of the bluff. One cannibal in the center of the pack screamed to those around him but it was too late.

Pan-do launched the first of the flaming spears. It crashed into a pile of dry debris Pan-do had spread across the width of the canyon, beyond the last male. The flame popped and sparked, found its food, and spread. Those at the back laughed. They thought Pan-do missed.

Simultaneously, at the canyon's front, Sa-mo-ke's blazing shaft landed in similar dry stubble spread earlier across the gorge. It too exploded and quickly dispersed from one side of the gorge to the other.

The cannibals stopped, confused as to what they should do, and then reversed but behind them, a wall of flames roared. More fires popped up in strategically placed debris piles within the group until finally, pandemonium broke out. The cannibals shrieked, frantic for a way out. Those who bulled their way through the fire were cut down by the People's warriors. Some tried to climb the rocks only to be skewered by those above.

It didn't take long before the one-sided battle was over. Pan-do walked through the charred bodies, kicking some to be sure life had left, taking any weapons that appeared usable. Only when he'd convinced himself that no one survived did he lead his warriors back to the People's cave and the plan's next step. They hid in a copse of trees and watched. A cluster of Those-who-eat-Others clambered up the hill behind the cave and dropped into the back entrance. No one knew about that opening except Pan-do, Xhosa, and the Cave Dwellers.

Pan-do motioned to Kasiika, "Those-who-eat-Others are going to be disappointed."

The remains of the People, mostly females, children, subadults, and elders now carrying spears as they did in their youth, had left when Pan-do did, leading the warriors to the gorge. By now, this group was well on their way to the Islander's homebase.

Pan-do watched the cannibals mill around in front of the cavern, confused by its emptiness. After a long time, one of them smelled the stench of burnt flesh coming from the canyon, yelled at his groupmembers, and sped toward it.

Pan-do and his warriors caught up with the rest of the People. He motioned to Kasiika, "Maybe they'll forget about us for a while."

Kasiika, responded, "Or forever."

Chapter 31

Path to Viper's homebase

"Xhosa! Our cave is burning!"

Eyes wide, breath ragged, salt tingeing his lip white, Bone was closer to panic than she had ever seen him. A cool breeze did nothing to offset the sweat-soaked pelt clinging to his chest. He yammered about the clouds of smoke by the People's cave, the noxious stench of burned flesh he could smell even from this far, the gathering flocks of carrion birds.

Xhosa wanted to let him talk through his frenzy but gave up. "Bone!"

He'd been looking around the area, at everything and nothing, and now, at his callsign, his head snapped to attention.

"Pan-do did well, Bone. Now it is up to us."

Moon left and reappeared. The group led by Viper ran hard every day, sleeping soundly most nights. The sigh of a chill wind through the odd spiky leaves promised even colder nights. They finally reached the edge of Viper's homebase but didn't slow, sprinting past a patch of radiant yellow flowers atop fuzzy stalks. Such beauty seemed out of place with the battle Xhosa knew was coming. A raptor circled overhead, waiting its turn to scavenge some predator's kill.

That fit Xhosa's mood.

While the warriors paused to catch their breath, Bone continued on a roundabout path to see how close the reinforcements were who would assist Thunder and Nightshade. Bone didn't return until Sun was well across the sky. He must have run most of the way because he could barely stand and when he tried to speak, could only gulp noisy mouthfuls of air.

Xhosa didn't care if he was tired. She shook him and forced his eyes to hers. "Are they here?"

He nodded, spraying sweat into the chill air. "Thunder, Nightshade, and handfuls of warriors."

Xhosa turned to Wind. "Your brother, what do you think he's planning?"

"He will use Nightshade's hatred of the People to find out how to defeat you. Once he's taken everything he needs from Nightshade, he'll kill him. Your former Lead Warrior is crazy. My brother will never trust him."

Betaaka gazed from Xhosa to Wind and back. "You two together, there are times I think you read each other's thoughts."

Xhosa didn't need to look at Wind to know he made a subtle flick with his hand, so unobtrusive, no one would notice it if they weren't looking for it, which apparently Betaaka was.

"Like that."

Within another finger of Sun's travel overhead, Xhosa picked up the aroma of freshly spilled blood and opened guts. Viper stopped, hand out but low and ducked behind a wall of foliage where she could see into her People's homebase.

She motioned to Xhosa, "All I see are Big Heads."

She whistled a callsign, so much like a natural sound, the Big Heads didn't turn. Viper smiled when an answer came back, a bird calling its mate.

"My Lead Scout. I taught him birdsong before I left," and Viper translated for her warriors who didn't understand, "He suggests the fight start tomorrow, at Sun's arrival."

The warriors withdrew far enough they couldn't be seen or smelled. There was no moon, just cold howling winds. Distant lightning flashed and thunder sounded, but the storm burned itself out before reaching them. Without a fire or a cave for warmth and with thoughts of tomorrow's battle whirling through their minds, few slept. It wasn't lost on Xhosa that Viper and her People were in trouble because Thunder hated Wind and Nightshade hated everyone, and that tomorrow, for many, would be their last day.

Xhosa crouched at the edge of the Mountain Dweller's homebase, behind a screen of low-growing plants. When Morning Bird greeted Sun, the battle began, the People's warriors on one side, Viper's on the other, and the enemy in the middle. The two-sided barrage confused the Big Heads at first but soon, they responded with a vengeance. It didn't take long for the Mountain Dwellers to exhaust their supply of spears and turn to lobbing rocks and dirt clods. Many launched them from the treetops but once they ran out of missiles, unable to change their position, were knocked out of the limbs. If the fall didn't kill them, spears did. Betaaka and his warriors fought valiantly but not fast. Few were killed but most injured and unable to fight any further. They crawled off to find a place to hide until the enemy left or the battle ended.

Soon—too soon—only the People remained. They'd expended all their spears but not the throwing stones. These, in their hands, were deadly weapons, launched at vulnerable points like the temple, the eyes, behind the ears, and the dangling parts, always hitting their mark. Finally, the enemy withdrew to protected locations. It became a standoff until a stout muscular warrior with dark lined skin and eyes like molten rock, pristine in the lack of blood on his body, dragged Viper into the open area. She bled from a handful of cuts but fought him for every step.

"Come out, Xhosa, or Viper dies," he motioned one-handed in the gestures of the People.

"Nightshade," Xhosa muttered to herself.

Wind recognized the voice also. "Don't trust him!"

But she strode into the open. "This is between us, Nightshade. Let her go."

He laughed. "No, we won't do it that way."

His arm moved so quickly, she had no chance to dodge the rock. Pain shredded her head. She managed to hiss at Wind to stay back.

Nightshade sauntered up to her side—*How'd he get there so fast?*—and jabbed a spear tip into her chest. She almost winced but bit her lip instead.

Nightshade cackled. "You forget I can read your mind," and then he shouted, "Show yourself, One-called-Wind or your Leader dies. If any of the People's warriors remain, drop your weapons."

Instantly, Wind revealed himself. His eyes flicked from Nightshade to a spot somewhere behind him.

Nightshade snickered. "I won't fall for that, One-called-Wind. Many have tried to distract me and none succeeded."

Wind ignored the cocky warrior and focused beyond him. "Brother." Wind spoke the callsign, voice strong but vibrating with concern.

Thunder swaggered toward him. "Yes, your brother and Leader of your People. I knew this primitive would draw you out."

Then Thunder did what no one expected. He stepped to Nightshade's side and slashed his throat. The once-mighty fighter gurgled something Xhosa didn't understand and then fell over dead.

"Your Lead Warrior, Xhosa, is crazy. He hates you more than I hate Wind. It surpasses any loyalty he could ever give me and negates any trust I could ever allow him. Once he showed me how to get here and entice you into the open, he became unnecessary. His biggest concern was the wolf who travels with you and it appears he didn't join you." He leered at her. "I have no additional need for you, either, but rather than death, I will enslave you."

A rustle behind Wind announced the arrival of Betaaka, his head high, warrior presence radiant. Thunder turned toward him.

Which was a bad mistake.

Despite her wooziness, Xhosa snatched a handaxe from her neck sack and assaulted Thunder. He shoved her down but she dragged him with her and they fell in a tangled heap of legs and arms. Handaxe still in her fist, she slammed his hand flat on the ground and slashed mercilessly. Her aim wasn't exact but her power was unforgiving. She severed first one finger and then another. He froze, eyes on the pulsing stumps as they glowed red against his dirt-encrusted skin.

He smirked, barely acknowledging the pain. "You won't quit."

"No," and she slammed her handaxe into the ragged remnants of his gory fingers.

As though on a signal, the vestiges of the People's and Betaaka's warriors charged. Thunder fled but turned back when he was out of range.

Head high, blood a glistening red pelt over his hands, face dark with rage, he bellowed, "You will never escape me, one-called-Xhosa. Nor will you, brother, if you remain with her! It will end in your death!" And he abruptly walked into the foliage and vanished.

Wind and Betaaka both yelled, "Leave him! We must protect those still alive!"

Viper strode toward Xhosa, the young female's cheeks and forehead blackening where Nightshade hit her, but her spirit undaunted.

"Not many of us remain but those who do wish to join the People, if we may."

Bone interjected, "His reinforcements are less than a day away."

Xhosa nodded and Wind motioned, "We must leave now. Thunder's destroyed hand will make him angrier."

Chapter 32

Islanders' camp

Betaaka led the survivors on a circuitous route to his homebase, where Xhosa assumed Pan-do would be. They sloshed through freezing water, trundled along talus slopes, and walked in each other's footprints, all designed to hide their tracks. Bone stayed well behind, searching for pursuers and never saw even one. When they were far enough to feel safe, the group gathered for a meal, though without fire. As they ate, Wind explained the situation.

"Don't underestimate Thunder because he is injured. I have seen him wounded often and it just makes him more perilous. Rest assured, we will beat him, in part because he overestimates himself but also because he underestimates us."

The People's warriors slapped the ground as Wind talked, grunting in rhythm with the thump of their hands. His cold flat glare said he and Xhosa would lead them to victory. The hard set of her mouth told Wind she was tired of running.

When Wind paused, Xhosa stood. "We have a plan." Her words were greeted with grins and more thumps. "It will stop not only Thunder but Those-who-eat-Others. Right now, the most important thing we must do is rejoin the rest of the People."

Xhosa's birdsong calls never received a response on the trail home. She knew why this could happen—for example, Pan-do and Isaalka were too far away or they couldn't spare scouts to wait along the backtrail—but it still worried her. She and Wind quickened the pace. Most of the group couldn't keep up but she didn't care. If Pan-do needed help, it was her duty to get there as soon as possible. First, Viper's females and children dropped back, then the remaining few Mountain Dweller warriors, and finally Betaaka's warriors, saying they would protect those traveling slowly. None of Xhosa's warriors dared slow though a chorus of wheezes and gasps replaced what should be silence. Noise wasn't allowed before or after a battle but Xhosa didn't have time to correct them.

The bedraggled group finally hunkered at the outskirts of Betaaka's cave while Xhosa and Wind scanned the surroundings, analyzing and rejecting odd shadows and sounds. A stiff wind blew their scent into the mouth of the cavern but that didn't worry Xhosa. Only those who were no threat would recognize it.

And she was right.

Ocha scampered out of the cave, tail raised, nose in the air. She skidded to a halt, snapped her muzzle to the side, and howled. Spirit sprinted past her and leapt on top of Xhosa while Ocha stood on her hind legs and slapped her paws against Wind's chest. The rest of the People spilled out of the cave into the cool air. Xhosa's legs shook with exhaustion but she greeted everyone, ticking off all except Pan-do.

As she scratched between Ocha's ears and rubbed the fur on the wolf's back, she asked, "Where's your pack leader, Ocha?"

Ocha huffed and Pan-do appeared. "I was up there," and pointed to the bluff over the cave. "checking your backtrail."

He answered the question in her eyes with a head shake. That bothered Xhosa as much as if he'd seen Thunder. Where were the Big Heads?

His shoulders were strained but eyes calm. "I heard your birdsong but I didn't want Cucu'tez to know."

"He's back?"

"No." His stiffened arms and widened stance told Xhosa what she suspected. Cucu'tez was now an enemy.

She moved on. "Nightshade is dead," and fell silent. There was nothing else to say about her failed Lead, the one her People had called Leader in her absences, the male who would have been her pairmate, and the only member of the People ever to kill one of their own.

Pan-do didn't ask how. Why would he? He thought he knew. Xhosa would explain later. Now, she needed to discuss the group's plans.

"You succeeded," she gestured, remembering the billowing smoke and the rancid smell of burning flesh.

"In part, but Those-who-eat-Others knew you left." He paused, saw Xhosa understood, and continued, "They split their force. Honestly, I misjudged them. I won't again." Though his hands were calm, a tightening around his eyes told Xhosa how much this bothered him. "Can you tell me the rest of your plan yet?"

"Yes," and she shared her strategy to rid the People of both Thunder and the cannibals.

For the first time since she returned, Pan-do grinned. "That could work."

Xhosa released a long slow breath while her eyes moved over her warriors. Many injuries had gone untreated in the rushed retreat from the Mountain Dweller's homebase. Viper had run most of the way with a spear in her side, unable to search for the honey and moss she needed to treat it. Rocks had shredded many feet which Siri was already treating. Honey tended a deep cut in someone's arm. Her usual graceful movements were awkward, wrong-handed.

Pan-do followed her gaze. "Honey lost a hand. The cannibal who took it lost his life courtesy of Ant. He has practiced non-stop with his weapons and is more skilled than before his finger was chopped off. He is helping her adjust."

Pan-do started to go and then turned back. He pulled a fungus she recognized from his neck sack and handed it to her. Neither said a word but Xhosa's eyes misted as she accepted help with a problem she couldn't handle alone.

Then they parted ways, each with their own duties, all critical to preparing for Thunder's arrival.

The next day and the next, everyone worked Xhosa's plan until they knew their part perfectly. A storm forced them to shelter inside for a full day. Its harsh icy wind roared, bending the slender trunks of the saplings and thrashing their bare branches.

Xhosa squatted on her haunches by the fire, shivering while she pounded roots, thinking about what else she must do, when Seeker appeared.

"I have something for you." He led her outside, up the snow-and-ice-laden slope of the hill behind the cave. He wore a thin pelt and no foot coverings but as usual showed no reaction to the frigid air. Xhosa secured a pelt she'd taken from an Okapi around her chest and hips, wondering how the scrawny boy didn't tremble uncontrollably.

Once at the top, he lay down in the wet snow, quickly buried to his ears by the pristine white flakes. Xhosa settled in beside him but not without an involuntary shiver.

He breathed in and out, deliberately, eyes focused above. "Scooping Hand remains opposite Butterfly. Both revolve around Always-there Star."

Then he talked about other stars that had moved, animals who prepared for the cold time, the resilience of life—on and on. She asked no questions because any distraction delayed his point, whatever that was.

The warmth of the snow around her body, Seeker's mellifluous voice, and fatigue lulled her to drowsiness. She pinched herself to stay awake.

Seeker smiled. "You wonder why we're here."

This calm, aware Seeker was not the boy-male she first met at Hawk's. Every part of that boy—legs, arms, head, chest, even his hair—burst with boundless enthusiasm as he described what he saw to anyone who listened or to no one. This new Seeker, hardened by life, challenged by death, and awed by his pairmate, Lyta, accepted that most of his groupmates' worlds differed from his.

"Remember not long ago, the stars fled across the sky from your old homebase to beyond this new one, the message telling us we would not stay here, that our homebase lay somewhere else? Tonight, they offer new guidance."

Within a breath, a fiery blob brighter than Moon and larger than Scooping Hand streaked through the sky. Behind it streamed a sparkling tail that changed colors from red to the darkest blue and then blended into the blackness like a snake that had shed its iridescent skin.

"They tell us to stay."

That's not what Xhosa wanted to hear and she couldn't hide her frustration. "That's the opposite of what they said before!"

"You misunderstand. Stay longer but not forever."

"How long? Till the warm air returns? Until my plan works?"

Seeker seemed to consider her questions. "Maybe. They say you have more to accomplish. I suppose that could be your plan. Oh, you will get one more message and it will arrive at a time you most need it."

"What does that mean?" But Seeker was already lost in the night sky.

Xhosa went back to the cave and rubbed the fire's warmth into her arms. Qu'tez was deep in conversation with Wind but she decided to interrupt them.

"Qu'tez. Do your former groupmembers still trust you?"

He nodded and she explained what she needed.

He stood straighter, growing in maturity as she watched. Finally, he answered, "I will find them, tell them a big tribe of large individuals has arrived from the mountains. All that food— they won't pass it up."

"It will be risky, Qu'tez."

The subadult motioned, "So are warring tribes intent on our death."

Wind asked, "Will they believe you?"

"Yes. They know I always tell the truth."

She showed her respect by nodding.

"If I don't make it back, Xhosa—and Wind —take care of Re'ez for me." Something offhand and hopeful filtered through his expression. "I will stay in touch with birdsong."

The next morning was drizzly and cold but without snow. Qu'tez left before Sun awoke. The boy-male who had never impressed her as brave now carried spears in both hands, a warclub over his back, a neck sack stuffed with stones, and the responsibility for the People's future in his hands.

A day passed and another, and another. A blizzard coated everything in ice. The watering holes froze and adults warned the children not to step on them. No word came from Qu'tez. Xhosa, Pan-do, Wind, Mbasa, the Leads and their Seconds, practiced until their bodies performed Xhosa's plan without thought.

When Thunder struck, and he would, success relied on everyone performing their part perfectly.

"Thunder is here!"

Betaaka snapped awake and sped outside. Xhosa stood, arms crossed and fists clenched.

Bone swallowed, chest heaving. "They came from the mountains!" *Not from Viper's homebase as we all expected.* "They're right behind me!"

And then he gurgled and fell forward, a shaft embedded in his back. Shock turned Xhosa's face white. If Bone hadn't been standing to her side, she would have been skewered.

Rul'ez shrieked, joined by a strangled cry from Asal'rez as both flopped into the refuse ditch, spears through their throats.

And then, everyone did as they'd practiced. Siri and Tuuka led the females and children the opposite direction of the enemy, intending to circle back when it was safe. Betaaka and his warriors charged down a predetermined trail toward a narrow canyon, followed by Thunder's fighters. The Islanders acted disheveled and frightened, as though roused from deep sleep, and repeatedly peered over their shoulders, faces panicked. Once in the narrow confines of the chasm, they didn't have far to run before reaching a dead end. Betaaka had argued with Wind that not even arrogant Big Heads would expect his warriors to madly pursue a path they should know had no exit but Wind assured him they would. His former groupmembers considered all Others not Big Heads to be stupid and unskilled. This time, they would be proven wrong.

And Wind was right. The Big Heads laughed at Betaaka's predicament, not noticing Wind above them on the cliff's precipice. He couldn't shower them with burning sticks this time, not with his own People trapped below, but he could do something almost as deadly. As soon as all the Big Heads were stuffed into the gully, Wind, Zvi, Stone, Betaaka, Pan-do, and Sa-mo-ke pushed massive boulders over the edge. They rumbled down the cliff into the gorge and exploded with thunderous crashes atop the Big Heads. Those who tried to escape ended up beneath the next boulder.

But not as many had followed as Wind hoped. Betaaka peered back toward the opening and saw why.

Pan-do shook his head. "There's more fighting out there than in here. He's as smart as Wind said. Let's go!"

Betaaka paled. "I don't think it's smartness. Something else is going on," but he didn't have time to figure it out. He leaped over the crushed bodies and shattered boulders and flung himself into the skirmish.

"Over here!" Wind bellowed, backed up against the stone wall by a Big Head.

Mbasa growled. "I'll finish here and help you!"

"I can't wait long."

The Big Head males advanced, warclubs gripped in muscular hands, the conflicted look on their faces telling Wind they hadn't forgotten how often his warclub ensured they survived.

One whispered, "I can't do this, not for Thunder," and left, accompanied by others until no one remained.

Wind breathed a relieved sigh and sprinted toward Mbasa. She was down to the last assailant. "It's handled. Go find your own prey."

That didn't take long. Wind recognized the lean wiry build of Scorpion, his long-time Big Head partner. He held a cutter the length of a hand, leaves wrapped around the bottom. It was his favorite weapon, one that ended many lives in the time Wind fought with him.

He slapped Scorpion's head. "Stop."

He gawked at Wind wide-eyed. "But you are us!"

"Not anymore," he growled, "You complained more than I about Thunder. Why do you still support him?"

He answered by brandishing his odd cutter until someone seized his wrist from behind.

Wind grinned. "Scorpion, meet Stone, one of my new partners."

Stone squeezed until the fragile bones ground together. The Big Head let out an involuntary gasp and lost his grip on the cutter. Stone snatched it from the ground.

"I can use this," and then swung his warclub. Scorpion's ribs cracked as two enemy came to his defense, though too late. One flung himself at Stone and ended up on the tip of a sharpened antler. The other—Storm—caught Wind around the neck with one arm and raised the other to slice his throat. Wind twisted away and slammed the butt of his spear into Storm's hand. His fingers popped opened and the cutter dropped to the ground.

"Give up!" Wind asked.

Storm answered by reaching his good hand for his warclub. "Don't do it."

But he did which left Wind no choice. He shattered Storm's jaw and then collapsed his skull. Storm's eyes showed surprise, that his fellow warrior would be the one to end his life.

"Argh!"

Wind jerked toward the sound. "Mbasa!"

One of Thunder's warriors held her wrist and she his, her face crimson with effort. His arm bled from a deep puncture wound which explained why the smaller female managed to hold him off.

Without interfering, Wind jostled into position facing the male. "I see you met Mbasa. You should surrender because she won't."

As though on cue, a barrage of stones was unleashed into the Big Head's temples, cheeks, and eyes. He swatted at the projectiles which allowed her to stab him in the stomach. The male crumbled to the ground.

Mbasa pulled in a deep breath. "You took your time, El-ga."

Wind motioned to the youngster hidden behind a boulder, "You are excellent with stones."

The boy pretended to shrug off the praise. "I did what must be done," but his eyes glowed.

Before they could find the next enemy, the Big Heads fled.

El-ga started after them. "We must catch them."

Wind waved him away. "No. Let them go. They realize we won."

The People treated the wounds of the injured, threw the dead far enough away that they wouldn't attract predators, and then gathered to groom, eat, and sleep. Mbasa motioned El-ga to her side. He sat without a word, as though he belonged. Sun disappeared and with it, the air's warmth. The fire felt good.

That's when Wind realized Xhosa was missing. He shouted her callsign to no avail. Everyone searched the area in case she'd been injured but Wind knew they wouldn't find her.

"Thunder didn't retreat. He got what he came for and left."

Chapter 33

Islanders' camp

Pan-do would stay at the base and Wind, Betaaka, Tor, Mbasa, and Ocha would follow Thunder when daylight resumed.

Wind understood the reasoning but would make a different choice.

The next morning, before Sun awoke, he strapped his warclub to his back, looped his sack around his neck, and took a spear in each hand. Energized by the crisp chill in the air, he and Spirit set out following the Big Head tracks. It didn't surprise Wind that Thunder left a clear trail. He wanted his brother to follow.

"But why does he go to the flatlands?" He muttered silently, and then it struck him. "He doesn't know the cannibals live there."

He was still struggling to unravel if that would be for the better or worse when a bird chirped.

"Qu'tez!"

No one had heard from the subadult since his departure. Many thought he deserted but not Re'ez. The two had talked often about pairmating once she bled. They both looked forward to it.

The subadult's birdsong said Those-who-eat-Others had found Thunder and were stalking him. He was shocked to see

Xhosa a captive of the Big Heads and would do all he could to keep her safe.

Wind sprinted forward at a ground-eating pace. He kept that speed until day turned to night and then slept in an abandoned wolf den, warmed by Spirit's dense fur.

"Wind—we must go!"

Wind shook the sleep from his brain and crawled out of the cozy, dark cave. The sunlight filtered through the leaves causing the dew to glow.

He wasn't surprised by Mbasa's voice. "You ran hard to catch up."

She greeted him with a nod, as did Betaaka and Tor. "Spirit and Ocha are already gone. They want to find Xhosa as much as we do."

Betaaka added, "We heard Qu'tez's message. That boy—I judged him wrong."

Tor gestured, motions as tense as Wind had ever seen from him, and the group set off.

By the time they reached a river, Wind's shadow was nothing more than a dark puddle at his feet. A light rain had fallen earlier, turning the hard-packed path into mud, but now, the clouds had left and Sun glowed. Spirit and Ocha returned from their mission, one Wind suspected had to do with spying on the Big Heads.

Wind pointed to piles of dung. "Steam's still coming off some of them. Our quarry is close."

Mbasa dipped noiselessly into the water and swam across, a murky shadow until she climbed out on the opposite side and faded over a rise beyond the river. By the time the rest of the People crossed, Mbasa was back, with news.

"Thunder's ahead, with his warriors and Xhosa."

She crawled up the rise and then ducked behind a dense thicket. Before Wind could catch up, he saw movement downstream.

Cucu'tez!

Unaware of the People's presence, the suspected traitor dawdled along the waterway. His gaze jumped between his backtrail and the Big Head camp.

He's watching for the cannibals.

A plan formed in Wind's brain.

When Tor reached him, Wind motioned back along the river, "Watch Cucu'tez," and then crawled up to Mbasa, flattened himself to the ground, and peered through the foliage.

Thunder's warriors, Wind's former groupmates, milled around a small clearing. To the side, by herself, was Xhosa, hands tethered, head hanging, chin on her chest, sleeping or passed out. Her arms prickled with cold. Wind glanced around and saw no fire pit. As he studied her body for injuries, her eyes cracked open a sliver, found him, and tweaked her head to the side.

Spirit! He was nestled behind her, hidden. Then, Xhosa tipped her head forward across the site. Qu'tez was here, too, behind a thick wall of foliage. Wind doubted Qu'tez knew Cucu'tez was in the river, waiting for Those-who-eat-Others, so warned him with a birdsong, then sang to Xhosa, "Be ready."

She acknowledged with an almost invisible twitch of her hand. Qu'tez blinked and then coughed, saying he'd heard Wind.

Thunder paced, never glancing at Xhosa, never wondering about the sudden presence of birds around their camp. His hand was swollen and red against his dark skin but you'd never know it hurt. Wind knew, though, because Thunder never would have missed not only the unusual birdsong but the out-of-place slosh of Cucu'tez crossing the river. Wind grinned to himself. That might be the advantage he needed.

Time to make something happen.

He motioned cryptically to Mbasa, "Spirit will protect me. If he can't, be brilliant."

Without waiting for a response, Wind moved into the open space. Xhosa was ready for anything so he focused on Thunder. His brother and greatest enemy radiated hate as a fire did heat.

"I've expected you."

Wind raised the corners of his mouth. "How is your hand, brother?"

Thunder guffawed, a wild look in his eyes. "Turns out I don't need it to stop you. All it took was your pairmate."

"Well, there is the whole fighting thing," and Wind pretended to clumsily raise his spear and drop it.

Thunder's eyes narrowed, becoming savage pools of rage.

Wind interrupted whatever Thunder was about to say, his gestures broad and high enough for all to see. "Your leadership of my People ends here, brother. I challenge you."

He had chosen these words carefully, signaling his intentions to the warriors. Any could challenge and it must be respected but such a fight was not issued lightly. The winner would become Leader and the loser would die.

Thunder's warriors fell silent and backed away, leaving room for the brothers.

Wind spoke now as much to his former groupmates as to Thunder, "You are an insult to the reputation of our father, brother. He was a good and fair Leader who fought Others if necessary, avoided them when possible. He never used his warriors for a personal grudge. I must stop you so our People can find a worthy Leader!"

As Thunder sneered, Spirit padded to Wind's side, hackles up. Ocha slipped to his other side and Red Wolf behind. Though young, the pup's size intimidated.

Wind hid his surprise. *When did Red Wolf arrive?*

The Big Head warriors hissed. Never had they seen feral animals work with Others. Thunder squeezed his spear with an awkward wrong-handed grip. Spirit saw this as a threat to his pack. His ears flattened against his head and a growl rolled from deep in his chest.

Wind motioned to the wolves and they all lay down one leg bent, ready to spring.

One eye on Thunder, he nonchalantly stepped to Xhosa's side and slashed the vine around her hands.

"She is not part of this. It's between you and me."

Thunder slapped his hands on the ground. "How stupid you still are."

Spirit leaped to his feet and snarled, canines bared. Wind again stopped him with an open hand, never removing his fiery glare from Thunder. With Thunder's attention on the wolf, Wind opened his hand and the cutter fell into Xhosa's lap.

Thunder motioned, "The winner gets One-called-Xhosa as well as our father's tribe. The loser dies."

"I accept," though Xhosa was not Wind's to give. If he lost, Xhosa would explain that to Thunder.

Wind was an excellent fighter but he spoke truthfully when he told Xhosa he'd never beaten his brother. Thunder's strength and endurance knew no limits, his treachery no bounds. Today must be Wind's first win.

Out of the corner of his eye, Wind saw Cucu'tez, attention now fixed downstream. The stench of cannibal drifted across Wind's nose and made him sneeze. He reverted to his brother, now grinning maniacally, face alight with the fervor of blood. Though unlikely Wind would survive, he had a greater purpose than simply one life. He would make this battle last as long as possible, giving Mbasa time to free Xhosa, and all of his People a chance to escape before the cannibals arrived.

"Brother. Even if you beat me, you can't defeat your next adversary, and he is here already. You and I are both dead. The question is who will go first."

Thunder frowned in confusion but only for a moment. "I chased you farther than I knew existed. Today, you die. Then, my People return to the homebase of our father. There, One-called-Xhosa will be my slave!"

Wind shook his head. "That's not how this will end."

One of Thunder's warriors started forward but Fire, Lead for Wind's father, held him back.

"This challenge is between brothers for leadership of our People. The winner will decide our future. We must let it play out."

Thunder motioned, "Because you worry about my ability to defend myself, throw your weapon away. That will level this battle."

Wind did as asked, albeit hurriedly, and Thunder attacked. He immediately pinned Wind with his damaged arm and snatched a handaxe someone had tossed his way with his good one.

Wind shouted, "Mbasa—Tor—Xhosa—run!"

Thunder guffawed and prepared the death stab but Xhosa roared, now standing, Spirit and his wolf pack at her side, "One-called-Thunder! Look around you! Even you can't defeat the opponent you now face!"

Thunder glanced around, seeing the cannibals for the first time. There were at least two for each of them. Wind sighed his relief at not seeing Tor, Mbasa, or Betaaka anywhere.

Xhosa's hair billowed in the cool air, body sparkling with energy. Face to Wind, her eyes said it all. With Thunder distracted, Wind tossed him off and scrambled to his feet. Shoulder to shoulder, the brothers faced the new nemesis.

Thunder's eyes blazed. "Your escape is temporary. I will destroy these and then we finish our battle."

Wind grunted as Qu'tez strode from the milling throng of cannibals, a blood-encrusted wound on his stomach, and motioned, "You are slaves. You will only die when the time is right."

Without warning, pain shot through Wind's head. The ground buckled beneath him and everything went dark.

Chapter 34

Something jabbed Wind's ribs and a damp red fog washed over him. He threw up and it hurt to open his eyes. Now he understood the agony Xhosa suffered from her head pains. His nose wrinkled at the rancid stench of too many Others who didn't use the refuse ditch. Behind that oozed the sweet odor of cannibals.

Another stab, this one harder.

"Wind! Wake up!"

He shook to clear the dizziness from his head but now it throbbed. His lips trembled from the cold every time he breathed. He still wore his pelt but wished it covered his entire body the way Spirit's did. Sluggishly, he catalogued the bruises, cuts, and scrapes on his body. Most, he didn't remember.

"Those-who-eat-Others kicked you, a lot, after you passed out. That's what hurts." A root bundle plopped to his side. "Eat that. It'll dull the ache."

Odd the cannibals left her neck sack with not only the herbs but travel food and throwing stones. Well, not so odd. They probably didn't know the bladder was used to carry items because Cucu'tez had fallen asleep during that lesson. For the first time, rather than anger at the boy's laziness, Wind felt relief.

Wind swallowed another wave of nausea and ate the nodes as Xhosa ordered. She was right. The misery stepped back. He imagined this was how the shore felt when the water pulled away from the sand. He forced his eyes open and his spirit lightened. Xhosa was tied up at his side, close enough to touch. Across the clearing, Thunder glared at him, eyes burning, seemingly oblivious to the reality that he and his warriors were captives, his promises of vengeance meaningless.

There was no sign of Betaaka, Mbasa, or Tor among the captured or the dead bodies piled in the middle of the open space. Nor were the wolves anywhere. Wind stifled a smile.

My plan may have failed but I will die beside Xhosa.

Xhosa nudged him. He saw her confidence, unswayed by the difficulties they faced.

Never mind dying. She's not done.

When he thought about it, none of what had happened negated Xhosa's plan to destroy both the Big Heads and the cannibals. No doubt, Mbasa and Tor were already adapting to the revisions. He must be ready.

First, he'd find one of Thunder's warriors who realized he was fighting on the wrong side, someone who would work with the People. He scanned through the trussed males and stopped at Fire, his brother's Lead. More gray streaked Fire's head hair than Wind remembered and blood seeped from a handful of wounds, but still he radiated power and confidence, his eyes alive.

When Fire finally looked his way, Wind tapped his hand. A faint smile limped across the Big Head's face as he remembered their last time together, before Thunder ejected Wind, how Fire broke his hand in battle but still wouldn't quit.

A growl turned Wind's attention to Thunder. "You caused this, brother-no-more. I will escape and destroy you!"

He fought the vines around his hands and shouted that nothing would stop him. Blood crusted his head. His arm with the missing fingers hung loosely and a deep gash cut his chest. Despite himself, Wind respected the warrior in his brother. He would never give up, even now when it appeared hopeless. To Those-who-eat-Others, Thunder appeared to be a valiant opponent, worthy of living as a slave, maybe even a member of their tribe. If they realized how disruptive he was, they would kill him immediately.

Out of nowhere came beautiful birdsong and a soft growl, missed by the captors. Xhosa smiled. The sound of the People, coming to their rescue.

Qu'tez wandered over to Wind and whispered, "I told them you and Xhosa are considering joining Those-who-eat-Others. Your strength would make them even more formidable. If they didn't think there was a chance you'd say yes, they would end your life immediately."

Which was better than being eaten a piece at a time. "Qu'tez. Cause a distraction."

Without acknowledging, the subadult began to taunt Thunder, first with words, then by poking a spear in his chest, and finally, he peed on him. Wind laughed at his brother's helplessness. No one treated him that way without repercussions. Each assault enraged him more until he couldn't help but to writhe wildly—and violently enough Wind worried he might free himself. The cannibals guffawed at Thunder's rabid helplessness. More joined Qu'tez taunts, their backs to Wind and Xhosa.

Using a cutter Xhosa had slipped to him, Wind started to slice away his bindings until Thunder screamed and pointed at his brother. A cannibal rushed over and kicked Wind savagely, snatched the cutter, and rejoined his comrades.

Qu'tez wandered over, mimed a vicious kick at Wind also, and motioned, "I have a plan. It starts when Sun sleeps." The boy's gestures were hard to interpret and Wind made him repeat his message before finally nodding, *Yes, I understand.*

Qu'tez took on the gruesome task of arranging the corpses for easy access. All day, he shoved and sorted bodies in the communal pile as cannibals dribbled in, mouths drooling at the massive supply of captured Others. Additionally, Qu'tez checked on the prisoners, slapped them or spit on them to entertain his fellow cannibals which gave Xhosa and Wind time to talk.

Finally, the birdsong Wind had been waiting for rang through the air—*Be prepared.* A breath later, Zvi spun into the field, clomping heavily, arms flapping as she twirled and twisted. Red Wolf pranced at her side, paws clawing the air, sharp-toothed muzzle huffing. Wind eyed Xhosa and she shrugged, "*I didn't know Zvi was here, either.*"

Zvi brandished a flaming spike while she sang a beautiful birdsong, mesmerizing all, exciting Wind who understood the message.

Qu'tez rushed forward with a yowl and began to spin and twirl with Zvi, ever faster in dizzying circles. All eyes watched, wondering how they stayed on their feet. Without warning, both froze, arms stretched upward, heads thrown back, eyes closed. A moment, another, and then Zvi took a long ragged breath and howled.

Overhead, a swath of stars streaked across the dark night sky and left a trail of red and yellow in its wake. All eyes followed the anomaly, awed and frightened. By the time the spell broke, Wind and Xhosa stood at Zvi's side, shafts made from bone in their hands, tall and proud, confident and energized. Spirit padded to one side, Ocha the other. The wolves searched the crowd and settled on the Lead cannibals. Thunder screamed for his brother to free him so he could slaughter him. Fire dipped his head while his shoulders shook, desperate to hide his laughter.

Xhosa muttered, "He should ask for help but instead, promises our doom. He *is* crazy."

Zvi and Qu'tez never turned away from the colors overhead. Finally, Qu'tez screamed. "It is a sign! We must let them go!"

As his entreaties became louder, Spirit, Ocha, and Red Wolf streaked through the cannibals, starting with the Leads, snapping and growling. Screams erupted all around and their captors fled, chased by what must seem to them a pack of rabid animals.

Except Cucu'tez. His face fell and breathing shallowed as he realized he'd chosen the wrong side. His gaze shot around the area in a panicked search for someone to trust and found Thunder.

Wind screamed, "Don't do it, Cucu'tez. He's not who you think he is!"

But the boy was beyond listening. He scrambled over to Thunder and cut the vines that tied hands and feet.

"I free you, One-called-Thunder—kill Wind—do what you want—just take me with you!"

Once unleashed, the crazed male backhanded Cucu'tez so savagely, the slender boy flew through the air and slammed head-first into a boulder. A loud wet crack made Wind cringe and Cucu'tez collapsed into a motionless heap. Thunder laughed and then freed Fire who released the rest of his warriors.

Thunder strode to his brother, mouth in a sneer, eyes blazing. If either was afraid, they hid it well.

Wind stepped forward and spread his stance. "Brother. You are not strong enough anymore to push me around. Take your warriors and go before the cannibals return."

The Big Head males gathered behind Thunder, stances wide, eyes on Wind. Behind them was a growing crowd of the cannibals. Wind stiffened, prepared for what must come next, but they simply watched, eyes glazed, faces slack, arms loose at their sides. One after another, they slumped over, no longer caring.

Wind motioned to Qu'tez, "What's wrong with your People?"

The boy spit. "They aren't my People." Fury blazed in his eyes. "I sprinkled the carcasses with the poisonous mushrooms I learned about from Xhosa. They've consumed them all day. I started to think they weren't working," and then grinned, proud of his deceit.

Xhosa rubbed her eyes. "They will pass out and be unconscious for many hands of Sun's travel. Or if they ate too many, forever."

Wind glowered at Thunder and shouted, "It's time to finish our argument."

Thunder leered. "As I recall, I was about to slit your throat."

He raised his arm to swing his warclub but instead, grimaced. He reached over his shoulder as he fell forward. A spear protruded from his back. Behind him stood Fire, the one who insisted the brothers be allowed to confront each other without interference. His eyes glowed with rage.

"He has been trouble since you left, Wind." He motioned behind himself, "Any who wish to challenge Wind, the new Leader, do so."

Wind wanted to object but would wait until his father's People were safe. When no one stood, he motioned, "It's time to leave, before these monsters awaken. We go to the Islander's camp."

As Fire organized the remnants of his People, Wind pulled Xhosa to his chest, tears rolling down his cheeks. "Was this your plan all along, to lead the cannibals to the Big Heads? Were you always supposed to be the bait?"

Xhosa kept her face neutral. "Plan or not, it worked, didn't it?"

Wind gripped her closer. "I need you, Xhosa. Captured together, dying together, that was better than living without you. But don't ever do that again!"

That confused her. No one needed someone or cried at the thought of their loss. Still, swathed in his arms, her nose filled with his scent, her strength blending with his—this felt good. A tingle inside made her want to stay right there, not move. If that's what he meant, she agreed.

Xhosa looked into his moist eyes and said, "Never worry about that."

As they set out, Xhosa asked Zvi how she got here.

"I know what you're asking, Xhosa. I haven't been away from Seeker since we met but he explained about the stars falling and their colored tails and how that indicated danger. He insisted on coming but I changed his mind. Seeker is easily distracted by everything around him. We both agreed I would move faster by myself."

"Did Red Wolf come with you?"

Zvi shook her head. "No, she left right after Ocha, by herself. She's more loyal than any creature I have ever met but other than her pack, she doesn't mind being by herself."

Lone wolf. Xhosa smiled. That must be Red Wolf's name.

Xhosa set a ground-eating pace, one she and the People could maintain forever and the cannibals couldn't. Qu'tez struggled but managed to keep up. His many hunts with the People had developed within him uncommon stamina and an attitude to match. Zvi offered to carry him but he demurred. Fire and those who could followed. Those who couldn't walk, crawled. No one wanted to stay by the sweet smelling carcasses. Sun slept and Moon arrived and the People hurried onward. The heavy pelts and the speed kept them warm. Mbasa and Tor watched the backtrail but only Big Heads drifted along behind, intent on following the trail left by Fire. Qu'tez assured Xhosa that the cannibals would leave the People alone until hunger again overcame them. Xhosa intended to be gone by then.

The exhausted collection of Big Heads, People, and wolves finally straggled into the Islander's camp. Zvi carried Red Wolf, now known as Lone Wolf, on her back. Males helped others who couldn't walk on their own. Re'ez pulled Qu'tez aside and motioned something that made him grin. A woof of excitement greeted the wolf pack as one of the pups leaped into Zvi's arms to lick Lone Wolf's face.

Pan-do rushed up to Xhosa and Wind, hands jerking with emotion.

Xhosa motioned, "Cucu'tez is dead, as is Thunder."

Pan-do swept the comment away. "But you are healthy." He breathed a sigh of relief and then twitched his head toward the Big Heads, confused.

Wind pulled Fire over. "This is Fire, the Big Head's Lead Warrior and a friend who helped us escape. His warriors want to follow us—or at least, Fire."

As everyone gathered in the fire-warmed cave, Xhosa left. She needed time to think. How did Nightshade, once as important to her as her own life, go this wrong? How did she not see what was happening? She had no answers, just guilt, and wriggled aside to make room when Wind pushed onto the slab with her, still warm from the day's sun. He said nothing, simply lent his support. She stared into the darkness in contemplative silence, eyes on the twinkling stars until the cold drove them into the cave.

Daylight spilled over the landscape, chasing the darkness away, at least for a while. Xhosa gathered Wind, Pan-do, Betaaka, Viper, and Fire to work out a plan.

She caught Betaaka's eye and then gestured, "My People—we won't be staying. The cannibals will strike again when they run out of food."

Wind motioned, "They don't care how many of their own die stopping us."

Betaaka motioned, eyes meeting Xhosa's, "It is a good decision. We are leaving, too, returning to our former homebase. Come with us, with your People. These pelts, the fire, what you have taught us, we can survive—even thrive—there."

Fire motioned, eyes on Wind, "My People want to return to the land of Xhosa's People. Wind, will you lead us?"

Wind smiled. "The Big Heads are not my People anymore. I give you the Leadership, Fire. Any may challenge you but I support you."

Fire nodded, not surprised, and motioned to the group around him, "All are welcome to go with us, in friendship. No one will cause you any trouble."

It was Xhosa's turn to smile, her thoughts on Seeker and the stars, their many messages leading her one place.

"Thank you but we join Betaaka."

Fire turned to Viper. "We will travel through your homebase. You may go with us. Maybe some of your People remain."

She found Stone, at the back of the group, his gaze fixed on her. "No. Xhosa's People—these People are now mine and the Mountain Dwellers. We will stay here."

Betaaka slapped his thighs. "It's settled then. We leave tomorrow."

Chapter 35

Leaving the Islander camp

Betaaka led, following his People's backtrail based on descriptions from the long-dead elders. Xhosa tried to see what he did—an odd-shaped tree or unusual boulder—but all the trees looked unusual to her and snow buried most of the big rocks. He said it didn't matter. There was really only one way across these mountains. Once in the foothills on the opposite side, following the shore of Endless Sea would lead them to the land bridge. They'd take that over the Endless Sea and from there, find his former homebase.

He grabbed a green stalk sticking up through the snow as they walked and chewed it. "The hard part will be if the land bridge no longer exists." He swept the snow from his pelt. "We'd have to find another way to our island."

Betaaka set the pace, Xhosa and Wind at his side, Pan-do mixed in with the rest of the travelers. Siri and Zooka carried their babies in slings that allowed the children to watch the world while their mothers walked. Siri's child, born a handful of days ago, had Pan-do's solemn eyes and gentle countenance. He was content to watch everything around him without comment, except for the occasional gurgle.

The group wound its way up, the terrain steeper with each step, moving through the passes and valleys, the ridges always sharper, slopes always slippier, branches always burdened with thick layers of snow, and everything accompanied by the incessant bitter wind. The day's migration began with light and ended with darkness. The scouts had no problem finding caves where the People could burn a fire, groom each other, and sleep, awakening to do the same the next day.

Some days were better than others. Today was not one of them. Xhosa fought her way up the ice-coated surface, slipping as often as she didn't. She leapt over crevices and lost track of how many times she almost lost her spear as she scrabbled her way up. Wind often held out his hand to balance her, as she did for him. They talked more than at any point since she'd known him. Surrounded by craggy cliffs, the wind whistling along the slopes and rustling through the branches, they didn't worry about being overheard.

Once, when she was silent for longer than usual, he asked, "Are you alright?"

Without looking at him, she chopped an abrupt, "Yes," not adding, *except for a fist clamped around my stomach and an overwhelming fatigue that grows continually worse. And the constant snow storms, the howling wind, and the pelting ice shards. Oh—and the nights too cold for the fire to warm me. Other than those, yes, I'm alright.*

But if it exhausted her, what did it do to her People?

"I'm fine."

To continue upward, they must first descend into a narrow valley, trek around a deep gorge that blocked their route, and climb a different side to eventually rejoin their original ascending trail. Xhosa reached the bottom, hurried forward, rounding a bend before realizing she'd gone too far. Rather than go back, she'd find the least dangerous place to re-climb the rock face.

A drop of water hit her forehead. The hair on her neck stood up and a shiver ran through her as she tipped her head back. All she could see were dark clouds.

"Wind! Betaaka! Hurry!"

Suddenly, sky fire struck the earth accompanied by a loud crack and a rumble. Her gaze jerked toward the walls on both sides and found what she expected—a line etched into the face partway up and over her head.

"Climb! A flood!"

Xhosa sprinted for the wall, picking out the best upward path as she ran, one most could handle. Then, she climbed, scrambling over jutting protrusions, ignoring their sharp edges, barely noticing when she passed the high water mark, not slowing until she touched level ground. When she looked back, the People were struggling upward with as much speed as they could muster. A frothy deluge cascaded toward them. A tree cracked, ripped apart by the thunderous water, its limbs snapped as though dry twigs. Lightning split another in two and it burst into flames. A scream rent the air, ending with a wet smack below. Another howl but this of anguish, then another, and another. Ngili tossed a vine to his pairmate, Hecate, big with a baby. The climb for her should have been impossible but Hecate never gave up on anything. Finally, all were above the water line.

When Xhosa turned back to their forward trail, she gasped at the sight of another narrow valley in front of her, bounded by more steep walls.

Bird had gone ahead to find somewhere the People could shelter for the night. Now, she raced for Xhosa, shrieking, "A snow flood!" as a wall of snow and ice chased her, pouring down the valley, flattening everything in its path, scrubbing the stone walls clean of life.

Dust yelled, "There is a cave not far from here. It's protected by a boulder bed."

Xhosa yelled for everyone to follow Dust, waving them on, helping those who fell. Stone and Zvi manhandled a boulder over the cave's mouth leaving a narrow gap stragglers could slip through. Once the last of them tumbled in, Xhosa jumped through, snow layering her back, and Zvi slammed the final boulder into place.

Siri built a fire from the twigs and debris blown into the cavern over time. Quickly, the interior warmed and the People congratulated each other on surviving.

Wind asked Xhosa, "How many didn't make it?"

She opened and closed a hand.

The next day, sun glowed in a cloudless sky and the migration continued. The People wound their way up the mountains, past the point where trees no longer grew, into the rugged barrenness of crevasses and dirt slides. The higher they got, the thinner the air until they wheezed with each steamy breath. The snow blinded them at times, often accompanied by gusty winds, so they wrapped their faces with skins and rubbed their arms.

Xhosa squinted against the fine grains of snow stuck to her lashes, barely able to see through the glare of Sun reflected off snow. Spirit seemed unaffected so she trusted him to find the path. Steam boiled from the wolf's nostrils, as he, Ocha, Lone Wolf, and the pups picked their way uphill, oblivious to the extreme cold because their dense undercoats protected them. Not until the snow froze to their fur did their tails tuck beneath their bodies. Xhosa frequently stopped to break away the balls of ice that formed between the pads of their paws but rather than be impressed, Spirit gave her the bored look as if to say, *I forgive you for taking this long!*

Although Dust and Bird always reported no one following, Xhosa still searched the outcroppings and the snowy white drifts. At one point, a flock of birds burst from the ground and she stopped everyone, continuing only after assuring herself that the disruption was because of them, not someone following. Over time, she acclimated to the normal sounds of those who called this home and was alarmed only by their silence or noises not them.

Finally, the frozen assemblage reached the mountain's crest. Xhosa's breath came in ragged gasps as she beheld her future. Betaaka glowed with excitement, oblivious to fatigue, frustration, or the doubt that crept into most of the People's minds about this never-ending migration. White clouds poured from his nostrils.

"There." Betaaka indicated a winding stream well down the mountain's flank. "We follow that to the base."

It started as a trickle growing little by little to a river, its muscular currents coiling back and forth, its surface shimmering in Sun's light like Snake's scales.

Descending was worse than ascending. Several perished in falls and avalanches. Finally, the People dropped below the stark gray cliffs into the groves of narrow trees with spiky leaves that scratched Xhosa's face and shredded her hands. It took more handfuls of days before they found themselves along the shore of Endless Sea. Xhosa walked on the wet sand, the salted water stinging her ragged feet.

She motioned to Betaaka, "Does this look familiar?"

He nodded. "We can rest here, start again at first daylight. It will take all day to reach the next resting place."

And it did but no one complained.

As they sat the next night in a cave around a fire, Betaaka looked outside. "There's fruit over there and nuts and berry bushes. Tomorrow, we eat well."

Chapter 36

Xhosa stretched. Eyes no more than slits, she padded outside to relieve her water while studying the clouds.

"What will Sun throw at us today?"

Before she could answer her own question, a scream broke the morning. She ran inside the cave and found Hecate leaning against the wall, face red, legs spread.

Xhosa motioned to herself, "I guess now I know."

One more howl rent the quiet, followed by the high-pitched yelp. When the People left the next day, Hecate curled her new baby in a sling against her chest, secure as she walked.

The wind blew ruthlessly all that day but the fish were abundant, berries everywhere, and no one but the People seemed to eat the never-ending supply of eggs. As Sun peaked overhead, Betaaka caught Xhosa's arm.

"See the land bridge jutting into Endless Sea?"

Xhosa peered into the haze of low-hanging clouds. All she saw was a long narrow smudge that sat atop the water. It must be what Betaaka referred to so she answered, "Yes."

"That's where we're going."

Xhosa wasn't sure how to respond and settled on, "It drops into Endless Sea?"

"No." Betaaka smiled. "Onto my homebase."

It took the rest of that day and part of the next to reach the bridge. Waves lapped its sides, at times washing over it. Xhosa stood, skeptical of taking the narrow land bridge to a place no one could see.

"Why can't we go that way?" She indicated the direction they were going, the one that veered away from the upcoming land bridge.

Betaaka motioned, "Within a Moon, you come to a wall of ice, too cold to walk on, without life of any type."

Xhosa thought of the Ice Mountain Invaders who drove the People from their good homebase.

Wind handed her a vine. "Tie this around yourself. Anyone who falls off can be dragged back."

"As Mbasa and Tor did on the rafts crossing Endless Pond," Xhosa added.

That done, the group headed across. Spirit shook from muzzle to tail and then stood stiff-legged at the entrance, hackles raised, tail tucked between his legs.

Zvi squatted. "Shall I carry you?"

The wolf moaned and then padded onto the bridge, pressed against Zvi's legs. Ocha whined but followed, which meant so too did Lone Wolf and the pups.

When they reached the opposite side, Betaaka's eyes glistened, his cheeks wet. He continued forward until stopped by a stream, its shores choked with tall narrow-trunked trees, their flat leaves fluttering in the constant breeze.

His hands shook and his breathing became short inhalations, as though he forced each breath in and out. Finally, he managed, "See these bare spots on the trunks. That's where Gazelle ate chunks of the bark because they couldn't find any other food. That means we missed the cold time."

Betaaka waded across the waterway and through a screen of barren branches that revealed a long broad meadow. Spindly-legged creatures, maybe this area's version of Gazelle, raised their heads and studied the two-legged upright creatures lazily. Assessing them as no threat, they went back to munching.

Betaaka motioned, "This is the first of many herds. We will eat well."

Xhosa pointed to the distant hills. "They aren't white. Is it not cold up there?"

Betaaka grinned. "The wind blows so hard, it cleans the snow off."

They crossed the meadow, through air laden in familiar fragrances. Without a word, Betaaka sprinted toward a smudge ahead and then skidded to a stop by a cave, hands clenched.

He motioned, eyes shining, chest puffed out, "We're home."

Inside, traces of prior habitation still lingered but the cavern was roomy and empty. Siri started a fire while some of the males explored the back tunnels. That night, rain thundered against the ground but the stone walls kept them dry and the bouncing flames provided as much warmth as they needed. By morning, yesterday's shallow stream now rushed. Xhosa, Wind, and Betaaka followed it through a valley grazed by hairy mammoth, odd-looking bison, pigs, and something that looked like Equiis but not quite. The air drizzled nonstop except for brief breaks to let Sun drench them with warmth. Betaaka promised it would dry out before the air got cold.

During the next days, the females and subadults, even the children, found seafood in the many mudflats by Endless Sea— swimming worms, fish with shells, and seaweed. Others walked along an inlet fed by rivers filled with fresh water and prey like the hairy mammoth, huge rhinos and hippos, giant deer and more of the odd-looking bison. All were stalked by sabertoothed cats, lions, wolves and hyaenas.

And now, the People.

Their new home was surrounded on two sides by water, one by the land bridge, and the last by naked peaks that blocked the Ice Mountains Betaaka claimed were on the other side. It took a Moon, maybe two, for Xhosa to adjust to this place bereft of the blazing heat, dry scrub, and desiccated ground she was accustomed to. The cave was large enough for each tribe to claim separate spaces. Outside, the clearing in front abutted to an open valley surrounded by forests. Betaaka said once this area was filled with Others but now it seemed to be only them.

Xhosa worried about finding the hard stones for spear tips and handaxes until Betaaka took her to a river. He dug around in the freezing water until he found a particular rock, smacked it against another, and with a grin, revealed a hidden stone as solid as those found by Fire Mountain.

The surest sign that this was to be their new home turned out to be Seeker. Again, the boy-male floated through the days. Every sound, every odor engaged him.

Finally, as Xhosa stood alone one day, her thoughts overflowing with the abundance of this amazing place, she murmured, "Father, we are home."

Epilogue

Two years later

The pale mist of Sun's arrival had long since vaporized. Xhosa headed out with the hunters, eager for fresh pig or goat after such a long cold time. Though she'd seen no trace of Others since arriving here, she carried not only her spears but a warclub. She would always be a warrior, prepared for anything. She kept her wealth of glistening hair loose for warmth throughout the cold but now wrapped it with a vine.

In the time here, her opinion of the land had changed from "miserably freezing" to "tolerable-but-cold" to "exquisite." In fact, she'd come to love the hills that overflowed with an abundance of plants, the many forests, the rare sun, and the endless rain. Creeks cut the countryside delivering fast-running water and fat fish to many parts of the land. Canyons broke up the hills filled with fruit, nuts, and ground birds.

Xhosa gulped in the sight of this open country, awed by the immensity of her new home. She and her People had adjusted well to days lived in pelts with a fire always lit, where they were never hungry and never threatened by enemies.

Xhosa's two children, Ruul and the second yet unnamed, hurried after Pan-do's oldest, Kish, and Siri to gather berries. Siri eased her overgrown body down to pick the fruit. Hecate and Ngili's child, Tian, already wielded a tiny shaft with a sharpened tip. Stone and Viper's first child often played with Baj and Betaaka's, Ank, each determined to outdo the other. And Qu'tez and Re'ez would soon add their own child to the growing pack.

Seeker spent most nights peering up at the night sky, the dull glow of Moon pale between thinning clouds. The stars no longer talked to him and Lyta showed the first signs of a baby within her.

Betaaka's People had moved to their own cave with one of Ocha's pups at the mouth of a river. Towering cliffs surrounded the lush valley, home to the sure-footed mountain goats who made their way into the upper meadows and back. These creatures maneuvered the narrow outcroppings that none of the People could, which meant Others could never sneak up on them.

"Xhosa, fruit blooms. Seeker and I are going to collect it."

She nodded as Lyta left. Spirit and Ocha bounded after her, flying down the gentle slope, on the lookout for a hare or pig slipping through the thick undergrowth and clumps of sedge.

With everyone busy, Xhosa could pursue her own plans. Last night, for the first time since arriving to this Island, Lucy visited her dreams. The two walked this terrain—green, vibrant, and alive—in search of the prints of another Upright Lucy seemed to know. Xhosa wanted to rest but Lucy pushed her onward, telling her it was important to reach their destination soon.

Xhosa trotted into the grove of narrow trees with spiky leaves, over a carpet of ankle-high leaves that muffled her footsteps. Her feet made a soft swishing noise as she walked, like the murmur of streams. The trees themselves issued a peculiar musty odor that reminded Xhosa of decaying mulch. She broke the ice along the edges of a pond and drank thirstily as she and Lucy did in her dream. Steam from the warmer water rose to meet the light dusting of snow that filtered down.

She picked her way through the thatch of brown tufts of sedge and dead wild flowers until tracks of an Upright appeared, as they had in her dream. They frightened her not because she didn't recognize them, but because she did. After following the footprints, a hand of Sun's passage overhead, she arrived at a cliff. She listened and heard silence.

"I guess I better see what's over the edge," and she crouched down, knees on the precipice, and tipped forward. She did this in her dream but awoke without discovering what lay down there.

The wall was steep and seemed to go down forever. It took her a long time to find below what didn't fit.

It was a body, eyes closed. Xhosa went cold.

"Zvi?"

The eyes popped open.

Afterword

Several hundred thousand years after taking refuge in the land we now call Britain, Xhosa's descendants were again driven away by what was called the Anglian Glaciation. This was a time when a heavy sheet of ice buried about two thirds of Britain making it too cold for even humans with fur pelts and fire to survive.

Coming up next in the *Man vs. Nature* saga

The last two books of the *Dawn of Humanity* trilogy, *Laws of Nature* (working title) and *In the Shadow of Giants* (working title). Expected publication for Book 2 is 2021. Sign up for our newsletter to be notified of its progress.

Do you want to see what happened next to Xhosa's People? Sign up to be the first to be notified of the sequel trilogy to *Crossroads,* expected publication 2023.

Preview of *Born in a Treacherous Time*

Book 1 in the *Dawn of Humanity* Trilogy

Read this before Book 2 comes out in 2021

Chapter One

The scene replayed in Lucy's mind, an endless loop haunting her days and nights. The clear sun-soaked field, the dying Mammoth, the hunters waiting hungrily for its last breath before scavenging the meat, tendons, internal organs, fat, and anything else consumable—food that would nourish the Group for a long time.

But something went horribly wrong. Krp blamed Lucy and soon, so too did Feq.

Why did Ghael stand? He had to know it would mean his death.

Lucy wanted to escape, go where no one knew what she'd done, but Feq would starve without her. He didn't know how to hunt, vomited at the sight of blood. For him, she stayed, hunting, scavenging, and outwitting predators, exhausting herself in a hopeless effort to feed the remaining Group members. But one after another, they fell to Snarling-dog, Panther, Long-tooth Cat, Megantereon, and a litany of other predators. When the strangers , Feq let them take her.

By this time, Lucy felt numb, as much from the death of her Group as the loss of Garv. Garv, her forever pairmate, was as much a part of her as the lush forests, Sun's warmth, and Snarling-dog's guidance. Now, with all the other deaths, she could leave his memory behind.

Forests gave way to bushlands. The prickly stalks scratched her skin right through the thick fur that layered her arms and legs. The glare of Sun, stark and white without the jungle to soften it, blinded her. One step forward became another and another, into a timeless void where nothing mattered but the swish of feet, the hot breeze on her face, and her own musty scent.

Neither male—not the one who called himself Raza nor the one called Baad—had spoken to her since leaving. They didn't tell her their destination and she didn't ask, not that she could decipher their intricate hand gestures and odd body movements. She studied them as they talked to each other, slowly piecing together what the twist of a hand and the twitch of a head meant. She would understand it all by the time they reached wherever they headed.

It was clear they expected her to follow. No one traveled this wild land alone. Her reasons for joining them, submissively, had nothing to do with fear. Wherever the strangers took her would be better than where she'd been.

Lucy usually loved running through the mosaic of grass and forest bleeding one into another. Today, instead of joy, she felt worry for her future and relief that her past was past. She effortlessly matched Raza's tread, running in his steps at his pace. Baad did the same but not without a struggle. His sweat, an equal mix of old and stale from the long trip to find her and fresh from trying to keep up, blossomed into a ripe bouquet sending its fragrant scent past her muzzle. She found comfort in knowing this strong, tough male traveled with her.

Vulture cawed overhead, eagerly anticipating a meal. From the size of his flock, the scavenge must be an adult Okapi or Giraffe. Even after the predator who claimed the kill—Lucy guessed it to be Megantereon or Snarling-dog—took what it needed, there would be plenty left. She often hunted with Vulture. It might find carrion first but she drove it away by brandishing a branch and howling. While it circled overhead, awaiting a return to his meal, she grabbed what she wanted and escaped.

Feq must smell the blood but he had never been brave enough to chase Vulture away. He would wait until the raptor finished, as well as Snarling-dog and whoever else showed up at the banquet, and then take what remained which wouldn't be enough to live on.

Sun descended toward the horizon as they entered a dense thicket. They stuck to a narrow lightly-used animal trail bordered by heavy-trunked trees. Cousin Chimp scuffled as he brachiated through the understory, no doubt upset by the intruders. Only once, when a brightly-colored snake slithered across her path, did Lucy hesitate. The vibrant colors always meant deadly venom and she didn't carry the right herbs to counter the poison. Baad grumbled when her thud reverberated out of sync with Raza's, and Cousin Chimp cried a warning.

Finally, they broke free of the shadows and flew through waist-high grass, past trees laden with fruit, and around the termite mound where Cousin Chimp would gorge on white grubs—if Cheetah wasn't sleeping on top of it.

I haven't been back here since that day...

She flicked her eyes to the spot where her life had changed. Everything looked so calm, painted in vibrant colors scented with a heady mix of grass, water, and carrion. A family of Hipparion raised their heads, found no menace, and turned back to their banquet of new buds.

As though nothing happened...

Lucy sprinted. Her vision blurred and her head throbbed as she raced flat out, desperate to outdistance the memories. Her legs churned, arms pumped, and her feet sprang off the hard earth. Each step propelled her farther away. Her breathing heaved in rhythm with her steps. The sack around her neck smacked comfortingly against her body. Her sweat left a potent scent trail any predator could follow but Lucy didn't care.

"Lucy!"

Someone far behind shouted her callsign but she only slowed when the thump in her chest outstripped her ability to breathe. She fell forward, arms outstretched, and gasped the damp air into her tortured lungs. Steps thumped louder, approaching. She kept her eyes closed. A hand yanked her head back, forcing her to look up.

Despite the strangeness of Raza's language, this she did understand: *Never do that again.*

Feq followed until Lucy had reached the edge of her—Feq's—territory. Here, he must let her go. Without Feq, the Group's few children and remaining female would die. She threw a last look at her brother's forlorn face, drawn and tired, shoulders slumped, eyes tight with resolution. Lucy dipped her head and turned from her beleaguered past.

Maybe the language difference made Raza ignore Lucy's every question though she tried an endless variety of vocalizations, gestures, and grunts. Something made him jumpy but Lucy sniffed nothing other than the fragrant scrub, a family of chimps, and the ever-present Fire Mountain. Nor did she see any shift in the distant shadows to signal danger.

Still, his edginess made her anxious.

What is he hiding? Why does he never relax?

She turned toward the horizon hoping whatever connected sky to earth held firm, preventing danger from escaping and finding her. Garv credited Spider's web with this task, said if it could capture Fly, it could connect those forces. Why it didn't always work, Garv couldn't explain. Herds and dust, sometimes fire, leaked through, as did Sun at the end of every day. Lucy tried to reach that place from many different directions only to have it move away faster than she ran.

Another truth Lucy knew: Only in Sun's absence did the clouds crack and send bolts of fire to burn the ground and flash floods to storm through the canyons. Sun's caring presence kept these at bay.

A grunt startled her back to the monotony of the grassland. At the rear of their column, Baad rubbed his wrists, already swollen to the thickness of his arm. When she dropped back to ask if they needed help, his face hardened but not before she saw the anguish in the set of his mouth and the squint of his eyes. The elders of her Group suffered too from gnarled hands. A common root, found everywhere, dulled the ache.

Why bring a male as old and worn as Baad without the root to rid him of pain?

Lucy guessed he had been handsome in his youth with his commanding size, densely-haired body, and brawny chest. Now, the hair hung gray and ragged and a white line as thick as Lucy's finger cut his face from temple to ear. In his eyes smoldered lingering anger, maybe from the shattered tooth peeking through his parted lips.

Was that why he didn't try to rut with her? Or did he consider her pairmated to Raza?

"Baad," she bleated, mimicking the callsign Raza used. "This will help your wrist," and handed him a root bundle from her neck sack. "Crack it open and swallow the juice."

Baad sniffed the bulb, bit it, and slurped up the liquid. His jaw relaxed and the tension drained from his face, completely gone by the time they passed the hillock that had been on the horizon when Lucy first gave him the root.

"How did you know this would work?" Baad motioned as he watched her face.

Why didn't *he* know was a better question. Lucy observed animals as they cared for their injuries. If Gazelle had a scrape on her flank, she bumped against a tree weeping sap so why shouldn't Lucy rub the thick mucus on her own cut to heal it? If swallowing certain leaves rid Cousin Chimp of the white worms, why wouldn't it do the same for Lucy? Over time, she'd collected the roots, blades, stems, bark, flowers, and other plant parts she and her Group came to rely on when sick.

But she didn't know enough of Baad's words to explain this so she shrugged. "I just knew."

Baad remained at her side as though he wanted to talk more.

Lucy took the opportunity. "Baad. Why did you and Raza come for me?"

He made her repeat the question as he watched her hands, body movements, and face, and then answered, "Sahn sent us."

His movement for 'sent' looked odd. One finger grazed the side of his palm and pointed toward his body—the backtrail, the opposite direction of the forward trail.

"Sent you?"

"Because of the deaths."

Memories washed across his face like molten lava down the slopes of Fire Mountain. His hand motions shouted a rage she never associated with death. Predators killed to feed their families or protect their territory, as they must. Why did it anger Baad?

"Can you repeat that? The deaths?"

This time, the closest she could interpret was 'deaths without reason' which made no sense. Death was never without reason. Though he must have noticed she didn't understand, he moved on to a portrayal of the world she would soon live within. His location descriptions were clear. In fact, her Group also labeled places by their surroundings and what happened there—stream-where-hunters-drink, mountains-that-burn-at-night, and mound-with-trees. Locations were meaningless without those identifications. Who could find them if not for their surroundings?

His next question surprised her.

"Why did you come?"

Bile welled in Lucy's throat. She must not tell him how she failed everyone in her Group or explain she wanted a better life for the child she carried. Instead, she grunted and pretended she misunderstood.

That night, Lucy slept fitfully, curled under a shallow overhang without the usual protection of a bramble bush barrier or a tree nest. Every time she awoke, Raza and Baad were staring into the dark night, faces tight and anxious, muscles primed.

When Sun reappeared to begin its journey across the sky, the group set out, Lucy again between Raza and Baad. She shadowed the monotonous bounce of Raza's head, comforted by the muted slap of her feet, the thump in her chest, and the stench of her own unwashed body. As they trotted ever onward, she became increasingly nervous. Though everything from the berries to the vegetation, animals, and baobab trees reminded her of home, this territory belonged to another group of Man-who-makes-tools. Before today, she would no sooner enter or cross it as they would hers. But Raza neither slowed nor changed direction so all she could do to respect this land-not-hers was to move through without picking a stalk of grass, eating a single berry, or swallowing any of the many grubs and insects available. Here and there, Lucy caught glimpses of the Group that called this territory theirs as they floated in the periphery of her sight. She smelled their anger and fear, heard them rustling as they watched her pass, reminding her she had no right to be here. Raza and Baad didn't seem to care or notice. Did they not control territories where they lived?

Before she pondered this any farther, she snorted in a fragrance that made her gasp and turn. There on the crest of a berm across the savanna, outlined against the blue of the sky, stood a lone figure, hair puffed out by the hot breeze, gaze on her.

"Garv!" Lucy mouthed before she could stop herself. *He's dead. I saw it.*

No arm waved and no voice howled the agony of separation.

"Raza!" Baad jerked his head toward the berm.

"Man-who-preys?" Raza asked with a rigid parallel gesture.

Lucy's throat tightened at the hand movement for *danger.*

"Who is Man-who-preys?" Lucy labored with the callsign. "We don't prey. We are prey." Why did this confuse Raza?

Raza dropped back and motioned, "I refer to the one called Man-who-preys—upright like us but tall and skinny." He described the creature's footprints with the distinctive rounded top connected to the bottom by a narrow bridge. She knew every print of every animal in her homeland. These didn't exist.

"No. I've never seen those prints."

He paused and watched her face. "You're sure Mammoth slaughtered your males? Could it have been this animal?"

"No. I was there. I would have seen this stranger."

Raza dropped back to talk to Baad. She tried to hear their conversation but they must have used hand motions. Who was this Man-who-preys and why did Raza think they caused the death of her Group's males? Worse, if they followed Raza from his homeland, did that bring trouble to Feq?

Lucy easily kept up with Raza, her hand tight around an obsidian scraper as sharp and sturdy as the one the males gripped. Her wrist cords bulged like the roots of an old baobab, familiar with and accustomed to heavy loads and strenuous work. Both males remained edgy and tense, often running beside each other and sharing urgent hand motions. After one such exchange, Raza diverted from the route they had been following since morning to one less trodden. It's what Lucy would do if worried about being tracked by a predator or to avoid a group of Man-who-makes-tools. They maintained a quicker-than-normal pace well past the edge of her world. That suited her fine though she doubted Man-who-preys could be more perilous than what preyed in her mind.

Click to purchase

About the Author

Jacqui Murray lives in California with her spouse and the world's greatest dog. She has been writing fiction and nonfiction for 30 years and is an adjunct professor in technology-in-education.

You can find Jacqui Murray on her **blog**:

https://worddreams.wordpress.com

Twitter:

https://twitter.com/WordDreams

LinkedIn:

https://www.linkedin.com/in/jacquimurray

Instagram

https://www.instagram.com/jacquimurraywriter/

BIBLIOGRAPHY

Allen, E.A., The Prehistoric World: or, Vanished Races Central
    Publishing House 1885

Brown Jr., Tom, Tom Brown's Field Guide: Wilderness Survival
    Berkley Books 1983

Caird, Rod Apeman: The Story of Human Evolution
    MacMillan 1994

Calvin, William, and Bickerton, Derek Lingua ex Machina:
    Reconciling Darwin and Chomsky with the Human Brain
    MIT Press, 2000

Carss, Bob The SAS Guide to Tracking Lyons Press Guilford
    Conn. 2000

Cavalli-Sforza, Luigi Luca and Cavalli-Sforza, Francesco The
    Great Human Diasporas: The
History of Diversity and Evolution Perseus Press 1995
    Conant,

Dr. Levi Leonard The Number Concept: Its Origin and
    Development Macmillan and Co. Toronto 1931

Diamond, Jared The Third Chimpanzee Harper Perennial
    1992

Edey, Maitland Missing Link Time-Life Books 1972

Erickson, Jon Glacial Geology: How Ice Shapes the Land Facts
    on File Inc. 1996

Fleagle, John Primate Adaptation and Evolution Academic
    Press 1988

Fossey, Dian Gorillas in the Mist Houghton Mifflin 1984

Galdikas, Birute Reflections of Eden: My Years with the
    Orangutans of Borneo Little Brown and Co. 1995

Goodall, Jane In the Shadow of Man Houghton Mifflin 1971

Goodall, Jane The Jane Goodall Institute 2005
    http://www.janFriendshipegoodall.com/chimp_central/chi
    mpanzees/behavior/comunication.asp

Goodall, Jane Through a Window Houghton Mifflin 1990

Grimaldi, David, and Engel, Michael Evolution of the Insects
    Cambridge University Press 2005

Human Dawn: Timeframe Time-Life Books 1990

Johanson, Donald and Simon, Blake Edgar <u>From Lucy to
    Language</u> Simon and Schuster 1996
Johanson, Donald and O'Farell, Kevin <u>Journey from the Dawn:
    Life with the World's First
Family</u> Villard Books 1990
Johanson, Donald and Edey, Maitland <u>Lucy: The Beginnings of
    Humankind</u> Simon and Schuster 1981
Johanson, Donald and Shreve, James <u>Lucy's Child: The
    Discovery of a Human Ancestor </u>Avon 1989
Jones, Steve, Martin, Robert, and Pilbeam, David <u>The
    Cambridge Encyclopedia of Human Evolution</u> Cambridge
    University Press 1992
Leakey, Richard and Lewin, Roger <u>Origins</u> E.P. Dutton 1977
Leakey, Richard <u>The Origin of Humankind</u> Basic Books 1994
Leakey, Louis <u>Stone Age Africa</u>, Negro Universities Press
    1936
Lewin, Roger <u>In the Age of Mankind</u> Smithsonian Books 1988
McDougall, J.D. <u>A Short History of the Planet Earth</u> John
    Wiley and Sons 1996
Morris, Desmond <u>Naked Ape</u> Dell Publishing 1999
Morris, Desmond <u>The Human Zoo</u> Kodansha International
    1969
Rezendes, Paul <u>Tracking and the Art of Seeing: How to Read
    Animal Tracks and Sign</u> Quill: A Harper Resource Book
    1999
Savage-Rumbaugh, Susan, et al <u>Kanzi: The Ape at the Brink of
    the Human Mind </u>John Wiley and Sons 1996
Spencer Larson, Clark et al <u>Human Origins: The Fossil Record</u>
    Waveland Press 1998
Stringer, Chris, and McSahn, Robin <u>African Exodus: The
    Origins of Modern Humanity</u> Henry Holt and Co. NY
    1996
Strum, Shirley C. <u>Almost Human: A Journey into the World of
    Baboons</u> Random House 1987
Tattersall, Ian <u>Becoming Human: Evolution and Human
    Uniqueness</u> Harvest Books 1999
Tattersall, Ian et al <u>Encyclopedia of Human Evolution and
    Prehistory</u>, Chicago: St James Press 1988

Tattersall, Ian Fossil Trail: How We Know What We Think We Know About Human Evolution Oxford University Press 1997

Tattersall, Ian The Human Odyssey: Four Million Years of Human Evolution Prentice Hall 1993

Thomas, Elizabeth Marshall, The Old Way: A Story of the First People Sarah Crichton Books 2008

Tudge Colin Time Before History Touchstone Books 1996

Turner, Alan, and Anton, Mauricio The Big Cats and Their Fossil Relatives: An Illustrated Guide to Their Evolution and Natural History Columbia University Press NY 1997

Vogel, Shawna Naked Earth: The New Geophysics Dutton 1995

Vygotsky, Lev The Connection Between Thought and the Development of Language in Primitive Society 1930

Walker, Alan and Shipman, Pat Wisdom of the Bones: In Search of Human Origins Vintage Books 1996

Waters, JD Helpless as a Baby http://www.jdwaters.net/HAAB%20Acro/contents.pdf 2001

Wills, Christopher Runaway Brain: The Evolution of Human Uniqueness Basic Books 1993

READER'S WORKSHOP QUESTIONS

Setting

- Where else have land bridges (that are now underwater) played into man's expansion, such as the connection between Alaska and Asia?
- How did the setting of the ancient Iberian Peninsula make life difficult?
- How about the frigid temperatures in ancient Britain?

Themes

- Discuss Xhosa's respect for all animals. Why do you think she felt this way?
- Why did Xhosa and her kind survive Nature's challenges?
- We know *Homo erectus* was replaced by the more-advanced humans, collectively designated archaic *Homo sapiens*. What characteristics and traits in this story help to explain why?

Character Realism

- What traits made Xhosa a survivor?
- Do you relate to Xhosa's predicaments? To what extent does it remind you of yourself or someone you know struggles to fit into a "man's" world, or survive a toxic environment?

Character Choices

- What moral/ethical choices did the characters in this book make? Discuss why the animals are referred to as "who" rather than "that" and why often they are addressed by proper nouns.
- Discuss how Xhosa's People raised children. Do other primitive tribes handle families in this way?

Construction

- Discuss how Xhosa communicated—with body language, gestures, facial expressions, and the rare vocalization. How effective do you think it was? How is it relevant today? What present-day animals communicate with methods other than words? How about sign language?

- Discuss how Xhosa described quantities (such as "Sun traveled a hand" or "ticked them off on her fingers"). Discuss number systems used by some primitive tribes today.
- How did early man make sense of the moon disappearing and reappearing over and over?

Reactions to the Book

- Did the book lead to a new understanding or awareness of how man evolved to be who we are today? Did it help you understand something in your life that didn't make sense before, maybe seemed a "gut feeling" or instinctual?
- Did the book fulfill your expectations? Were you satisfied with the ending?

Other Questions

- What do you think will happen to the characters in Book 3?
- Discuss books you've read with a similar theme or set in a prehistoric time period.

Printed in Great Britain
by Amazon